SHADOWS AND CURSES

WEEPING HOLLOW
BOOK ONE

WILLOW HADLEY

Edited by Taryn Gilliland

Cover Design by Maria Spada

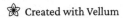 Created with Vellum

To Taryn and Kiersten for loving this book and these characters so much, and for encouraging me to keep writing this book even when writing was a struggle.

CHAPTER I
HARRIET

"Oh, look! Rosemary's Diner is still here. Your aunt and I used to get milkshakes there practically every day during the summers. And there's— Harriet! Turn that off. You're missing everything."

Internally rolling my eyes, I continue staring out the passenger window of our 1985 Jeep Wagoneer. I still have my headphones in, but I turned my music off as soon as I saw the town's welcome sign a few minutes ago. My mom doesn't need to know that. The more she prattles on about what a terrible daughter I am and how teenagers are all the same these days, the harder it is not to roll my eyes or make a snide comment. It's stupidly easy and way too satisfying to piss her off.

While I pretend to ignore my mom, I continue to look out the window and take in the scenery of Weeping Hollow, Massachusetts. Despite the creepy name, it's one of those quaint, picturesque New England towns people like to idealize because the leaves are just *so pretty* in the fall. My mom and her twin sister used to spend every summer and school break here visiting their grandmother Sylvia.

I've heard so many stories about this place over the years that I feel like I know it already. I recognize every shop we pass without my mom having to say a word. I'll never admit this out loud, but a big part of me is excited. All the houses we've passed are old-fashioned and unique, every shop appears to be local, and there are Halloween decorations literally everywhere.

It shouldn't be surprising, considering the history of this place. Plus, we're only about two hours away from Salem. Even if regular people don't believe in witches anymore, most people love that sort of spooky stuff this time of year. When we turn onto Hazel Lane, it takes everything in me not to press my face against the glass in excitement.

The street is lined with old Victorian homes. Some of them are smaller, some of them are straight up mansions, but all of them are gorgeous and have obviously been well kept over the years. Most of them appear to be residential, but there are a few that have been turned into businesses. A law office, a dentist, a clothing boutique, not one but *two* antique shops, and a bed and breakfast.

It's obvious we've reached the house when my mom squeals in delight. I give up every pretense of acting like a bratty, brooding teenager and turn to grin at her. I've waited my entire life to see the historic home that's belonged to my family since it was built in 1852.

A couple of minutes later, I find myself standing with my arms crossed on the sidewalk beside my mom as we look up at the Abbot House. This thing is a *monstrosity*. It's three stories tall with a huge wrap-around porch, complete with balconies and spires. Unlike every other house in this neighborhood, this place has *not* been well kept. The once-white paint is peeling, most of the shutters are broken or falling off, and the entire house is covered in thick black and green scum. The yard is even worse, if possible. The grass is at least waist-high, and there are several overgrown bushes and trees. Some of them completely cover parts of the house, and I wouldn't be surprised if there are tree roots and vines growing inside. The black wrought iron fence surrounding the property makes the whole thing look even more ominous and unwelcoming.

"Wow, mom. It's even better than you described."

She smacks my arm lightly as she pulls her phone out of her purse to check the time. "Oh, be quiet. We knew it would need a little work. Where on Earth is your aunt? We only have a few minutes before the curse is broken."

"Oh yeah, just a little work." I snort, holding my arms out in an exaggerated shrug. "I'm sure it'll be nothing. A piece of cake."

Ignoring my sarcastic remark, my mom turns her head to look down the street. "Here she is."

A bright yellow taxi appears further down the street, and we watch with excited anticipation as it approaches and parks behind our Wagoneer. My aunt steps out of the car with a grin on her face. I stand back with my arms crossed and watch as she greets my mom, grabs her suitcases from the trunk, and pays the driver.

After the taxi drives away, Aunt Flora smiles and waves me over. "Get over here!"

"It hasn't been *that* long." I laugh when she pulls me into a tight hug. Flora never stays in one place for too long, but she usually visits me and my mom every few months. We just saw her earlier this spring to celebrate Beltane.

Flora snorts and pulls away with her eyebrows raised. "Long enough for you to grow at least two more inches. You must be almost six feet tall by now!"

Shoving her away, I quickly smooth my hair down and scowl at her, hoping my cheeks aren't flushed. My height is a

3

major sore spot my mom and aunt never fail to pick at. "I'm five-ten." And a half, but that's irrelevant.

My mom sighs at my 'bad attitude' and waves her hand at me. "Help your aunt with her bags."

It's not worth arguing with her, so I roll my eyes and pick up one of the two suitcases my aunt has with her. "Is this really all you brought, Aunt Flora?"

She adjusts her glasses and grabs the other bag. "Yeah, you know I don't hold onto much with how often I travel. Besides, the house is still full of furniture and all of Grandma Sylvia's things!"

She's probably right, but there's no way to know what sort of condition the inside of the house is in. If the outside is anything to go by, it doesn't look good. The Wagoneer is completely full of mine and my mom's stuff, and the trailer we towed all the way from Canty, Oregon is even more packed. I still have no idea how we managed to pack up our entire house, minus the furniture, in less than a week. But here we are.

My mom gestures wildly at her phone and squeals, "Okay! One minute left and the curse will be broken!"

The front gate is hanging off one of the hinges, and Flora cautiously pushes it open the rest of the way. The three of us wordlessly stride into the disaster-zone that is the front yard, carefully walking up the cracked stone pathway leading to the porch. My mom and my aunt each take a deep breath and clasp their hands together before simultaneously walking up the rickety front steps. I know this is a pretty emotional moment for them, so I try to stay back and out of the way.

The Abbot House has been cursed for twenty-three years, since the day my Great-Grandmother Sylvia died. The circumstances behind the curse and her untimely death have always been a mystery, and my mom and Flora have waited more than half their lives for answers. They loved Sylvia dearly. She was more present in their lives growing up than their mother ever was. I've never even met my Grandma Helena. All I know is that she lives somewhere in Japan. She sends the occasional birthday card and gift, though never actually *on* my birthday, and that's really the only contact I've ever had with her.

Exactly one week ago, on the anniversary of Great-Grandmother Sylvia's death, my mother and Flora received matching letters in the mail with no return address. The letters had been written by Sylvia when she was still alive, and a copy of her will was included. My mom and Flora have inherited the Abbot House, along with my Great Grandma's entire fortune. They simply had to wait for the curse to end to claim everything.

Since the curse went into effect, nobody has been able to set foot inside the house. My mom and Flora have tried to break in several times over the years, along with help from other witches, but it's been a pointless endeavor. The house has been magically protected and locked up tight until now. While my mom counts down the seconds under her breath, I glance around the yard again and shake my head in disgust. Sylvia could have at least added some sort of spell or charm into her curse to make sure the property didn't fall completely into disarray.

"Della!" my aunt says my mom's name in a hushed, reverent voice.

I spin around and face the front door. It's covered in mold and grime, like everything else I've seen of the house so far. My mom and aunt both take a sharp intake of breath, but I don't feel or notice anything until a large, ornate brass key suddenly materializes in the keyhole of the door. I huff and roll my eyes. Granny Sylvia was obviously a show-off with her magic.

Flora's hand trembles as she reaches forward and slowly turns the knob, building the anticipation even more. *Finally,* the door opens all the way with a loud creak. It's too dark inside to see much of anything, but I don't hesitate to follow my mom and aunt into the house.

The second I step inside, I start coughing. There's so much dust. It covers literally every surface, and our few steps into the house have kicked up giant clouds of it. I keep walking forward, running straight into a spider's web. Still coughing, I wildly brush my hands over my face and hair trying to get the damned thing off of me. With one final, exaggerated cough, I turn to glare viciously at my mom and her twin sister. They're looking around with smiles on their faces and tears brimming in their eyes.

"This place is a fucking mess! It reeks in here, and I can't even breathe! There's no way we can sleep here tonight."

Flora finally loses the stupid, starry-eyed expression and nods as she looks around more critically. But my mom puts her hands on her hips and fixes me with one of her *angry faces* that are way too ridiculous to take seriously.

"Harriet Abbot, watch your mouth!" She takes a deep breath through her nose and softens her expression slightly. "I know it's not fair to you, uprooting you and making you leave the only home and friends you've ever known, and I'm sorry. But your aunt and I have waited a long time for this day to come. We've always dreamed of coming back here and settling down. I know you'll end up loving it here as much as we do. Please give it a chance."

To be fair, I'm not that upset about moving here. It did really suck having to say goodbye to my best friend Sage, but she's already planning on visiting. I've always been curious about this place and my Great-Grandmother Sylvia. I never thought I'd get to see the famous Abbot House and the charming town of Weeping Hollow that were so often featured in the stories from my childhood.

But that doesn't mean this whole situation doesn't completely blow. In just a couple of days, I'll be starting school as the new girl. And if the kids here are anything like they were at my old school, I'm not exactly going to fit in. Plus, it's October, which means I'll probably end up getting a ton of bogus make-up assignments in whichever crappy left-over classes I get stuck with.

"I'll try," I scoff with another exaggerated eye-roll.

My mom smiles and claps her hands together, happy enough with my response. "Thank you. Now, we clearly have some work to do. We'll have a look around, and you can pick out your bedroom, Harriet. I think we—"

I stop listening when I get a tingly feeling on the back of my neck, and I turn around with a loud groan. I already know what I'm going to see, even before I feel a slight pressure between my eyes and my nose starts to itch.

"There's a ghost in here."

My mom and Flora gasp excitedly, staring vaguely in the right direction. Flora hesitantly asks, "It's not Grandma Sylvia, is it?"

Shaking my head absently, I look over our new house-mate and cross my arms as the creepy-shivery feeling continues to wash over me. The ghost looks like an old lady, and it's clear she's been dead for a while. She's nearly translucent, and her eyes are completely black. She's staring at me with a horrific, toothless smile while she giggles softly to herself.

"No, she's, like, super old. Her clothes look like something out of a Charles Dickens novel."

"Great-Great-Grandma Josephine, maybe?" my mom asks, sharing a look with Flora.

Raising my eyebrows, I silently ask the ghost to introduce

7

herself. Or to say *anything*, really. Ghosts tend to either keep entirely to themselves, or else they never shut up. Seeing as this one made an appearance as soon as we walked in, I have a feeling she'll be the annoying type.

Her giggling slowly raises in volume until it becomes cackling, and she keeps smiling and tilting her head side-to-side while she wrings her gnarled hands together. And then she speaks in a high, nearly angelic tone:

"There was a crooked man, and he walked a crooked mile.
He found a crooked sixpence upon a crooked stile.
He bought a crooked cat, which caught a crooked mouse.
And they all lived together in a little crooked house!"

"Oh, Goddess." I rub my hand over my forehead and shut my eyes tightly. "She's creepy as shit. She just sang some old ass nursery rhyme or something."

Flora laughs until she's red in the face, and my mom gently grabs my arm to lead me further into the house with an amused smile on her face. "I'm sure she's harmless. Just try to ignore her for now, and hopefully we'll find an old photo album so we can figure out who she is."

I glance over my shoulder, scowling when I see Old Creepy following us. "Yeah, easy for you to say."

CHAPTER 2
HARRIET

"This is a fucking joke."

I drop the box in my hands, and it lands with a loud, satisfying thud at my feet. Of course, my mom chooses that moment to walk by. Her eyes narrow at the box as she angrily hisses, "Be more careful, Harriet! You're going to break something."

"We're witches," I scoff, even though she's already walking away. "If something breaks, you can just fix it with magic."

Old Creepy hums a sad, melodic tune from behind me, and I scratch my nose as I turn around to face her. "I know, right?"

She pauses her humming to giggle quietly, offering me another of her horrifying, toothless smiles. Fresh goosebumps creep up along my arms, but I barely notice at this point. Old Creepy has been following me around, practically glued to my side since we got here. My mom, Flora, and I have been cleaning for hours now, and we've barely made a dent in the house. At least now I have a bedroom that's dust-and-spider free for the most part, and the kitchen and main upstairs bathroom are habitable.

My mom and aunt are doing a spiritual cleansing to get rid of any lingering remnants of the curse, and I'm stuck bringing in boxes before it gets too dark outside. Spiritual cleansing, my ass. It's obvious the curse is completely broken, and Old Creepy is the only spiritual entity I've picked up on. I'm pretty sure my mom and Flora just want a break, and they're using some pointless spell as an excuse while I get to do the hard, non-magical labor.

I point down the hallway in the direction my mom went, lowering my voice in case she's still near enough to hear me. "If it sounds like bullshit, that's because it probably is."

Old Creepy sways back and forth, humming her tune again, and then she lifts her hand to point in the same direction I was.

"Wynken, Blynken, and Nod one night, sailed off in a wooden shoe.

Sailed on a river of crystal light, into a sea of dew."

"Yeah." I sigh. Old Creepy might be a ghostly old-lady weirdo who only speaks in rhymes and riddles, but at least she's sympathetic.

I head back down the intricate, winding staircase and out the front door. There are more people out and about now than when we first arrived. People are walking on the sidewalk across the street, staring and pointing at the Abbott House, and cars continually slow down as they drive by and ogle our U-Haul trailer and the open front door.

Grimacing, I wipe my grimy hands on my pants. I knew people would be curious about us moving in since the house has been the town's biggest mystery for so long. But the attention makes me feel more nervous to start school in a few days.

I quickly make my way down the front steps, through the overgrown path and the rusty front gate. I grab a few more boxes from the trailer, once again wishing I had help to make this go faster. I carry the stack of boxes precariously in my arms and attempt to navigate my way back to the front door without dropping anything.

When I'm about halfway up the front path, there's rustling in the tall grass to my right. I immediately go still and widen my eyes, worried it's a snake. The grass is so thick, I wouldn't be surprised if there were hundreds of snakes hiding out around here.

Before I can rush the last few steps to the porch, a tiny mewling sound comes from the grass. A small, black cat steps onto the path, blinking up at me with bright yellow eyes.

I scoff and begin making my way into the house again, annoyed that I was scared of a stupid cat. The mangy thing follows me all the way into the house. Old Creepy is still waiting for me in the foyer, and I kick at the tiny black monstrosity when it starts purring and rubbing against my ankles.

"You're a cliché." The cat only purrs louder, apparently extra determined to piss me off. "Get out of here!"

Flora walks into the foyer from the kitchen, fixing the messy bun on top of her head. "Aww." She smiles at the cat. "How cute! Where'd it come from?"

I make an ugly, hissing noise to spook it. It finally takes the hint and sprints back outside.

"Harriet!" My aunt furrows her eyebrows and places her hands on her hips. "You know black cats are good luck."

"I hate cats." I set down the boxes I carried in and shrug. "Almost as much as I hate ghosts."

Flora rolls her eyes, promising they're almost finished with the cleansing spell and will be able to help carry boxes in shortly. That lifts my mood enough that I smile at Old Creepy when she starts chanting another nursery rhyme.

For the next twenty minutes, I carry as many things from the car and trailer as I can, and I ignore the growing number of spectators driving and walking by. While I'm working, I imagine how I'm going to decorate my room here. The bedroom I picked is on the third floor, and it has two windows facing the front yard and street. The furniture in there is wicked old, but not too hideous. I'm sure I'll be able to do something cool with the space.

As I pull out a couple more boxes from the trailer, a large pick-up truck slows down, stopping right in the middle of the street beside me. I glare at the old dude driving the truck, and he frowns back and forth between me and the house as he rolls his window down.

"You and your family moving in, kid?"

I roll my eyes, ignoring him and his rhetorical question.

"Hey!" he shouts when I start to walk away. I turn back to scowl at him, and he shakes his head. "Are you crazy? Don't you know that house is haunted?"

I flip the guy off, holding the boxes unsteadily with one arm. "Fuck off, you creepy old pedo."

His face reddens, and his eyes blaze angrily. He doesn't respond before quickly speeding away down the street. I get a better grip of the boxes and head back to the house. I'm completely over this, and I just want a break. I desperately need a shower and something to eat.

Some more rustling in the grass catches my attention. I turn my head, expecting to see that stupid cat again. Instead, I find two teenage guys hiding behind an overgrown shrub in the yard next door. One of them has a pair of binoculars up to his face, and the other is holding his phone up in my direction.

"Oh, shit." The guy holding the phone makes eye contact with me before quickly ducking further behind the shrub. His accomplice follows his lead and does the same.

Heat creeps along my cheeks and neck in anger and embarrassment. They've just been creepily watching me with *binoculars* and taking pictures of me on their phones? While I'm all gross and sweaty and working my ass off? What kind of sick people live in this town?

"I can still fucking see you!" I shout, even though I can't actually see them. But I know they're still there, and they can definitely hear me.

I stomp up the walkway furiously, intent on never leaving the house again. Not tonight, at least. I only make it a few feet before something crashes into the backs of my legs, and I fall forward. I land hard, only managing to half-catch myself on one of the boxes while the other falls several feet away. I also bite my tongue when I fall, so the taste of blood coats my mouth while my right arm throbs painfully.

It takes everything in me not to cry, but I'm completely humiliated and everything hurts. The chances that those guys with the binoculars witnessed me wipe out are extremely high. It's the last thing I should be worrying about, but I can't help it.

The black cat from earlier appears, brushing its tail against my face as it sits in front of me. I narrow my eyes and watch the little demon make itself comfortable, purring as it casually licks its paw.

"Did you trip me?" I whisper angrily. Like the cat will answer back.

The cat stops purring and stares at me with its big, yellow eyes. It flicks its tail for a few more seconds, and *I swear* the thing smirks at me, before suddenly rushing off and disappearing into the tall grass.

Groaning in pain, I get up and carefully pick up the boxes I dropped. Inside the house, I set them down next to the staircase and glance over at Old Creepy. She's humming again.

"You win. I officially hate cats *way more* than I hate ghosts."

"Oh my Goddess." My aunt laughs happily. "Everything in here looks exactly the same."

I look around Rosemary's Diner with my arms crossed defiantly. It's exactly how I imagined it from all of the stories I've heard over the years. Black and white checkered floor, red and white vinyl booths, waitresses wearing poodle skirts, and chrome finishing on everything. It's the perfect definition of 1950s diner aesthetic.

But just because I've always wanted to eat here doesn't mean I'm happy to be here *now*. After the incident with that stupid cat outside, I was adamant about not leaving the house. The healing potion my mom gave me may have fixed the cut on my tongue and the scrapes on my arm, but it did nothing to help my severely bruised ego.

"It looks just like any old diner anywhere," I say.

Aunt Flora wraps her arm around my shoulders and leads me to an empty booth. "You might think that now, but just wait until you try their blueberry pancakes."

I try to fight a smile, but it still slips through. It's hard to pretend to be mad at Flora, and she knows I'm secretly stoked to be here. I just wish we could have ordered pizza tonight instead. I'm dreading running into those guys with the binoculars again. I have a feeling I'll probably see them at school in a few days, but there's nothing I can do to avoid that. The most I can hope for is that I won't see them in the diner or anywhere else in town before then.

My smile drops when we reach an empty booth in the

middle of the diner, and I groan as I rub my suddenly itchy nose and blink against the slight pressure I feel between my eyes.

"Here? Really?" my mom asks, rubbing my arm soothingly.

I nod and glance sideways at the bar in front of the kitchen area where a ghost sits on one of the stools. He's an older man, but he looks solid enough that I don't think he's been dead very long. A few years, at best. He meets my eyes and glares before quickly turning away, like I'm the one bothering *him*.

"Whatever." I roll my eyes and slide into the booth across from my mom and aunt. "Looks like he'll leave me alone, at least."

While we're waiting for someone to bring us menus, my mom and Flora discuss our plans for the house tomorrow. When they were younger, my mom and aunt used to talk about turning the first floor of the Abbot House into a bakery or tea shop. Now that the house is officially theirs, they're hoping they'll be able to do just that. That dream is still a long way off though. Right now, their priority is getting the house back in order to simply live in it.

There's still so much cleaning to do, not to mention unpacking. The thought makes me want to curl into a ball and cry. Grandma Sylvia was totally the most selfish witch ever. She locked the house up with her curse knowing it would fall into decay like this, and my mom and aunt can't just use their power to instantly clean and fix everything. Magic takes so much energy and only goes so far.

Resting my elbows on the table, I mumble a promise that I'll start on the yard tomorrow. Not just because I'm scared of snakes or stupidly sneaky cats. Old Creepy seems to have a thing about not leaving the house, and even though she's really not that bad, my head is seriously killing me after being around her all day. This old, douchey diner ghost isn't helping things either.

Tuning out the rest of the conversation, I glance curiously around the diner. It really is awesome here, though I'll never admit it. Most of the tables are full, and the atmosphere is filled with happy chatter. I can see a couple of waitresses walking around taking orders and refilling coffee mugs. I also notice a guy around my age bussing tables not far from us. A really cute guy.

Instead of wearing some cheesy uniform like most of the staff I've seen so far, he's wearing black slacks, a black tee shirt and apron, and converse sneakers. He's got jet-black shoulder-length hair that's pulled back into a short ponytail. I'm dying to text Sage, but she's still camping with her family, so her cell service is basically non-existent.

"Della and Flora Abbot? It can't be!"

Tearing my eyes away from the cute bus boy, I find a woman my mom and aunt's age smiling at us. My mom's eyes completely light up as she exclaims, "April! Oh my god, it's so good to see you!"

After a quick introduction where I learn April was friends with my mom and aunt as kids—and also that she owns the diner now—the woman asks, "Are you visiting? It's been so long since I've seen either of you around here."

"We're here for good, actually." Flora smiles.

April raises her eyebrows, surprised but clearly happy at the news. She hands a few menus to my mom and says, "Wow! That's amazing. Listen, we're a little busy tonight, but I would love to catch up with the two of you soon."

She exchanges numbers with my mom and Flora, all of them promising to make plans soon. Before she walks away from our table, she says, "I'll be around, so let me know if you need anything. Spencer will be with you in just a minute to take your order."

The moment April walks away, Flora opens her menu with a smirk on her face. "Hmm, I wonder if Spencer is the guy Harriet was checking out."

"I wasn't—" I stop myself mid-sentence and quickly look around to make sure that bus boy isn't nearby. When I don't see him, I sneer at my aunt. "I was *not* checking anyone out."

"You don't need to deny it, Harriet." My mom rolls her eyes and smiles slyly. "You're still a stunning girl, even with your gray hair."

She and Flora laugh, and my cheeks warm in embarrassment. I settle a vicious glare on both of them and run my fingers through my hair. My mom and her twin sister share the same thick, luscious ebony locks and sapphire blue eyes. I didn't inherit either trait. I ended up with flat, mousy brown hair and dull, gray-blue eyes. I'd blame my biological father, but I have no clue who he is or what he looks like.

Just before moving here, Sage helped me magically dye my hair. She was aiming for blonde, but it came out silver by mistake. I can't really complain. I can't do any magic, so she's leaps and bounds better than me. Plus, the silver turned out really cool, and it suits me better than any shade of blonde would have. The silver brings out my eyes so they don't look so dull, and the spell is permanent so I won't have to redo it or legitimately dye it. My hair grows this color automatically now —at least, it has for the past six months.

"It's silver," I correct my mom and sniff indignantly. "It's not my fault you guys don't understand fashion."

Flora and my mom burst out laughing until they're interrupted by a smooth, masculine voice.

"Hey, I'm Spencer, and I'll be your waiter tonight. Can I get you ladies started with something to drink?"

WILLOW HADLEY

I look up to meet a pair of chocolate brown eyes and a blinding white smile. Spencer is a million times cuter up close, and all I can do is stare at him like an idiot.

"Oh! *Spencer,* hello!" My mom flashes me a smug smile, and then flutters her eyelashes obnoxiously. "This is Harriet. Do you think she's pretty?"

Oh, Goddess. Please just kill me now.

Spencer looks surprised, but he smiles down at me again with a glimmer of amusement in his eyes. Even with the teasing expression on his face, he manages to sound genuine when he replies, "Yeah, very pretty."

My cheeks flame and my stomach flutters as I glare at the stupidly-cute boy. My aunt kicks me under the table and says with a laugh, "That's good, because Harriet was totally staring at your butt earlier."

The wonder twins completely lose it, falling all over each other while they laugh at my humiliation. I cringe and quickly open my menu, holding it up in front of myself so I can hide my reddening face. Too late, I realize I'm holding the fucking thing upside down.

I'm so angry. The entire day has been shitty, and I'm about two seconds away from begging my mom to send me back to Oregon so I can live with Sage's family until graduation. I know she'd never actually let me do that, but I can still try. If I thought falling down in front of the binocular boys was embarrassing, that was nothing compared to how I feel now. The chances that Spencer goes to my new school are pretty high, and I guarantee he'll never forget this. I'll have to avoid him for the entire year, or else I'll die of embarrassment.

"Hey." Spencer startles me, pulling my menu back gently with the tips of his fingers. I look up to find him staring at me with an adorable, crooked smile. "Do you know what you want to order yet?"

18

My first instinct is to say something sarcastic, but my brain completely freezes while I gape at him. When I finally regain my ability to speak, I say the first thing that pops into my head. "Blueberry pancakes."

His eyes crinkle and his smile widens, lighting up his entire face. "You got it."

He scribbles my order down and tucks his pen behind his ear. After promising to be right back with our food and drinks, Spencer smiles at me one last time and walks away.

I slap my menu down on the table and glower at my mom and aunt. They're wearing identical smirks, and I hiss at them as I cross my arms in front of me.

"I would totally put a curse on both of you right now if I could."

CHAPTER 3
HARRIET

Between the pitter-patter of rain beating against the windows and the cackling laughter coming from my mom and Principal Di Rossi, I'm pretty sure I'm going to have a migraine for the rest of the day. School was supposed to be my break from the never-ending headache I've had from spending days with Old Creepy, but it seems my mom and her old friend are determined to make sure I have no peace. I rub my temples and slump down lower in my seat, peering disdainfully out the window to my left.

The latest laughing fit slowly dies down, and I raise my eyebrows hopefully. We've been sitting in this dusty old office for half an hour. At this rate, I'm going to miss the entire school day instead of just first period. I wouldn't normally care, but I'd rather stay home with Old Creepy than waste another minute listening to my mom and her friend reminisce about the good old days. I'm quickly learning that my mom knows everyone in this town—witches or not—so it's no surprise to learn that she and my new principal used to be close when they were my age.

Principal Di Rossi's eyes squint as he grins excitedly across his desk at my mom. "Remember the time when—"

"Please, Goddess, no." I groan, not bothering to be subtle about my suffering any longer.

"Harriet!" my mom yells in a shrill voice.

"No, she's right." Principal Di Rossi smiles apologetically and shuffles some papers on his desk. "I could sit here all day talking like this, but I should probably get some work done."

He hands me my schedule, and I frown down at the crisp, white paper while he and my mom exchange numbers and make plans to get together. As soon as we step into the main administrative area of the office, all of my nerves about starting at a new school hit me again. I almost wish I'd kept my mouth shut so I could continue hiding out in Di Rossi's scholarly little man-cave. Headache or not.

While my mom and Di Rossi continue laughing quietly together, I try to ignore them and glance anxiously around the room. There's a woman on the phone and another office worker is behind her desk with a stern expression plastered to her face as she types furiously at her computer.

"I can't have Saturday detention this weekend. I have plans."

"Maybe you should have thought about that, Mr. Baxter," the secretary hisses through her teeth without looking away from her screen.

"Please, I just..." The guy trails off when he notices me standing there, and his eyes widen the slightest fraction.

It's *him*. One of the guys who was spying on me outside my house with binoculars the other day. I'm almost certain he's the one who was holding his phone up. It takes everything in me not to react. Goddess, I desperately want to scream at him for being a perverted asshole, and I also want to run away so I don't have to deal with the humiliation of reliving that incident. But my mom will be a million times more pissed if I say something, so I stay quiet. The guy must think I don't recognize him because he slowly relaxes and flashes me an obnoxiously flirtatious smirk.

Heat trails across my neck and face, and my eyes narrow in outrage. He's a little shorter than I am, by at least a few inches, and he has a mop of dark, curly hair hanging in his eyes, freckles scattered across his golden-brown skin, and a small, jagged scar right above his top lip.

"What seems to be the problem here?" Principal Di Rossi asks in a stern tone when the secretary starts screeching.

The guy tears his eyes from mine and gives the principal a pleading, puppy-dog expression. "I was just joking around, sir. It's not my fault Ms. Askew gets offended over every little thing."

The secretary adjusts her glasses and clears her throat, holding up a slip of paper for everyone to see as she reads, "Mr. Matthew Baxter made 'finger guns' at another student and called them a 'thick ass boy.'"

A giggle slips out of my mouth before I can help it. I try to cover it up, but Matthew catches on right away and flashes me a bright, smug grin.

I cross my arms and turn away from him before he gets any ideas in his stupid head.

"Alright, how about this." Di Rossi claps his hands together and smiles warmly back and forth between me and this Matthew kid. "Harriet is a new student here. If you show her around, help her find her classes, and take her under your wing while she's settling in, I'll let the incident slide this time. Deal?"

"Deal?" Matthew blinks and shakes his head like he's in a daze. He swipes the curls off his forehead and turns to face me again with another of those stupid, flirty smiles. "It would be

0

an honor to take this Amazonian Goddess under my wing, Mr. Di Rossi."

I scoff and flip him off, which only makes the asshat smile wider.

"Harriet!" My mom hisses my name under her breath, giving me yet another disapproving look. "Can you please try to be nice? He's offering to help you."

Except he didn't offer. Di Rossi bribed him. And maybe if my mom knew me at all or cared to pay attention, she'd realize there's a reason I don't want to spend time with this particular guy. Why can't she ever be on my side?

"Whatever," I grumble and roll my eyes, cutting a disgusted glare at Matthew as I move to leave the office.

I've barely made it a few feet into the empty hallway when Matthew runs after me and shouts, "Wait up! Do you know where you're going?"

I grudgingly stop and turn to face him with a scowl. He stops in front of me, smiling up at me like a lunatic. Up close like this, I can see that his eyes are the prettiest forest-green color. The second the thought crosses my mind, I want to slap myself. Huffing angrily, I shove my schedule at him.

If he's offended by my attitude, he doesn't say so. He quickly glances over the paper and exclaims, "Oh, shit! We have two classes together, dude!"

"Great." I snort.

Matthew completely ignores my sarcasm, smiling at me while he responds in a cheerful tone. "First and second period. We still have a while before class ends, so I can show you your locker and stuff before we head to history class."

"Whatever." I shrug, looking away. I already suck at talking to guys, and I'm nervous as shit about meeting more of my classmates. Even though he's being nice, all I can think about is catching Matthew and his friend spying on me.

"Cool." Matthew laughs awkwardly and motions for me to follow him. "I'm Mattie, by the way. My friends call me Mattie, I mean. Not Matthew. Do you have a nickname, or...?"

Hearing the uncertainty in his voice makes me feel bad. Well, almost. Enough to decide I should stop being a complete bitch and answer him without any sarcasm, at least. Only, when I open my mouth to respond to his question, a ghost pops out of the wall right in front of me.

The ghost meets my eyes and blinks, like he's unsure if I'm really seeing him or not. Before I can move out of the way quickly enough to make it seem natural, he glides closer and waves his hand right in front of my face. Pain explodes behind my eyes while I sneeze several times in a row.

Ghost Boy steps back and furrows his eyebrows in concern. "Um..."

I grit my teeth and glare at him when the sneezing finally subsides, and he gapes at me like a deer in headlights. He couldn't have been much older than me when he died. And he looks almost completely solid, like he couldn't have died more than a few months ago, if that.

"Can you see me? I can't tell."

The tone in his voice is so heartbreaking that I almost forget myself and answer him aloud. Luckily, Mattie reminds me that I'm in public by gently touching my arm and asking, "Dude, are you okay?"

I seriously cannot believe my luck. I've been in Weeping Hollow less than a week, and I've already seen three ghosts. Home, the diner, and now here. Back in Oregon, I'd go months without running into any spirits.

"Yeah," I answer both Mattie and the ghost, shaking Mattie's hand off. "I get these weird allergy attacks and migraines sometimes. It's not a big deal." He doesn't look totally convinced, so I clear my throat and answer his original question in an attempt to change the subject. "And Harriet is fine."

"Cool!" Mattie continues leading me down the hallway.

He points out a couple of classrooms while we're walking, but I'm having a hell of a time paying attention. Ghost Boy is gliding beside me, nearly brushing his elbow against mine while trying to catch my eye. I don't normally feel anything more than mildly irritated when I meet ghosts, but the fact that this ghost is so young is really getting to me. Even though I've been able to see ghosts my whole life, I don't see them all that often. And I've never seen one so young before. Part of me is curious enough to want to talk to him, but his close proximity is making my head hurt enough that I also want to yell at him to fuck off.

"This is your locker," Mattie says, stopping in front of a wall of them. There's a tense, awkward silence between us, but I don't know how to make that go away. Or if I even want to. There's nothing for me to put in my locker yet, so I take a few seconds to make sure the combination I was given works. While I do that, Mattie leans against the locker next to mine and asks, "So, you just moved here from Oregon, right? And you're staying in the Abbot House?"

The fact that he's suddenly brave enough to bring it up so casually pisses me off to no end. My face flushes when I remember how humiliated I was to discover him watching me from the bushes. He also saw me wipe out when that mangy cat tripped me on the sidewalk. Mattie and his friend have probably been laughing at my expense for days.

"I know it was you," I whisper threateningly.

"Uh, what?" he asks with an awkward chuckle.

Leaning in close, I glare at him and hiss through my teeth, "You and your fucking friend, watching me from the bushes outside my house the other day."

"That wasn't us!" He holds his hands up and shakes his head back and forth in an idiotic effort to defend himself. When I cross my arms and scoff, he grimaces and caves. "Okay, it was us. That was super messed up on our part, and I'm sorry. My cousin and I have been geeking out over the Abbot House for years. We were really excited to see who was moving in and to meet you..."

The bell rings, and students begin swarming the hallways. Nobody's paying attention to us, but I really don't want to continue having this conversation in front of other people.

"Let's just go to class, okay?" I sigh. I'm still irritated, but at least he apologized.

Mattie nods and gestures for me to follow him. Ghost Boy stays on my heels, staying quiet for the time being.

"Seriously, Harriet." Mattie lowers his voice and grimaces up at me. All traces of that flirty smirk are gone. "Can we please pretend like that didn't happen? My cousin has been a nervous wreck. He feels really bad. We weren't sure if you'd be in school with us or not, but he's gonna shit himself when he meets you later."

"You know, you guys could have just—"

"Mattie!" A girl squeals and throws herself into his arms, cutting me off mid-sentence. One glance at her gives me a tingly feeling on the back of my neck that helps me recognize her as a fellow witch.

I'm only a little annoyed by the interruption at first. Mattie's got this ridiculous, lovesick look on his face, and he's staring down at her like the sun shines out of her ass. But when she glances at me over her shoulder with venom in her eyes and a spiteful smirk on her lips, I decide right then and there that I absolutely fucking hate her.

"Hey, Amethyst," Mattie says with a lovesick sigh.

Amethyst pulls away from their embrace and gives me a

fake-surprised smile. "Oh, I'm sorry! I didn't see you standing there." She giggles and holds her hand out for me, flipping her ebony hair over her shoulder. "I'm Amethyst. Amethyst *Redferne*."

It takes everything in me not to roll my eyes at the emphasis on her family name. The witch community in Weeping Hollow is fairly large, so I knew I'd be going to school with other witches. Principal Di Rossi even made a point of mentioning there were several in the same year as me here. It just fucking figures the first fellow-witch I meet happens to be a bitch and a walking cliché. She's decked out in all black—a short, pleated skirt, a too-tight long-sleeve black tee, thigh-high stockings, Doc Martens, and a little black choker with a pentagram charm on it. Her makeup is way too dark and dramatic, but I have to admit that her eyebrows are on point.

The moment I put my hand in hers, the sleeve of my jacket bursts into flames. It doesn't hurt, and it's obvious she's made sure nobody else can see the illusion she just cast, but it pisses me off to no end. I raise my eyebrows at her and try my best to look as bored as possible.

"Harriet Abbot. Sorry, I'm not familiar with the name Redferne." That's a total lie. The Redferne family name is super well-known in our society. Just like I expected, the look on Amethyst's face is fucking priceless.

"Hmm." She purses her lips, turning away from me to give Mattie a dazzling smile. "I'll see you around!"

Ghost Boy pats my arm where Amethyst's fake flames are still blazing, and I yank my arm away from him and hiss through my teeth. "Cut it out, will you?"

Luckily, Mattie's totally oblivious as he stares after Amethyst with a dreamy look in his eyes. Ghost Boy shoots me this bright, heartwarming smile. "You really *can* see me."

"God, she's so hot," Mattie says, joining me in the present

moment once more. "My best friend dated her for a while last year, and he's still kinda hung up on her. Otherwise, I would totally ask her out."

I breathe through my nose in annoyance and respond in a dry tone, "Thanks for sharing."

Mattie blinks up at me like he's just remembered who he's talking to. He lets out a short, embarrassed laugh and says, "You're really hot too, obviously."

Ghost Boy snickers, and I honestly just want to die. Why is every moment spent in Mattie Baxter's presence so fucking humiliating? I'm so ready for this day to be over, and I haven't even made it to class yet.

"For the record," Ghost Boy says when Mattie and I begin walking silently together again. "He and his cousin *have* been talking about you obsessively the past couple of days."

"Good to know," I grumble and roll my eyes.

"What did you say?" Mattie asks curiously. When I shake my head, he shrugs it off and grins as he points his thumb at our classroom door. "Here we are! I normally hate school, but Miss Camelli makes this class kind of fun. Do you want to sit next to me?"

He may be an idiot with awful taste in girls, and he's definitely seen me in way too many embarrassing situations. But at least he's making an effort to be nice. I still think he might be a creep, but maybe I should give him a chance? It's not like I have much choice, anyway. I don't know anyone else here, and hanging out with Mattie is better than being alone when there are catty witches walking the halls.

With an exaggerated shrug, I sigh. "I guess so."

CHAPTER 4
HARRIET

"What are you doing? Hurry up!"

Ghost Boy shrugs and steps into the girls' bathroom behind me with an embarrassed expression on his face. "I wasn't sure you wanted me to follow you in here."

I roll my eyes and sigh, quickly bending down to make sure all the stalls are empty. History class has been agonizing. From the moment I walked in with Mattie, everyone has been staring at me while pretending they aren't. I expected it, being new here, but it still sucks. My run-in with Amethyst in the hallway probably didn't help. But honestly? Mattie and Ghost Boy are the ones making class unbearable. They keep staring at me—*openly*—with these creepy smiles, and Mattie keeps leaning over to ask if I need help with anything pretty much every few seconds. I couldn't get out of there fast enough. Asking for a bathroom break was the only excuse I could think of. When Ghost Boy followed me, I figured I might as well try to figure out what his problem is.

"Okay." I spin around to face Ghost Boy, holding my hands

29

out in a placating manner. "Now that we can finally talk, why do you keep grinning at me like some kind of psycho?"

"Oh," Ghost Boy says dejectedly, his smile faltering. "I'm just excited to have someone to talk to. It's been a long time."

I look him over again and frown. Most of the ghosts I've run into have been more like Old Creepy. Kind of fuzzy or see-through. I can usually tell how long a ghost has been dead by how solid they appear and by how black their eyes are. Ghost Boy looks like a totally average high school guy. He's about my height with shaggy blond hair and blue eyes, and he's wearing a plain gray tee shirt, jeans, and Converse.

"It can't have been that long," I insist. "When did you die?"

Ghost Boy shrugs. "I don't know. A year? Ten years? Things start running together after a while."

Ten years? "No freaking way." I shake my head in denial. "Have you ever seen other ghosts? You look like you just keeled over yesterday."

Ghost Boy laughs, his eyes crinkling in both shock and amusement at my morbid joke. "I haven't. I can't leave the school grounds, and I've never met anyone who could see me before. I'm assuming you're a witch based on your name and that little squabble with Amethyst Redferne. But how come you can see me when the other witches can't?"

He's not able to leave the school? While I've been able to see ghosts my whole life, I'm not exactly an expert. I've never heard of anything like this. Sure, ghosts are typically stronger in their place of death, but they can usually still leave if they want to. Since I'm not sure where to begin with my questions, and we don't have a lot of time before I need to get back to class, I answer him with a shrug and a roll of my eyes.

"I just can. I don't know why, but I can't do magic like other witches. I can talk to ghosts, and that's all. It's literally the most useless gift ever."

"Not useless to me." Ghost Boy's eyes light up as he reaches for me. His hand goes straight through mine, causing goosebumps to rise all over my skin. "I can't tell you how happy it makes me that you can see me, or that you're talking to me right now."

Staring into his eyes and seeing the heartfelt, genuine warmth there makes me feel like the worst person on the planet. My head is throbbing and my nose is itching like crazy, but I don't have the heart to tell him how uncomfortable it is to even be around him.

"Well, we can probably talk for a few more minutes." I clear my throat and glance behind me at the bathroom door. "But if I talk to you in front of people, I'll look like a lunatic."

"That's okay," he says. "I can still talk to you, right? You can just listen?"

I nod my head, part of me already regretting it. Between Ghost Boy at school and Old Creepy at home, it looks like I'll have to get used to having a constant migraine. My mom—let alone any other witches who know about my supposed gift—has never been able to find or mix a potion that helps with ghost-related headaches, and regular medicine doesn't work either. It majorly sucks.

"What's your name, anyway?" I rub my hand over my itchy, tingly nose. I have got to stop calling him Ghost Boy.

"It's Ryan. Nice to officially meet you, Harriet Abbot."

BACK IN CLASS, MATTIE IS WAITING FOR ME WITH ANOTHER OF HIS wide, flirtatious grins. As soon as I sit down, he leans close to my seat and whispers, "I thought you might have gotten lost. I told Miss Camelli she should let me go check on you, but she said no."

I sigh and look to the front of the room at my new history teacher. She's one of two teachers I have who's a witch, and she seems okay so far. At the very least, she kept Mattie from finding a way to embarrass me for a little while. "Thank Goddess for that."

Ryan snickers, hovering behind me. I force myself not to glare at him or pay him any mind. Miss Camelli is talking about the Salem Witch Trials of all things, and I seriously want to laugh at the bored looks on everyone's faces. Weeping Hollow was literally settled by witches, and even today, it's still one of the most populated witch towns outside of any metropolitan area in the country. The fact that so many of the kids in this class are oblivious is probably amusing to the other witches. I know it is to me.

When I glance at Mattie from the corner of my eye, he seems to be one of the few students who's actually paying attention. He scribbles notes furiously, and he even raises his hand to ask the teacher questions a few times. Since this is a subject I'm very familiar with, I decide to tune the teacher out and write notes to Ryan.

As soon as I start writing, he leans forward until I feel him brush against my back and shoulder. I shiver and grind my teeth, silently cursing the pain in my head. I can't deny I'm extremely curious about his death and his weird limitations.

"Were you a witch?" I figure that's an easy question to start with, especially since he knows at least enough about witches to pick up on my name and not be surprised by Amethyst's showboating.

Ryan tilts his head sideways, appearing to contemplate my question. "I don't think so. But I must have known about witches when I was alive because it's easy for me to notice them. Well, that, and there's not much else for me to do except eavesdrop on people's conversations."

I huff out a quiet laugh without meaning to, and Mattie turns to smile at me. Yikes. Once again, he's caught me doing something embarrassing. I try to ignore him and go back to scribbling in my notebook. *"That's not creepy at all."*

"Trust me, you'd do the same thing. Being dead is boring," Ryan says. He points his thumb at Mattie and grins. "Lately, I mostly hang out with him and his friends. They're more interesting than most of the other kids around here. Sometimes it feels like they're my real friends too, as pathetic as that sounds."

Swallowing the lump in my throat, I stare down at my paper so Ryan doesn't see the pity in my expression. I don't think that's pathetic of him, but it is really fucking sad. I'm not used to feeling this much empathy for a ghost, and fuck if it's not throwing me off. In an attempt to change the subject, I quickly scribble another question. *"How did you die?"*

When he doesn't answer right away, I turn to look at him. He's staring back at me, a strange expression on his face that gives me major goosebumps. I've never been truly afraid of a ghost before, but for the first time in my life, I wonder if I should be. Ryan's already made it clear that he's different from any other spirit I've ever encountered.

"I don't remember," he whispers. The melancholy sound of his voice makes me shiver, and I raise my eyebrows in alarm and confusion. Before I can scribble another question, he lets out a sad laugh and shakes his head. "Sometimes I get these flashes. Faces that seem familiar, fleeting memories of playing baseball or kissing a guy in the locker room. But it's like everything about my life when I was alive is fuzzy, and the longer I'm like this, the harder it is to remember. I'm surprised I could even remember my name when you asked.

It's been so long since I've said it out loud or heard anyone else say it."

Goddess, is that true for all ghosts? I'm realizing I don't know as much about ghosts as I've always assumed I do. Shit, I've never had such an elaborate conversation with one either. The only ghost I've spent more time with than Ryan is Old Creepy, and she doesn't exactly *talk*. But maybe this is a good thing. For the first time ever, I can't help feeling like maybe my gift isn't so useless after all. There has to be some way I can help Ryan. Even if all that means is talking to him any chance I get.

"Harriet? You okay?"

I turn and blink at Mattie, realizing belatedly that everyone is packing up their things. Heat trails across my face and neck when I realize how fucking weird I probably looked to everyone while I was gaping at Ryan.

"Yeah." I stand up and cram everything into my backpack haphazardly. "I just spaced out and didn't hear the bell ring."

Mattie flicks his hair out of his eyes and smiles up at me. "Do you want to borrow my notes? I can try to help you with any makeup homework you get too."

That's really nice of him to offer. Even if he's only being nice because Principal Di Rossi told him to be. Plus, he probably still feels bad about creeping on me outside my house a few days ago.

"I'm good, thanks."

Mattie's smile falters, but then he shrugs. "Okay. Just let me know if you change your mind. What class do you have next again?"

I pull the crumpled paper from my pocket and read, "Forensic Science."

"Fucking lucky!" Mattie groans. He holds the classroom door open for me, and I follow him down the hallway. "I wanted that class so bad, but my chemistry grade was shit last year. I'm pretty sure my cousin and my best friend are in the same class as you."

My stomach flips over nervously at the thought of meeting more people. With my luck, Mattie's cousin is going to be just as annoying as he is. Besides, I haven't forgotten the binocular incident. Ryan catches my eye and gives me two very enthusiastic thumbs up, which makes me feel even surlier.

While following Mattie through the hallways, I catch sight of someone I recognize and stop in my tracks. Spencer, the guy from the diner I swore to avoid after thoroughly embarrassing myself in front of him, is standing outside a classroom door less than ten feet from me. He's talking to another student, so he hasn't noticed me yet. How pathetic is it if I find somewhere to hide?

Mattie latches onto my arm and drags me closer to Spencer and my imminent mortification. "Yo! What is up, my dudes?"

Spencer and the other guy look up, and Spencer smiles broadly the moment our eyes meet. "Harriet!"

I stare at him like an idiot without saying anything. I couldn't tell in the diner since I was sitting down, but he and I are the same height. I always get flustered around any cute guys, but it's usually worse when I meet a guy who's my height or taller than me. If I wasn't blushing before, I definitely am now.

"Wait, how do you two know each other?" Mattie asks, frowning back and forth between us. "I thought I was the first one to meet her!"

"Chill out, bro. I met her at work." Spencer laughs, never once taking his eyes off mine. "I was hoping I'd run into you today. I would have asked for your number if I knew you'd just moved here, but I didn't find out until you and your family had already left the diner."

Oh, Goddess. A cute guy just implied he might want my number and all I can do is stare at him like a moron. If Sage was here, she'd know what to do. I let out an embarrassing, nasally laugh and shift my gaze to Ryan. He gives me an encouraging smile and nods his head, but I don't know if he's helping or making me feel more awkward.

Mattie looks slightly irritated, but he quickly shakes the expression off and shoots me one of his flirty smiles. "Alright, so you know Spencer, but you haven't officially met my cousin yet. This is Nolan."

When I look at the guy beside Spencer, I see that his entire face is beet-red as he stares at me in absolute horror. His dark hair is curly like Mattie's, but they don't share many other physical similarities at first glance. Nolan is a few inches taller than me, and he's paler and skinnier too. His light-brown eyes are hidden under thick brows and a pair of black-framed glasses. I seriously cannot believe that Spencer is friends with the guys who were spying on me. It's like the universe is actually trying to find a way to make sure I die of embarrassment.

Having all of their eyes on me at the same time makes me feel nervous and prickly, and my head is still killing me from having Ryan by my side for the past hour. Without thinking it through, I sneer at Nolan and say, "Nice to meet you, Binocular Boy Number Two. I'm Harriet."

Mattie widens his eyes and shakes his head frantically at me, and Nolan's face turns even redder. He makes a terrible choking sound and stumbles over his words. "Oh, god. I'm so sorry. I—I just...fuck."

"Binocular Boy?" Spencer laughs in surprise, glancing between me and his friends. "Hold up, what did I miss?"

Crap. I didn't expect Nolan to react as badly as he did, and Mattie was kind of sweet earlier when he apologized and asked me not to mention the incident to his cousin. Then again, how messed up is it that *I* feel bad when they're the ones who did something wrong in the first place?

Crossing my arms defensively, I glare at Mattie and Nolan. "They were watching me with binoculars and taking pictures from the bushes outside my house the other day when I was moving in."

Spencer howls with laughter, as does Ryan—unbeknownst to everyone but me. Nolan hunches his shoulders and stares at his feet, his cheeks turning just as red as I imagine mine are.

It seems like Mattie is embarrassed too, but he's doing a way better job of hiding it. He holds his hands out and laughs nervously. "Okay, in our defense, Harriet lives in the Abbot House. The fucking *Abbot House*! We were gonna tell you and Owen right away, but Nolan made me swear not to mention it after Harriet caught us."

"For real?" Spencer stops laughing, staring at me in awe. "What's it like? Are there any ghosts in there?"

I can't tell if he's joking or not, and it's not like they'll believe me anyway. So, I answer truthfully. "Just one."

Mattie and Spencer chuckle in surprise, and even Nolan looks up at me. He looks like a sad, scared little puppy. Plus, I *do* feel kind of bad. I offer him a small smile. That seems to freak him out because he grimaces and turns away from me again.

The bell rings, and Mattie jumps. "Shit, I'm going to be late. Uh, I'll meet you after class, Harriet."

"Don't worry about it. I can take her to class," Spencer says.

Mattie frowns at his friend before turning to sprint down the hallway. Even if he was blackmailed into helping me, I figure I should still let him know I appreciate it. I quickly call out to him before he gets too far. "Thanks, Mattie!"

He goes still and slowly turns to face me with a huge, cheesy grin on his face. "You're welcome."

As I shuffle into class behind Spencer and Nolan, Ryan stays right on my heels. He's still laughing about the conversation that just happened in the hallway, and it's taking everything in me not to turn and flip him off. My eyes fall on the rest of the class, which is only about half-full. The back of my neck tingles, signaling there's at least one other witch nearby. I glance quickly around the room and find three of them sitting together at a table in the back of the room. They're glaring at me, no surprise, and they all look like they came straight from Hot Topic. Just like Amethyst. I roll my eyes and head to the teacher's desk so I can get a textbook and any makeup work she has for me. I was taking a pretty similar class at my old school, so I don't think it will be difficult for me to catch up.

I'm pleasantly surprised when Spencer waves me over and offers me the empty seat between him and Nolan. But I'm still nervous to be around both of them, and I pray to the Goddess that I don't do anything else to embarrass myself in front of either of them again.

While I grab a notebook and pencil from my bag, Spencer leans close and whispers, "You really live in the Abbot House? It's been empty for years."

"Yeah, it belonged to my great-grandma. She left it to my mom and my aunt in her will, but we weren't allowed to move in until now."

"That's so fucking cool!" He grins, making his eyes all squinty and adorable. "Nolan and Mattie live really close to you too."

I peer at Nolan from the corner of my eye and rack my brain for something to say. Why do I suck so much at talking to people? He beats me to it, mumbling quietly so the teacher doesn't hear, "I really am sorry, Harriet. We've always been interested in your family's house, so we were excited to see that someone was moving in."

"You guys are such idiots." Spencer snickers. "You could have just walked up and introduced yourselves, or even offered to help her move shit."

That's exactly what I'd been thinking, but Nolan looks like he wants to disappear. His apology seems genuine, and I totally get them being curious about the house. "It's okay. I haven't been able to do much in the yard since it's been raining the past couple of days, and the inside is still almost as bad. But you guys can come over whenever. If you still want to look around."

Spencer practically blinds me with his smile, and Nolan gives me this adorably timid crooked grin. He adjusts his glasses and asks, "Really?"

Ryan laughs, reminding me of his ghostly presence. "Trust me when I say they're playing it cool right now. Their group is obsessed with anything supernatural, but especially the Abbot House. You could have just told them they won the lottery, and I doubt they'd be more excited."

Before I can wonder if I've maybe made a mistake by inviting these guys over so quickly, Ryan startles me by touching my arm. The sudden cold makes me hiss and drop my pencil, and I glare at him over my shoulder when I move to pick it up.

"Oh, let me get that for you." Nolan bends down at the same time I do, and his fingers brush against mine. I look up through my eyelashes, both embarrassed and alarmed to find that his face is only a few inches from mine. Nolan's cheeks redden when our eyes meet, and he makes this crazy choking sound before jumping back and flailing his arms. He somehow manages to slam his elbow against my nose, causing pain to erupt across my face.

A few drops of blood land on the desk and floor before I bring my hands up to cover my nose. The warm, sticky blood pooling in my hands makes me feel nauseous, and I squeeze my eyes shut in pain. I've never had a serious nose-bleed before, and I don't know how to stop it.

Someone touches my arm, and several people talk over each other to ask if I'm okay. I don't open my eyes until I hear the teacher's voice in front of me. I've already forgotten her name, but she looks seriously frazzled by the situation.

"You need to go to the nurse, sweetie. Spencer's going to show you where that is, okay?"

I shake my head and grunt. I'm afraid my nose might be broken, so I'd rather get it fixed by a witch. Principal Di Rossi never mentioned whether the school nurse was a witch or not, and I'd rather not take my chances. I manage to grit my teeth and get my words out clearly enough for the teacher to understand. "I wanna go alone."

"I'm not sure that's the best idea," she says. But I don't care what she thinks. I walk out of the classroom without looking back, Ryan hovering worriedly by my side.

CHAPTER 5
HARRIET

"I've never been the best at healing spells, I'm afraid." Principal Di Rossi smiles apologetically.

I tenderly touch my nose. It still hurts, but nowhere near as much, and it isn't bleeding anymore. Still, it's good I came here. Apparently, the school nurse isn't a witch, and my nose was actually broken. I hate admitting to other witches that I'm incapable of doing magic, but Di Rossi didn't hesitate to help me when I stumbled in here a few minutes ago. Knowing my luck, I wouldn't be surprised if my mom already told him about my *deficiency*. Today has been one embarrassing moment after another.

"Thank you, sir," I mumble, averting my eyes.

"Of course." When he gestures to my blood-stained shirt and jacket a bit awkwardly, I nod. He quietly murmurs an incantation under his breath, and the stains slowly fade until they're no longer there.

When he turns to his desk to write me a hall pass, Ryan grins and nods enthusiastically. He's been hovering a few feet away since we came in, unbeknownst to Di Rossi. "Looks good.

You've still got a little dried blood on your face, but it should wash right off."

I self-consciously brush my fingers underneath my nose, but I don't say anything. I'm not sure if my mom told Di Rossi about my ability to see ghosts or not, but I'm not about to tell him there's a ghost kid roaming his halls who may or may not have died under mysterious circumstances.

"What exactly happened?" Di Rossi asks as he hands me the hall pass.

"It was an accident." I shrug. As pissed as I am at the Binocular Boys, I know Nolan didn't knock into me on purpose.

Principal Di Rossi gives me a long look, like he's not sure if he should press for more information or not. "Your mother and I used to be very close. I know being a new student isn't particularly fun. I hope you feel comfortable coming to me for anything. Please let me know if anyone here ever bothers you."

It takes so much effort not to roll my eyes. No way am I going to snitch on anyone, even if they mess with me on purpose. I nod my head absently and wait a few more awkwardly-silent seconds until I'm dismissed.

Ryan follows me out of the office, and this time he doesn't hesitate to follow me into the closest bathroom. When I finally get a good look at myself in the mirror, I curl my lip in disgust and groan dramatically. There's dried blood all over my face— under my nose, around my mouth, on my chin, and even a little on my neck. Gross.

"I know you were obviously distracted at the time," Ryan says, grinning at my reflection in the mirror. "But you should have seen Nolan's face when your nose started bleeding."

I grab a handful of paper towels and wet them under the tap before vigorously scrubbing at my face, rolling my eyes at Ryan in the process. "Maybe I'll get lucky, and those guys will avoid me after this."

He shakes his head and chuckles. "I doubt it. You invited them to see the Abbot House. They're obsessed now." When I make another face in the mirror, Ryan raises his eyebrows. "Oh, come on. You even told Di Rossi you knew it was an accident. You're not seriously pissed at Nolan, are you?"

"No." I shrug defensively. "Not really. I'm still irritated about the spying thing, but I think he meant it earlier when he apologized."

"What's the issue, then?" Ryan leans close, looking into my backpack while I dig around for my makeup bag.

The closeness makes my temples throb. Combined with the pain from breaking my fucking nose and the fact that I've had a ghost-induced headache all damn day, I feel like I'm going to explode. I glare up at Ryan and snap, "Have you not noticed that I'm entirely incapable of talking to cute guys without thoroughly embarrassing myself? Goddess, every second I've spent in those guys' presence has been humiliating!"

Ryan gives me an obnoxious, Cheshire Cat grin. "You think they're cute, huh?"

No way does that question deserve a response.

"Well, what about me? You've been talking to me all day." Ryan wiggles his eyebrows at my reflection.

"You're dead." I roll my eyes hard. "I don't exactly have a reason to impress you, do I?"

The second the words are out of my mouth, I feel guilty. Rather than being offended, Ryan grins wider and squints his eyes in amusement. "You basically just admitted you think I'm cute."

"Ugh!" I spin around and shove him without thinking, nearly tripping over myself when my hands go right through him.

He howls with laughter, and we spend the rest of the class

period hanging out in the bathroom, talking while I finish fixing my makeup.

THE HALLWAY IS CROWDED, AND PEOPLE KEEP EYEING ME CURIOUSLY. Ryan stays glued to my side as he leads me to my English class. I'll never tell him this, but it's actually kind of comforting having him with me. The migraine is almost worth it.

"Shit," Ryan mumbles, and I look up to see what's caught his attention. It takes everything in me not to groan out loud when I see Amethyst standing with a couple of other witches outside my classroom.

Weeping Hollow is a small town, and this is a pretty small school. Running into her and sharing some classes shouldn't come as a surprise, but it still blows. I avoid looking directly at her or her friends, hoping to slip into class without any trouble or another stupid showdown.

I barely make it a few steps before I feel their stupid, prickly-witchy eyes on me. Witches love to show off, and they especially love to challenge each other. I brace myself for some kind of idiotic, magical act—like Amethyst's trick with the fire illusion earlier—so I'm at least somewhat prepared when tiny, electric shocks break out across my skin, and I seemingly trip over nothing. These kids have no way of knowing I can't fight back, but they're still major dickheads for messing with me.

An embarrassingly-weird yelping sound escapes my throat when someone roughly grabs my arms to stop me from falling. The person who caught me grabbed me hard enough to leave bruises, but that's still preferable to face-planting in the middle of the hallway.

44

"Harriet!" Amethyst screeches, cackling loudly with her friends. "Goddess, you're so clumsy!"

I ignore her, instead focusing on the large hands that are still holding me in place. I spin around and come face to face with a crazy-tall guy, and he drops his hands to his sides. We stare at each other silently, and my face gets warmer and warmer with every passing second. In my head, I want to say *thank you*. But he's—*Goddess*, he might be the hottest guy I've ever seen in my life.

When I say he's tall, he has to be at least 6'5. I have to tilt my head back a little to meet his gaze. His icy-blue eyes contrast beautifully with his bronze skin, and he has short, straight black hair.

"Uh..." I attempt to say something. Anything.

His eyes sweep over me carefully, and he never smiles or shows any expression. Without warning, he turns away and walks into our classroom. I exhale slowly and try to calm my rapidly-beating heart. I must have some seriously bad karma considering all of the shit luck I've had since moving to this town. I don't think I can handle any more embarrassment today.

"That was adorable." Ryan snickers.

I glare at him as I quickly shuffle into class. My new English teacher is this tiny, ancient lady named Mrs. Townsend who enthusiastically introduces me to the class and shoves a copy of *Alias Grace* into my hands.

The only open seat just happens to be next to that crazy-tall, *crazy-hot* guy from the hallway. At the very least, I'm relieved I'm not stuck next to those catty witches—though Amethyst's seat is only two tables behind mine.

As I slide into my new seat, Ryan grins and points dramatically at the cute guy beside me. "His name is Owen."

I glance sideways to subtly steal another look at him, but

Owen is already watching me unabashedly. I've never had anyone look at me so intently. Especially not such a cute guy. It makes me feel ten million times more flustered. I try to appear totally cool and casual by brushing my hair over my shoulder, and I open the front cover of *Alias Grace* with what I hope is a curious expression. Honestly though, what's the point of reading this when I can just watch the Netflix adaptation?

The first fifteen minutes of class pass by uneventfully. Mrs. Townsend seems passionate about her subject, and she's very engaging with the other students. I'm practically sweating while I try to keep up and take notes, desperately hoping she won't call on me for anything. English has never been my best subject. Grammar is stupidly hard, and reading is so boring. Ryan hovers quietly nearby, and I pretend not to notice Owen glancing at me from the corner of his eye every few minutes.

Unfortunately, I'm concentrating hard enough that it completely throws me off guard when my chair slides a few inches back. I clumsily mark a line across my page and curse under my breath. When my chair moves again, I glare over my shoulder to find Amethyst smirking at me. She and the girl beside her giggle loudly when I meet their eyes.

My face burns from anger and embarrassment when I turn around in my seat, and I have to bite my tongue to keep myself from lashing out. I'd love to walk back there and smack that asinine look right off of Amethyst Redferne's pretty face more than anything in the world.

"Why are they picking on you?" Ryan whispers, even though nobody else can hear him.

I scoot my chair in and start to write out a response to him, but my hand jerks as soon as my pen touches the page. Those petty witches giggle again, just loud enough for me to hear, and I grit my teeth when I feel their magic settle against my skin. I have absolutely zero control as my hand jerks back and forth across the desk, drawing jagged lines all over my notebook and on the desk. Angry tears prick at my eyes. I know Owen is watching me, and he probably thinks I'm a fucking lunatic.

Owen's hand suddenly closes over mine, stalling my erratic drawing. I make this awful, mortifying squeaking sound as my eyes dart up to meet his. He's still not showing any emotion, but I'm sure he's annoyed he got stuck sitting next to the weird new girl.

Instead of telling me to act normal or demanding that the teacher move me to another seat, he calmly reaches over and grabs my notebook with his other hand and sets it in front of him. While keeping my hand enclosed in his, he begins taking notes in *my* notebook for me, flicking a glance up front at the board every few moments to keep up with the lesson like this is the most normal thing in the world.

My hand feels clammy under his, but I'm terrified to move. I don't know what to think, and all I can do is stare at him like a gaping idiot.

"Wow." Ryan moves to hover in front of my desk, glancing back and forth between me and Owen with a comical, surprised look on his face. "He must really like you, Harriet. Owen doesn't talk to people outside of his friend group. I've never seen him pay attention to anyone like this."

"What?" I ask before I can think. Owen immediately stops writing and turns to look at me.

"Sorry." He lets go of my hand, but he doesn't give my notebook back. The corner of his mouth curls into a half smile, and he says, "I'm Owen."

"Harriet." I introduce myself automatically, cringing when I realize I'm making heart-eyes at the guy. He's only being nice because he thinks I'm mentally deranged. I awkwardly gesture at my notebook. "Thank you, but you, uh, really don't need to do that."

"It's fine." Owen shrugs. He continues taking notes for me like there's nothing weird about me or this situation.

I look up at Ryan helplessly, and he grins at me like he's never been more amused.

WHEN CLASS ENDS, I FEEL SHY AND UNSURE OF WHAT TO SAY OR DO with myself. Owen and I didn't talk after initially introducing ourselves, but Amethyst didn't mess with me again either. I'm dreading going to lunch since I'll probably run into Mattie, Spencer, and Nolan. Just thinking of dealing with them again gives me a headache. On top of the headache I already have.

"Thank you," I say quietly when Owen stands up and hands me my notebook. I brush my hair over my shoulder, feeling self-conscious.

Amethyst *accidentally* bumps into me as she walks past, and the witch beside her laughs obnoxiously as he wraps his arm around her waist. I breathe angrily out of my nose, but I'm careful not to react otherwise or look in her direction.

Owen's gaze flits toward the front of the room, and he frowns. "Ignore them. Amethyst Redferne and her friends are assholes."

"Yeah, I got that impression." I laugh, grinning up at him.

He smiles back, and my stomach flutters like crazy. I feel shy again, so I drop my gaze and make my way out of the classroom behind everyone else. I'm so distracted that I almost forget about Ryan until I feel his freezing touch against my arm.

"You should look at what he wrote." Ryan waves his hand at my notebook and wiggles his eyebrows suggestively.

I stop in the hallway and hesitate, especially when Owen stops beside me rather than leave to meet up with his friends. But my curiosity wins out, and I flip open the book to the last page Owen wrote in. His handwriting is neat, and it looks like he expanded on the notes a bit instead of just copying what was on the board. At the very bottom, underneath all of the notes he took for me, I find what Ryan wanted me to see.

You're the most beautiful girl I've ever seen in my life. Want to go out sometime?

His name and phone number are scribbled under the short note. Holy crap, I'm going to explode. Or squeal, or do something else ridiculously humiliating. In the end, I let out a high-pitched, girlish giggle and look up at Owen half in awe, half in embarrassment.

He smiles, blushing faintly. "I didn't think you'd notice that until later."

I cannot, for the life of me, figure out how to respond. Anything I say is just going to sound awkward, and I'm totally going to ruin whatever's happening between us.

"Harriet!" Someone calls my name, saving me from embarrassing myself for the time being. I look up to find Mattie jogging toward us. When he reaches us, he throws his arms around me in a way-too-familiar hug, causing me to immediately tense up.

"What are you doing?" I ask, horrified. I'm not a big hugger, and he really caught me off-guard. Maybe I should feel bad for snapping at him, but he didn't even fucking warn me.

"I was worried, dude! Spencer told me that Nolan broke your nose during third period."

"What?" Owen exclaims, his voice thick with concern as his icy-blue eyes scan my face worriedly.

Mattie turns and blinks like he's only just now noticed Owen's presence. "Oh, good. You found Owen. That means you've met the whole crew."

Wait. Mattie, Nolan, and Spencer are friends with Owen? Goddess, I can't decide if this is a good thing, or if this is the universe's idea of a joke at my expense. I narrow my eyes and look back and forth between the two boys who couldn't seem more different. And then I turn my glare on Ryan. He's barely kept his mouth shut all day. He could have at least given me a heads up. Ryan grins and shrugs, not bothering to answer my silent question.

"Your nose doesn't look broken." Mattie muses as he peers up at me quizzically.

"It was just a nosebleed," I lie. "I'm fine now."

Mattie beams, beckoning for me and Owen to follow him. "In that case, let's go to lunch. Nolan and Spence are probably looking for us. We have a million questions for you, Harriet!"

CHAPTER 6
HARRIET

"We spent most of class analyzing the blood spatter from your nose-bleed after you left."

I make a face at Spencer as he sets his lunch tray down on the table across from me. "That's disgusting."

"It was actually kind of awesome." He grins. "Right, Nolan?"

Nolan coughs and makes a point of not looking in my direction. I know he feels bad for earlier, and probably for the binocular thing. But I'm not about to sit here and console him or tell him I'm not mad. He stutters at Spencer's question, "Uh, it was, um..."

Owen sits down on my right side, and my cheeks flush. He's not sitting so close that we're touching or anything, but I'm still reeling from what he wrote in my notebook. I can't help thinking he was playing a joke on me. He hasn't said a word since I walked to lunch with him and Mattie a few minutes ago.

"Look at how flustered he is! The poor thing." Ryan

snickers at Nolan. He's sitting across from me, beside Spencer, grinning like a jackass at the guys. I would totally flip him off if I could get away with it without looking like a crazy person.

Mattie slides into the seat on my left. But unlike Owen, he has no clue what personal space is. He sits close enough that he's practically glued to my side. I grit my teeth together and turn to glare at him, but then he yanks my lunchbox from my hands and rifles through it. "Ooh, this looks delicious!"

My eyes widen in outrage. I try to grab it back, but he keeps my lunch too far from my reach. "What the fuck is your problem? Have you seriously never heard of personal space?"

He completely ignores me, pulling out a wrapped sandwich and a small box of pale orange macarons. "Look how adorable Harriet's lunch is, guys!"

The mocking tone in his voice makes me blush harder. Forget the fact that Mattie Baxter was somewhat nice to me earlier. Clearly, he's intent on making my life unbearable. I consider getting up and leaving, and I cast my angry gaze around the cafeteria. Amethyst is sitting with a group of witches at the other end of the room, and they probably expect me to beg for a spot with them since it's supposed to be where I belong. You couldn't pay me to sit with any of those assholes. Besides Sage, I never really got along with other witches my age back home either. Since I haven't talked to anyone else in this school besides the four boys surrounding me, and I don't feel like hiding out in the bathroom with Ryan like some kind of loser, I guess I'm kind of stuck here for now.

"Cut it out," Spencer chides his friend. He takes my lunch from Mattie and places it back in front of me, offering me an apologetic smile.

He's so cute, but the words get stuck in my throat when I try to thank him. Instead, I open the macarons and hand him one. "My mom really loves to bake."

His eyes light up, and he beams at me as he pops the treat into his mouth. "Sweet, thanks!"

I'm about to put the rest of them aside, but then I glance sideways at Owen. He's watching me the same way he was in class, and my stomach flutters nervously. I pass him a macaron before I think too hard about it, and he gives me a radiant smile as he wordlessly takes it from my fingers.

Everyone sits quietly, none of them eating. It makes me feel anxious and flustered, and before I know it, I begin rambling as I unpack the rest of my lunch and tear open the sandwich my mom packed for me. "It'll probably take a while since the house needs so much work, but my mom and aunt are going to convert the first floor of the Abbot House into a bakery and tea shop. My mom's always wanted to open her own bakery, and she always wanted an excuse to move back here."

The guys exchange looks. I can't even guess what they're thinking. For once, Ryan is silent, being no help at all.

Surprisingly, Nolan is the first one to break the silence. "That's a good idea. There's not anything like that in town, or even close by that I know of."

"What's the house like on the inside? Like, what sort of work does it need?" Spencer tucks his hair behind his ear and leans forward with his elbows on the table.

"It's really gross. It's been sitting and rotting for twenty-something years, and everything is covered in dust and mold." I shrug and take a bite of my sandwich, relieved to see Owen, Spencer, and Mattie finally begin to eat as well.

Instead of eating like everyone else, Nolan places a small black pouch on the table and pulls out what looks like a thick pen. There's a clicking sound when he holds it against his fingertip, and there's a tiny prick of blood on his skin when he pulls it away. I watch with morbid fascination as he presses his bleeding finger to a tiny strip of plastic, and then inserts the strip into a small machine.

Nolan frowns when he catches me watching him, and he mumbles, "I have diabetes."

I quickly avert my eyes and pretend to be totally engrossed with my own lunch. I feel like such a jerk for staring at him, but I was only curious to see what he was doing. At least I didn't offer him a macaron and make things even more awkward.

"So, the Abbot House." Spencer redirects my attention and smiles when my eyes meet his. "It's been empty for so long, like you said. Why's your family just now moving in?"

It's not like I can tell them about the curse, so I shrug and give them just a little bit of the truth. "My great-grandma's will was only discovered recently, and she left it to my mom and her twin sister."

"Do you know how she died?" Mattie asks with a creepy-excited smile on his face. When I raise my eyebrows at him in disbelief, his smile turns into a grimace. "Sorry. We're just curious."

"Which of these guys do you think is cutest, Harriet?" Ryan interrupts. He floats closer to Spencer and pokes his cheek, but his hand goes right through the other boy. Spencer doesn't notice, and Ryan turns to grin at me while he wiggles his eyebrows. "Normally my vote would be on Mattie, but Spencer just pulls off that sexy-emo-boy look so well. Then again, you and Owen seem to have some mad chemistry, and Nolan's pretty adorable too."

I choke on a bite of my sandwich and glare menacingly at Ryan before I catch myself. Owen looks in Ryan's direction and raises an eyebrow at me in confusion. I cringe and look away from him. Goddess, will I ever stop embarrassing myself? Owen already saw me acting like a psychopath in class, and now this! Ryan looks so alive, and he doesn't act like any other ghost I've ever met. It's too easy to forget I'm the only one who can see him.

When Owen doesn't call me out, and the other guys pretend not to notice my weird behavior, I shrug and answer Mattie's question. "Technically, her death was ruled as a heart attack. But it was super weirdly planned out. My grandma Sylvia already had a bunch of stuff set up and taken care of before it happened."

"Well, she was pretty old, right? It would make sense for her to have some kind of plans for after her death," Nolan says. He pushes his glasses up on his nose and pulls his own packed lunch from his backpack.

"But!" Mattie holds his finger up and grins triumphantly. "There have always been rumors that she might have killed herself."

Owen hums thoughtfully and adds, "It could have been something else though. You said she had some stuff planned, but that they only recently found her will? That's pretty unusual."

Spencer, Mattie, and Nolan stare at Owen in shock. I don't see how his comment or question are any weirder than Mattie's, so I shrug it off and nod my head in agreement. "Exactly! She dropped her cats off at a shelter and checked into a hotel, which is where she was found when she died. And she set up these bank accounts for my mom, my Aunt Flora, and my grandma Helena with some money. But the house was all locked up, and I'm pretty sure the will was purposely hidden."

"Oh, these guys love a good conspiracy theory." Ryan chuckles, rubbing his hands together like a villain from a cheesy movie. "Nice going, Harriet."

I force myself not to glance in Ryan's direction, but his comment makes me blush. I didn't mean to sound so keen or get excited about the subject. It's just that the Abbot House and my Grandma Sylvia's death have always been such a mystery to me, and Sage is the only person I've ever been able to discuss my questions and theories with.

Before I can apologize or try to change the subject, Spencer asks, "Did anyone try to hire a lawyer to deal with the property when the will wasn't originally found?"

Obviously, I can't tell them about the curse, or about the politics of witches. My mom and Flora would have done anything to get into the Abbot House before now if they'd been able to. While they've always told me all sorts of charming stories about Weeping Hollow and our family home, they've never talked to me much about Sylvia's death. I don't know if they're still too sad about it, or if they really believe she died naturally from a heart attack. But I've always thought the whole story sounded sort of peculiar, and just a bit too mysterious.

"Why are you guys so interested in my house, anyway?" I narrow my eyes at the four boys suspiciously.

Nobody answers right away, and Ryan gets this crazy-obnoxious grin on his face. Spencer and Nolan exchange a look, and Owen clears his throat before he finally answers me. "We're a paranormal investigative team."

My mind goes totally blank, and I stare at Owen like a moron. There's no way I heard him right. Mattie jabs me in the side with his elbow and enthusiastically says, "You know, like ghost hunters! We like to explore haunted places, and we've been trying to get into the Abbot House for years."

A grin slowly spreads across my face, and I stare back and forth between the four of them before finally focusing on Ryan. No wonder he's been so amused by my interactions with these guys, and why he considers them some of his favorite people to ghost-creep on in this school.

"You're kidding," I squeal, finally giving into the giggles

that have been building in my chest. Goddess, if they only knew how ironic this was. They're *ghost hunters* sitting right next to a fucking ghost who follows them around on the regular.

Too late, I realize the guys look embarrassed. Spencer gives me a tight smile and shrugs. "I know it sounds nuts, but something like forty-five percent of people believe in ghosts. Weeping Hollow is kind of known for having an occult history, and there are tons of places in New England that are supposedly haunted too."

He's right about Weeping Hollow, considering the town was established by witches. The Abbots were one of the first well-known witch families to settle here, along with Amethyst Redferne's ancestors.

"We're going to check out this abandoned insane asylum this weekend." Owen slides his hand just a tiny bit closer to mine on the table, and he smiles when I turn to meet his icy-blue eyes. "Do you want to come with us?"

"Yeah, that would be fucking sweet!" Spencer exclaims. "Do you think your mom would let you?"

I get this warm, fuzzy feeling all over, and a genuine smile forms on my lips. I barely know these guys, and I've acted like such a clumsy idiot in front of all of them. But they're already acting like they want to be my friends, and there's something kind of amazing about finding four people who are interested in ghosts. Maybe Ryan's right. Seeing ghosts might not be such a terrible gift to have.

But then I catch Nolan shaking his head from the corner of my eye, and the fuzzy feeling vanishes. Maybe he doesn't want to be friends or invite me along on his ghost-hunting adventures just yet, but that's okay. I'd be apprehensive if I were Nolan too, and it's not like it matters.

"I can't. My mom and aunt invited a bunch of people over

this weekend, and I have to stick around for that." They're trying to reconnect with some of the witches in town, and I can't say I'm exactly thrilled about the unofficial coven meeting. "But you guys can still come over anytime if you really want to see the house, or if you want to do a paranormal investigation or whatever."

"For real?" Mattie asks reverently. I swear the guy has literal heart-eyes. When I shrug nonchalantly, he throws his arms around me and hugs me tightly with his cheek pressed against mine. "You're the fucking greatest, Harriet. I'm so glad I made that deal with Principal Di Rossi."

I shove him away as roughly as I can, and I know I'm probably blushing again judging by Ryan's laughter. I can't stand being touched or hugged by people I don't really know, and Mattie's lack of respect for personal space is starting to get old.

"What deal?" Nolan asks quietly, glancing quickly between me and Mattie.

Mattie sits up straight and scoots close again, totally unfazed by me shoving him away. "Principal Di Rossi said if I showed Harriet around, I wouldn't have to do Saturday detention."

He launches into the whole story of how he and I met in the office this morning, and what he did to get himself in trouble in the first place. While everyone's attention is focused on him, I stay quiet and eat my lunch as I reflect on the events of the day. I still have three classes after lunch is over, and I'm already exhausted. I know I'm probably feeling extra drained from being around Ryan all day, which seriously sucks.

I still have no idea what's up with him—why he looks so corporeal, why he's supposedly unable to leave the school, and why the hell he can't remember much about his past. I know ghosts are typically stronger and more coherent if they stick close to where they died, but they're not usually stuck, per se. Ryan doesn't even seem that interested in figuring out why he is the way he is or what happened to him. He's just happy to have someone to talk to, and he's weirdly invested in this group of amateur ghost hunters for some reason.

"Do you have a boyfriend, Harriet?"

Mattie's voice brings me back to the present, and I whip my head around to frown at him. I may have been spacing out, but where the hell did that question come from? "No, why?"

He smirks mischievously and pushes his curly hair away from his pretty eyes. "Just wondering."

I stare at him for several long seconds and seriously debate punching him in the mouth. After a few moments of deliberation, I decide against it, rubbing my temples as I groan in frustration. "Goddess, you're giving me a headache."

Spencer, Owen, and Ryan chuckle. If only I was joking. I'm not looking forward to going home because Old Creepy will probably stay glued to my side after missing me all day.

"What class do you have next? We only have a few more minutes until lunch is over," Spencer says.

Ryan snorts and floats around the table until he's hovering just behind me. "How much you wanna bet you share your next class with at least one of them?"

I mentally roll my eyes and dig in my backpack for my schedule, and then I hand it over to Spencer.

CHAPTER 7
HARRIET

"You don't see any of them, do you?"

Ryan cackles and shakes his head. "I think you're good. I don't get why you're trying so hard to avoid them."

I glare at him, and then I glance over my shoulder at the school to make sure Owen, Spencer, Mattie, or Nolan aren't anywhere nearby. I was lucky enough not to share my last class of the day with any of them, and now I'm outside waiting for my mom to pick me up.

"It's fucking awkward, that's why. I've embarrassed myself enough for one day."

After lunch, I had psychology with both Spencer and Owen. However, the teacher, Mr. Carrington made me sit with the other witches on the complete opposite side of the room from Spencer and Owen. It was fucking awful. The only saving grace was that Amethyst wasn't one of the witches, and the pretentious fuckers didn't bother talking to me or messing with me in front of Mr. Carrington.

My next class was pre-calculus, which I shared with Nolan.

He didn't bother talking to me, so I feel like I got off pretty easy humiliation-wise for the rest of the day compared to how my morning went. Still, if I can make it home without any more incidents, I'll call it a win.

"Thank Goddess," I groan when I catch sight of my mom's ugly Jeep Wagoneer pulling into the pick-up lane.

Ryan brushes his hand against mine, making me shiver, and I turn to find him looking at me with a sad smile. "Before you leave, I just wanna say thanks for letting me follow you around all day."

My throat suddenly feels thick as I stare back at him. After spending the last six hours with Ryan glued to my side, it feels weird to think I won't be able to talk to him until I come back to school tomorrow. I totally consider him my friend, even if I won't admit that out loud. If he wasn't stuck on the school grounds, I would offer to let him come home with me. At least then he would have Old Creepy for company when I can't be around.

"I didn't let you," I scoff and roll my eyes before I accidentally say anything too sappy. "You followed me around without permission. Besides, I'll see you tomorrow."

He grins and shakes his head in amusement, clearly not offended in the slightest. When my mom parks beside the front curb, he follows me to the car and hovers close as I climb into the passenger seat.

"Hi, sweetie!" My mom grins. "How was it? As bad as you expected it to be?"

I shrug and open my mouth to tell her it was fine, and also to introduce her to Ryan even though she can't see him. But before I can get a word in, she keeps talking. "Kamal Di Rossi hasn't changed a bit. He's so great, isn't he? Please tell me you behaved after I left. That Matthew boy seemed very nice, and

Kamal mentioned there are several other students here who are witches."

My mom knows damn well I've never gotten along with witches my age, and she knew I was nervous about starting school today. Why can't she just be nice and think about me for once? As usual, she's focused on herself, and she's worried about me tarnishing her image. Why doesn't she realize that things don't come as easily for me as they always have for her? It's not fucking fair. I suddenly have no desire to share anything about my day with her, and I turn my head to look out the window with a scowl.

"Yeah, whatever." I wave to Ryan as my mom pulls away from the curb, and he offers me a comforting smile as he waves back. My headache dissipates as soon as I get some distance from him.

She doesn't ask me any more questions about my day the entire drive home. She drones on about the cleaning she and Flora did in the house and talks incessantly about one of the neighbors. I pretty much tune her out. I'm too hurt by her dismissal that I don't care at all to listen to anything she has to say.

The moment we arrive home, I kick my shoes off by the front door and stomp upstairs. Flora calls my name, but I ignore her. I have no doubt she'll take my mom's side. There's no sign of Old Creepy in my room, thank Goddess, and I slam my door closed and collapse on top of my bed face down.

I spend a few minutes convincing myself not to cry. I made it through the day, after all, and I even made a friend if you count Ryan. I'm not counting the other guys I met. Every time I start to think of Mattie, Spencer, Nolan, and Owen as potential friends or acquaintances, something else horribly embarrassing happens around them. I might still sit with them during lunch at school, but only to avoid being a total loner-weirdo.

Rolling over onto my back, I grab my phone out of my pocket and sigh as I pull up Sage's info. Unless her family changed their plans at the last minute, she should be heading home today. I miss her so much, and I need to talk to someone who's alive and not related to me about everything that's been going on since I came to Weeping Hollow.

"Come on, Sage," I whine quietly to myself while I wait for her to answer the FaceTime call. To my surprise and relief, she answers on the fourth ring. I grin broadly when I see her pouting back at me through my phone screen.

"Oh my Goddess, Harriet, I was just about to text you!" she practically shouts into the phone. I can still barely hear her because her three younger brothers are screeching and laughing obnoxiously in the background. "I'm still in the car, but I'll be home in a couple of hours!"

"Ugh, you have no idea how much I've missed you." I can't stop smiling like an idiot, and I feel like I'm a few mortifying seconds away from bursting into tears.

"I can't even hear you!" Sage groans, and I watch as she turns her head. I can't see what's happening for sure, but I think she might have punched one of her brothers based on the wail that follows her sentence and the muffled admonishment I hear from Sage's mom a few seconds later.

Sage rolls her eyes on screen again and grimaces at me. "I'll call the second I get home, okay? I want to hear absolutely everything!"

She hangs up before I can say goodbye, but I don't mind. Her family can be nuts, and I'd much rather have some privacy when we get a chance to talk. Besides, I already feel better just from seeing her and talking to her for a few seconds.

Just when I start to feel happy and peaceful for the first

time all week, my nose starts to itch, and goosebumps break out across my skin as my temples begin to throb.

> *"There was an old woman lived under the hill,*
>
> *And if she's not gone, she lives there still.*
>
> *Baked apples she sold, and cranberry pies,*
>
> *And she's the old woman that never told lies."*

Sighing in defeat, I frown at Old Creepy as she floats into my room. She's wringing her hands together and staring at me with a horrifying, toothless smile.

"Hey, Old Creepy." I pat the spot on my bed beside me, inviting her over. She's gonna hover even if I ignore her, so I might as well give in already. "I missed you too. School was even worse than I thought it would be."

She hums a melancholy tune and joins me on the bed, floating so it looks like she's sitting next to me. She pats my hand as she hums, and I smile at the gesture. I can't feel anything other than a slightly painful, freezing burn where my skin comes into contact with her. I shiver slightly, but I don't pull away. She's doing her best to comfort me, and that's more than I can say for my own mother.

"I met another ghost," I whisper. "He might be the weirdest ghost I've ever met, and that's saying something."

Old Creepy cackles, and my smile widens. She totally gets my humor. My head pounds, making me cringe and rub my temples desperately. These past few days in Weeping Hollow have me thinking this whole seeing-ghosts thing might not actually be so bad, if only I could do something about these damn migraines. I don't know how much longer I'll be able to take it, especially if I'm gonna be around ghosts on a daily basis from now on.

My bedroom door slowly creaks open. I look up, expecting

to see my mom or Flora, and gasp in anger when I see a tiny, mangy black cat peek its stupid little face into my room instead.

"Who let you in here, you little monster?"

The cat ignores me and waltzes into my room like it owns the place. I purse my lips and narrow my eyes, silently cursing Aunt Flora and her ridiculous idea that black cats are somehow good luck. The cat walks the perimeter of my room, all the while ignoring me while I yell and hiss at it. Even when I throw my backpack in its direction, intending to scare it rather than hit it, it only looks up with a judgmental, unimpressed look on its face.

I groan and get up from my bed to shoo it out of my room. I'll pick it up and throw it out in the hallway if I have to. Just thinking about touching the ugly little beast makes my skin itch. It's probably riddled with fleas.

"Get out of here!" I nudge its side with my foot and make another hissing sound at it to scare it off.

The black cat blinks up at me with unsettling yellow eyes, and then it pounces forward and starts scratching like mad at the floor in the corner of the room.

"Hey!" I screech. I grab at the cat to try and get it to stop, but the fucking thing is determined. It scratches rabidly at the floorboard with its sharp claws. "That's original hardwood, you little demon!"

It mews and scrapes its claws against the wood as I pull it away. I'm about to freak out and go off on my mom and aunt for letting this animal into the house, but Old Creepy claps her hands and laughs her ass off while pointing at the floorboard the cat was scratching at.

I turn around and take a closer look at the floor. There are a few scratches in the wood from the cat, making it easier to notice that the floorboard is loose. Feeling curious, I crawl closer and dig my fingers into the tiny crack that's visible and pry the board the rest of the way up.

Beneath layers of dirt and dust, there's a small tin box with a frayed and faded ribbon tied around it. I pick the tin up, wipe it off, and cough from the insane amount of dust entering my lungs. The tin is plain with no decorations other than the crappy ribbon, but I'm still careful as I untie it and open the lid.

Old Creepy leans close, practically brushing against me while she tries to get a better look. The cat walks over too, sitting beside me calmly as it purrs and stares at the tin in my hands. Very rarely do I ever feel my 'witch's intuition' kick in, as my magic never works the way it's supposed to. But for once, I feel that tingly feeling of rightness that I'm on the right path set for me by the Goddess.

Inside, there's an old, white handkerchief folded up with an envelope underneath it. I pick up the handkerchief, intrigued to discover there's something wrapped inside of it, and then I gasp when I see my name written in old-fashioned calligraphy on the front of the envelope.

There's nothing else. No address or stamp or anything. Just my first name. I set the handkerchief aside and hold the letter up for Old Creepy to see. She clasps her hands together and grins as she nods her head vigorously.

I'm terrified I'm going to rip the envelope, but I don't have time to search through the house for a letter opener. My curiosity is practically burning me up. I delicately slide my fingernail under the wax seal on the back, and I nearly squeal when it opens easily without tearing.

With shaky hands, I pull the letter out of the envelope and unfold the paper. It's so thin and totally ancient. There's no date written anywhere on it, and nothing to help me guess how long it's been hidden here. The letter is short. It's only a few sentences, but it's addressed to *me*. I read it aloud to Old Creepy and the black cat:

"*DEAREST HARRIET,*

My sister Ruth and I found this stone by the river this afternoon while we were scrying, and we both agreed it's meant for you. True adder stones are rare to find, but we have the strangest feeling you're in more need of one than we are.

Yours truly, Esther."

THE CAT BRUSHES AGAINST MY ARM AFFECTIONATELY, STILL PURRING loudly. I scratch the top of its head and carefully set the letter down, picking up the handkerchief to gently unfold it. Folded inside the old handkerchief, I find a smooth, flat black stone with two naturally-created holes through it with a black cord tied with an intricate knot through one of the holes.

"Holy shit," I whisper excitedly as I run my finger over the smooth stone. Witch stones, or adder stones like Ester called them in the letter, are fairly difficult to find. People used to think you could see fairies when looking through the holes of the stones, but now they're used more as good luck charms or talismans for powerful witches.

I slip the necklace over my head, and I feel a drastic difference immediately. Even though Old Creepy is sitting right next to me, I don't feel cold or numb anymore. Best of all, I don't have a fucking headache. For the first time in days, my head feels clear. I almost want to cry in relief.

Old Creepy hums, but it's a happy tune rather than a melancholy one like she usually seems to prefer. She gives me one of her horrifying smiles, and I grin back at her like a lunatic. She pats my arm, and her hand goes right through me like always. But for the first time, her touch doesn't feel cold or unpleasant. It's just a little tingly.

The black cat moves closer to me and rubs its head affectionately against my hand. I scratch its head again and sigh. It still desperately needs a bath, but I guess not all cats are really so terrible. This one seems too smart for its own good, but I can't be mad at it anymore after it helped me find the solution to my ghost-migraine problem.

"Alright, you can stay." I continue petting it, and I giggle when the cat starts purring even louder.

CHAPTER 8
HARRIET

N othing. Absolutely fucking nothing.

"It just doesn't make any sense," I whisper irritably.

Old Creepy giggles, but she's not paying attention to me. Apparently, my new cat can see ghosts too. She's amusing herself and my ghostly roommate by batting at her translucent ankles. I sigh and close my laptop, feeling dejected and irrationally angry.

For the past hour, after finding the adder stone necklace left by my ancestors, I've been searching for anything related to Ryan's death. He didn't give me much to go on, but I figured something was sure to come up by searching his name, death, and Weeping Hollow. I even searched through graduation class groups on Facebook from the past ten years to see if there were any pictures or posts about his death. But there isn't a single mention of a high school student dying in Weeping Hollow over the past decade.

I'm starting to think Ryan lied to me about how much he knows. Any time I tried asking him more questions during school, he was vague or said he didn't remember. Either that, or someone did a very good job of hiding the evidence and sweeping the whole thing under the rug. I'm more determined than ever to get to the bottom of this, with or without Ryan's help.

"Harriet!" My mom's voice calls through the house, interrupting my thoughts. I suspect she's using magic, considering I can hear her clearly and I'm pretty sure she's still downstairs. "You have some visitors!"

The cat and Old Creepy turn to look at me, and I raise my eyebrows at them. I have no idea who'd be visiting me, but I'm too curious not to investigate further. It's probably better for me to take a break from my so-called research on the dead guy I'm sort of friends with at school.

I make my way through the long hallway and down the stairs. When I make it about halfway down, I freeze and widen my eyes. Spencer, Owen, Mattie, and Nolan are standing in the foyer with my mother. Owen looks up and smiles at me, but the other guys appear too distracted. They're staring around the house with awestruck expressions, and I totally don't miss the fact that Mattie's holding his phone up.

"Um, hey." I slowly walk the staircase, my eyes roaming over each of the guys. Mattie, Spencer, and Nolan finally look up at me, and I try not to grimace when I feel myself blushing. "What are you guys doing here?"

Spencer chuckles as he raises his hand in a wave. "You invited us, remember?"

Oh, right. I did tell the guys they were welcome to come over anytime so they could check out the house. I just didn't think they'd show up like this, especially after I did my best to avoid them after lunch today. Mattie lowers his phone like he's trying to hide it from me, and I nearly snort at his lack of subtlety. He's probably taking pictures or a video of their first glimpse inside of the Abbot House, just like he was taking pictures of me from the bushes the other day.

The other guys are each holding some sort of object too. Owen has a fancy-looking camera around his neck, Spencer's holding a thick, leather-bound notebook, and Nolan has a weird electronic device in his hand that kind of looks like a remote control.

"I guess I just didn't expect you to come over so soon," I mumble, feeling somewhere between amused and anxious at being around them again. At least I'm feeling more clear-headed now that I'm not practically dying from a ghost-inflicted migraine.

"Harriet didn't tell me she made friends already," my mom says. She gives each of the guys a calculating look and turns to face me with a mischievous smile. I tense up even before she speaks again. "I'm so proud of you, sweetheart! I told you your new school wouldn't be so bad."

It takes everything in me not to snap at her. Why is she trying to embarrass me? I had the crappiest day ever, and she knows how nervous I get around guys. I bite my tongue and turn away from her, hoping the guys will be quick about looking around.

"Who's this little furball?" Spencer crouches down to scratch the cat's head when she makes an appearance.

If my mom's surprised to see a random stray cat roaming around the house, she doesn't say anything. She probably agrees with Flora that black cats are good luck or some bullshit like that. Seeing Spencer petting the little menace is pretty adorable though, and I can't help smiling when he glances up at me from the floor.

I've been tossing ideas for names around since I agreed to let the cat stay, and I make up my mind on the spot as Spencer waits for my answer. "Her name's Circe."

His grin widens as he stands. "Like the Greek Goddess? Nice."

I'm super impressed he knew that, but there's no way in hell I'm going to let myself nerd out in front of a cute guy. Scratch that—cute *guys.*

"Uh huh." I nod once, feigning nonchalance. "How do you guys wanna do this?"

Mattie flicks his hair out of his eyes and smirks. "That's what she said."

I meet his gaze dead-on as I flip him off, and Owen and Spencer snicker quietly. My mom is entirely not amused though, and she puts her hands on her hips as she gives me one of her angry-faces.

"Harriet! Be nice." When I don't respond, she sighs and turns to walk away. "I'll be in the kitchen if you need anything."

As soon as she's gone and I'm left alone with the guys, I feel both relieved and also ten million times more nervous. I have no idea what to say or do next. There's an awkward silence before Owen smiles softly at me and saves the day. "Normally in a house this big, we start from the top and work our way down. Just let us know if there's anywhere we're not allowed."

"Yeah, okay." I nod and spin around to head back up the stairs. There's really not much I'm afraid of them seeing or finding, and I'm extremely curious to see what they look for when doing their paranormal investigations. "There are still a bunch of rooms we haven't looked in yet. We've mostly been focusing on the main living areas so far."

Mattie rushes past the others up the stairs so that he's right beside me and grins. He's holding his phone up again, pointing it at everything. "That makes it so much cooler. You're seriously the fucking best for letting us do this."

"No problem." My face flushes happily at the stupid

compliment, and I get that same bubbly feeling I had at lunch earlier. Like I've found people I might actually fit in with. "What exactly are you going to do?"

At the top of the stairs, I pause for a split second when I see Old Creepy hovering outside my bedroom. She tilts her head at the guys and giggles as she wrings her hands together, but she doesn't come any closer. The four of them were totally oblivious about Ryan at school, but I wonder if they'll be able to pick up on a ghost's presence when they're prepared.

"We didn't want to freak you or your family out too much, so we didn't bring all of our equipment like we normally would," Spencer says, not looking at me. He flips open his notebook and glances around the upstairs hallway and second-floor balcony as he jots something down.

His handwriting is too small and scratchy for me to read without getting closer, but I can't deny that I'm super curious. I pass by my bedroom and head up the smaller, winding staircase that leads to the third floor. There's not much up here —just a couple of rooms crammed full of old boxes and furniture, and the access panel to the attic. I haven't had a chance to search through the attic yet, but I have a feeling the dust and spiders will be a million times worse there than they've been in the rest of the house.

Spencer scribbles furiously as soon as he reaches the third floor, and Mattie walks slowly through the rooms with his phone up as he continues recording. "Holy shit, guys. We could probably spend hours in just one room. Have you looked through any of this stuff yet, Harriet?"

My attention is divided between the four of them, so it takes me a second to answer. "Uh, not really." My eyes follow Nolan as he shuffles into one of the storage rooms, and Owen snaps photos with his fancy camera. "I've glanced in them, but that's it. My aunt said a lot of this stuff was stored up here like this even when my great-grandmother was alive."

The four of them are quiet for a few minutes, completely lost in their own world. Even though it's my house, I feel incredibly awkward and in the way. When Circe brushes against my legs, I pick her up and cradle her to my chest without hesitation. She purrs quietly, which makes me feel a little bit better.

"Hey." Owen's voice startles me, and I spin around to see him standing just a couple inches behind me. I have to tilt my head back to meet his eyes since he's so damn tall, and he smiles. "Sorry we're boring you. Wanna head down to the second floor while they finish up?"

"What are they doing?" I whisper as I lead him down the winding steps. It's probably a bad idea to leave the other guys alone, but Owen's right about me feeling bored and weird. Still, my gaze flits back up the stairs anxiously.

"They won't touch anything," he assures me with a chuckle. "They're just taking basic notes right now. Nolan's checking the EMF meter for any anomalies, Spence is mapping out the rooms and taking notes, and Mattie's taking a video on his phone for us to look at later in case we missed anything in person."

"Huh." I click my tongue and look around the hallway on the second floor with new eyes. "Think you guys will find anything?"

"Maybe." Owen takes a photo, and I blink when I realize he was aiming the camera at me. "You told the guys you have a ghost, right?"

Old Creepy giggles from my bedroom doorway, and I force myself not to turn and look at her. My cheeks heat up in embarrassment at Owen's question. Sometimes other witches don't even take my gift seriously, so I certainly didn't expect four non-magical teenage guys to believe me.

"I was kidding when I said that."

He gives me this amused half-smile. "Okay."

Butterflies writhe in my stomach and my face feels even warmer than before. It feels like he's teasing me, like he really believes I was telling the truth about the ghost. It also kind of feels like he's flirting with me, and I can't get that moment out of my head when Ryan pointed out what Owen wrote in my notebook during English class. He not only called me beautiful, but he also asked me out and gave me his freaking phone number! And all I did was giggle like an idiot.

Since I suck at talking to guys and I get embarrassed way too easily, I quickly change the subject and point at his camera. "What's your job then? What's the point of taking pictures when Mattie's already recording on his phone?"

Owen raises his camera and snaps a photo of me, and I blink in surprise. "Sometimes things show up differently in photographs, especially when they're developed in a darkroom."

When he takes another photo of me, I drop Circe to the ground and I cross my arms defensively. "I think taking pictures of me is kind of missing the point of this little project."

He bites his lip and smiles bashfully, and I practically melt when his gorgeous blue eyes meet mine. "Yeah, well, I think I'd rather take pictures of a beautiful girl than a bunch of old antiques or a potential ghost."

A mortifying squeaking sound escapes my throat, and Owen's smile widens. Oh, Goddess. What do I even say to that? How do I respond? Sage would know what to do, but I'm a fucking moron. I can't do anything other than gape at this crazy-attractive dude while he calls me beautiful to my face!

"Girls and boys, come out to play,

the moon doth shine as bright as day."

I look up when Old Creepy starts one of her creepy-as-fuck rhymes, my eyes following her as she floats behind Owen. I want to slap myself the second I realize what I'm doing. The guys may be into ghost hunting and paranormal shit, but I still don't want them to think I'm a weirdo.

Owen's gaze follows my line of sight, and quicker than I can blink, he spins around and starts taking photos rapidly of the same spot where Old Creepy is standing. I inhale sharply and stare at Owen in alarm as I realize something. He really, truly believes in ghosts, and he might even think I can see them.

There's a question on the tip of my tongue, but I'm just not sure how to ask him what I'm thinking. Before I say something I might regret or make myself look even more foolish, the sound of footsteps on the stairs behind us causes Owen and me to turn around.

"Find anything down here?" Spencer asks with a grin as he steps into the second-floor hallway.

Owen shrugs but doesn't answer verbally. He simply walks across the hallway and gestures at one of the closed doors until I nod to let him know he's allowed to open it. Spencer smiles at me and follows Owen into the room. It's dusty and full of junk just like the rooms upstairs, but eventually we're going to make it into a sitting room.

Mattie and Nolan come downstairs next, and Mattie gleefully enters the room after his friends while talking a mile a minute about how fucking cool the house is. I'm still anxious about the moment I just shared with Owen, but I can't help smiling at Mattie's enthusiasm. I kinda like that I was able to make these guys happy so easily, just by letting them come over like this.

Nolan pauses in the hallway beside me, fiddling with the EMF meter in his hands as he avoids eye contact. "You know, Owen doesn't really talk to people. Not since his mom died, at least. I haven't heard him speak at school in more than two years."

My heart drops into my stomach at his words. I would have never guessed something like that, considering how nice Owen has been to me all day. I mean, he definitely seems quiet, but he's still talked to me a fair bit. I want to ask when and how his mom died, and if that's why Owen believes in ghosts. Mostly, I want to ask what made him want to talk to me of all people if he normally stays silent.

Instead, all I manage to say is, "Oh."

Nolan meets my eyes, adjusting his glasses as his cheeks redden. "Thanks for letting us do this. I know you probably think we're a bunch of losers, but this is still really cool of you. I'm sorry if I was a jerk earlier, and even sorrier for making your nose bleed and for the uh, the binocular thing."

Now it's my turn to be embarrassed, and I avert my gaze when I feel like my face is going to explode from blushing too hard. "It's fine, Nolan."

He nods, hesitating for a moment, and then he follows the other guys into the future sitting room.

"BEST AFTERNOON EVER!" MATTIE EXCLAIMS, PUMPING HIS FIST IN the air as the five of us step outside.

It's not raining anymore, but the ground is soggy. I frown

at Circe as she darts through the tall grass making up the jungle in the front yard. When she comes back later, I'm giving her a bath. I'll have to talk to my mom about taking her to the vet and getting her shots and flea medicine and stuff too.

"Agreed," Spencer says. "Thanks for hanging out with us, Harriet."

I turn my head to meet his gaze and roll my eyes. "I don't know if you can call it hanging out when you guys just walked through all the rooms in the house silently taking notes and pictures. But okay."

Nolan and Mattie exchange a look, and I immediately feel ashamed. I didn't mean for my comment to sound as snarky as it did. It did feel like hanging out. Especially when they were done looking around, and the five of us sat around in the kitchen eating the cookies my mom made for us. Plus, all four of the guys took turns talking to me during their preliminary investigation. The whole thing turned out way better than I expected.

"That's fair. Next time, we'll make a point to hang out longer without talking about anything paranormal." Nolan pushes his glasses up higher on his nose, and he even gives me the smallest, cutest smile when he does.

I don't try to hide the smile that forms on my face. It's a relief to hear that they even want to hang out at all, and not just to look around my family's creepy house. I follow them down the rickety steps of the front porch. Nolan's mom's van is parked outside. From what the guys told me, she lets Nolan and Mattie drive it sometimes. Mostly whenever they do their paranormal investigating stuff. I know it's getting late, but still. I'm bummed to see them leave. It almost feels like these guys might become my friends after all.

"You're gonna sit with us at lunch again tomorrow, right?" Spencer asks.

"Yeah." I smile. "I hope the Abbot House was everything you guys hoped. I still think it's funny that you tried to break in for so long."

"Dude, you don't even realize." Mattie shakes his head and widens his eyes. "It was impossible to get in here. Even though I just spent the past couple of hours inside, I still almost can't believe it. Check this out!"

Somehow, I don't expect what happens next. Mattie steps around the porch while the rest of us follow, and then he picks up a brick from one of the overgrown flower beds and hurls it at the Tudor-style front window.

I gasp and throw my hands up to cover my mouth, staring in shock as the glass shatters. There's a screech from inside, and Spencer and Owen curse while Mattie and Nolan stare at the broken window in horror.

"Harriet, I swear to fucking god..." Mattie swallows audibly and turns to look at me with a terrified expression. "I've been throwing shit at these windows for years trying to break them, and this has never happened before! Oh fuck, your mom's going to kill me. My aunt is going to kill me! Holy shit."

Hysterical laughter bubbles up in my chest, and it takes so much effort to stay quiet. It's not like I can blame Mattie. He has no idea that the windows were only unbreakable because of Sylvia's curse, and he obviously doesn't know that my mom and aunt will be able to fix the window pretty easily with a spell.

My mom pokes her head out the broken window and frowns sternly at me and the guys. "Does anyone mind explaining what just happened?"

I don't think my mom would actually get mad at Mattie, but I don't want to take the chance that she might not let him or the guys come back here to do any more of their paranormal investigating. It hardly matters if she gets pissed at me.

"This house is ugly as fuck already. I was just trying to prove to the guys that a broken window might actually be an improvement." I sneer and cross my arms.

My mom purses her lips and narrows her eyes. "Harriet Abbot, say goodnight to your friends and come inside this instant."

I roll my eyes and walk past the guys back to the front door. I glance at the four of them over my shoulder and wave. "See you guys tomorrow."

CHAPTER 9
HARRIET

"Are you kidding me? That movie wasn't even scary!"

"I never said it was scary, dumbass." I roll my eyes hard. "I said it was fucked up."

Mattie grins at me across the lunch table like he enjoys nothing more than riling me up. Every time I start to think he and I might actually be becoming friends, he says something stupid or purposely starts an argument with me.

"What are you two fighting about now?" Spencer sets his tray on the table and takes a seat beside me.

Owen sets his tray down at the same time and sits beside Mattie, across from us. Nolan's sitting on my other side a few feet away with a book propped open in front of him. I've eaten lunch with these guys every day this week, and it's always the same. Mattie starts an argument with me while Spencer and Owen wait in line for the school's lunch, and Nolan mostly keeps to himself.

"Your love-hate thing with Mattie is so hot." Ryan snickers.

I manage to ignore him, but it's getting harder and harder to do so. Ryan's always at my side, from the moment I arrive at school to the moment I leave. He's an annoying pain in my ass, and he says embarrassing shit constantly. Still, I'd be lying if I said I wasn't growing ridiculously attached to him.

He was behind me, but when he doesn't get a reaction out of me from his comment, he floats above the table and hovers like he's lying on his stomach and stares down at me and the guys with his hands under his chin and a psychotic grin on his face.

"Horror movies," Nolan answers Spencer's question without looking up from his book. "Mattie's giving Harriet shit because he doesn't think *Midsommar* was scary."

"That movie was crazy," Owen says quietly.

He smiles at me, giving me butterflies. We haven't talked about the note he wrote to me during our English class on Monday, and he hasn't made any more flirtatious comments since the guys came over to my house to do their preliminary paranormal investigation. That doesn't mean I haven't thought about those moments almost constantly the entire week. I haven't been able to find the courage to text or call him, and I'm even more terrified to say something in person. Sage says I'm being silly, but I can't help feeling like Owen was only messing around.

It doesn't help that the catty witches in this school continue to make me look like an idiot at any possible opportunity. I 'trip' in the hallway multiple times per day, and I always manage to 'accidentally' drop things or blurt out something inappropriate in any classes I share with my fellow witches.

Amethyst is the worst. She hasn't spoken to me since my first day here, and she won't touch me with her magic during English so long as Owen's holding my hand or taking notes for me—which he's done every day this week. But she's always glaring at me, and I've quickly learned that the other witches here at Weeping Hollow High will do pretty much anything Amethyst says. All the petty shit they've done to me this week has been ordered by her.

"I haven't seen it." Spencer turns to me and grins. "I didn't know you liked horror movies."

Maybe it's hypocritical of me, since I called Amethyst a walking-cliché for her choice of wardrobe, but I've always been drawn to all things creepy and occult. "I love horror movies! My best friend Sage and I used to do horror-movie marathons every Friday night."

"That's fucking awesome. What are some of your favorites?" Spencer asks.

I'm distracted from answering right away by two witches who stop beside our table. Blaze and Celeste are in a couple of my classes, and they've been assholes to me just like the rest of their coven. Blaze has his arms crossed and Celeste's hands are on her hips while they scowl at me.

"Can I help you?" I sneer up at them.

Blaze narrows his eyes, and I feel a tiny jolt of electricity tingle over my skin. It stings, but I don't let myself react. That only seems to piss him off more, and he practically growls as he asks, "Why haven't you asked to sit with us?"

"Are you serious?" I laugh. "You and your friends have been cunts to me all fucking week. Why would I ever want to sit with you?"

Celeste flips her blood-red hair over her shoulder and scoffs. "You're not better than us just because you're an Abbot."

Instead of responding, I take a huge bite of my chicken salad sandwich and chew with my mouth open in a way that I hope looks disgusting while I stare at Celeste and Blaze. I know they've been fucking with me and casting petty spells all week as a way to test me. The Abbot family name used to be really well-known, and I'm sure the witches here expect me to be stupidly powerful. It's probably driving them insane that I haven't retaliated or admitted that they're stronger than me by begging to be part of their group.

At this point, I would rather die than let any of them know that I'm incapable of doing magic the way they can. I'd rather put up with their bullying every day until graduation than face that kind of humiliation.

Ryan floats down until he's sitting across from me beside Owen. He grimaces and shakes his head at me. "Next time, maybe find a different way to piss them off? Your ghost-hunting boys are going to change their minds about wanting to fuck you if you do gross shit like that."

I clamp my mouth shut and turn my head to glare at him without thinking. Owen's the only one who seems to notice my bizarre behavior. He turns his head and stares directly at Ryan, and then turns to look at me again with his eyebrows raised. My heart stutters in my chest, and I only hope I don't look as panicked as I feel. Owen is way too observant. That's another reason I'm insanely nervous to be around him.

Having not noticed my weird interaction with Ryan, Celeste huffs at me as she pulls Blaze away from our table. "Enjoy Amethyst's leftovers!"

Spencer was already tense when they first stopped beside our table, but he goes completely stiff at Celeste's quip. He coughs and shoots me an apologetic look. "Sorry, Harriet."

I breathe angrily out of my nose and roll my eyes. "It's not your fault."

After eating lunch with the guys that first day, I quickly discovered that Spencer is Amethyst's ex-boyfriend. Mattie mentioned to me that his friend used to go out with Amethyst before I met the other guys, but I didn't think much of it at the time. Since I've been seen interacting with Spencer, despite the fact that he hasn't acted romantically interested in me, every piddling witch at this school has done their best to rub it in my face that he and Amethyst used to go out.

I've done my best not to show any interest or ask any questions. I know why he liked her. She's hot. Mattie reminds me of that fact every morning when we pass her in the hallway between first and second period. He's careful not to mention his crush in front of his other friends, so I keep my mouth shut even though I wish I could slap some sense into the guy.

"Still, this is getting ridiculous," Spencer says. "We broke up more than six months ago."

I know he feels embarrassed by the constant reminders, and that sucks. I know he feels guilty too, even though he's not the one bullying me or bringing up his past relationship. I just wish I knew if Mattie was right about Spencer being over her or not.

"What's their problem with you?" Nolan closes his book and looks over at me, pushing his glasses up on his nose. "They barely ever talk to people outside of their group."

"My family used to be well-known around here like Amethyst's family is." I shrug defensively, keeping my gaze focused on my food. "It's stupid."

Mattie taps his fingers against my thermos of iced tea to get my attention, and I look up to find him staring at me with a bashful smile. "Are you sure you can't come with us tomorrow? The asylum's gonna be so sick."

Nolan grunts from beside me and goes back to his book. He's usually nice to me at school, and he doesn't seem to mind me sitting with them at lunch. But he's made it pretty obvious he doesn't want me anywhere near their paranormal investigations. I don't really understand why, especially considering I let them do an investigation at my house and gave them an open invitation to come back any time.

"Nah." I sigh in response to Mattie's question. "I have to mow the lawn in the morning, and then I'll be busy the rest of the day with my mom and aunt's stupid friends."

"What about tonight?" Spencer asks. I raise my eyebrows in question, and he turns to face me better as he grins. "Are you busy?"

Other than sitting around watching Netflix with Old Creepy and Circe, I don't have any plans in mind for my first Friday night here in Weeping Hollow. I'm certainly not about to tell the guys that.

"Not really." I shrug nonchalantly.

Spencer's grin widens and he raises his hand to push his hair back from his face. "I know it won't be the same as your weekly tradition with your best friend, but would you want to come over to my place to watch scary movies?"

I feel my cheeks flush as I stare at him, dumbfounded. Ryan wolf-whistles and loudly says, "Holy shit, he's totally asking you out. You're gonna say yes, right?"

Goddess, can he please shut up? There's no way Spencer is asking me out, even if I kind of wish he was. His offer is really sweet though, and I do love horror movies. I don't have any reason to say no, so I give Spencer a small smile and say, "Yeah, sure."

He exhales and lets out a quiet chuckle. "Cool."

"Are you fucking serious?" Mattie grumbles. When we look up at him, he widens his eyes and gives me a sheepish glance before huffing at Spencer. "What about Shiloh? You know Zoe gets pissed when we let him watch that kind of stuff."

Spencer shrugs defensively. "Zoe has a date tonight, and Shiloh's dad is picking him up for the weekend."

There are a few questions at the tip of my tongue that I'm dying to ask, but Mattie looks pissed off and I have no clue why he even cares. I subtly glance at Ryan, hoping he'll be helpful for once.

To my relief, he catches my eye and grins. "Zoe is Spencer's older sister, and Shiloh's her son. Spencer's parents aren't in the picture, so Zoe has custody of Spencer. Looks like you two will have plenty of privacy tonight."

It dawns on me that Spencer hasn't invited the other guys to our movie night. Is it a date then? I've never been on one, and I really didn't think Spencer was interested in me that way. I have no idea what I'm supposed to think or feel. I mean, Spencer is cute. One of the cutest guys I've ever met, but...

My gaze shifts to Owen before I finish my train of thought. He's staring back at me, those stunning blue eyes brighter than ever. His expression is blank, guarded even, as he watches me unabashedly. Butterflies stir in my stomach and my cheeks flush again. Owen asked me out too, technically, and I never answered him. Is it stupid for me to feel guilty?

A familiar tingle runs up my arm and across my skin, and I curse under my breath when I realize what's happening. My hand raises without my consent, though I try to fight against the spell, and I slam my palm down on the table, smashing the remnants of my sandwich and making a huge mess in the process.

Several people cackle loudly from somewhere behind me, but they're far enough away that they can easily argue they aren't laughing at me. Fucking Amethyst and her coven of cunt-bags. I curl my hand into a fist and blink away angry tears as I stare down at the table. I can feel the guys watching me, just like they always do after one of my 'episodes.'

It's amazing, really, that they hang out with me at school at all. I'm lucky they haven't shunned me.

When I glance sideways at Spencer and see the troubled look on his face, I'm convinced there's no way in hell he'd ever ask me out. He probably feels bad for me, just like Owen does. Still, I'd be stupid to throw away any possibility at friendship. Two years with nobody to talk to aside from the occasional ghost would be unbearable.

"I'm sure we can find at least one movie neither of us has seen yet," Spencer says quietly, bumping his foot against mine.

My lips curve up into a genuine smile. "I can't wait."

AFTER SCHOOL, I STAND OUTSIDE THE MAIN ENTRANCE WITH RYAN BY my side while I wait for Spencer. Apparently, Spencer lives close enough to walk to and from school. When I texted my mom earlier to ask if I could hang out at a friend's house, she was more than happy to let me go. I think she's relieved that I'm making an effort here when she probably expected me to act like a spoiled brat about the move. As much as I miss Sage and my old house in Oregon, I've never been against moving to Weeping Hollow.

"Don't be so nervous. It'll be fine!" Ryan says cheerily.

I bite my lip and turn to face him with a sigh. He's been hyping me up about my horror movie date with Spencer all afternoon. Even though I'm adamant it's not a date. If Spencer likes girls like Amethyst, I certainly don't stand a chance. Still, while I'm nervous to hang out with a new friend, who just so happens to be a very cute guy, Ryan has made me feel way more at ease about the whole thing.

Sighing again, I purse my lips together and quietly admit, "I'm gonna miss you."

A grin stretches across Ryan's face, and his eyes practically sparkle. "Aww, getting sentimental on me now, are you?"

"Shut up." I roll my eyes and chuckle. "Seriously though. It's gonna be weird not seeing you all weekend, especially knowing you're stuck here by yourself."

I'm still not any closer to finding out how Ryan died or why he's stuck in his place of death. Every time I try to bring it up with him, he changes the subject or tells me not to worry about it. I know time has probably lost all meaning to him if he's been dead for as long as he thinks he has, but I can't help thinking of how he feels after school ends and he's here alone. He doesn't have the ability to move things, even slightly, so it's not like he can chill in the library and read. Plus, as far as I know, ghosts don't sleep.

A deep sadness overwhelms me as I stare at the boy in front of me. I can't begin to fathom how lonely he is.

"You don't need to worry about me," he says in a softer tone. He reaches his hand out to touch my shoulder, but all I feel is a slight tingle. "I'm gonna miss you too though. I can't wait to hear all the salacious details about your date night!"

"Shut up!" I repeat, laughing quietly under my breath.

"Who are you talking to?"

I spin around to find Spencer watching me with a crooked smile. I'm a little embarrassed he caught me talking to Ryan, but I shake it off quickly. The guy's seen me in way more mortifying situations than this one the past week, so this is nothing.

"Nobody." I shrug.

Spencer doesn't question me further. He adjusts his backpack over his shoulder and asks, "Ready to go?"

I nod and follow him down the main pathway leading away from the school. I peer back at Ryan over my shoulder and subtly wave goodbye, and he waves back while grinning at me like a lunatic.

"Have you been able to explore much of the town yet?"

89

Spencer asks as we walk side-by-side.

The further we get from school, the more nervous I feel. I try to keep my eyes forward instead of glancing repeatedly at Spencer like I want to. "Not really. Other than the diner my first night here, I haven't been anywhere other than school."

"There's really not much else, honestly." He chuckles. "Unless you like antique shops. The diner is cool though. The guys and I used to hang out there more often before I started working there."

"My mom and aunt used to go there all the time when they stayed here during their summer breaks. They talked it up for years, so I was actually excited to finally see it for myself."

"And then they embarrassed you and ruined the experience," he says matter-of-factly.

I grimace, staring straight ahead rather than at him. "Yep."

Spencer laughs. "My sister's the same way. She uses any opportunity she can to humiliate me."

I'm still low-key pissed at my mom and Flora for calling me out that first night at the diner when Spencer was our waiter. At least he's taking the whole thing lightly.

"You live with your sister, right?" I ask.

He nods. "One of the guys told you?"

Technically, Ryan told me. He's basically one of the guys, right? I shrug, and Spencer seems to take that as an affirmative response.

It's quiet between us for a few moments, and then Spencer peers sideways at me with an unreadable expression on his face. "My dad's in prison, and my mom took off a couple years ago. Zoe's only five years older than me, but she fought to get custody of me so I wouldn't go into foster care."

"Holy shit." I cringe when the words fall from my mouth, feeling like a completely insensitive asshole. "I'm so sorry. It's really messed up that you had to deal with that."

"It's okay." He smiles, laughing quietly to lighten the mood. "I mean, it's *not* okay. It's definitely a fucked-up situation, but I'm okay. Zoe's great, and I'm really lucky to have her as my sister."

I don't know what else to say. I feel really bad for Spencer, and I feel awful for bitching about my mom all the time when other people have it way worse than I do. My mom and I may not see eye-to-eye on a lot of things, and she might not ever really get me, but I know she loves me and she'd never abandon me. And who cares that I've never met my dad? Plenty of kids grow up with only one parent, and they turn out fine.

Spencer changes the subject. We discuss some of our favorite horror movies, along with our favorite and least favorite horror movie clichés. Spencer seems to prefer gorier movies, and he's a big fan of the classic slasher films. I don't mind gory stuff at all, but I like psychological horror better.

It doesn't feel like we've been talking long, but soon enough, Spencer stops in front of a small one-story house. It has white siding, a red door, and a simple, manicured lawn. Butterflies swirl around in my stomach again as I follow Spencer up the front path. I shove my hands in my pockets while he unlocks the front door, and I look around at all the kitschy Halloween decorations adorning the front porch.

"No jack-o-lanterns?" I ask teasingly. There are lights, fake cobwebs, and bats hanging on strings, but no pumpkins anywhere I can see.

Spencer pushes the front door open and steps aside to let me through first. "Not yet. My nephew Shiloh is very particular about certain things. He doesn't want us to carve pumpkins until a few days before Halloween."

"How old is he?"

I follow Spencer's lead and set my backpack, jacket and

shoes beside a hall tree near the front door. Spencer leads me through the house into a small kitchen where he opens a fridge, and he answers, "Shiloh just turned six."

Wow. That means his sister was really young when she had him, if she's only five years older than Spencer. I gain a new appreciation for Zoe, who I've never met, and look around the tidy kitchen in awe.

"Do you want a soda or anything?"

"Okay." I smile nervously.

Spencer hands me a coke and suggests we make popcorn, which I whole-heartedly agree with. It's stupid and cheesy to think this way, but I can't help feeling lucky and happy. Spencer's been nice to me all week, and he's made an effort to include me in conversations during lunch and the classes we share together. But now, with him opening up like this, it feels like we're becoming friends for real. It felt like that when the guys came over to my place to do their ghost-hunting stuff too, but I worried they were only being nice and trying to appease me so they could check out my family's house. This feels more real than that.

While we're waiting for the popcorn to finish in the microwave, we talk about school. Spencer asks me what my house and school were like back in Oregon. He seems a little surprised to hear that the town I'm from is almost as small as Weeping Hollow, and my house was nowhere near as grand as the Abbot House.

Once the popcorn's finished, Spencer leads me into a small living room and settles onto a comfy red sofa. I sit close enough so that we can share the popcorn between us, but not so close that we're touching. Despite the awkwardness at lunch when Mattie freaked out, and all of Ryan's dumbass comments, I'm still not picking up on any romantic vibes from Spencer. On one hand, that sucks because I do think he's really cute. On the other hand, it makes me feel way more comfortable to just be myself around him.

"Can I ask you a question?" I shove a handful of popcorn into my mouth to hide how curious and stupid I feel.

"Yeah, anything."

I watch him turn the TV on and pull up a streaming app. I reconsider asking him the question that's been bugging me, but I'd rather hear it from him than from one of the witches from school.

"Why did you and Amethyst break up?"

He pauses with his hand above the popcorn bowl and raises his eyebrows in surprise. "Nobody's told you?"

"The more I pretend I'm not interested in anything they say or do, the more pissed off Amethyst and her friends get. All I know is that you went out with her last year, and she clearly doesn't want any other girls going near you."

He grimaces and takes a sip of his soda before answering. "She cheated on me."

"What?" I ask in outrage.

His cheeks redden, and I can tell he feels embarrassed, or maybe ashamed. "Amethyst was my first girlfriend. I felt so fucking lucky when she agreed to go out with me, and I was always worried I was gonna do something to fuck it up. My sister hated her, and she was always super shitty to my friends. But I just...I liked her, and she made me feel important. So, I always made excuses for her. We'd been together almost eight months when I found out she'd been cheating on me with multiple people during our entire relationship."

"Are you kidding me?" If I thought Amethyst was a cunt before, that's nothing compared to what I think of her now. "Goddess, I want to punch her so bad!"

"Trust me, I know." Spencer ruffles his hair, giving me a

sheepish smile. "The worst part was, she made me feel stupid for being upset about it. Like I should have just accepted it."

"I'm sorry. That's so messed up. Nobody deserves to be treated like that."

His pretty brown eyes bore into mine, and he stares at me for a moment like he's waiting for something. I stare back at him, unsure what else to say, feeling horrible because I somehow keep bringing up really deep and uncomfortable subjects with him.

"You're really different than I expected you to be." His lips slowly curve into a wide, bright smile, and I furrow my eyebrows in confusion. Before I can ask what he expected instead, he asks, "What about you? Any ex-boyfriend drama back in Oregon?"

"No." I snort. I wish I could open up to Spencer the way he's opened up to me, but there's no way in hell I can tell him I'm a witch or that I can see ghosts. "I've never had a boyfriend, and Sage was pretty much my only friend back home. I'm boring."

"Now that's definitely not true." He snickers, reaching his hand out to brush a strand of my hair through his fingers.

My heart does a somersault as I stare back at him in shock. That's totally a flirty move, and I wasn't expecting it at all. An embarrassing giggle escapes my throat before my brain catches up with my mouth, and Spencer grins smugly.

"Do you know what movie you wanna watch yet?" He picks up the popcorn bowl and sets it in my lap, sliding closer so that our legs are touching while he throws his arm over the back of the couch behind me.

Okay, we're not, like, *cuddling*, but this feels like a very couply way to sit. Spencer seems so fucking confident, and I have no idea what to do with my hands. I feel like I missed something, and I replay our conversation over in my head. I don't think I said or did anything that would make him think I like him, but what do I know about guys and dating? Goddess, does Spencer even like me? Why would he? I act like a moron every time I'm around him, and—

"Harriet?"

"Huh?" I blink and turn to look at Spencer. He has the most adorable, crooked smile, and his eyes are shining with laughter.

"Anything in particular you want to watch?" he asks again.

"Oh, no, I'm fine with whatever." I shrug, trying really hard to regain my cool as I shove a giant handful of popcorn into my mouth. It's better for both of us if I can't talk right now.

Spencer scrolls through our options on the TV screen for less than a minute before the front door opens. He tenses up in surprise, but doesn't move from his spot beside me.

"I have Shiloh with me, so you'd better be decent!" a girl calls from the front entryway. A few seconds later, a short brunette walks into the living room with a small, dark-haired boy behind her. She crosses her arms and glares at me and Spencer. "Dammit, Spence, you can't just bring girls home without asking me!"

Spencer rolls his eyes and glances at me apologetically before responding to his sister. "You told me I'd have the house to myself tonight."

When Zoe focuses another disapproving glare on me, I panic and blurt out, "I'm Harriet."

She ignores me. "Something came up, and Danny won't be able to pick Shiloh up until tomorrow morning. I need you to babysit."

"What? No way!" Spencer stands up angrily, quickly turning to mumble to me, "Sorry, I'll be right back."

Zoe disappears from view, but I can still hear her as she walks through the house with Spencer following her. "Yes, way. This is the first night I've had off in months, and I *need* to go out. You know I hate asking you to watch him, Spence, but I don't have any other options."

Spencer's reply is muffled. I sit up, wondering if I should text my mom to come pick me up. It's not Spencer's fault our movie night has to be postponed, but I don't want to make things awkward or uncomfortable between him and his sister.

"Are you Spencer's new girlfriend?" A quiet voice grabs my attention, and I look up to see Shiloh still standing in the same spot his mom left him.

"Nah, we're just regular friends."

Shiloh watches me for a few seconds, and then he slowly walks into the room and takes a seat on the couch next to me. When he reaches his tiny hand into the popcorn bowl, I hold it at a better angle for him. I haven't been around many kids besides Sage's younger siblings, but I always secretly loved helping Sage babysit them. Shiloh is probably one of the cutest kids I've ever seen. He's small with adorable chubby cheeks, dark, almond-shaped eyes, and thick, shiny hair so dark it almost looks black. I idly wonder if his dad is Asian, because Shiloh looks like he might be multiracial.

"Is that your real hair color?" He asks quietly.

"No." I shake my head, picking up a strand of my silver hair. "My friend dyed it for me because my real hair was ugly."

Shiloh giggles and pats the top of his head. "I want to dye mine purple, but my mom said I'm not allowed to."

I ruffle his hair, making him squeal and laugh louder. "Maybe when you're older. But my mom has your hair color, and people are always jealous of it. I used to wish I had hair like hers."

"It's so pretty now though." Like a typical six-year-old, he changes the subject out of nowhere. "What are you going to be for Halloween?"

"A witch." Sage and I have dressed up as witches every Halloween for as long as I can remember. It's probably only funny to us, but there's no way I'm breaking the tradition just because we're apart. "What are you going to be?"

He shrugs sadly and stuffs his mouth full of popcorn. Suddenly appearing shy, he whispers, "My mom says she doesn't have enough money for a costume this year, and Spencer said dressing up is for babies."

"First of all, Spencer is lame, so don't listen to him." I scoff, rolling my eyes. Shiloh giggles, and I smile in relief. I hate seeing kids get all sad and mopey. "Second of all, you don't need to spend money on a costume. Makeup and accessories will do ninety percent of the work."

"Makeup?" he asks curiously.

"Yup." I wave my hand around my face and grin. "Doing makeup is one of the few things I actually think I'm really good at. I bet I could do your makeup for Halloween, no matter what you want to dress up as, and you'd look ten million times cooler than all the kids who buy generic costumes from Halloween stores."

Shiloh stares at me critically, like he's assessing my makeup and my words. "What does generic mean?"

Sage's youngest brother Everest is smart and inquisitive like Shiloh is, and I used to love talking to that kid. "It means boring, like when everyone looks and dresses exactly the same."

He eats a few more pieces of popcorn, and then grins at me like he's finally decided I might be right. "Okay! Can you do my makeup so I look like a mermaid?"

Goddess, I fucking love this kid so much already. "Heck yeah! Do you want to look cute or scary? I bet I could make it look like you got a fish hook stuck in your mouth."

I take my phone out of my pocket and pull up Pinterest.

Before I finish typing anything into the search bar, Spencer walks back into the room with a sour look on his face.

"Sorry I took so long, Harriet. I don't think we're gonna be able to do horror movies tonight." I'd figured as much, but I feel bad that he seems so put out about it. He furrows his eyebrows when he realizes Shiloh and I are sitting huddled over my phone together. "What are you guys doing?"

"Harriet's going to do my makeup for Halloween so I don't have to buy a costume. She's gonna make me look like a really creepy mermaid with fish hooks coming out of my mouth!"

Creepy it is, then. I chuckle at Shiloh's enthusiasm, even if the stunned expression on Spencer's face is making me feel nervous.

"Really?" Spencer asks.

"Uh huh. Apparently, someone told Shiloh that dressing up is for babies, and I need to prove that person wrong."

He grins in response and sits on the floor since there's no room on the couch with me and Shiloh. "You don't need to stick around if you don't want to, Harriet. Zoe says you can if you want to, but please don't feel obligated."

"No!" Shiloh whines, turning to give me the most pathetically-adorable puppy dog eyes. "Please don't leave. I can watch scary movies with you guys!"

"No way, dude. Your mom got so pissed at me the last time I let you watch something scary with me."

I don't want to leave yet if I don't have to. There's nothing waiting for me at home except for a night of watching movies with Circe and Old Creepy. I like them, but they're not always the greatest company. Plus, I feel a lot closer to Spencer after talking earlier, and Shiloh is fucking precious. Who wouldn't want to stay and hang out?

"Have you guys seen *Over the Garden Wall?* It's cute, and it definitely has some spooky vibes."

CHAPTER 10
NOLAN

"Well, that was a fucking letdown." Mattie slumps down in the passenger seat and crosses his arms. When Spencer and Owen mumble their agreements, I sigh quietly in defeat. They're not wrong. I'm disappointed too. We spent weeks researching this asylum and planning this trip. Spencer was able to find the original blueprints of the building and enough information to draw a general map of the place to reflect what it looked like when it was last open several decades ago. Mattie and I did about a million chores around the house so my mom would let us take the van tonight. We even bought some new equipment just for this trip.

Everything should have gone perfectly. We overprepared. After a nearly two-hour drive, we made it to the place and quickly realized it would be harder to break in than we anticipated. Not because the dilapidated building is heavily guarded—no more than most abandoned schools, hospitals, and asylums are, at least. But because all the doors and windows on the first floor were barred and completely impenetrable. Luckily, we found a broken window that had been boarded up on the second floor and somehow managed to climb up there without killing ourselves and break in with all our shit in tow.

Not-so-luckily, once we got inside, we found literally nothing of interest. Nothing! We explored every inch of the building where the floors weren't rotted away—which was only about a fourth of the building, but still. Almost all the furniture and supplies often left behind in old asylums like this one were gone. Other than a few random chairs or tables, there were no cool artifacts for us to take note of. Even worse, I didn't pick up any activity on my EMF meter or thermal camera. Mattie didn't pick up any useful audio or video either, and Owen's fairly certain nothing will show up in his photos when he develops them in his dark room.

"We should have brought Harriet with us," Mattie whines.

I frown at him from the corner of my eye, gripping the steering wheel tighter. "How would that have helped?"

He shrugs. "Would have been more fun."

I roll my eyes and bite my tongue before I remind him that Harriet went out with Spencer last night. Well, sort of. If going over to Spencer's house to Netflix and Chill counts as *going out*. I'm surprised my cousin hasn't brought it up or picked a fight with Spencer over the situation yet. Hopefully, he doesn't start now that Harriet's name has been mentioned.

"We should ask her if we can do another investigation at her house," Spencer suggests.

My heart leaps at the same time a flush spreads across my neck and face. Getting a look inside the Abbot House was hands down one of the coolest things I've experienced in a long time. We found a ton of interesting stuff in some of those old, dusty rooms that I'd love to get another look at. Plus, I got a ton of feedback on my EMF meter the whole time we were there. It seemed like the most activity was on the second floor near Harriet's bedroom. Mattie swears he picked up some faint laughter on video that wasn't from us or Harriet's mom or aunt. It's the best find we've ever had during an investigation, and it would be a dream to get back in there.

"I don't know," I say, clearing my throat. "I don't think that's a good idea."

"Why not?" Owen asks. I meet his eyes through the rearview mirror, surprised to hear him speak up. He's never been all that chatty, but he rarely talks ever since his mom died. Even when the four of us are alone, he's quiet and only speaks if it's to say something important.

Then again, he's been talking to Harriet all week. The guys and I have tried not making a big deal of it, but I know it was a shock for all of us when he started talking at school a few days ago. Maybe it's a coincidence and this is simply a turning point for Owen in his grieving process, but I think Harriet has a lot more to do with his sudden willingness to talk and open up than anyone's ready to admit out loud. Bad news for Mattie. He was already pissed at Spencer for making a move on his latest crush. It'll be that much harder for him if Owen's crushing on her too.

"Guys." I laugh awkwardly, darting a quick glance over my shoulder at Spencer and Owen. "Harriet already thinks we're losers. Showing up at her house to do another investigation is only gonna make things worse."

My cousin and two best friends loudly disagree, all talking over one another. When they quiet down enough to talk at a normal volume, it's Spencer who scoffs first. "Dude, she doesn't think that. She's our friend."

"Harriet loves ghosts and paranormal stuff," Mattie says vehemently. But does she really? Because I very vividly remember her laughing her ass off when we told her about our club and what we like to do in our free time.

I don't really blame her. Most girls think I'm a loser, and my friends don't usually have much better luck with girls than I do. Spencer going out with Amethyst last year was a weird fluke. At least, I thought so until Harriet agreed to go out with him yesterday. Like me, Owen and Mattie have never had girlfriends before. Shit, I've never even kissed a girl.

"She's new here." I shake my head. "She's only been hanging out with us because she doesn't know anyone else. Plus, you know she's...different. Maybe she thinks nobody else will accept her."

"Different." Mattie scoffs. "Who cares if she's a little schizo? She's hot, and she's so fucking cool. I think you're wrong, Nolan. Harriet wants to be friends with us because she's just as weird as we are. You just don't get her. I mean, come on. You talk to her less than the rest of us do. Even Owen talks to her during lunch."

My hands clench the steering wheel tight enough that my knuckles turn white. Shit, I really don't want to have this fight again. All week, the guys and I have been fighting about how to handle Harriet's disorders. I highly suspect she has Tourette syndrome and that she might be schizophrenic. I also suspect she's not taking the right medication or hasn't been diagnosed properly. Every time she has an episode in front of me, it takes all of my self-control not to drag her somewhere private so she doesn't embarrass herself in front of other people. Or bother her with questions of how I can help. But I know how I feel whenever people say something ignorant about my diabetes or give me unwanted advice for how to handle my disease, and I don't want to do the same thing to Harriet. I especially don't want her to know how much I pity her.

Every time I bring the issue up with the guys, they argue

with me. Mattie insists that Harriet is perfect and it doesn't matter if she shouts obscenities at random, makes a mess with her lunch or schoolwork, or that sometimes she looks at things that aren't there. He thinks that if Harriet's brave enough to go through life like nothing's wrong with her, then we should respect that. Owen and Spencer just say it's none of our business and we shouldn't bring it up unless Harriet does.

"Fine," I mumble. It's a losing battle. If my friends want to bug Harriet about the Abbot House, I'll just have to deal with the humiliation of knowing a beautiful girl thinks I'm a raging fucking loser. Glancing at the clock, I realize we'll probably make it back to Weeping Hollow in about an hour, just before eleven. It's way earlier than we anticipated getting home, but there was no point sticking around the asylum longer than the hour we spent there. "It's probably too late to go to her house tonight."

"Obviously," Mattie says, turning in his seat to face the other guys. "Text her, Spence. Ask if we can come over tomorrow morning."

There's a moment of silence. Since I'm driving, I can only assume Spencer's busy texting Harriet. But then he snorts and says, "I don't have her number, dude."

My eyebrows shoot up in surprise. It's too dark for me to read Spencer's expression through the rearview mirror. Before I can bite my tongue, words tumble out of my mouth. "How do you not have her number? Aren't you guys going out?"

"Uh, no." Spencer laughs. "What the fuck? I would have told you guys if we were going out."

Mattie looks over at me. I see surprise, frustration, and hope flash in his eyes. I'm pretty sure I'm the only one in this vehicle who knows just how obsessed my cousin has become with Harriet over the past week. So, I know exactly how excited and hopeful he is about Spencer's confession.

"But you asked her out yesterday," Mattie says apprehensively. "She went to your house, didn't she? I assumed you guys hooked up last night."

Spencer groans. "Zoe came home like two minutes after we got to my house and dumped Shiloh on me. Harriet ended up helping me babysit, so yeah. Nothing happened. But seriously, dude. Just because I asked her to hang out once doesn't mean she's suddenly my girlfriend."

Mattie faces forward in his seat, but I don't miss the grin on his face that he's probably trying to hide from Spencer. I clear my throat and ask, "So, does that mean nobody here has Harriet's number? How is that possible when we've been hanging out with her every day for a week?"

"Well, I gave her my number, but I never got hers," Owen says.

I can practically feel Mattie and Spencer react with surprise. I want to turn around to look at Owen, but I force myself to keep my eyes on the road.

"When did you give her your number?" Mattie asks.

"On Monday when I asked her out," Owen responds nonchalantly.

Mattie whips around in his seat, and I watch him open and close his mouth a few times like he's struggling to find the right words. Spencer beats him to it and laughs incredulously. "What the fuck! Dude. Why didn't you tell me you asked her out? Now I feel like shit."

"What did she say?" Mattie asks quietly.

God, this is an Amethyst situation all over again. First, because Mattie's obsessing over another girl he's too scared to ask out while watching his best friends move in on her. And now? If she's agreeing to go out with Owen *and* Spencer in the same week, that doesn't exactly give me high hopes she wouldn't cheat on one of my friends the same way Amethyst cheated on Spencer.

"Nothing. I think she was embarrassed, but at least I put it out there." Owen grunts. "You don't need to feel like shit, Spence. Nothing wrong with letting her know we like her until she tells us to fuck off or decides she likes one of us back."

Mattie and I share a look. Is Owen serious? That sounds like a disaster waiting to happen. I adjust my glasses and grip the steering wheel, steeling myself for an argument. "Guys, I know Harriet's pretty. But she's new here, and she clearly has a lot of issues. She needs friends. Not for you guys to act like fucking cavemen around her or for us to bombard her with our ghost hunting shit."

"Whatever." Spencer chuckles. "If you're so worried about her, maybe you should talk to her and act like the friend you think she needs."

CHAPTER 11
HARRIET

Saturday morning, there's a beautiful lavender dress waiting on my bed for me when I walk into my room after taking a shower. I assume my mom left it here for me to wear during the coven meeting we're having. It's a really sweet gesture on her part, especially considering we haven't talked much this week. I've mostly been giving her the silent treatment, only telling her the most minute details about school and my new friends. She still doesn't know about Ryan, and I haven't mentioned any of the bullying from Amethyst and her bevy of sheep.

I quickly tie my hair up in a towel and set about getting dressed. I spent close to four hours in the yard this morning, and I'm exhausted. I'm happy to say the yard no longer looks like a snake-infested jungle. I've been dreading the get-together my mom and Flora have planned, but my mood is slowly improving as I stare at the dress in admiration.

When I slip it over my head, however, my good mood vanishes almost instantly.

Old Creepy floats through the wall into my bedroom,

humming a somber melody. I frown at her and sigh, crossing my arms in irritation as I turn around to face my mirror.

"Pretty clothes always fit me weird. It's not fair."

The color of the dress looks amazing against my hair and eyes, but everything else about it is so wrong on my figure. The sleeves are too short, hitting me at a weird spot on my forearms, and the hemline barely passes my butt. If I bend down even the slightest bit while wearing it, I'm definitely going to flash someone. I *could* wear tights with it, but there's nothing that will fix the unflattering way the fabric is bunched up around my boobs. It's *extremely* obvious in this dress that I'm the most unfortunately flat-chested girl in the fucking universe.

I nearly rip the dress when I angrily pull it up over my head, and I ball it up and throw it into the corner of my room. My mom always says I'm lucky, that I'm built like a model. Fuck her. Girls like my mom and aunt, and girls like stupid Amethyst Redferne, they have it easy. They're short and cute, clothes are made to fit them perfectly, and guys find them desirable.

"Lavender's blue, dilly dilly, lavender's green,
When I am king, dilly dilly, you shall be queen."

Old Creepy sways beside me, attempting to pat my arm consolingly while she continues singing her eerie little nursery rhyme. I wrap my fingers around my adder stone necklace and smile at her in thanks, and then I walk over to my closet in defeat.

After pulling on a pair of black skinny jeans and a hunter-green Henley shirt, something I know I'll feel comfortable in, I sit down in front of my mirror with my makeup bag. I may not be able to wear the lavender dress like I want to, but I can damn well make sure my makeup is killer.

A few guests have already arrived by the time I finish getting ready and make my way downstairs. My mom is cackling in the kitchen, and Flora is talking to a couple of witches near the front door. Old Creepy follows me halfway down the stairs, but she giggles nervously when she sees other people and retreats back to my room. I don't blame her. I'd totally do the same thing if I could get away with it.

"Harriet! Come in here, will you?"

I roll my eyes at my mom's shrill voice and head to the kitchen. To my dismay, Amethyst and Blaze are there, along with a few other witches my mom's age. Blaze smirks when he sees me, but Amethyst doesn't spare me a glance. I had a feeling some of my classmates would be here. The community of witches isn't that big, and all the older families tend to stay in contact.

Still, it fucking sucks seeing Blaze and Amethyst in my house. The only upside is that I know they won't mess with me while their parents and so many other adults are around. There's no way they're that brave.

"What are you wearing?" My mom furrows her eyebrows at my appearance. "Didn't you see the dress I left out for you?"

I shrug in response. I don't want to admit in front of everyone that the dress didn't fit, and I don't want to fight with my mom about it. It doesn't help that Amethyst looks stunning as ever. She's wearing a gorgeous sapphire dress that matches her eyes and shows off her figure in the most flattering way possible.

My mom sighs, clearly upset. "I don't know why I even try with you sometimes, Harriet."

"Oh, you know how teenagers are," a woman says with a chuckle. She offers me a friendly smile. "Your mother was the same way when she was your age. Your grandmother could never get her or your aunt to listen to a word she said."

I smile at the woman. She's sweet to try to diffuse the tension. My mom gives me another one of her looks, but she decides not to dwell on it and changes the subject. "Have you met Amethyst and Blaze? They're in the same year as you."

It takes everything in me not to sneer or flip my classmates off. I smile placatingly at my mom and say, "Yep. They're in a few of my classes."

"How wonderful!" My mom grins, completely oblivious.

For several minutes, I'm forced to stand in the kitchen and fake interest in the conversation my mom's having with her old friends. Amethyst and Blaze are quiet too, and Blaze even sneaks looking at his phone a few times. I wish I'd been smart enough to bring my phone downstairs to distract myself with.

Eventually, Flora joins everyone in the kitchen with a few more middle-aged witches. Principal Di Rossi is one of them, and he greets everybody cordially before handing my mother a bouquet of flowers. He barely takes his eyes off of her after that, and it's pretty clear everyone else has picked up on it.

Flora offers to give a tour of the house. I follow behind everyone else, careful to keep my distance from Blaze and Amethyst. A few witches try to talk to me, mostly asking questions to figure out how powerful I am and which elements I'm most capable with, but I answer vaguely and keep to myself. I already begged my mom and Flora not to tell anyone my embarrassing secret—that I can't do magic, and that I can see and talk to ghosts—but I'm paranoid someone will figure it out.

When my mom starts showing off some of her spellwork with the plants decorating the second-floor sitting room, I sneak back downstairs to get a snack from the kitchen. My mom and Flora made a ton of food, and it's going to waste.

I've just popped my third mini-quiche into my mouth when I feel a familiar tingling against my skin. Before I can turn around or do anything to stop it from happening, I'm forced to shove three more of the tasty morsels into my mouth until I start choking.

Amethyst and Blaze snicker cruelly and watch as I spit the quiches onto the floor, continuing to cough uncontrollably. My eyes are blurry with tears after choking and coughing so much, and I scramble to pour a glass of water at the sink.

"Goddess, you're seriously the most pathetic witch I've ever met. It's almost not fun anymore." Amethyst sighs like she's annoyed.

I glare at her over my glass, and slam it down on the counter when I finish drinking. "You're in my house, you fucking cunt. I can't believe you'd try that shit here."

"You're not giving us a choice, Harriet Abbot." Blaze steps closer to me, effectively trapping me against the counter. I'd have to physically shove him to get away. While we're about the same height, Blaze definitely has a lot of muscle on me, and I doubt he'd care if he hurt me or not. "Just show us what you can do. Literally anything at this point, and we'll leave you alone."

Fury blazes in Amethyst's eyes. "She's purposely not using magic or fighting back because she thinks she's better than us."

I scowl at the girl in front of me. She doesn't know me or anything about me other than my family's name, and she's made my first week at my new school miserable. If that wasn't enough to make me hate her, everything I learned about her from Spencer certainly did the trick. Amethyst Redferne is a liar, a cheater, and all-around one of the most disgusting people I've ever had the misfortune of meeting.

"I *am* better than you." I sneer at her. And then I try my luck and shove Blaze as hard as I can.

He stumbles back a few steps, but he immediately pins me against the counter again with a vicious smirk on his face. "Amethyst is jealous because her pathetic, human boy toys have been giving you attention. But the longer you go without retaliating, without talking to us, the more curious you're making the rest of us."

He doesn't bother whispering. All of the adults are upstairs with my mom and Flora, and Blaze clearly doesn't care about hurting Amethyst's feelings. She huffs indignantly at his words, but he ignores her and keeps his gaze locked on me.

"Fuck. *Off*." I try to shove him again, but Blaze's smirk widens as he captures my wrists with one hand.

"Counteract my spell, and I'll give you all the attention you could ever want."

I shiver at his promise, and not in a good way. If I scream for help, will my mom or Flora even care to check on me? Are Amethyst and Blaze smart enough to have put a soundproofing spell on the kitchen?

Blaze presses his body against me so I can't move, and he forces me to hold out one of my hands. A flame appears in the palm of my hand. Only, it's not fake like the illusions Amethyst likes to cast. I grit my teeth against the pain, and the flame slowly burns hotter and hotter. I feel blisters forming on my skin, and tears prick at the corners of my eyes. Blaze is stronger than me physically and magically, and I'm completely powerless against him.

Just as I'm about to give in and beg him to stop, somebody yells, "What's going on in here?"

The flame disappears from my hand, and Blaze jumps back in alarm.

"Nothing," he says defensively. "We were just talking."

I wipe my eyes, doing my best not to cry outright before I can find some privacy.

"Do you think I was born yesterday, Blaze Alden? I'll be having a word with your father. You can be sure of that." The kind woman who defended me to my mom earlier stares down Blaze with her hands on her hips and a no-nonsense expression on her face.

"Harriet started it!" Amethyst points at me, her voice pitched higher than usual.

The woman purses her lips and shakes her head. "I know that's not true. Now get upstairs and stay out of trouble before I decide to tell your mother about this too."

Blaze and Amethyst give me scathing looks, but neither of them says another word before leaving the kitchen and heading upstairs. Whoever this lady is, they're obviously afraid she's going to get them into trouble.

"Are you okay, sweetheart?" The woman lightly touches the hand I'm cradling against my chest.

I shake my head because I'm afraid I'll start sobbing if I open my mouth. Not just because my hand hurts, but also because Blaze honestly scared the fuck out of me. Even after all the crap the local witches at my high school have put me through this past week, I never thought any of them would legitimately hurt me or take things so far.

"Do you know any healing spells? Or do you want me to do one for you?" The woman speaks quietly as she rubs soothing circles on my back.

I swallow, trying so hard to keep the tears at bay. A small sob escapes me as I stutter, "I-I can't—"

She doesn't ask any more questions. She simply grabs a hand towel from beside the stove, wets it under the faucet at the sink, and takes me to the door in the kitchen that leads to the backyard. Now that the grass has been cut, it's way more practical to go outside here rather than using the front door.

We take a seat on the small porch outside the kitchen door. The lady places my burnt hand in her lap as she presses the wet towel against the wound and mumbles an incantation. I let a few tears cascade down my face and sniffle quietly as I watch her. My mom mentioned everyone's names in the kitchen earlier, and now I feel like an ass for not paying attention. The woman is really pretty though. She's short and curvy, and she has long, wildly curly copper hair and amber-brown eyes.

"There you go," she coos softly.

I stretch my fingers out, no longer feeling pain from Blaze's burn. "Thank you," I mumble. I'm still shaken, and I'm beyond embarrassed to have been caught in such a pathetic, helpless situation. But she needs to know how grateful I am that she stepped in. "What was your name again?"

"Iris." She peeks over her shoulder at the door to the kitchen, but nobody is coming to find us. She sighs and turns around to smile sadly at me. "Owen told me you've been having some issues with the witches at school, but I never imagined it would escalate like this."

At first, I assume I misheard her. "Owen?"

"My step-son, Owen Castillo?" At the shocked expression on my face, Iris chuckles in amusement. "He's so shy, I shouldn't be surprised. He gave me the impression the two of you were becoming friends."

"We are! It's just, he's..." I stumble over my words like an idiot. But what the actual fuck. "Owen knows I'm a witch?"

Iris cackles good-naturedly and nods. "He does. The Council is pretty strict about witches marrying outside of our covens, and Owen isn't supposed to interfere with our magic or politics. He was probably too nervous to say anything. I just assumed, since he seems so smitten with you..."

She trails off, and I feel my face flush. Owen knows I'm a witch, and his step-mom is sitting next to me telling me he's fucking *smitten* with me. I have no idea what to say.

"Have you told your mom about Amethyst and Blaze?" Iris asks, sounding much more somber and serious. When I shake my head, she asks, "What about Mr. Di Rossi?"

"No. I don't want anyone to know." I cross my arms and curl into myself a bit. I know Iris is just trying to help, but I feel so fucking weak and worthless, and I'm totally reeling over this new information about Owen.

Owen, who holds my hand and takes notes for me to stop Amethyst from messing with me during class. Who's called me beautiful more than once, who has never made me feel weird or called me out for acting like a lunatic when he sees me talking to ghosts or when Amethyst's friends cast spells on me.

"Thanks for healing my hand." I stand up and turn to head back into the house before Iris can ask me any more questions or decide she needs to involve my mom in what happened today.

The kitchen is still empty, thankfully. I quickly load a plate with snacks, grab a couple of sodas from the fridge, and manage to tiptoe upstairs and lock myself in my room without running into anyone. My mom can get pissed at me later if she wants, but there's no way I'm dealing with any more witchy bullshit or putting myself in a position where I need to face Amethyst and Blaze again. Seeing them at school on Monday will be awful enough as it is.

MUCH LATER, AFTER EVERYONE'S GONE HOME AND MY MOM HAS yelled at me for being rude and antisocial, I curl up on my bed with Circe and stare at my phone in distress. Owen gave me his phone number almost a week ago, and it's pretty late. I don't even know if he's home. He might still be at the asylum with Mattie, Spencer, and Nolan.

I have to call him though. There's no way I'll make it through the rest of the weekend without talking to him. My stomach flutters every time I think about him and the fact that he knows what I am. Part of me is annoyed he never said anything to me, but I get it. The Council of Witches is super strict when it comes to outsiders knowing about us.

My anxiety is out of control. Even though I've been thinking about calling him all day, I still have no idea what I'm going to say. My fingers shake as I dial his number, and I hold my breath when I raise my phone to my ear.

It rings, over and over again. My heart pounds louder and louder with every passing second. I'm about to chuck the fucking thing across the room when Owen finally answers.

"Hello?"

At the sound of his deep voice, I panic and blurt out, "I met your step-mom today."

There's a pause on the other line, and I grit my teeth as I smack my forehead. I'm such an idiot. He obviously has no idea who's calling him, as I never gave him *my* number.

"Harriet." He laughs, sounding surprised and delighted. "You actually called me. Fuck, I just, uh, I just walked through the door. Give me one second. Please don't hang up."

The line goes silent again, and an embarrassing giggle escapes my throat before I can clamp a hand over my mouth. I'm pretty sure he just put me on mute, but there's a possibility he can still hear me. Butterflies flutter like crazy in my stomach while I wait for Owen to come back. I'm so relieved that he sounds happy to hear from me.

I expect him to take at least a few minutes, so I jolt in surprise when I hear his voice again less than thirty seconds later.

"Are you still there?"

I bite my lip at the worry in his voice, and the butterflies in my stomach become even more vigorous. "I'm here."

He breathes out a sigh of relief, and then chuckles. "I can't believe you called. I know I sound like a loser, but I'd really given up hope."

"You don't sound like a loser." Another girlish giggle leaves my mouth, and I grimace at myself. Goddess, Owen isn't even in front of me, and I still can't get through a simple conversation without embarrassing myself. How do girls talk to cute guys so easily? I clear my throat and quickly change the subject, reminding myself of why I called Owen in the first place. "Your step-mom came to my house today."

"I figured she would," he says casually.

Seriously? That's all he has to say? I swallow the lump in my throat and press my hand against my chest, willing my heart to stop beating so furiously. "She told me that you, um, know about me. About my family."

"Yeah," he says, sounding embarrassed. "I knew as soon as Amethyst started messing with you in class on your first day."

I'm desperately trying to think of something to say, but I'm so nervous and agitated, and it feels like my tongue is stuck to the roof of my mouth. Maybe it was a mistake to call Owen. I'm totally not prepared to have this conversation.

"Harriet?" he asks softly. "I'm sorry. I know I should have said something, but I'm really not supposed to know any details or get involved in anything to do with witches. Plus, I was afraid I'd scare you off or make you angry."

"I'm not angry with you," I answer quietly. "It's just that I've never told anyone outside of the community, so I'm really anxious. But also kind of relieved, if that makes sense? I don't know. I keep trying to figure out what to say, but my brain is totally scrambled."

"That makes sense." I can practically hear the smile in his voice, and I slowly begin to relax.

"How long have you known? About witches, I mean."

There's a rustling sound from his end of the phone, and I imagine him making himself more comfortable. I settle more comfortably on my bed too, wrapping my blanket around myself and scratching Circe's head when she snuggles closer.

"Not long. My dad married Iris a little over a year ago, and she told me pretty soon after she moved in."

"Did you freak out?" I chuckle, still feeling a little jittery and nervous.

"Definitely." Owen laughs. "Sometimes it's still hard to wrap my head around."

At least he doesn't think I'm mentally deranged after witnessing all of my 'episodes' caused by the stupid witches at school. It's still pretty embarrassing that he's seen me be picked on so much, but I'd rather that than have him think I'm crazy.

"Do the other guys know?" I ask curiously. Owen seems close with Spencer, Mattie, and Nolan, but I have no idea if he'd risk telling them or not. They're really into paranormal stuff, but...

"Spencer knows," Owen answers without hesitation. I raise my eyebrows in surprise, and he continues, "Amethyst told him last year when they were dating. Nolan and Mattie have no idea."

I grimace and rub my hand over my forehead. "What do they think is wrong with me?"

Owen pauses, and then clears his throat. It's obvious he's embarrassed to tell me this. "They think you have Tourette's, and Nolan's pretty sure you're schizophrenic. He's worried you're not taking the right medications, and he's been trying to convince the rest of us we should sit down and have, like, an intervention with you."

"Oh, Goddess." I suspected they thought something like that, but it's so much worse hearing it confirmed. It's also fucking embarrassing to realize the four of them have discussed me and my issues together!

"Spence and I told him to leave it alone, that it's not any of our business. I'm sorry, Harriet."

"It's fine. I'd probably think the same thing if I was them." In a weird way, it's actually kind of sweet that Nolan's so concerned. I really didn't think he liked me very much. And Mattie, as annoying as he is, still wants to be friends with me even though he thinks I'm a schizo with Tourette's. "So, you and Spencer...you're fine with me being a witch?"

"Of course," Owen says, like the answer should be obvious. "Can I ask you a question?"

"Yeah, anything," I say. And I really mean that. Talking to Owen about this is overwhelming, but I can't deny that I'm feeling giddy about the whole fucking thing. Owen and Spencer are hands down some of the hottest guys I've ever met, but I also really like them and want to get to know them better. If they're okay with me being a witch, maybe they'll be okay learning everything else about me.

"Why won't they leave you alone?"

He's obviously talking about the other witches at school. I

groan in embarrassment. "They're challenging me. You probably already know this, but Weeping Hollow was established by four witch families, and the community here is larger than most places in the country. The covens here are extremely close because of that. The witches at school, well, they don't like me because I'm an outsider, and they want me to prove that I belong with them. It's a little more personal with Amethyst. She's the reason they haven't let up."

Owen hums thoughtfully. "I hate seeing it. It drives me crazy that I can't do anything to stop it."

The embarrassing, girly giggle makes an appearance again, and I feel my cheeks flush. "You've done more than enough."

"How much longer are they going to mess with you?" he asks worriedly. "Is it because you're hanging out with us?"

"No," I laugh humorlessly. "Don't get me wrong, I'm sure that pisses them off too. But they won't stop until I cast a spell in retaliation or do something to defend myself."

"Why haven't you?" he asks. For the first time, it sounds like he thinks I might actually be insane after all.

I wrap my blanket around myself more securely and bite my lip. It takes me a few moments to gain enough courage, and then I tell him the truth. "I can't do magic. I'm the first witch in my family in hundreds of years who can't cast a single spell or charm. All of the witches here expect me to be super powerful like my mom, and like my Great-Grandma Sylvia was. But I'm just...I'm a dud."

"And you don't want them to know?" he asks sadly. Again, I know he's talking about the witches at school, and I'm so glad he knows what I'm trying to say.

"It's embarrassing." I shrug defensively, even though he can't see me.

Owen's quiet, but I can hear him breathing, so I know he didn't hang up. Eventually, he grunts and says, "God, I can't tell you how much that pisses me off. I thought you were playing some fucked-up game with them, but to know you're completely defenseless? Harriet, they could really hurt you."

"They won't." After what happened with Blaze today though, I'm not so sure. All I know is that I don't want Owen to be upset, even if it does make me feel stupidly happy to know he's worried about me.

"Will you tell me if they do? Please?"

"I will," I promise, lowering my voice to a whisper. "Can I tell you another secret?"

"You can tell me anything you want, Harriet Abbot."

The way he says my name makes me feel like I'm literally going to explode from the number of butterflies assaulting my stomach, and my heart does this crazy little backflip thing that makes me want to throw up.

Before I lose my nerve, I quickly blurt out, "I can't do magic, but I can see ghosts."

CHAPTER 12
HARRIET

"Are you sure you want to keep her?"

Circe purrs when I scratch the top of her head. Ever since I gave her a bath the other day, her fur has felt so soft. She's also been an absolute angel since she found my adder stone for me. She doesn't venture far from the house, and she always wants to snuggle whenever I'm in my room.

"Yeah, I'm sure." I chuckle. I still hate cats, but I've decided to make an exception for Circe.

My mom pulls on her coat and smiles at me proudly. "You know, it's a pretty special thing when an animal takes a liking to a witch. Even more so when it's a black cat. You'll need to take good care of her."

I have no clue why Circe took a liking to me, but I can't deny she's exhibited some pretty weird behavior for a simple animal. It's also really nice that for once, my mom's actually proud of me as a witch. I shrug and pick Circe up, hoping she'll be calm in the car. I don't have a kennel for her yet.

"We're heading out now, Flora. Text me if you need

anything!" my mom says, twirling her fingers in the air. Aunt Flora's upstairs, but my mom's spell will make sure she hears.

Luckily, Circe doesn't squirm too much when I get into the car. It's a twenty-minute drive to the vet's office, and she does fine as long as I pet her. My mom talks about the coven's get together and how nice it was to see everyone. I try not to roll my eyes. She still has no idea something happened with Amethyst and Blaze.

"How do you know Iris?" I ask, just for the sake of making conversation. My mom hasn't found a reason to get mad at me today, and I'm not in a hurry to change that. Owen wants to hang out later, and I don't want to give my mom a reason to keep me locked up at home.

"Her family's been in Weeping Hollow for generations." My mom shrugs. "I was never as close with her as with some of the other girls in town, but we still hung out whenever your aunt and I came here during our summer breaks."

She doesn't add anything else, and I debate for a moment whether I should say anything or not. But she'll probably appreciate the gossip. "My friend Owen is her stepson. He was one of the guys who came over to the house the other day."

"Really?" she asks excitedly. "That's so sweet! Why didn't you tell me your friends knew about witches? Your aunt and I wouldn't have been so careful to hide our magic when they came over."

"I didn't know until Iris said something yesterday. And besides, it's just Owen. The other guys don't know." I figure it's best not to mention Spencer. I haven't talked to him yet, and he's technically not supposed to know, anyway.

"Still, I think it's wonderful you're making friends here. Especially with people you can be yourself around."

"Yeah." A smile forms on my lips, and I pretend to focus on petting Circe.

"Owen's awfully cute, too."

"Mom!" I groan and roll my eyes.

She teases me a little more, and I grudgingly admit I think Owen is cute. I don't mention our phone call last night, or the fact that I *still* haven't responded to him asking me out. For the first time all week, my mom and I have a normal, pleasant conversation. I tell her about my classes, my teachers, the guys, and their ghost hunting obsession, but I don't tell her about Ryan or the bullying I've experienced. Baby steps, right?

"Here we are!" My mom parks in front of a small, white building. There's an old man walking a beagle outside, and he waves at us apologetically when his dog barks.

Circe tenses in my arms, but I whisper to her that everything's fine. It's a struggle getting out of the car while cradling her in my arms, but I manage. My mom holds the door to the clinic open, and I step through.

The receptionist smiles when we walk in. "Hello! Do you have an appointment?"

My mom checks us in and confirms the vaccinations Circe needs. We're shown to a room and told to wait for the vet tech. I can tell Circe's nervous, and I do my best to soothe her. Before the vet tech comes in, my mom's phone rings.

"It's Kamal," she says, holding her phone up for me to see. "Do you mind if I step out for a moment, sweetheart? I shouldn't be long."

Ugh, gross. My mom's totally going to start dating my principal. I mean, he seems nice, but that's going to make things so much more awkward for me at school. Especially when they inevitably break up. I wave her off and tell her I'll be fine.

The vet tech walks in seconds after my mom leaves. She's bright and cheery, and she talks nonstop while she checks Circe's temperature and other vitals. She asks me a bunch of questions I don't really know the answers to, considering Circe was a stray cat. As far as I know, anyway. I have no clue how old she is or where she came from.

"Dr. Reichardt will be with you in a few minutes," the vet tech says.

After she leaves, the room is quiet. Circe seems content to sniff around the room on her own. I have no clue how long it's going to take the vet to come in, so I take my phone out to check my messages. Nothing new, but I smile at the texts Owen and Sage sent me this morning.

I haven't completely updated Sage on the Owen situation yet, but she knows how cute I think he is and that I'm hanging out with him later today. She seems positive he likes me, and she thinks Spencer likes me too. I'm such an idiot though, and I have no idea what to do or how to act with either of them. All I know is I'm absolutely giddy at the thought of seeing Owen later, and I'm stupidly anxious to talk to Spencer now that I know he knows I'm a witch.

The door to the exam room opens, and I look up to find a middle-aged man frowning at me. He's wearing a white lab coat and holding a clipboard, so I assume he's the vet. He's tall with graying-brown hair, a beard, and glasses. He looks irritated. I stand up straighter as I shove my phone back into my pocket.

"You're not Della Abbot," he says.

"Uh, no." I shake my head slowly. "That's my mom. She just stepped outside."

He nods and lets out a heavy sigh, stepping fully into the room. "I should have known she'd move back to town eventually. How long have you been in Weeping Hollow?"

I'm not sure whether I should be insulted or intrigued. This guy is the first person I've ever met who doesn't seem completely enchanted by my mother. It's obvious he knows her, but he doesn't sound thrilled at the prospect of seeing her again.

"A week," I tell him truthfully.

He hums in acknowledgment and points at Circe, who's still sniffing around on the floor. "And who do we have here?"

"This is Circe." I pick her up and set her on the exam table, petting her to keep her calm. "She just needs a regular check-up and vaccinations. She was a stray until a few days ago, and I took her in."

He checks her over, much like the vet tech did, only a lot more in depth. He doesn't say anything or ask any questions, which is just fine with me. He frowns again when he touches her stomach, and he asks me to assist him in holding her down so he can get a better look.

"Is something wrong with her?" I ask worriedly. Circe hasn't acted weird or hurt, but what do I know about cats?

"I think she might be pregnant," he says, running his hand over her stomach again. He smiles softly at me and adds, "See how her nipples are slightly red and enlarged? It's not your fault. If she was a stray, like you said, this might not even be her first litter."

Circe meows pitifully and flicks her tail back and forth. I stare at her in shock. "You little ho! You totally tricked me into keeping you so you'd have a cushy place to have your kittens. Didn't you?"

Dr. Reichardt chuckles. "I can give you some pamphlets and the name of a rescue that can help you adopt the kittens out, if you'd like."

"Yeah, I guess that's fine." I'm kind of freaking out. I just got Circe. What am I going to do with a bunch of kittens? How will I be able to tell if something goes wrong?

He continues his examination, explaining he'll have to skip the vaccines today and wait until after she's had her kittens.

He explains the risks of vaccinating a pregnant cat and gives me all sorts of tips and things to look out for during her pregnancy and with the newborn kittens. I mostly nod without saying anything, trying not to show how anxious I feel. Even though I got the impression this guy doesn't like my mom, I still wish she'd come back. She'll know what questions to ask.

Speak of the devil. The door opens, and my mom walks in.

"I'm so sorry, sweetie! Has the vet been in—Henry!" She gasps, pausing in the doorway when her eyes land on Dr. Reichardt.

"Della," he says without looking up.

Oh, Goddess. I take it back. Why couldn't my mom have waited outside? The tension in the tiny exam room is so thick, I feel like I'm suffocating.

"I see you've met Harriet," she says cheerily, letting the door close behind her. Dr. Reichardt meets my eyes for a split second before focusing on Circe again. "Are you the lead veterinarian here?"

He mumbles at me to hold Circe again while he finishes examining her. I figure he's going to ignore my mom's question completely. She's standing behind me, and I'm glad I can't see the look on her face.

"I own the vet clinic," he finally says.

"How wonderful!" my mom exclaims. She steps closer and pats my arm, giving Dr. Reichardt a charming smile. A smile he definitely does not reciprocate when he looks at her. "I'm so glad you followed your dream. I wasn't sure you would after you knocked up Audrey Pickingill."

"Dammit, Della!" Dr. Reichardt growls. "I'm trying to be professional here for your daughter's sake."

Holy shit. I'd give anything to disappear right now. I pretend to be completely oblivious, avoiding both his and my mom's eyes while I pet Circe. Thank Goddess the appointment is almost over.

"Our daughter, actually." My mom giggles. My heart fucking stops, and I look up to find her smiling viciously at him. Her eyes flit over to me briefly, and her smile widens. "Harriet, dear, this is your father, Dr. Henry Reichardt."

"What?" I squeak.

My mom has never mentioned my father. She's never told me his name or where he lives. Hell, until this moment, I always assumed she didn't even know who he was. Witches have this stereotype of being kind of slutty, and my mom's always fit that. She's beautiful and she dates a lot, but she's never been close to marrying anyone. I rarely see her boyfriends, and I've never worried much about it. My mom and aunt didn't grow up with a dad either, so I've never felt like I was missing out on much.

But now? This might be the cruelest thing she's ever done. If she's lying, that's seriously fucking low to use me like this. All because of a feud with her stupid ex-boyfriend. If she's telling the truth? I don't even know where to start. Does he know?

"That's impossible," he hisses through his teeth.

"Is it?" My mom asks nonchalantly. I can't react. Can't move or say fucking anything. "Let's see. The last time we saw each other was April 2005, and Harriet will be seventeen in January. Look at her eyes and her nose, Henry! Goddess, sometimes I swear she looks and acts just like you!"

Before I have a nervous breakdown, I grab Circe and leave the room. I can't look at my mom, and I definitely can't look at *him*. My vision is blurry—either from unshed tears or from sheer fucking panic, I have no idea. I force myself to pause beside the receptionist's desk and hope I don't look like a lunatic.

"Uh, do you guys have any, like, kennels or anything I can carry her in?"

The last thing I need right now is for Circe to squirm out of my arms and run away. We're too far from the house, and I don't trust she'd be able to find her way back from here.

"Sure, sweetie." The receptionist quickly assembles a temporary cardboard carrying case for Circe, and I gently place her inside.

My mom and Dr. Reichardt must still be arguing. Neither of them comes out into the lobby, and I'm glad for it. I walk outside at a brisk pace, pass by my mom's car and turn left on the sidewalk. I have no clue where I am or how to get home, but I don't care. As long as I get far away from my mom, I'm good.

I've walked for less than ten minutes when the town basically ends, and all I see along the rest of the road are woods. I set Circe down and pull my phone out of my pocket, glancing around nervously. My anxiety's at an all-time high, and *Goddess*, I wish Sage was here. She'd know what to say.

But she's not here. My fingers tremble as I pull up Owen's number. I trust him. I just wish I didn't have to let him see me in such a pathetic, helpless situation.

He answers after the second ring. "Hey, what's up?"

Just like last night, he sounds so happy and surprised to hear from me. He's got to be the sweetest guy in the universe. Tears fill my eyes again, and my voice breaks.

"I—I'm sorry. I just, *Goddess*, I don't even know where I am and just—"

"Hey, hey, it's alright. Are you hurt?"

A pitiful whimper escapes my throat, and I clutch my adder stone necklace between my fingers. "No, I'm not hurt. This is so embarrassing. I just don't have anyone else to call."

"Don't be embarrassed," he says softly. "I'm glad you called me. What do you need? How can I help?"

"Can you pick me up?" Last night he mentioned he has a truck, but I still feel like a jerk for asking him. "I took Circe to the vet. And the vet, well, my mom just dropped a fucking bombshell and told me the vet is my dad. I took Circe and left, but I don't know the area. It's kind of far from my house."

Owen doesn't ask me for more details, and there's absolutely no judgment in his voice. "Can you share your location? I'll be there as soon as I can."

"Thank you," I whisper.

"Spencer's with me," he says uncertainly. "Is that okay?"

It's not totally ideal. I'm humiliated enough having one person witness my moment of weakness. But I like Spencer, and I want us to become better friends. Besides, I'm sure Spencer and Owen together will easily be able to distract me from what just happened with my mom.

"Yeah, of course."

We end the call, and I share my location with him. Circe makes a pitiful mewing sound from her makeshift carrier. I sigh as I pick her up, and I turn to go back in the direction of the vet. I'm pretty sure I passed a coffee shop, and I figure it's better to wait there than the side of the road.

My phone rings, and I sneer at my mom's name on the screen. I consider letting it go to voicemail, but I don't want her to call the cops and say I'm missing, or something stupid like that.

"What?" I spit into the phone.

"Where are you?" she asks, sounding only slightly alarmed. "The receptionist told me you were waiting outside."

"I left. I don't want to spend a second with you if I don't have to."

"Goddess, Harriet." She sighs. I can picture the stupid,

exasperated expression on her face. "I can't deal with this right now. Come back to the clinic so we can talk. Henry wants you to take a paternity test."

"You're an evil, selfish bitch. Do you know that?" I practically screech. "I don't give a fuck what you or *Henry* want. I'm never speaking to you again!"

I hang up, block her number, and send a quick text to Flora to let her know I'm hanging out with Owen and Spencer. If my mom needs to say anything to me, she can say it through my aunt from now on.

Fifteen minutes later, a gray Chevy truck pulls up beside the curb in front of the coffee shop I found. Spencer rolls down his window and grins at me.

"Are you looking to be rescued?"

A smile forms on my lips, and I snort as I stand up. Spencer opens the passenger door, jumps out, and holds his hand out to take Circe from me.

"Thank you," I mumble.

"Don't mention it." Spencer reaches out to stroke a strand of my hair between his fingers. His smile widens when our eyes meet, and I feel my cheeks flush. "Shit, I am so fucking relieved I can finally admit to knowing you're a witch."

That awful, embarrassing giggle makes an appearance, just like it always does whenever I talk to Spencer or Owen. Goddess, please kill me now.

Spencer chuckles and gestures for me to get into the truck. Owen's sitting behind the wheel, and he smiles shyly when I scramble into the front seat beside him. When Spencer moves to get in beside me, I realize there's no back seat. I scoot super close to Owen until I'm pressed against him, and I giggle awkwardly.

"Sorry, I know it's kind of cramped," Owen says.

"It's fine," I lie, even as Spencer scoots in close enough that our legs are pressed together too. He balances Circe's carrier on his lap and closes the truck door.

I'm completely squished in between them, which is making me feel giddier by the second. Before I blurt out something mortifying, I turn my head back and forth to meet both their eyes. "You guys have no idea how much I appreciate this. Seriously, thank you."

"Anytime." Owen smiles. He puts the truck in drive, and I try really hard to keep my hands in my lap. "Is there anywhere in particular you need to go?"

"Does your mom at least know we're not kidnapping you?" Spencer asks before I can answer.

"Yeah." I sigh. "I talked to her briefly, and I texted my aunt to let her know I'm with you guys. And, uh, I need to drop Circe off at my house, but otherwise I don't care where we go. What were you guys doing when I called?"

Spencer settles his arm against the back window behind my head. It's like he almost has his arm around me but not quite. "Owen picked me up from work not long before you called. We were just gonna chill at his house until you were free."

I'm glad I didn't mess up their plans much, if they wanted to hang out with me, anyway. I smile in relief and relax in my seat.

"How did Circe's appointment go?" Owen asks. When I turn to look at him, he grimaces. "I mean, before the, uh, crap with your mom."

I open the top of Circe's cardboard carrier, and she pokes her head out. Spencer scratches the top of her head, making her purr. She seems calm enough that I'm not worried she'll jump out or act crazy in the cab of Owen's truck.

"Apparently, the little slut cat is pregnant." The guys chuckle, and I smile too. "My mom dropped her bomb before I could get a ton of information. I have no clue what I'm gonna do with the kittens."

"I'm sure you'll figure it out," Spencer says. He clears his throat. "So, what happened with your mom? Something about the vet and your dad?"

And because I really like and trust these guys, I decide to tell them the whole story. They already know so much about me, and they've accepted me so far. When my voice catches and my eyes get teary again, Owen threads his fingers through mine, and Spencer places a comforting hand on my knee. I don't know if they realize they're each doing it, but it feels nice. It feels like they care, and like they want to make me feel better.

By the time I finish telling them what happened, we're back in the main part of town. I recognize the shops we drive past, all decorated for Halloween.

"Fuck them," Spencer says. I raise my eyebrows at him, and he gives me a half-smile. "As someone who has extremely sucky parents, I empathize with you. What your mom did is really shitty, but you can't let it affect you. I know that's easier said than done."

"Definitely easier said than done." I sigh. "I don't even want to go home, let alone talk to my mom ever again. Honestly, I don't even really want to think about this vet guy being my dad, either. It's so fucking crazy, I can barely wrap my mind around it."

"Understandable," Owen says. He turns left onto Hazel Lane and parks outside my house.

My mom's still out, but my aunt's car is in the driveway. I don't want to see or talk to her yet, but I don't want to leave Circe outside. She's had a traumatic day too, being poked and prodded by a stranger. Spencer gets out first and hands Circe to me.

I slink up to the front door and open it just a crack to let Circe in. She meows and takes off up the stairs. I leave the cardboard carrier by the front door, and then I quietly slip outside. My mom and aunt have charms set on the house, so Flora definitely knows I'm here. She doesn't appear or call out to me though, so I retreat back to Owen's truck, feeling completely relieved.

"You okay?" Owen asks quietly when I slide in next to him again.

"Yeah." I sigh, and I smile at him. He smiles back and threads our fingers together, even though there's no excuse for him to do it this time.

"So, what do you wanna do?" Spencer asks, closing the passenger door behind him as he scoots in.

"Whatever you guys want." I shrug.

The guys lean forward slightly to make eye contact, silently conveying something impossible for me to understand. Spencer's cheeks redden when he looks at me, and his smile turns bashful. "My sister invited us to go to the pumpkin patch with her and Shiloh. She told me I don't need to go, but I know she wants to apologize to you for Friday. Plus, Shiloh will not fucking shut up about you. If you'd rather not do that, we can chill at the diner or Owen's house."

"The pumpkin patch sounds fun." I grin.

"Okay, awesome." Spencer stares at Owen's hand entwined with mine. I'm about two seconds from panicking because I don't know what to do. But he doesn't comment on it. He just throws his arm around my shoulders. For real this time, rather than resting against the window. "Now, can we please talk about the fact that you can see ghosts? And how that's the coolest fucking thing I've ever heard?"

Cue another embarrassing giggle. How can he expect me to talk right now? Both guys are touching me and being all cute and couply in front of each other, and he brought up my biggest secret so fucking casually.

"Um, well..." I trail off, wishing I wasn't such an awkward disaster. "What do you want to know?"

"Owen told me there's a ghost in your house and one at school. Have you seen any more around town?" he asks excitedly.

A warm, tingly feeling runs through my whole body. Owen was the same way on the phone last night. He didn't doubt me or my gift for a single second, and he showed just as much enthusiasm as Spencer. They just want to learn more. I smile brightly, only a little nervous.

"There's one at the diner too. Some old, grumpy guy. He doesn't look like he's been dead long."

CHAPTER 13
HARRIET

"Hey, let me see your phone." Spencer holds his hand out, giving me a crooked smile.

Owen squeezes my hand, reminding me our fingers are still intertwined. Like I could forget. Just like I can't forget the fact that Spencer still has his arm around my shoulders. My skin tingles where he keeps rubbing his fingers over my arm, even through my tee shirt and jacket. It's hell sitting squished between these guys. I love the attention and the way my heart keeps skipping around, but I feel like an idiot who is completely inept to deal with this situation.

"Oh, um, sure," I mumble, realizing I've been staring at Spencer's hand without answering for several seconds. He chuckles, and my cheeks flush in embarrassment.

I pull my phone from my jacket pocket and hand it to him. He thanks me, tapping on it quickly. It takes me way too long to process the fact that he's adding his number to my contacts. When I see him press the call button, presumably so he can add my number to his phone too, I nearly let out another of those awful, high-pitched giggles.

"There." He hands me my phone back. His voice sounds smug, but his smile is almost shy. "Now you can call me instead of Owen whenever you need help. Or if you just want to talk or hang out."

"You can still call me." Owen grunts, squeezing my fingers tightly as he glances at me sideways.

Spencer laughs, pulling me closer to his side. "Just letting her know she has options."

Owen turns his head and glares at Spencer, but there's no real heat behind his expression. When both guys chuckle a few seconds later, I realize they're teasing each other.

What the hell is going on? Do they even like me? They keep flirting with me and acting like it, but surely most guys would get jealous or mad if their friend was hitting on the same girl as them. Right? Goddess, am I reading this entire situation wrong?

Desperate to change the subject—because I am not flirting back or responding to any of their cute, flirty moves until after I've talked to Sage about how the hell to handle these guys—I clear my throat and look at Spencer. "So, why the pumpkin patch today? I thought Shiloh was picky about when he wanted to carve jack-o'-lanterns."

"He is." Spencer laughs. "But today is the only day Zoe and Shiloh's dad have off work, and they like doing stuff like this together with Shiloh if they can. They had to promise him that just because we're getting pumpkins today, that doesn't mean we have to carve them yet."

A smile spreads across my face. Halloween is only two weeks away, so it's not like Shiloh will be waiting long either way. "Is Shiloh's dad in the picture much, then?" I ask curiously.

"Oh, yeah," Spencer says. "His name's Danny, and he's definitely still in love with my sister. His parents were not supportive of Zoe's pregnancy while she and Danny were in high school, and you know my parents aren't around. Even when they were still here, we were pretty much on our own. Zoe broke up with Danny after she had Shiloh and said she'd never forgive him if he didn't graduate and go to college like they both originally planned on doing. Danny goes to university in Boston, so he's not too far. He works a lot and sends my sister money too, and he comes around whenever he can. He's a good guy."

Something settles in my chest, knowing Shiloh has two great parents who love him. I can't imagine how hard it was for Zoe, getting pregnant so young and without any real support system. She didn't seem to like me much the last time we met, but Spencer said she wants to apologize, so maybe I'll have another chance to make a better impression.

Thinking about Zoe and Shiloh's dad makes me think about my morning at the vet. About the fact that I apparently have a father too. Is Henry Reichardt a good guy? It feels wrong to judge him by our first interaction when he had no clue who I was other than my relation to my mom. And after the way shit hit the fan, I can only assume he has some very good reasons not to like my mom. If he wants to go through with the paternity test and wants a chance to get to know me, do I owe that to him? Do I owe it to myself?

"Zoning out on us?" Owen asks teasingly.

I give him a bashful smile and shrug. "Yeah, sorry." I think about leaving it there, but maybe I should open up. Owen's already proven to be a good friend. He showed up for me without question. Spencer too. "It's just weird, I guess. I've gone my whole life never worrying about having a dad, and now it's, like, all I can think about."

"Makes sense." Owen nods.

"Goddess, I think I have a sibling." I pinch the bridge of my nose. "My mom made a comment about him knocking up some other witch before I was born."

Owen and Spencer are sweet and supportive during the rest of the drive, letting me vent and also offering me advice on how to talk to my mom whenever I feel ready to face her. By the time we reach the pumpkin patch, I feel like a weight's been lifted off my shoulders, and I feel a million times more willing and prepared to process the situation with my mom and Dr. Henry Reichardt.

After Owen finds a parking spot, he grabs his camera from the back of his truck—pausing to take a quick photo of me, which makes me laugh—and the three of us walk to the front entrance to meet up with Zoe, Shiloh, and Danny. Neither Owen or Spencer holds my hands or anything like they did in the truck, but they walk much closer than casual friends should.

"Harriet!" Shiloh screeches when we approach, pulling away from his parents to make a beeline for me. I laugh and stumble backwards as he crashes against my legs, bending down to return his enthusiastic hug.

"Hey, buddy." I grin.

His parents approach behind him. Zoe smiles tightly, like she might not be entirely thrilled at my being here. Did Spencer totally lie about her wanting to meet me again under better circumstances? Beside her is a cute Asian guy her age who I presume is Danny. He holds his hand out for me to shake and gives me a bright smile.

"Hi. Harriet, right? I'm Danny, Shiloh's dad." Before I can answer or confirm my identity, he reaches down to playfully ruffle Shiloh's hair and says, "The kid hasn't stopped talking about you all weekend."

Shiloh squawks in indignation, swatting his dad's hands away while denying the claim that he talked about me *all weekend.* His embarrassment is completely adorable, and I can't help giggling softly. After finally introducing myself properly, I make small talk with him, Zoe, and the guys standing on either side of me for a few minutes.

While Shiloh rambles enthusiastically about what qualifies as a perfect pumpkin and how he wants to decorate his jack-o'-lantern, Owen gently taps my arm. I turn to look up at him in confusion, and he gives me this sweet, bashful smile that instantly makes me remember all the reasons I like him.

"Do you want a cup of hot apple cider?" he asks, pointing at a little tent where they're selling drinks. "Or maybe a hot chocolate?"

I feel a goofy smile slide across my face as my cheeks warm. "Sure. I'd love some hot apple cider." Luckily, it's just chilly enough outside to warrant drinking the warm treat.

Before Owen can step away, Spencer punches him playfully in the arm and gives him a feral grin. "What about me?"

Owen's lips twitch as he rolls his eyes. "Don't worry. I'll get you a drink too, sweetheart."

A giggle escapes me, and both guys look at me like they've won the lottery. When Owen steps away, Danny grins at his back before turning to me.

"So, I hear you just moved here?" Danny asks.

I nod, nervously brushing a strand of hair behind my ear. "Yeah, just over a week ago now."

"You're living in the Abbot House, right?" Zoe asks. When I nod, she chuckles quietly. "Man, I don't know how you can stand it. That place is so creepy. Unless you're into that kind of stuff, like Spencer is."

Spencer makes a fake offended sound, and I give his sister a half smile and shrug. "It's not so bad now that my family's cleaning it up."

"Do you have any pets?" Shiloh tugs on my jacket sleeve,

and I look down to see him giving me puppy-dog eyes. "I really want a dog, but my mom says we can't have one at our house."

Goddess, this is why I love kids. It's impossible to figure out how exactly their train of thought works. I give Shiloh a big grin and nod. "I just got a cat when I moved here. Her name is Circe, and she's all black."

"Oh my god!" Shiloh bounces on the balls of his feet. "Like a witch's cat?"

Spencer snorts beside me, and I have to try very hard not to glare at him or elbow his side before I answer his nephew. "Yeah, like a witch's cat. And guess what? I took her to the vet this morning, and I found out she's having kittens!"

That leads to a whole slew of excited questions from Shiloh. To my pleasant surprise, Zoe gives me a real smile for the first time and tells her son that maybe they can visit to see the kittens after they're born. The idea of Circe having kittens is still a bit overwhelming, and I have absolutely no clue what I'm going to do with the kittens after they're born, but it's exciting to talk about it all hypothetically.

When Owen returns with apple cider for me, Spencer, and himself, Spencer puts his hand on the small of my back and gently begins leading me away from his family. "Alright, this has been fun. We'll talk to you guys later."

I glance over my shoulder at Zoe, Danny, and Shiloh, frowning slightly once the guys and I are several feet away. "I thought you wanted to hang out with your family?" I ask Spencer.

"Not really." He shrugs. "Just wanted to say hi and let Shiloh see you again. Owen and I would much rather hang out alone with you. Right, dude?"

Owen's knuckles brush against the back of my hand, and he hums quietly in agreement. I glance back and forth between the two boys shyly, lifting my apple cider to my lips to hide my nervous smile. If I was alone with just one of them, this might feel like a date. But they probably just want to hang out so we can talk about ghosts and witch stuff. That's what I have to tell myself, anyway, or else I'll go crazy from worrying I'll do something stupid.

"Okay." I stop in front of a decorative sign that lists all of the activities the farm has to offer. There's a pumpkin patch, of course, and there's also a giant corn maze, a petting zoo, a small farmer's market, and hay rides. Back home in Oregon, we had a pumpkin patch similar to this one, but it was much smaller. Just like everything else I've seen in Weeping Hollow, this town loves to go all out with anything Halloween or fall-related. "What do you guys want to do first?"

CHAPTER 14
OWEN

"Don't you think you've taken enough?"

Harriet sighs exasperatedly, and I smile as I raise my camera to snap another photo. If she were right in front of me, I know my fingers would be itching to brush away that adorable furrow between her eyebrows. I think I understand her well enough now to know she's not really irritated. Embarrassed, maybe. But not irritated.

"Just a few more," I say, wishing for the millionth time I had my film camera with me instead of a digital one. The way the light is hitting Harriet with all the fall colors in the background would come out so much better after developing the photos in my dark room. But these will still turn out great, I'm sure.

When Harriet sighs and adjusts the pumpkin she's cradling in her arms, Spencer chuckles quietly beside me. "You really can't help yourself, can you?"

No, I can't. I feel like I've been losing my mind since I met Harriet last week. I have no control over every idiotic word out of my mouth or every ridiculous thing I do around her. How

I've managed to convince this girl to be my friend is beyond me, but I'm certainly not complaining.

Shiloh runs over to Harriet, already talking a mile a minute, so I slowly lower the camera. If Spencer's sister is getting ready to leave, there's probably no reason for us to stick around much longer either.

"Hey, listen," Spencer whispers, nudging me. I glance sideways at him, not wanting to tear my gaze away from Harriet entirely. "I'm gonna head home with Zoe and Shiloh. You should ask Harriet to hang out longer though. Just the two of you."

That gets me to turn and face him fully, my eyebrows shooting up in surprise. I know he likes Harriet too. Shit, I'm still surprised he hasn't told me to fuck off so he can make a real move on her.

"Are you sure?" I ask.

"Yeah." He shrugs. "She's never gonna admit to liking either of us while we're both hanging around. Besides, I'm the one who jacked your whole day you had planned with her."

"I—" I clear my throat. My words always seem to fail me when there's something I want to say. Unless I'm talking to Harriet, for some reason. "I don't think she likes me. Not like that, anyway. So, you shouldn't worry."

And I mean that. Sure, I'll keep shooting my shot and acting like an idiot for as long as Harriet allows, but I sincerely doubt she likes me as anything more than a friend. She only called me last night after she realized I know she's a witch. Pretty sure she would have left me hanging indefinitely otherwise. Which is fair. She doesn't owe me anything just because I'm kind of obsessed with her.

Spencer laughs and slaps my back. "Sure, man."

Without another word, he walks over to Harriet and pulls her into a hug. I can't hear what he says to her, but her face turns beet red. When he pulls away, he bends down to grab Shiloh, tickling the kid until he squeals from laughter.

Steeling my nerves, I walk over to stand beside Harriet. She glances up at me with a shy smile, her silver eyes and hair glinting in the sunlight. I smile back at her, looking like a lovesick fool, I'm sure. If Spencer and his family weren't lingering nearby, I'm sure I'd have blurted out something humiliating already. Instead, I stay quiet and wait for them to leave. As Zoe, Danny, and Shiloh begin walking toward the parking lot, Spencer tells me and Harriet that he'll see us tomorrow. Giving me a final, unreadable glance, he quickly leans forward and kisses Harriet's cheek before turning and jogging after his family.

Harriet slowly raises her hand to her cheek, staring after Spencer with a bewildered expression. When she turns to me, she frowns. "Are you ready to head home too?"

I try really hard not to let the fact that she sounds disappointed go to my head, but I know I fail miserably. "Actually, I was going to ask if you still wanted to hang out. Maybe you can come over? I've been dying to show you the photos I took at your house last week."

"You want me to come over to your house?"

"Yeah." I shrug, wishing I didn't feel or sound so dumb. "If you want to, I mean. It's okay if you just want me to take you home."

"No, that sounds cool. Let's do it."

I grin again, taking the pumpkin from her arms so I can carry it to my truck for her. She's quiet as we get settled in the truck. I glance down at the middle seat between us, wishing I had a plausible excuse to ask her to sit close to me again like she did when Spencer was with us. Holding her hand and feeling her leg pressed against mine on the drive here was everything.

"So, that was a lot of fun," Harriet says quietly, twisting her hands in her lap. "Way nicer and more festive than any pumpkin patch I ever went to back in Oregon."

"Really?" I laugh. "I would think fall in the northwest would be similar to here with all the forests and mountains. Plus, I'm pretty sure *Halloweentown* was filmed in Oregon. How can there be no overzealous pumpkin patches there?"

She giggles, which is quickly becoming one of my favorite sounds in the world. Forget *kind of* obsessed. I'm definitely fucking obsessed with this girl. "That's true. Maybe there are bigger and better pumpkin patches and fall festivals places other than where I lived, but Weeping Hollow just goes totally nuts for anything fall or Halloween-themed. I love it, but it's pretty crazy."

"Must be all the witchy influence," I tease.

She rolls her eyes and smiles, turning to stare out the window. Not for the first time, I wonder what it is about her that draws me in. I know plenty of other witches. All the ones I go to school with, I've known practically my whole life. Not that I'm friends with any of them. Still, Harriet is nothing like any of them, from what I've seen. She never seems conceited or arrogant, and she never acts like she thinks she's superior to other people. Most baffling of all, she seems to have no idea how attractive she is. I don't know if it's because she grew up somewhere different than here, or if it's because she doesn't have the same powers other witches do. I want to ask more about her lack of magic, but I get the feeling it's a sore subject.

The first day I saw her, I seriously considered the idea that she might be using some sort of charm on me to make me want her. After witnessing some of the other asshole witches in our class bully her, I thought it could have been one of *them* using a spell on me in a roundabout way to fuck with Harriet more thoroughly. I still haven't entirely ruled out that theory, if I'm honest, but I've decided I'm past the point of caring. Harriet's beautiful and interesting, and I'm pretty sure I'd like her regardless of any magical influence.

"What do you miss most about Oregon?" I ask.

For the rest of the drive to my place, she tells me all about her old house, her old school, and her best friend Sage. I greedily latch onto every detail that comes out of her mouth, committing everything I'm learning about her to memory. By the time we reach my house, I can't decide if I'm more nervous or excited to have her here. She wouldn't still be hanging out with me if she didn't want to, right? I know she was looking for an escape from her family situation this morning, but I'm positive she had fun hanging out with me and Spencer.

She gets quiet when I park the car, so I'm sure she's nervous too. I'm determined to make her feel more at ease, but I'm not sure how to do that yet. Luckily, my dad and stepmom aren't home, so I don't have to worry about forcing Harriet into any awkward small talk with either of them.

The first thing Harriet says when we step inside the front door is, "Do you have any siblings?" When I turn to look at her, she smiles bashfully. "Sorry if that sounds random. I was thinking about it earlier when we were talking to Spencer's sister, and I realized I've never asked. About you, Nolan, or Mattie."

"Nope, I'm an only child." I shrug. "Nolan has a younger sister. Katie. She's twelve."

I don't mention Mattie or what happened to his family. That's his story if he ever wants to tell her.

After grabbing her something to drink and giving her a quick tour of the house—which is nowhere near as impressive as hers—I lead her upstairs to my darkroom. My dad let me convert my mom's old office about a year ago, and I spend an unhealthy amount of time in here whenever I'm home.

"Wow." Harriet frowns when she walks in behind me. A frown settles on her face as she looks around. The faint red light makes it harder to read her expression than usual. I wish I could tell what she's thinking. Does she think I'm completely lame for this? Nolan seems to think Harriet's dubbed our entire group as a bunch of losers. Right now, I can't help but worry he's right.

"Too much?" I chuckle, rubbing the back of my neck.

She looks up to meet my eyes, appearing bashful. "No, no. That's not what I meant. I guess I just didn't realize people still used these. How did you even learn to develop photos this way?"

Relief makes me laugh. "Yeah, no, you're right. They're not used very often. I'm just a nerd, I guess. I got into digital photography a few years ago, but when I learned about developing film, that's when I got really obsessed. It's, like, a lost art. Photos developed in a dark room always feel more magical somehow, like they show you something different than you'd ever see from anything digital."

God, I never talk this much. And I certainly never ramble on and on like an idiot. What is this girl doing to me?

"That's amazing!" The smile she gives me is almost blinding, and my heart stutters in my chest. "I don't really know anything about photography, but I love that you're so passionate about this. The fact that you even have a room like this in your house is insanely cool."

"Thanks." My fingers twitch at my side as I fight the urge to reach out and touch her. Or kiss her. Still, the compliment from her feels like everything. Clearing my throat, I gesture to a table in the corner. "Did you still wanna see the photos I took at your house?"

"Will I even be able to see them in here?" She squints at the faint red lights. I think she's teasing me, but she has a point.

Not everyone is accustomed to sitting in a dark room for hours at a time like I am.

I grin broadly. "We'll look at them in here first, and then we can take them to my room. Trust me, the effect is worth it."

Her lips twitch with a smile as she nods, following me over the table along the far wall. I pick up the folder I labeled *Abbot House* with the date the guys and I did our preliminary investigation. I want Harriet to see all the photos I took, but especially the ones tucked at the back of the pile. It's impossible to hide my excitement as I flip open the folder and hand it to her.

She takes the stack of photographs carefully, like she's afraid of ruining them. She doesn't need to worry, but I secretly love seeing her soft side. Every time she does something sweet or caring, even when it's followed by a sarcastic remark, it feels like I'm chipping away at the guard she has up and seeing more and more of the real Harriet.

The first few photos are of the exterior of the Abbot House. Harriet and her family still hadn't cut the grass or worked on the yard at that point, so the aesthetic of the photos is creepy as fuck. When we drove by her house earlier to drop off Circe, it was a shock to see the house looking almost...normal. I don't think it could ever look a hundred percent not-creepy, but the yard has been tamed and the entire exterior of the house looks like it's gotten a fresh coat of paint. I'm sure some magic was involved to make the changes happen so quickly, but that only makes the transformation even more amazing.

I watch with building anticipation as she slowly looks through the stack of photos, gently setting the ones she's finished looking at down on the table. She seems embarrassed every time she sees a photo of herself, but I have zero shame. She's gorgeous. Stunning. Hot as fuck, as Mattie likes to say. Why wouldn't I photograph her any chance I get? When

Harriet finally reaches the last few photos at the end of the stack, I make sure I'm watching her face so I don't miss her reaction.

Her eyes widen, and she inhales sharply. Without looking away from the photo, she says, "I can't believe you actually managed to get a picture of her. This is..."

She trails off, and I snort out a laugh. "Nightmare fuel?"

Giving a tiny smile, she turns to me and nods. "That's one way to put it. I've never seen such a clear photograph of a ghost before. I didn't think it was possible. She barely even looks translucent here. Is that because of the dark room stuff, or are you just a super talented photographer?"

"I've got a theory about that." I take the first photo from her, staring down at the horrifying image of the ghost who haunts the Abbot House. "The guys and I have been to plenty of places that we're fairly positive are haunted. I've captured wisps or vague outlines of spirits in photos before, but nothing like this. I think it's because you're in the photo too, and your powers somehow allow you to...I don't know, amplify the ghost's presence. I want to take some photos of you with Ryan tomorrow, if that's okay, so we can test the theory further. And maybe that ghost from the diner too."

Just thinking about it makes me pumped. The supernatural stuff has always been a geeky hobby the guys and I enjoy, but Harriet being around makes it all so much more real and exciting.

"I don't have any powers," she mumbles.

Forcing my eyes away from the photo of Old Creepy, as Harriet affectionately calls her, I frown at the girl beside me. There's a furrow between her eyebrows as she pretends to focus intently on the photos in her hand. I hate that she feels sensitive and insecure about this power thing.

"Sure you do," I say, trying to keep it light. I give into the temptation to reach out and smooth her soft, silver hair away from her face until she meets my eyes. "Maybe your power is different from other witches, but it's still fantastic. You can do something remarkable."

It's too dark to tell if her cheeks are red, but I have a feeling she's blushing. She blushes a lot, and it's fucking adorable. After staring up at me for a few charged seconds, she bites her lip and shrugs.

"Maybe. It's just really hard to think about seeing ghosts as something useful or special. When I first started seeing them when I was little, my mom freaked out. There were a few times I overheard her talking to friends about how she wished I was normal and how she couldn't wait for my real powers to manifest. When they never did, she didn't say anything, but I know she was disappointed. I'm sure she still is. She and my aunt are better about that and the ghost thing now, but it's not something we've ever talked about or that I've explored. Until I moved here, I only saw ghosts briefly every once in a while. It was never like this, the way it's been since I moved here."

It takes everything in me to keep my thoughts to myself. The more I learn about Harriet's mom, the less I like her. What kind of mother makes their kid feel like that? Like they're not *normal?* Not to mention the shit she pulled today with Harriet's bio dad. God, I just want to protect this girl and let her know I'm here for her. For whatever she needs.

"Let me help prove it to you," I say. Her eyebrows furrow, and I give her a crooked smile. "Prove that it's a valuable, badass gift, I mean. I bet Ryan and Old Creepy think your power is way more useful than anything your mom can do. Guaranteed."

She giggles softly and nods. "Yeah. Good point. I really, really want to figure out how Ryan died. I'm just not sure where to start."

"I'll help you," I say, probably sounding way too eager. "So will Spence. We can't wait to meet Ryan at school tomorrow. I still can't believe he's been following us around for who knows how long."

While Harriet told me a little about her ghostly acquaintances over the phone last night, she was much more open and animated talking about them to me and Spencer at the pumpkin patch today. He and I already have tons of ideas of how we can help her investigate Ryan's death without drawing attention, and we've started making a list of places we wanna take her where she might see more ghosts. Part of me wishes we could tell Nolan and Mattie too. Nolan especially. He's even more into the paranormal stuff than Spencer and I are. But I know it's not smart or safe to bring them into the loop. Spencer's not even supposed to know about witches, so we'll need to be careful going forward.

Harriet's quiet for a long time, staring down at my photos with a thoughtful expression on her face. Eventually, she looks up at me again and asks, "If I'm really amplifying their presence like you think I am, do you think there's something I can do to help Ryan get some of his memory back? Or to help Old Creepy talk in actual sentences?"

"Maybe. I'm sure that depends on how they died, at least partially. But we can always try to test that too. We'll just take one step at a time with them."

She grins and surprises the hell out of me by leaning forward to give me a hug. It only lasts a second, and it's not exactly romantic. But fuck if I don't feel the biggest, goofiest smile spread across my face.

"Thanks, Owen. You've been so amazing to me."

"Yeah, well..." I chuckle and rub my hand over the back of my neck. Should I ask her out again? Or bring up what I wrote in her notebook on her first day of school? No, no. I need to just keep on playing it cool. She knows I'm into her, and I don't need to keep pressuring her. "I'd be an idiot not to be nice to a beautiful girl, let alone someone as interesting and badass as you."

Dammit. That was *not* playing it cool. Why am I such a dumbass?

Harriet makes this squeaking sound that makes my lips twitch with a smile. She's gotta be blushing now. "I-I, um..."

After she stutters and trails off, I gather up the rest of the photos from this batch and tuck the folder under my arm. I don't want her to feel uncomfortable around me, so it's probably better to just change the subject and pretend like I didn't say anything moronic. "Did you still wanna look at these in better lighting?"

She nods, staying quiet. I lead her from the darkroom, making sure to close the door tight behind us, and walk with her down the hallway to my bedroom. There's nothing impressive in here. Just a bed, a dresser, a desk, and a bookshelf full of horror books. I notice that my bed's made and that all my dirty laundry has been cleaned off the floor. Thank god for my stepmom.

"Wow, you've got a lot of books." Harriet's eyes trail across my shelf as she walks over to sit on my bed with her legs crossed. When she gestures for me to hand her the folder of photographs, I slowly walk over and sit beside her, careful to keep a few inches between us so I don't accidentally freak her out all over again.

"Yeah." I chuckle, leaving it at that. I know Harriet doesn't like to read. She mentioned it during lunch one day last week. I've already forced my photography hobby onto her. She doesn't need to listen to me geek out about my favorite authors too. "So. Are the photos any better out of the dark room?"

She flips open the folder and looks through the collection

again, quicker than she did the first time. There's a smirk on her face when she glances over at me. "Okay. I see what you mean. It was definitely a different vibe looking through them in there. They're still incredible though. You're really talented."

"Thanks."

Harriet holds up one of the photos of her and Old Creepy, leaning a little closer to me. I lean closer to her too, even though I can see the photo just fine. I've looked at all of these about a million times already on my own, so I know I'm not going to notice anything new. When I first developed the shots of Old Creepy, I swear I nearly shit myself. I had an inkling Harriet was being more truthful about her ghost than she originally led us to believe, even before I knew about her power, and I was certain I'd catch something in these photos. But when this ghost's horrifying face showed up? Yeah, definitely not what I was expecting. Hearing Harriet talk about the ghost so fondly makes it even more nuts.

"Have you shown these to the guys yet?" she asks. "I can't believe they wouldn't say anything to me or ask to come over again to continue their investigation after this."

A snort escapes my throat, and she turns toward me. My heart stutters when I realize our faces are only a couple inches apart now, and it would be too easy to lean down and kiss her.

"Nah, I haven't shown them." I clear my throat. "I wanted to show you first in case you didn't want us coming back. Once they see this, they will never leave you alone or stop showing up at your house. Besides, at first, I wasn't sure if you really wanted us to know about the ghost or not. It's hard to tell when you're being sarcastic sometimes."

"A character flaw of mine," she says with a little half smile. "I think you should show them. I, um, really didn't mind you guys coming over like that. To do ghost hunting stuff. I feel a little stupid for not knowing as much as you guys do about ghosts and spirits when I can literally see them, but it would definitely be cool to learn."

"We'll show them tomorrow then." Mattie and Nolan are going to lose their minds when they see this. Hell, Spencer probably will too. Harriet described Old Creepy as this little old lady who floats around singing nursery rhymes. *Not* as this terrifying, skeletal creature with gnarled hands, empty black eyes, and a nightmarish smile.

"Sounds like a plan."

A COUPLE HOURS LATER, AFTER DROPPING HARRIET OFF AT HOME, I walk through the front door of my house and immediately smell dinner cooking. I grin and head into the kitchen, unsurprised to find Iris stirring something at the stove while she hums softly under her breath. My dad's nowhere to be seen, but I'm sure he'll join us in here soon.

"Hey, sweetie." She turns and offers me a loving smile. "How was your day?"

I sit at the breakfast bar and watch her for a few seconds. I was a little dubious when my dad first started dating Iris. It seemed too soon. They met barely a year after my mom's death. But Iris has always given me a good feeling. Being around her makes me feel calm and happy. I know part of that is her being a witch, but I think most of it's just her and who she is.

It's not like Iris replaced my mom. That would be impossible. Iris was adamant when she moved in that she never wanted it to feel that way, and it hasn't. She and my dad met at a support group for grieving widows, and I think they just found comfort in one another after losing someone they loved. Iris has been good for us, and I think we've been good for her too.

"It was good," I finally answer. "I hung out with Spencer and Harriet. And, uh, Harriet came over here for a bit while you guys were out."

Iris's eyes light up. "Oh, that's wonderful. She seems like such a sweet girl. I'm glad you guys are getting closer and spending more time together."

"Me too," I admit. Iris knows all about my pathetic crush on Harriet. The first day I met her, I came home and immediately spilled my guts to my stepmom about the new witch in school and my embarrassing attempt at asking her out.

My stepmom's expression turns thoughtful and slightly concerned as she turns to focus on dinner again. "I know you mentioned some of the other witches at school were hazing her, but after catching them at their nasty little games yesterday, I'm worried it's escalating into something dangerous. Do you know if any of your teachers have stepped in? Or even Principal Di Rossi?"

Shaking my head, I clench my fist in anger. Those asshole witches at school piss me off on a good day, but the way they've been treating Harriet makes me sick. Now that I know Harriet's not a willing participant in their 'games' and that she can't even fight back, I'm gonna try a million times harder to protect her while we're at school.

"Don't say anything to anyone in the coven," I plead. Iris nods, raising an eyebrow at me. I take a deep breath, hoping I'm making the right call in telling her Harriet's secret. "Harriet admitted to me that she doesn't have typical powers like most witches do. Like, she can't cast spells or anything. Nothing at all. So, every time the assholes at school mess with her,

Harriet's completely defenseless. I've been making it harder for them, getting in their way when I can, but I'm not really sure what else I can do."

Iris's face falls. "I was afraid it might be like that. Of course I won't mention it to anyone in the coven, but I feel like I should at least speak to Harriet's mother. Does she have any idea what her daughter's been dealing with at school?"

"I doubt it. I'm also not convinced that woman will do anything to stop it either."

It's impossible to keep the anger out of my voice, and Iris definitely takes notice. She sighs deeply and nods. "Della was always a little vain and self-centered. Even when we were kids."

Somehow, I'm not surprised. The kitchen gets quiet again, and Iris goes back to her humming while she cooks. It only takes a few minutes for me to feel calm again, even though I doubt I'll ever stop feeling pissed off about the way other witches treat Harriet.

My dad pops into the kitchen for a moment to say hi and to check on dinner's status before heading back into his office. Once I'm alone with Iris again, I decide to ask her the question that's been hovering in the back of my mind since I met Harriet.

"Iris?" I ask hesitantly. She looks up attentively, and that warm, calm feeling I always get around her washes over me. "Can I ask you a question? It's...a little embarrassing."

"Of course, sweetie." She turns off the burners at the stove and walks over to sit beside me at the breakfast bar, giving me her full attention. "What is it?"

The words stick in my throat. It's usually easier to talk to Iris than it is most people, but it's still not as effortless as it is with Harriet. At least I know Iris won't laugh at me, even if I end up sounding like a complete moron.

156

"Why do I like her so much?" I whisper. Iris's lips twitch, but I force myself to continue before she has a chance to respond yet. "It's—it's like an obsession. All encompassing. When I'm with her, I can't stop staring at her. And when I'm not with her, she's all I can think about. The way I feel about her just doesn't seem...normal. Especially considering I've only known her a week."

"Well." Iris taps her fingernails against the countertop and tilts her head thoughtfully. "Witches are naturally very sensual creatures. If there's a mutual attraction between a witch and a human, it's normal for the human involved to form a strong attachment in a short amount of time. More so if the witch feels just as strongly or if the human accepts the connection without fighting or questioning it. Do you think Harriet likes you as much as you like her?"

"No." I chuckle awkwardly. "At least, I don't think so. I've asked her out, and I flirt with her. Mostly, she seems embarrassed anytime I say or do anything that shows her how I feel. It's enough that she wants to be friends though. I'm happy being friends. Being around her at all is just...it makes me feel like I've won the lottery."

"Hmm." A sly smile spreads across Iris's face. "I wouldn't be so sure she's not just as smitten as you are."

Grimacing, I ask her the more pressing question that's been bugging me. "So, you don't think someone put, like, a spell on me? Or used a love potion to make me feel like this? Not Harriet, necessarily, but maybe one of the jerks who keep messing with her?"

Iris furrows her eyebrows and waves her hand over me while quickly muttering something under her breath. When she shakes her head definitively, I exhale in relief.

"No, I don't sense any hexes on you," she says. "Some girls Harriet's age will use charms to make themselves more appealing to those who already find them even mildly attractive. Sort of like a temporary love potion, usually mixed into their perfume. But if that were the case, your feelings would be very fleeting, and they certainly wouldn't last away from Harriet's presence. I don't think you have anything to worry about."

I didn't realize how worried I was about my theory, not until now. I feel like a weight's been lifted off my shoulders, and hope flares bright in my chest at the thought that Harriet might very well like me back. She's probably just shy and inexperienced, which isn't a problem for me. I'm shy and inexperienced too.

"Thanks, Iris."

CHAPTER 15
HARRIET

"You have to talk to your mom sometime."

I roll my eyes and lean my head against the passenger window, watching the scenery pass by in a blur. "No, I don't think I do, actually."

Flora sighs. It's obvious she's taken my mom's side and thinks I'm acting like an obnoxious teenager. But she's wrong. What my mom did at the vet office yesterday was repulsive, and right now, I don't see how I can ever forgive her. If I have to talk to her through my aunt for the next two years until I graduate, then so be it.

"She's sorry, you know," Flora says. I snort and give her a look, and she shrugs. "It's true. Maybe it doesn't seem like it now, but that's why you need to talk to her. Let her explain herself. She never intended to hurt you. I'm sure she never planned on telling you about Henry at all."

I wasn't planning on saying anything. Really, I wasn't. But her words make me snap. I whip my head around to glare at her and scoff. "And you don't see the problem with that? It shouldn't have been her choice. I don't care what sort of history she has with that guy. She should have told him about me. More importantly, she should have told me about him! But as usual, she can't help being fucking selfish."

My aunt purses her lips. I grip my backpack tight in my lap, prepared to demand she pull over so I can walk the rest of the way to school when she inevitably defends my mom and continues to take her side like always. Instead, she surprises me by reaching across the center console to pat the top of my hand.

"I'm sorry, Harriet. I know this is hard on you, and you didn't deserve for it all to come out this way. I still think you should talk to your mom."

There's no chance in hell that's happening, no matter how many times my aunt pleads with me. But I'm done arguing and wasting energy on this. I have other things to worry about today. Like checking on Ryan after not seeing him all weekend. I asked Flora to drive me to school early this morning with the excuse that I have a makeup test. But really, I just wanted some extra time to track down Ryan and catch him up on the situation with Owen and Spencer before they get to school.

The rest of the drive is quiet, thankfully. When Flora pulls up in front of the school, I can't jump out fast enough. She calls after me before I can take more than two steps away, and I grudgingly turn around to scowl at her.

"Do you need me to pick you up too?"

I hesitate, wondering how pathetic Owen will think I am if I beg him to drive me home instead. Even if he says yes today, it's not like I can expect him to drive me to and from school every single day after this. As much as I would prefer that. Still, if I manage to get up the courage, I'm going to ask him.

"I'll text you and let you know," I tell Flora, turning away without another word as I storm into the school.

I'm almost an hour early, and it's eerily quiet in the

hallways. A few cars are in the parking lot, and the front doors are unlocked, so I'm sure some staff members are here already. At first, I feel super weird about being here and slightly worried I'll get in trouble somehow, until I pass by a student sitting in a hallway doing their homework.

After dropping my stuff off at my locker, I look around, feeling totally lost. I have no clue what part of the school Ryan typically haunts whenever he's not following me around. Every day last week, he was waiting by the front doors for me before school started. I didn't stop to think he wouldn't know to wait there earlier for me today. Part of me can't help worrying that he's somehow forgotten about me or lost more of his memories after being left alone with no one to talk to for the past two days. That's stupid though, right? He was dead long before I met him. I'm sure two days feels like nothing to him.

Gripping my adder stone necklace between my fingers, I take a few steps down the hallway, looking around in case he randomly decides to pop out from the walls like he did the first time we met. Maybe he'll hear me if I say his name? How does ghost hearing work, anyway?

"Ryan?" I whisper, and then snort derisively at myself. This is dumb. No way will he hear me whispering when he could be floating around on the opposite side of the school. I should just go outside and wait for him by the doors. He'll show up out there eventually.

I spin on my heel to head back outside, nearly smacking into Ryan as he pops out of nowhere. I yelp in surprise, and he grins back at me as he holds his arms out like he's waiting for a hug.

"You called, babe?" he asks, smiling flirtatiously.

"Goddess, you scared the crap out of me," I groan, reaching out to smack his arm. My hand goes right through him, my skin immediately breaking out in goosebumps as a shiver runs up my spine. He stares at the spot on his arm my hand passed through, his eyebrows furrowing. Ignoring his weird look, I chuckle awkwardly. "Did you really hear me? I was so quiet."

He meets my eyes, looking at me like he's confused about something. I panic for a moment, assuming I was right about his memory loss getting worse. Has he seriously forgotten who I am?

"No, I—" He hesitates, and then quickly shrugs off his weird mood and gives me his usual, charming smile. "It was weird, but I somehow *felt* you calling for me. Like, a tugging sort of feeling that led me here to you. Fuck, I missed you, Harriet. Time used to have no meaning, but this weekend felt like it lasted for years. Years! It was only two days ago that I saw you, right? Time is weird when you're dead."

Relief washes over me. Thank Goddess he remembers me! I laugh and barely hold myself back from hugging him. All that would accomplish is potentially tripping over myself in the process and feeling like I was splashed with freezing cold water.

"Yes, it was only two days." I look around the hallway, remembering that I need to be more careful so I don't look like an absolute freak talking to myself. I lower my voice and lean closer to Ryan. "I have so much to tell you."

He wiggles his eyebrows and gives me a suggestive smirk. "Hooked up with Spencer after all, did you? I knew you had it in you."

"What? No!" I smack my forehead and sigh. Nope, I definitely didn't have anything to worry about. Ryan's just as obnoxious and crude as he was when he followed me around last week. "Let's just go somewhere we can talk without worrying about people walking by or overhearing us."

"They really wanna meet me, huh?" Ryan grins.

He's hardly stopped smiling since I started telling him about my whirlwind weekend. I rushed through telling him about the crap with Amethyst and Blaze at my house, and I vaguely mentioned the drama with my mom and possible father. But only to explain how I ended up calling Owen in the first place Saturday night, and then how I wound up hanging out with him and Spencer yesterday.

"Are you alright with that?" I ask, just in case Ryan feels weird about being studied or talked to by people who can't actually see them. "They said they're gonna help me figure out what happened to you."

Ryan's smile softens, and he scoots closer to give the impression that our legs are touching. We ended up coming to the library and hiding out in the back of the stacks where there's very little chance of any students coming by this early in the morning. The librarian only gave me a bored, tired look when he saw me walk in, and I feel confident he's not going to worry about checking on me any time soon. The side of my leg tingles and feels cold, but I don't move it away.

"Of course I'm alright with it. They already feel like my friends after eavesdropping and following them around for as long as I have."

He still doesn't seem sure of exactly how long that is, but it can't have been longer than the past couple of years since the guys are juniors like me. Spencer also made it clear that there's no way Ryan passed away in that time because he's sure they would have remembered a student dying.

My phone buzzes, and I reach down to pull it from my pocket. When I see a text from Owen, I feel butterflies in my stomach.

"Any chance you're at school yet?" he asks.

After a short conversation, I relay to Ryan that Owen and Spencer just got to school and want to meet up. Ryan excitedly punches the air as I laugh softly and let Owen know to find us in the library. It still seems like the safest place to hide and have a conversation about ghosts.

It's only a few minutes later that I hear them walk into the library. Spencer's laughter reaches me first, and I hear him mumble something to the grumpy librarian. I stand up, quickly brushing my hands through my hair and straightening my jacket. Ryan teases me for it, but I ignore him. While I told him nearly everything about this weekend, I very purposely forgot to mention the fact that both guys sort of flirted with me yesterday and that I'm definitely, helplessly crushing on both of them at this point. Ryan will never shut up if I give him an inkling of my feelings.

Owen finds me first, pausing at the end of the row of books where Ryan and I have been hiding. A wide smile slides across his face as he takes me in. "Hey."

"Hi," I squeak, waving at him like a loser.

He strides forward until he's in front of me, just a couple of feet away. We stare at each other silently while I look up at him and pretend I'm not completely swooning. We hung out all day yesterday until he took me home just in time for me to have a tense, quiet dinner with Flora and my mom. And even after that, we texted for a while before we went to sleep. How can it feel like it's been such a long since I've seen or talked to him?

"Missed you," Owen whispers, brushing his knuckles against mine.

My heart pretty much explodes, and for a moment, I don't

even care that my face feels like it's on fire or that I probably look like an overexcited tomato.

"Oh my god." Ryan walks over to stand beside us, looking back and forth between me and Owen with a manic grin. "You guys hooked up, didn't you? I knew it! Well, maybe I was wrong about Spencer, but I knew something was going on with you and Owen."

I turn and glare at him, beyond irritated that he's ruining this moment for me. "Shut up," I hiss.

"Ah, right." Owen chuckles. He turns his gaze in Ryan's general direction and raises his eyebrows. "Ryan. Nice to meet you, I think."

Before I can properly introduce them or Ryan can make another stupid quip, Spencer appears at the end of our row. He smiles and waves, striding forward until he reaches me. Just like he did yesterday when he left the pumpkin patch, he leans forward and kisses me on the cheek.

"Hey," he says, smiling like kissing me on the cheek is completely normal and like I'm not gaping at him in awe. "Sorry. I was talking to Mr. Langley."

"That's okay," I squeak, assuming Mr. Langley must be the grumpy librarian. When I manage to force my gaze away from his, I find Owen staring at me with an unreadable expression. Worse, beside him, Ryan is grinning like a lunatic and floating in a way that makes him appear to be bouncing on the balls of his feet.

"Harriet Abbot. You lucky little minx," Ryan says gleefully. "You're hooking up with both of them! And fucking hell, they're both completely into it!"

My cheeks flame as I give him a withering glare and hiss, "I'm not hooking up with anyone!"

Owen and Spencer share a look and chuckle, and Spencer

crosses his arms as he grins in Ryan's direction. "Right. Our ghost stalker. Nice to officially meet you, man."

Ryan gasps in fake outrage—and I know it's fake because his eyes are full of delight and mischief. "Rude. Tell them I'm happy to meet them too, Harriet."

I sigh and quickly tell them what Ryan said. When Owen sets down his backpack and unzips it, I remind Ryan that Owen wants to take some pictures to see whether he'll show up in any of the shots or not. Ryan floats over to stand close beside me and attempts to throw his arm around my shoulders. The contact makes my entire body feel cold, and I can't disguise my shiver. Giving me an apologetic smile, he moves his arm so it's floating just above my shoulders without actually touching me.

"I'm gonna use a digital camera first since it's easiest," Owen says, lifting the camera.

Nothing shows up in the digital photos, but Owen doesn't seem surprised. He gives me one of his swoon-worthy smiles and tells me he's still going to keep the pictures. It makes me blush because I know he means it. I can try to deny a lot, but he's told me so many times now that he thinks I'm beautiful and he genuinely seems obsessed with taking my picture.

"You bring your film camera?" Spencer asks Owen. And once again, it boggles my mind that he doesn't seem bothered by Owen's not-so-subtle flirting. Especially after the kissing-me-on-the-cheek thing. I'm pretty sure I'm never gonna figure these guys out.

Owen nods as he rifles through his backpack. "I did, and I definitely want to take some photos with it no matter what. But I'm going to try with a polaroid first."

The polaroid camera is bigger and clunkier than I expected, so I assume it's pretty old. When he lifts it up, I force another grimacing smile onto my face. At the last second, Ryan blows a tiny gust of freezing air at me. It forces my hair to move in a way that tickles my neck, and I let out a tiny, screeching giggle just as Owen snaps the photo.

"That was cute." Spencer laughs.

I huff in annoyance and glance sideways at Ryan with a frown. "Why did you do that?"

He shrugs and gives me a lazy smirk, lifting a hand to my hair so I can feel the barest hint of his cold touch. "Just trying to get you to stop looking so grumpy in our photos."

It takes a few minutes for the polaroid photo to develop. To my surprise and excitement, Ryan shows up perfectly in the photo. Even better than the ones with Old Creepy. He looks alive and whole beside me, like any regular high school kid. And even I can admit the way we're posing and smiling is pretty cute.

Owen and Spencer are even more impressed than I am. They're practically on the verge of freaking out and exclaiming about the evidence of a real live ghost right here in front of them. I imagine it is pretty wild from their perspective. They were taking a huge leap of faith by trusting me about being able to see Ryan, and I'm relieved that it's more real for them now.

After Owen takes several more polaroid photos and about a million pictures with his fancy film camera, the four of us settle onto the floor against the shelves with Ryan and me sitting across from Spencer and Owen. Taking advantage of the time we have left before the first bell, the guys jump right into enthusiastically asking Ryan a ton of questions. I have to relay everything Ryan says, of course, and I do my best to filter the more obnoxious comments out of the conversation. Spencer even writes everything down in a notebook.

All the questions they ask Ryan about his past and his death are very well thought out. We don't learn much more information than I already got out of Ryan last week, but he seems to be making a genuine effort to answer their questions and to remember things from his past. It makes me feel equal parts excited and stupid. Excited because I think we might have a real chance of solving the mystery of Ryan's death and the circumstances of his ghost being stuck here. Stupid because it's glaringly obvious that Spencer and Owen are way smarter than I am and much more knowledgeable about ghosts and spirits despite this being my gift.

When the first bell rings, there's a collective groan from all of us. Honestly, I could probably sit here with Ryan, Owen, and Spencer like this all day and be entirely content. Dealing with the normal parts of the school day, and facing Amethyst and Blaze again after what happened over the weekend, sounds miserable in comparison.

"You want us to walk you to class?" Spencer asks me on our way out of the library.

A big part of me wants to say yes, but I also want a few minutes to talk to Ryan again without the guys around. Just to make sure he really is alright with them pushing him about some of their questions. And maybe to emphasize the point that I am *not* hooking up with Spencer or Owen.

"No, thanks." I give him and Owen a nervous smile. "But I'll see you guys later?"

They agree, and I quickly head in the opposite direction from them so that Spencer doesn't have a chance to kiss my cheek again. I can only take so much of that sort of thing from the guys I'm hopelessly crushing on.

As soon as I'm sure we're far enough away that Spencer and Owen won't hear me, I turn to look at Ryan. Luckily, he's following right on my heels like he always does. "Well?" I ask. "How was that? Too weird? Are you alright?"

He snorts and gives me a look like I'm going insane.

"Weird? I'm pretty sure everything about us and this entire situation is weird. But yeah, of course I'm fine. Your concern for my well-being is adorable, especially considering the fact that I'm dead."

I roll my eyes. Excuse me for feeling protective of him. Maybe I'm being ridiculous, but I feel strangely responsible for Ryan and for figuring out what happened to him. And for some reason, the longer I'm here and the more I talk to him, the more determined I feel to help him.

"Hey, I'm just teasing." Ryan bumps his elbow against mine—or at least, attempts to. "I'm fine. Happy. Everything felt so empty before I met you. And now I have multiple people who *know* me. Who want to talk to me. It's probably stupid to get my hopes up, but..." He trails off for a moment, giving me a sheepish look. "Do you really think you'll be able to figure out who I was and how I died? Maybe even how to get me out of this stupid fucking purgatory so I can move on?"

My throat feels thick at the thought of Ryan being gone. Like *gone,* gone. Forever. But he deserves that. He certainly doesn't deserve to live for an eternity in high school as a ghost. Nobody deserves that. Pushing aside my own stupid, selfish feelings, I can't also help but think it's sad that he's finally admitting that he wants to learn the truth. Last week when we met, he acted like he couldn't care less about how or why he ended up as a ghost.

"I think our chances of figuring it all out are much higher now that Spencer and Owen are helping," I say truthfully.

He nods, smiling cheerfully. "Yeah, you're right. Besides, it probably helps that they want to bang you. I imagine that's very motivating."

"Goddess!" I groan, throwing him a withering look. When we pass a few other students who give me odd looks, I lower my voice. "Would you shut up about that? I'm flustered enough when they start acting like that. You mentioning it only makes it so much worse! It's not like I can date them both, so I'm just going to ignore it anytime they flirt. I don't even know if they actually like me, or if this is just some sort of game for them."

Ryan sighs exaggeratedly. "You're no fun."

CHAPTER 16
MATTIE

When Harriet glances sideways at me, I quickly turn my head and pretend like I'm concentrating on whatever the hell Miss Camelli is writing on the board. I've been staring at Harriet for too long. Way too long. Fuck, I'm pretty much always staring at her when she's nearby. No wonder she still thinks I'm an annoying creep.

We're still discussing the Salem Witch Trials in class, as well as some other lesser-known witch hunts that took place in the United States around the same time in the 1600s. I'm already pretty knowledgeable on the subject, so I don't feel too bad about ignoring the lesson even though history is my favorite subject.

"Have you ever been to Salem?" I whisper to Harriet, leaning closer to her. She bristles but doesn't move away or tell me to back off, so I consider it a win. "The Salem Witch Museum is really cool, and the memorial is really something. I mean, it's sad, obviously, but interesting. All of the people killed during the trials weren't even witches. Well, some of them could have been, I guess, but they still didn't deserve what happened to them."

Harriet stares back at me without saying a word. She doesn't even smile. Although, I've learned it takes a lot to make her smile, so this time probably isn't personal. Still, the longer she stares at me without responding, the stupider I feel. And whenever I feel stupid and flustered, especially around someone as hot as Harriet, my mouth keeps on yapping before my brain can catch up.

"They have other museums there too!" I rush out, still whispering. "There's a museum about the history of horror movies. And, uh, there's an art museum. Oh, and the House of Seven Gables! That's this weird, old house that Nathaniel Hawthorne wrote about in one of his books. That's Owen's favorite museum. I'm pretty sure he's read, like, every book in existence."

Shit. Why did I bring up Owen? It's obvious he has a crush on Harriet, which makes him my competition.

Very slowly, Harriet's lips curve up into a bright smile, and I forget how to breathe for a second. And then I want to shout with triumph. Fucking yes! I did it. I got her to smile. At me! God, I hope she's not just smiling because of what I said about Owen, but even then, it's still worth it to see this expression on her face. She's insanely hot all the time, but when she smiles? It's like I become re-obsessed with her all over again.

"All of that sounds really fun," she says quietly. "I've always wanted to visit Salem."

My heart races faster, and I blurt out, "We should go together." When Harriet's smile drops and her eyebrows scrunch together, I panic and add, "And the rest of the guys, obviously. Salem's not that far from here. Maybe after Halloween when it's not crazy busy with tourists."

"Yeah, okay."

I grin down at my notebook, wishing I could hide my expression from Harriet better. I don't want her to think I'm a lunatic, even though I feel like one whenever I'm around her. I realize how pathetic I am to be this excited over her saying yes to vague plans of hanging out with me and my friends. But at least she's willing to hang out with me outside of school.

Really, I need to just muster up the courage to ask her out for real. I honestly don't think she'd say yes—most of the time, she acts like she can't stand me. But it's only a matter of time before Spencer or Owen ask her out again. Neither of them seems worried that things didn't work out the first time they tried asking her out. I wish I could be as confident as they are. It was a relief to find out over the weekend that neither of them even has her number yet, but I know she likes them better than she likes me. This week, I need to figure out how to change her mind about me. To make her at least see me as a friend.

When the bell rings and we walk out of class together, my fingers twitch with the urge to hold her hand. Or to do something really corny like offer to carry her backpack. I can just imagine the horrified scowl she'd throw my way if I did either of those things, so I quickly shove my hands into my pockets to avoid temptation.

"So, uh, how was your weekend?" I ask, desperate to have some form of conversation flow between us. We talked a little in first and second period, but mostly about school stuff. Or whatever idiotic babble fell out of my mouth. "I never asked how the thing with your mom's friends went. Was it as bad as you expected?"

She groans and gives me a look, almost like she's pouting. It's stupid hot. "Worse. It was pretty much torture. Luckily, the rest of the weekend turned out better. Yesterday, I—"

My brain suddenly goes fuzzy. I vaguely recognize that Harriet's still talking to me, but there's something more important for me to focus on. Amethyst Redferne. *Amethyst, Amethyst, Amethyst.* I spin around until I spot her a few dozen feet away, standing by her locker with a few of her friends.

It feels like I'm stuck in a dream, like time slows down, as I watch Amethyst talk and laugh. As she runs her delicate fingers through her shiny, raven black hair. As her short skirt swishes around, drawing attention to the thin line of her thighs visible between her hemline and her stockings. My throat feels thick as I swallow the urge to call out to her. To tell her I love her and that she's the most beautiful girl in the universe. How did Spencer ever catch her attention? How could he be stupid enough to break up with her? Doesn't he realize how lucky he was to have her in the first place? God, I'd do anything to get her to notice me. And I mean *really* notice me.

She turns around and heads in my direction. I pull my sweaty hands out of my pockets, hastily rubbing them over my jeans as I smile in the hopes she'll glance in my direction when she walks past. I normally see her in the halls between first and second period, but I missed her this morning. This is a lucky break.

When Amethyst is only a few feet away, she looks up and meets my eyes and her entire face lights up with a stunning smile. "Mattie! Hi!"

Holy shit. Yes! She noticed me! My cheeks hurt from smiling so big. "Hey, Amethyst. You look hot today." It's true, obviously, but I quickly clamp my mouth shut before I say anything else embarrassing.

To my shock and delight, Amethyst steps forward and hugs me. I wrap my arms around her, loving how short she is beside me. And fuck, the way she's subtly rubbing against me, the way her tits are pressed against my chest, it's gotta be the hottest thing I've ever experienced. My dick is hard by the time she pulls away just a few seconds later.

"You should DM me," Amethyst says, waving at me over her shoulder. "Maybe we can hang out sometime."

And then she walks away, and I stand there watching her and feeling like the luckiest guy in the world.

Until I suddenly don't. The second Amethyst is out of sight, it feels like I'm snapped out of my dream and real life comes rushing back. The noise from everyone walking through the hallways is nearly deafening, and I blink as I spin around to find Harriet. God, please, I hope she didn't walk away.

Luckily, she's still standing behind me. Not so luckily, she's scowling at me and her arms are crossed. Shit. How could I be so stupid? How is it that every time I see Amethyst, it's like I forget about everything else around me, including Harriet? I had a huge crush on Amethyst in middle school and freshman year, and yeah, I was insanely jealous of Spencer last year when he first started dating her. But I got over that shit. For the most part, at least. I like Harriet way more than I ever liked Amethyst. And honestly, Harriet is a million times hotter and definitely more interesting than Amethyst is. There's no competition between them.

"Uh," I scramble to remember what Harriet was saying before my brain decided to take a vacation to Amethyst-ville. "What were you saying about your weekend?"

"Nothing." Harriet sighs. "Let's just go to class."

It's usually hard to read her, but I know I'm not mistaking the hurt expression on her face. My heart drops into my stomach as she breezes past me. Shit. Just when I feel like I'm making progress with her, I fuck up. Harriet was willingly talking to me. She was agreeing to make plans with me! I am the world's biggest idiot. Amethyst never even spoke to me once before last week when she first saw me with Harriet. Now, she says hi to me almost every morning. I'm not completely oblivious to the fact she's only doing it to bother

Harriet. I just don't understand why I respond to her the way I do, when I normally never think about Amethyst otherwise.

"Look, I'm sorry." I rush after Harriet. Her next class is nowhere near mine, but I still walk with her every day. Just for the chance to spend a few more seconds with her, whether she wants me around or not. "I didn't mean to ignore you like that. I just...got distracted."

Harriet stops walking, and I nearly bump into her as she spins around to glare at me. I have to look up slightly to meet her silver-gray eyes. I never thought I'd have a thing for a girl noticeably taller than me, but I'm very into it. Everything about this girl is sexy, and it's like she doesn't even realize it.

"I know, Mattie. You tell me every day that Amethyst is the hottest girl you've ever seen in your life. I get it, alright? I don't need to keep hearing about it."

My face burns with shame. I want to tell her it's not true. I want to tell her that *she's* the hottest girl I've ever seen. But I know she won't believe me or appreciate the words. It will just sound like I'm full of shit. Why am I like this? Why the fuck would I talk to another girl and blather on about an old crush to the girl I'm currently very interested in getting to know better? Forget the fact that Spencer and Owen are into Harriet too. I'm sabotaging myself, making sure there's no chance in hell Harriet would ever consider going out with me.

By the time we reach Harriet's forensic science class, I'm in despair. Seeing Nolan and Spencer waiting outside for us only makes me feel worse. Using the excuse that I'm going to be late to class, I take off before either of my friends can talk to me.

THE NEXT FEW HOURS BEFORE LUNCH PASS EXCRUCIATINGLY SLOWLY. I spend nearly all of that time moping and obsessing over Harriet while trying to think of how I can make it up to her. I still have no idea how I'm going to do that when I walk into the cafeteria, and my mood only gets worse when I see Harriet standing in the lunch line with Owen. She brings her own lunch to school, so she doesn't have any real reason to wait in line with him other than because she wants to.

"Hey, what's wrong?" Nolan walks up beside me and bumps his elbow against mine.

I sigh and turn to face him, shrugging desolately. "Just that I'm the world's biggest moron."

He snorts and rolls his eyes, pulling me over to our usual table. I sit beside him and practically slump over the table the second I sit down. My cousin frowns at me and quietly asks, "For real. What's going on? Why do you think you're a moron?"

Peering over to make sure Harriet and Owen are still in line and that Spencer isn't about to sneak up on us, I grimace. "Because Harriet thinks I have a crush on Amethyst. Amethyst has been coming up to me in the hallways between classes whenever I'm with Harriet. I know she's only doing it to be an asshole, but for some reason, it's like I lose my mind every time it happens. Jesus, I got a boner this morning just because Amethyst hugged me. How fucking embarrassing is that? Harriet is never going to like me at this rate. Not even as a friend."

Nolan's frown deepens, and he adjusts his glasses on his nose. "Uh, *do* you still like Amethyst? Because—"

"No." I cut him off. "I mean, I'm not blind. I still think she's pretty. But what she did to Spence last year was fucked up. I could never like somebody who treated my best friend like shit."

He nods slowly. "Good. Because that girl is poison, and she

177

and her friends have been really shitty to Harriet since she moved here. Have you noticed that? They're always making fun of her whenever she has one of her episodes."

Real anger flashes in Nolan's eyes. He usually tries to pretend he's not intrigued by Harriet, but he's terrible at hiding his feelings around me. It's also really obvious he feels protective of her, especially when it comes to her illnesses. I don't blame him. While I don't think Harriet needs to be protected, because she's a fucking badass on her own and handles her shit brilliantly, I agree that anyone who makes fun of a person for issues like Harriet's is fucked up. But hearing my cousin say what I already know only makes me feel more ashamed for making Harriet feel like I prefer Amethyst's company over hers.

"Harriet's going to hate me forever." I groan.

Nolan rolls his eyes. "You might annoy her sometimes, but I don't think she hates you." He pauses and gives me a pitying look. "I'm worried about how attached to her you are already though. Are you going to be okay if she starts dating Spencer or Owen? Apparently, they hung out with Harriet yesterday. Spencer flirted with Harriet pretty much the entire period in forensic science too, and she definitely didn't seem to mind."

My heart clenches painfully. I'm not surprised, but it still hurts to hear. Is that what Harriet was trying to tell me earlier before Amethyst interrupted us? That she hung out with Spencer and Owen over the weekend?

"Don't get me wrong, it would suck. I'll definitely be jealous if she dates either of them, but I'll get over it." I force a smile. "I'm glad she's hanging out with them. Maybe she'll want to hang out with us too. She's so fucking cool, and I want to be friends with her no matter what."

Nolan still seems apprehensive to consider Harriet a part of our group, despite how interesting he thinks she is. But that's not Harriet's fault. I know my cousin is just worried Harriet will turn out to be like Amethyst. A cheater and a liar who tries to drive a wedge between us and our best friends. I know he's wrong and she's not like that, but I can't blame him for being cautious.

"Hey, guys." Owen sets his lunch tray on the table across from us. Harriet sits beside him, holding a tray of her own.

I stare at the food on her plate instead of at her, still feeling a lingering sense of embarrassment for earlier and my behavior around her. "You didn't bring your lunch today?"

"Oh, I did." She sounds normal. Happy, even. Not like she's mad at me. I slowly look up to meet her eyes, and she gives me a tiny smile. Who am I kidding? She probably hasn't thought about me once since we separated before third period. "This is for Spencer. He texted me and Owen to let us know he's running late to lunch, so we figured we'd grab it for him."

So, they're texting now. Sometime after we got home from our trip to the asylum on Saturday night, Owen and Spencer managed to get Harriet's number. I'm glad Nolan gave me the heads up that our other best friends hung out with Harriet yesterday, otherwise I'd probably say something fucking stupid, abrasive, and humiliating.

"Nolan and I don't have your number," I whine. Well, fuck. Forget what I said about not saying something stupid and humiliating.

Harriet blinks and tilts her head slightly. "Uh, do you want my number?"

Owen huffs out a laugh and shakes his head at me, but I pretend not to notice him. I also pretend like I don't feel a blush rising to my cheeks and neck. Play. It. Cool.

"Yes!" I grin at her like a maniac, already pulling my phone from my pocket. "Are you one of those people who hate talking

179

on the phone? Or is it okay for me to call you? I send a lot of memes too, so I hope you don't mind."

Nolan groans quietly beside me, probably feeling some major second-hand embarrassment. Owen's not trying to hide his laughter either. Yeah, I'm definitely a moron.

Harriet looks horrified as she stares back at me, her cheeks reddening. I've embarrassed her, but definitely not as much as I've embarrassed myself. To my utter surprise, she reaches out and offers me her phone. "You can call me if you want, I guess. And memes are fine."

With her phone in my hand, I feel like I'm holding the Holy Grail. I have never managed to get a girl's number before. How the hell did I manage to get Harriet's? Especially after the garbage that just came out of my mouth? Still, no way am I wasting this chance. I quickly enter my number and text myself before Harriet can change her mind. And then I add Nolan's number too, since I did mention him not having her number either. He'll thank me later.

"Hey, guys." I look up from Harriet's phone to find Spencer walking over to our table carrying a huge stack of books. He sets them heavily on the table, sliding them closer to Harriet and Owen. "I got these from Mr. Langley. Figured they'd help us with our project."

The stack of books creates a barrier between me and Harriet, so I don't feel a bit bad about sliding the stack over so I can see her again. That's when I realize they're all yearbooks. From the past fifteen years or so.

"Oh my Goddess!" Harriet exclaims, staring at the yearbooks with wide eyes. To my astonishment, she turns and gives Spencer the most gorgeous smile I've ever seen on her face. "You're incredible! I can't believe I didn't think of this."

Spencer smirks, looking smug as fuck. I hate it, but I can't exactly blame him. If Harriet complimented me and looked at me like that, I'd be feeling pretty smug too. Spencer slides into the seat beside Harriet, leaning close to her and whispering something in her ear.

"What project?" I ask, almost shouting. Harriet and my friends look up at me, either alarm or amusement on their faces. I clear my throat and remind myself to *try* to play it cool. There's nothing I can do about Spencer or Owen flirting with Harriet, even if watching it happen makes me want to die inside. "What project are you working on?"

Harriet and Spencer share a look, but it's Owen who answers me. "Harriet has an old family friend who used to go here, but nobody remembers what year they graduated. And they're dead, so it's not like we can just ask them."

Damn. That sounds morbid and awesome as fuck. I want to help Harriet with her weird family project too. But I've stuck my foot in my mouth enough today. If she wants my help, she'll ask. Right?

While I'm staring at the yearbooks wistfully, wishing Harriet saw me as a good enough friend to help her with, well, anything, Harriet stands up and thanks Spencer again as she places her backpack on the table. She pulls her lunch box out first, and then her whole body stiffens. I know she's about to have one of her episodes. There are little tells I've picked up on over the past week. I lean forward slightly and watch her carefully, wishing there was something I could do to help or make it easier on her. At the very least, I'm prepared to step in if she does something to accidentally hurt herself.

She curses quietly under her breath and lifts her backpack upside down, shaking the bag jerkily until everything falls out and scatters across the table and floor around her. Owen quickly pulls Harriet down into her seat and wraps his arm around her shoulders, keeping her pressed close to his side. At the same time, Spencer bends down to collect any of her belongings that fell onto the floor.

They have the right idea of it. Harriet's face is red, and I know she's already embarrassed. But I don't want her to feel like that with us. Shit like this happening? It's not a big deal. I know she doesn't do it on purpose. To feel like I'm helping, I gather all her stuff that fell on the table and neatly stack her books, folders, and papers together. There are still a few things on the floor that Spencer can't reach, since they're closer to mine and Nolan's side of the table.

I bend down to grab the last few papers, pausing when I find a polaroid photo of Harriet and another guy. She looks so happy. Like, insanely happy. And the guy is smiling at her like she hangs the fucking moon. Was this one of her friends back in Oregon? Harriet said she doesn't have a boyfriend, but he could be an ex? Shoving my jealousy aside, I slide the photo between the other papers in my hand.

As I sit up, I glance at the top paper in my hands and blink as I try to figure out what exactly it is I'm looking at. A hopeful grin slides across my face as I turn to show the paper to Harriet. "Uh, what is this?"

Her face turns even redder than when she spilled all the stuff from her backpack, and she reaches across the table to snatch the paper from me. I quickly hold it back, too far for her to reach.

"Nothing!" She huffs. "I was just messing around."

Harriet's reaction completely proves that I'm right. And this is proof that she's secretly a big marshmallow on the inside once she puts her guard down. I smile even bigger, holding the paper up high so my friends can see it. "Guys, Harriet named our club and drew us a logo. Look at how fucking sick this is!"

"Did you really?" Nolan asks, gaping at the paper.

There are various scribbles all over the page until it looks like she finally decided on a final design for the logo. The words 'Weeping Hollow Informal Society of Paranormal Entities & Research' form a circle around a retro-style drawing of a full moon, a black cat, and a bunch of ghosts. The acronym WHISPER is also doodled all over the page. It's got to be the coolest, most clever name of a paranormal investigative team I've ever seen. I can't believe Harriet created this. For *us!* God, she really is the girl of my dreams.

"You guys don't have to use it or anything," Harriet says. "I swear, I really was just messing around."

Spencer jumps up and grabs the paper from me before I have a chance to stop him, and he scoots closer to Harriet while grinning at the drawings. Since Owen's still got his arm around Harriet, she's sitting practically squished between my two best friends.

"Babe, this is amazing," Spencer says. Babe! My eye definitely does not twitch when he calls her that. Spencer keeps on talking, oblivious to the fact that I'm over here still dying inside because I don't have the guts to ask Harriet out like he does. "I can't believe you made this. Of course we have to use it! Right, guys?"

Owen and I agree immediately, grinning ear to ear while we express how much we love the name and design. The only one who's quiet is my cousin, and we all turn to look at him after a few moments. We all know he's the unofficial leader of our team, which is why we haven't officially invited Harriet to be a part of it. We're all holding out for Nolan to agree.

Nolan slowly reaches across the table and grabs the WHISPER paper that Spencer set down. His mouth curves into a nervous smile, but it's easy for me to see the excitement in his eyes. He stares at the logo for a long time before he looks up at

Harriet. "I don't think we can use this unless you're part of our club too. If you want to be, that is."

"Really?" Harriet asks, smiling so brightly that her whole face lights up. I barely catch my jaw from dropping because *shit.* She's so fucking beautiful. I've never seen her smile like this. So open, happy, and genuine. "Yeah, I would love that."

"Now that's settled," Owen says, smiling at Harriet as he rubs his hand over her arm. He slowly pulls away from her, not seeming at all irritated when Spencer takes his place and throws *his* arm around Harriet's shoulders, and begins rifling through his backpack. "Harriet and I were talking about going back to her house for another investigation. I was waiting to show you guys these photos I took there last time to make sure it was okay with her."

Nolan leans across the table, and I stand up so I can lean further to get a closer look. Spencer looks just as interested as we do, so I'm pretty sure he hasn't seen these photos yet either. We all thought it was weird that Owen didn't show us anything from our first visit to the Abbot House. Usually, he can't wait to show off his newest batch of photographs, no matter what they're of.

Owen places a folder in the center of the table, gives us a roguish grin, then flips it open to reveal the first photo in the stack.

"What the fuck!" Spencer says, barely above a whisper.

Reaching out with shaking fingers, Nolan carefully grabs the top photo. There are more just like it underneath, so Spencer pulls the folder closer to himself to get a better look while I scoot closer to my cousin. The photograph of Harriet and what is clearly the ghost of an old woman is chilling. It's got to be the scariest, coolest thing I've ever seen.

"This can't be real," Nolan says. He's full of shit. I can see it in his eyes. He believes it's real, and he looks like he's never been more excited in his life. "Can it?"

"Of course it's real," Owen scoffs. "Harriet told us there was a ghost in her house, and you agreed with the rest of us that we definitely picked up on some potential spiritual activity."

"Holy shit." I laugh breathlessly. My heart is pounding with adrenaline. We've been into the ghost hunting shit for a few years now, but we've never seen anything like this. Even if I wasn't hopelessly obsessed with Harriet, I'd be begging my friends to go back to her house to see more of this ghost. Something occurs to me. Harriet *did* tell us she had a ghost. Like my friends, I assumed she was joking at the time and maybe making fun of us a little. But maybe she wasn't. "Wait, have you actually *seen* the ghost, Harriet?"

She nods slowly, like she's hesitant. "A few times, yeah. I call her Old Creepy." She smiles shyly down at the stack of photographs and says, "She looks terrifying, but she's not so bad. Like, she's friendly. She pretty much just floats around and sings these creepy old nursery rhymes."

I punch Nolan's arm excitedly, ignoring it when he hisses in pain and glares sideways at me. "I fucking told you guys I heard someone singing on my video!"

My cousin fixes a desperate look on Harriet and asks, "Are you sure you're okay with us coming back to your house to investigate? This is—wow, this is an incredible find. But I don't want you to feel pressured or feel like you have to let us over. You can still be in the club no matter what."

"Yeah, I'm sure." Harriet smiles. She glances at something between me and Nolan, blushing as she clears her throat. "Would you guys want to come over on Friday? We can do your investigation, and then maybe you guys could even sleep over? We can order pizza and watch horror movies. I know my mom won't care."

I'm pretty sure my eyes are practically popping out of my skull, and I have to bite my tongue from exclaiming *fuck yes* at the top of my lungs. I don't even care that three other dudes will be there. The girl I'm into just asked me to spend the night at her house. There is no way in hell I'm not agreeing to that.

"You're inviting us to a slumber party?" Nolan asks, his face turning red as he fucks with his glasses.

When Owen and Spencer snicker, Harriet's cheeks flush and she scowls down at the table. No, no, no! Are my friends stupid? They have to know how hard it is for Harriet to open up. It was probably so hard for her to invite us over, and now she's embarrassed because my friends can't help being assholes.

Slapping a hand over Nolan's mouth, I plead with Harriet. "Ignore my cousin. A sleepover with ghost hunting, pizza, and horror movies sounds like the best night ever. We're in."

Spencer smirks and gently tugs on a long, silvery strand of Harriet's hair. "You're such a little softie underneath all those scowls. Of course we'll come over Friday night."

Her expression softens, and then she does something I would never expect from her. She playfully sticks her tongue out at Spencer, making him laugh. It's so unexpectedly cute considering how serious she usually acts. That's what I want— for her to feel comfortable enough around me to open up and be herself, like she seems to with Spencer and Owen.

CHAPTER 17
HARRIET

I flip to the next page in the Class of 2011 yearbook, sighing when all the faces start blurring together. This is getting so tedious and frustrating. This is my second time looking through this one, and I've already gone through the rest of my stack twice. Owen and Spencer each took a few yearbooks home too, using the photos Owen took of me and Ryan to compare to photos in the yearbook. But they've had just as much luck as I have.

Meaning exactly none. None of us have found a hint of Ryan in any of the fifteen yearbooks Spencer scored from the school librarian. It seems impossible, unless Ryan's been dead way longer than I thought. I'm determined to look through them at least a couple more times before letting Spencer take this batch of yearbooks back to the librarian in exchange for older ones.

"Still no luck on your project?" Mattie asks.

"No," I groan, glancing up at him.

Not for the first time, I feel pleasantly surprised at how easy it is to hang out with him. Don't get me wrong. He's still fucking obnoxious and annoying a lot of the time, but he's definitely growing on me the more I get to know him. After giving him my number, I worried I was making a huge mistake by giving Mattie Baxter the ability to contact me whenever he felt like it.

But then he called me after school on Monday, and we talked while doing our homework over the phone. It was easy, effortless, and weirdly sort of fun. He did the same thing yesterday after school, and then again today. Except, today when he called, I sniped at him and said we might as well do our homework in the same room together since we live in the same neighborhood. Mattie immediately hung up and ran the two blocks to my house from his, ringing my doorbell incessantly until my mom let him in.

Now we've been in my room, sitting on the floor together for the past two hours while we do our homework, talk, and listen to *Beach House* play quietly through my Bluetooth speakers. I'm completely caught up with my homework and all the makeup work I was given last week. And I'm pretty sure Mattie is too, and that he's just messing around on his laptop so I don't have a good excuse to kick him out.

Not that I want to kick him out. I like him much better like this, outside of school. He's a lot more likable and easier to deal with away from all the noise and distraction, and especially away from all the cunty witches who have managed to convince Mattie and Nolan that I'm mentally ill.

"Maybe I could help?" Mattie asks, giving me a bashful smile as he brushes his hair out of his eyes.

I only hesitate for a few seconds before shrugging. It's not the worst idea. Owen already came up with that story about me looking for an old family friend. I might have to give Mattie a few more details for him to be able to help properly, but he doesn't need to know everything.

"Okay. That would be great, actually." I pull out my phone and text a picture of Ryan to Mattie's phone. It's one that Owen took the other day, except that I've cropped myself out. "This is the guy I'm looking for. His name is Ryan, but I don't have a last name or anything else to look up. He used to go to our school, and I think he, uh, died...sometime in the last fifteen years or so. But I haven't been able to find any reference to him or his death anywhere."

Mattie frowns at his phone for so long, I'm beginning to suspect he wants to back out of helping me with my 'project,' but isn't sure how to say so. I open my mouth to tell him it's not a big deal and he can still stay and hang out even if he doesn't want to help. But then he looks up at me with an unreadable expression. He's normally so energetic—either from being happy-go-lucky or else from nerves—and it's weird to see him look so serious.

"Harriet..." He trails off and clears his throat, glancing down at his phone for a quick second. "Isn't this—? Uh, who exactly is this? I saw a picture of you with him the other day when you spilled everything from your bag. You're telling me this person is dead?"

My face heats up. I've never had this feeling of being caught in such a complicated lie, and I'm not sure what to say. Should I deny it? Freak out and tell Mattie it's none of his business? Or should I risk it and tell him the truth?

I can't tell him I'm a witch. There are all sorts of laws about that. Spencer shouldn't even know, except Amethyst broke the rules for him. But seeing ghosts isn't *exclusively* a witch thing. My heart pounds at the thought of it, but I *could* tell Mattie about that without getting me or him into any trouble.

If he doesn't believe me, I guess I can fall back on his and Nolan's theory that I'm schizophrenic or whatever.

"I didn't mean to snoop," Mattie rushes out, chuckling

nervously. "And maybe I've got it wrong. I didn't even think. Maybe that guy from the picture I saw is a relative of the one you're looking for?"

He doesn't sound convinced, exactly. More like he's desperate to give me an out rather than make him leave. It's weirdly kind of sweet, and it makes the decision to tell him the truth a lot easier. Mattie *has* been a decent friend to me, after all. He thinks I have a severe disorder, and he never makes me feel weird about it. He's helpful, even when he's being obnoxious. And the past few days we've been talking on the phone and now hanging out, he hasn't once brought up Old Creepy or ghost hunting stuff. Almost like he's trying to prove he wants to be my friend, and not just because of the house I live in.

"No, you're right. It's the same person," I say breathlessly. Even after telling Owen and Spencer the truth, it's not any easier or less nerve-racking admitting this to Mattie. "Ryan is a ghost who's been following me around at school since my first day. He can't remember much about his life when he was alive or how he died, and I'm starting to think the whole thing was covered up for some reason. Because I can't find *anything* about him or a student ever dying at our school."

Mattie's jaw drops. It would be comical if I wasn't so fucking anxious about his reaction. Will he believe me? Or is he going to write it off as me being crazy or delusional?

"A ghost?" He gapes at me. "What the fuck. Can you see ghosts, like, all the time? What about the ghost you have in your house?"

"Um..." My eyes jump over to my bed where Old Creepy has been sitting and quietly humming since I got home from school. I'm so used to her presence when I'm home, it didn't feel all that weird for her to sit and watch me and Mattie doing our homework. "Yes? Old Creepy is sitting on my bed right now. Since before you got here."

Mattie spins around and stares at the spot I pointed out, and he begins laughing hysterically. My cheeks flush with embarrassment and the surety that he thinks I'm insane. But when he turns around to face me again, there's a huge grin on his face and an excited glimmer in his forest green eyes.

"Holy shit. Harriet! I knew you were fucking amazing, but this is..." He shakes his head at a loss for words. "Have you always been able to see them?"

I nod slowly, wringing my hands in my lap from nerves. "Yeah. But it's gotten worse since I moved here." Scrunching my eyebrows together, I shake my head. "Worse is probably the wrong word. I've just seen them a lot more often in Weeping Hollow than I ever have before."

"This town is full of creepy supernatural shit," he says, nodding like this all makes perfect sense.

The hope that he truly believes me, and that I've made another friend who fully accepts me for all my bullshit and weirdness, is nearly overwhelming. Feeling vulnerable and wanting to make sure he's not secretly making fun of me, I ask, "So, you believe me?"

He furrows his eyebrows and stares at me incredulously. "Of course I do. Why wouldn't I believe you?"

"Most people don't." I shrug. Or else they do, and they still think it's stupid and unimpressive compared to their own natural gifts. I look down at my hands and mumble, "Plus, I know you and your friends think I have...issues."

Mattie doesn't confirm or deny it. Instead, he scoots closer to me and grabs my hand, threading our fingers together. When I look up, he gives me a crooked smile. "Well, *I* believe you. And I'm guessing Owen does too since he took those photos."

Holding Mattie's hand doesn't feel weird. It actually feels nice, and I feel my guard drop a little more. "Owen is the first person I've ever told outside of my family." Outside of the witch community, at least. "And he told Spencer. It's been weird, having people know. But weird in a good way."

Uncertainty flashes in Mattie's eyes. I'm sure he's going to ask why his friends didn't want to tell him or his cousin too, and I don't have a good answer for that. He surprises me once again though, shaking his head and offering me a crooked smile.

"So, what are they like? Clearly, you're not freaked out, having them around all the time." Mattie darts another quick glance in Old Creepy's direction.

I laugh and shake my head. "Honestly? Most ghosts don't want to talk or be messed with at all. But Old Creepy and Ryan aren't like that. They're sort of, like, my friends. Old Creepy can't really *talk*, but she's sweet, and she hangs out with me every day whenever I'm home. Ryan's different. He's obnoxious and constantly says inappropriate shit, and he loves it when I embarrass myself in front of you and the other guys. But he's also sweet too, in his way. I've never wanted to help a ghost as much as I want to help him. It's like this obsession that's constantly hanging over my head, only getting stronger every day."

Mattie hums thoughtfully and flips through one of the yearbooks without really looking at it. "I get that. Can you tell me more about Ryan? Any weird, small details about him you can think of might be more helpful than you realize."

Spencer and Owen told me the same thing, which is probably why they've been asking Ryan all sorts of seemingly-random questions through me this week. I quickly and thoroughly list everything I know about Ryan, including the vague memories he's told me he still has. While I'm talking,

Mattie pulls a notebook out of his backpack and scribbles things down, like he's taking notes. It makes me smile and think of Spencer since he did the same thing.

I'm totally gonna have to tell Owen and Spencer about this. About the fact that Mattie knows at least most of my secret. Will they be upset? Does this mean I have to tell Nolan too? I'm not as close to him as the other guys. Like, we barely talk at all, though he has been nicer to me this week ever since the embarrassing discovery of the club's name and logo I created for my ghost hunting friends. But it also feels weird to purposely leave him out when all of his other best friends are involved.

"I've never had an actual mystery to solve like this," Mattie says, tapping his pen against his notebook after I finish telling him everything I can think of. "And your theory about his death being covered up is fucking scary. That kinda makes it harder to talk to other people. Like, we obviously can't just go around talking to random teachers in case they were involved."

"Right," I say, even though that never specifically occurred to me. I can't explain *why* I've been so intent on keeping Ryan a secret from everyone except for the guys. I easily could have told Principal Di Rossi multiple times. I haven't even told my mom yet either, even before I was angry with her.

"There are only two ways to become a ghost," Mattie says, scribbling another note. "If we can figure out the reason he became one, that would definitely help."

"Wait, what?" I blink. Goddess, I knew Spencer and Owen were smarter than me, but Mattie clearly is too. Like, way smarter. I've never once considered in my whole life that there was a *reason* people become ghosts. I just thought it happened randomly. Why have I never asked anyone or any ghosts I've ever talked to?

"Sure. Most people just, you know, *move on* when they die.

If everyone became ghosts, you'd probably be seeing millions of dead people walking around daily. To become a ghost, you've either got some major unfinished business that you're desperately hanging onto when you die, or else it happens because you're cursed."

My stomach churns with guilt. I've been so selfish. I've spent almost my entire life whining about my gift and wishing I could do 'real' magic like my mom and peers, when all along, I should have realized I could be helping all the lost souls I've come across. Surely, nobody *wants* to be a ghost if those are the only two ways to become one.

I glance across my room at Old Creepy. She's still sitting on my bed, casually humming an eerie tune while gazing languidly out the window. Why is she a ghost? Does *she* have unfinished business? Or was she cursed? Goosebumps break out across my skin at the thought.

"Harriet?" My mom gently knocks on my door, which is cracked open, and peeks her head in.

Rolling my eyes, I groan. "Mom, we have enough snacks."

She's been trying to make things up to me ever since the incident at the vet's office. Except, her version of making things up to me involves being overly sweet, doting, and excitedly encouraging my friendship with Mattie and the other guys. When he showed up earlier, she went nuts feeding us about a million cookies and muffins. The one thing she hasn't done? Apologize for what she did or even so much as acknowledge that what she did was fucked up.

Mattie grins and pats his stomach. "Speak for yourself. Your mom makes the best snacks in the universe."

My mom steps in, smiling anxiously at me. When I realize she's not carrying a tray of snacks, I narrow my eyes suspiciously.

"There's someone here to speak to you, Harriet," she says.

I sit up straight, glancing down at my phone. Surely, Spencer or Owen would text me if they decided to stop by. Even if it was them, I'm pretty sure my mom would have just let them in since Mattie's already here.

"Who is it?" I ask.

She sighs and gives me one of her looks. "It's Henry. The paternity test results came back, and he came over to speak with you." Her lips purse, and she adds, "He doesn't particularly want to talk to *me*, and he's refusing to come inside."

"Wow, I wonder why." I snort sarcastically. I glance over at Mattie to find him watching me curiously and with a hint of concern. The thought of talking to Henry again after everything makes me want to throw up, but I can't help the small, pathetic part of myself that wants to know him. To know if I'm more like him than my mom. I slowly stand up, giving Mattie a pleading look before I walk away. "Will you stay here and wait for me? Please?"

He gives me a soft smile and nods. "Don't worry. I'm not going anywhere."

Butterflies stir in my stomach at his words, but I quickly squash that feeling. I'm already crushing on two other guys. I don't need to add a third to my list just because he's being nice to me! Especially not a guy who's practically in love with Amethyst Redferne.

Still, Mattie's words do have a weird way of calming me and giving me a tiny burst of bravery. It lasts me all the way downstairs. At least until I open the front door and find Dr. Henry Reichardt pacing back and forth across the porch. Then I want to throw up again.

He looks up as soon as I step outside, a deep frown on his face. I didn't really *look* at him the last time we met for obvious reasons. But now I can see that my natural hair color is the same as his, and we do have the same eyes. He's also crazy tall, like me. It's such a weird realization that makes everything feel that much more surreal.

"Hi," I squeak.

My mom hovers behind me in the doorway, clearly hoping to listen in on our entire conversation. I turn and glare at her, slamming the door in her face. She has no fucking right.

A huff of laughter escapes from Henry's mouth, and I turn to give him a sheepish look. He clears his throat, sobering almost instantly. "Hello."

Goddess, this is awkward. I have no idea what to say, and he doesn't seem to have a clue either. He shifts his weight from foot to foot, peering anxiously at the front door and window.

"Do you mind if we step off the porch?" he asks.

I nod and hop down the steps and onto the front path in front of the house. I don't blame him for feeling jittery or worrying about my mom listening in. My aunt told me a few days ago when she drove me to the doctor to take the stupid paternity test that Henry is very aware that our family are witches. Apparently, his wife is a witch too. He probably suspects my mom will try to hex him or something, so it makes sense he wants to be cautious and stay as far from the house as he can.

There's an old, iron bench near the edge of the property I found the other day when I was working on the yard, and I lead Henry there, hoping it'll be easier to talk this far from the house. He sits beside me, on the far side of the bench opposite from me, and hums thoughtfully as he looks around.

"There used to be a garden over here. Your great-grandmother would spend hours out here every day, even when it was raining. I think the garden was her favorite thing about the Abbot House."

"Really?" I ask, looking around curiously. It never occurred to me that Henry knew Sylvia too, but I love hearing that little tidbit. I never knew she liked gardening. "Maybe I'll plant some stuff in the spring. That sounds nice."

My words are followed by an awkward silence. I wait patiently, squeezing my phone in my jacket pocket just so I feel closer to my friends while I deal with this. Sage, Owen, and Spencer have been really supportive and great about this whole thing. And now Mattie's waiting upstairs for me too, even if he doesn't know exactly what's going on.

"Listen, Harriet." Henry sighs, rubbing his hand over the back of his neck as he glances sideways at me. "I want to apologize. First, for my behavior the other day at my office. I was rude and took my feelings about your mother out on you, and you didn't deserve that. And second, I'm just so incredibly sorry for all the years we've lost. If I'd had any idea..."

Oh, Goddess. I am *not* going to cry. When I feel tears prick at the corners of my eyes, I blink furiously to hold them back.

"It's not your fault," I say, incapable of looking at him. "I know she didn't tell you. She never told me either. I always assumed she had no clue who my dad was. I never even thought about it. Not until she ambushed us the other day at your vet office."

He snorts, and I look up to find a slight smile on his face. His expression softens when our eyes meet, and he quietly asks, "You've had a decent life, then? Without having a dad around?"

"Sure." I shrug. It's not like it's that unusual these days for kids to be raised by one parent. I've never felt like something was missing in that regard, and even when we didn't have much money, I never really wanted for anything when I was growing up. It feels weird to say all that to Henry though, so all I give him is, "We lived in a small town in Oregon pretty much my whole life until we moved here a few weeks ago. I have friends, I do okay in school, and I've never gotten into any major trouble."

Henry chuckles, almost like he's surprised at every word out of my mouth. Or maybe it's just my existence he's still surprised at.

"Well, I'm glad to hear that."

I nod at him, and then the question I'm most interested in tumbles out of my mouth. "Do I have siblings?"

"Yes," he says, staring at me like he's not sure how I'm going to react to the news. I wish I could explain it to him, or to anyone, the way I feel torn between nervous excitement and absolute terror at the idea. Henry clears his throat. "My son, Dorian. He's your age. And my daughter, Elsie, who's thirteen. They're keen to meet you, as is my wife."

"They are?" I ask hesitantly. "So, they're not, like...mad?"

He gives me a look that's a mixture of guilt, frustration, and sorrow. "Nobody is mad at *you*, Harriet. I hate how this entire situation came to light, but I'm not angry or upset to find out that you're my daughter. I'm just incredibly sad that I've never had the chance to know you. I hope we can get to know each other now, and I hope you'll eventually feel comfortable with the rest of my family too. Because you'll always be welcome with us."

Blinking away a new batch of tears, I offer Henry a wobbly smile. "Alright. I'd really like that. Getting to know you and your family."

"Why don't you come over for dinner tomorrow night?"

Even though I just agreed that I would like to get to know him and I *do* want to meet my siblings, everything feels like it's happening so fast. I panic, thinking of what to say, and quickly blurt out, "Can I think about it?"

"Of course," he says. I feel bad, but he doesn't sound disappointed or anything. He's being super understanding.

Henry suggests we exchange numbers, which is only mildly awkward.

While I'm typing his number into my phone, Circe comes out from the bushes behind our bench and mews softly as she rubs against my leg and then Henry's. He chuckles and leans down to pet her. When she hops up on the bench to sit between us, Henry scratches the top of her head and turns to smile at me.

"How's she doing?" he asks. When I mumble that she's doing alright, he hums. "Know what you're going to do with the kittens after they're born yet?"

"No idea." I shrug. "Honestly, I used to hate cats until Circe pretty much bullied me into adopting her. And this week has been kind of nuts. I've barely thought about the kittens at all."

"That's understandable."

We make small talk for a little longer after that. Henry really does seem interested in getting to know me because he asks me all sorts of questions about school, my friends, and my hobbies. It's kinda nice, but that sense of everything being overwhelming never totally goes away. Eventually, Henry says he needs to get home, but hopes he'll hear from me soon.

After watching him walk to his car, parked along the sidewalk in front of the house, I sigh and head inside. I can hear my mom and Flora talking in the kitchen, and I'm sure my mom is feeling particularly nosy about how my conversation went with Henry. But I don't want to deal with either of them. Henry said he and his family weren't mad at *me*, but I can read between the lines.

I head upstairs, not bothering trying to be quiet so that Mattie can hear me coming. I know he said he'd wait, but I feel bad that I was gone for so long. Checking my phone, I realize I was outside for about half an hour.

"Hey, I'm so sorry," I say as I walk into my room. My

199

eyebrows raise when I see Mattie standing near my bed beside Old Creepy, holding his phone up like he's taking a picture or video of himself. "What are you doing?"

"Just messing around." He shrugs, grinning at me like he's been having the time of his life up here without me. "Your ghost roomie doesn't show up in pictures on my phone obviously, but her voice does. It's really quiet, but it's definitely there. She sang *Mary Had a Little Lamb* for me. Fucking awesome and creepy as shit."

A strangled laugh escapes me. Of course Mattie would spend the time I left him alone doing ghost hunting stuff. But at least it's further proof that he genuinely believes me. My laughter turns to a sob, and those stupid tears I tried so hard to hold back outside make another appearance.

"Crap." Mattie rushes over to stand in front of me, sort of flapping his hands around me while he stares up at me in alarm. "Did something happen? I know you don't like hugs, but shit. Is there something I can do?"

"No, no." I quickly wipe my eyes, hating the fact that I'm acting like such a baby in front of him. "I'm just sort of overwhelmed, I guess. I'm sorry for making you wait so long."

Mattie rocks back and forth on his heels, his hands twitching at his sides like he's still considering giving me a hug. After a short pause, he asks, "Do you want to talk about it?"

I realize that I kind of do. If he wasn't here, then I'd probably call Sage or Owen. Owen's so easy to talk to, but I already feel like I've dropped way too many of my problems on him over the past few days. And Sage is in a totally different time zone, three hours behind me. She's probably still in school right now.

"Yeah, okay."

We go sit on my bed instead of the floor like when we were

doing our homework, sitting a couple feet apart, facing each other with our legs crossed. Mattie gives me an encouraging smile, not rushing me to say anything. I pick at my nail polish, feeling anxious, and think through everything I'm feeling and want to say.

"I'm guessing Spencer and Owen didn't tell you about the stuff with my mom the other day?" I ask. He slowly shakes his head, his smile dropping. It makes me respect all the guys a lot though. They're really good friends, but they don't blab each other's business to one another without asking if it's okay. And they've been doing the same for me. I clear my throat and continue, "Well, I took Circe to the vet on Sunday. While we were there, I found out that the guy who owns the clinic is my dad. My mom never told me or him, and she dropped the bomb during the middle of our appointment just to be petty."

"Ahh." Mattie winces. "So, that explains the paternity test comment."

I nod, fidgeting slightly. "Yeah. It was such a fucking mess. I freaked out and ran off, and Spence and Owen came and picked me up. I've barely spoken to my mom since then. She refuses to apologize or admit she did anything wrong. I'm just, like, so fucking livid about it. I never cared about not having a dad around growing up. Like, I never dreamed about tracking him down like some stupid fucking Hallmark movie or anything. But just randomly finding out about him like that? Now I feel like I want to know everything about him, and I get so mad at my mom all over again every time I think about it."

"And I'm assuming today was the first time you've seen your dad since then?"

His voice is soft and full of patience. Goddess, I almost start crying again, but I'm determined not to embarrass myself. Not like that, at least.

"Yeah. It's still weird to think of him as that? But he seems nice. I don't know. He said he's sad he missed out on knowing me all these years, and he wants to get to know me now." I chuckle humorlessly and look down at my lap. "He invited me over for dinner tomorrow night. Apparently, I have siblings, and the whole family wants to meet me. I'm not against it at all, but it just feels like...a lot."

There's silence between us for a few moments, but it's not uncomfortable. I don't feel awkward telling Mattie all this stuff like I worried I might. Crazy how much my opinion of him can change after just a few days.

"Have any of the guys told you why I live with my aunt and uncle?" Mattie asks, breaking the silence.

His question catches me off guard as it's not remotely close to anything I expected him to say. Curious, I shake my head. I knew he lived with his cousin, Nolan. But truthfully, I never once considered why or even thought of it as something odd.

He gets a faraway look in his eyes. "My, uh, family died when I was twelve. My little brother had a soccer game, and I didn't want to go. I faked being sick so I could stay home to play video games, and my parents, brother, and baby sister all went without me. They ended up dying in a car wreck on the way there."

"Goddess, Mattie," I breathe out, reaching for his hands to twine our fingers together. "I'm so sorry."

"Thanks." He clears his throat and squeezes my hands, giving me a sad smile. "Anyway, I think you have every right to be mad at your mom. And I think it's completely understandable you're hesitant to let your dad in after going your whole life knowing nothing about him. But if something happened to either of them? I don't know, I just don't want you to regret holding a grudge or keeping your guard up for too long. I'm not saying you necessarily need to forgive your mom, but maybe talk to her?"

I don't even think about it before leaning forward and pulling him into a hug. He only seems surprised for about half a second before hugging me back tightly.

Later that evening, after Mattie is summoned home by his aunt and I'm left alone in my room with only Circe and Old Creepy for company, I take some of Mattie's advice. I text Henry to say that dinner tomorrow night sounds great.

CHAPTER 18

HARRIET

"Are you sure you want to do this?" Flora asks.

I roll my eyes and rest my forehead against the car window, watching the town pass us by. It's raining again, making everything look blurry and gloomy. It's not helping my mood, but I don't want my aunt to know I'm feeling anxious. Because then she'll go back and tell my mom.

"Yes, I'm sure." Even though I'm totally not.

I'm just going to blame Mattie. He made me all emotional yesterday by being weirdly fucking sweet and sentimental, and I made the rash decision to accept Henry's invitation to dinner. Now that I'm only a few minutes away from his house, I'm rethinking my decision. How awkward is this going to be? Are my siblings going to be assholes like other witches usually are to me? Or worse because of how their parents feel about my mom? Is Henry going to be nice again, or is he going to be different in front of his real family?

Unfortunately, I'm too stubborn to back out.

"Alright." Flora sighs. "Well, just remember you can call me to come and get you any time, okay? You don't have to stay if you feel uncomfortable or unwelcome."

The fact she seems so sure that I'm going to be *uncomfortable* and *unwelcome* makes me even more determined to go through with this. No matter how badly it turns out, I'm gonna act like this dinner tonight is the best night of my life just to spite my mom and Flora. I don't care how petty that makes me.

Mattie might have a point about moving on and at least talking to my mom, but that's much easier said than done. I still can't even look at her without feeling angry and betrayed. Hopefully getting to know my father a little will help, but I think it will take some time before I'm ready to have a candid conversation with my mom.

When the GPS on Flora's phone tells her our destination is on our right, my heart nearly beats out of my chest. All the houses on this block are cute. They're not super old and historical like the grand houses on my street, but all of them have a cozy feeling. The house Flora pulls up in front of is no different. It's a blue two-story with white shutters and trim, a big front porch, and a lush front yard. There are pumpkins on the porch, and a pretty fall wreath decorating the white front door.

Flora opens her mouth, but I open the passenger door before she can get a word out. Pulling my hood up to protect my hair from the rain, I tell her thank you over my shoulder and slam the car door shut. I rush up the front walk, wipe my boots on the welcome mat, and lift my hand to ring the doorbell. Before I manage to press it, the door swings open, and a young girl with light brown hair, freckles, and gray-blue eyes smiles up at me.

"Are you Harriet?" she asks. I nod, and she squeals as she

throws her arms around me in a hug. "Oh my Goddess! I've always wanted a sister, and now you're finally here! I'm Elsie."

I chuckle awkwardly and pat her arm, mumbling, "It's nice to meet you, Elsie."

It's definitely a much more enthusiastic welcome than I was expecting, so I can only hope this is a good omen for the rest of the night. Elsie grabs my arm and pulls me into the house, waving her hand behind her to magically close the front door.

"Mom and dad are in the kitchen, and Dorian's probably still sulking in his room. But you can sit next to me at the table."

"Okay," I say quietly, following her through the house while I gaze around. There are tons of family photos all over the walls, and everything is decorated to make the space feel cozy and warm. I'm already a little bit in love with the place. Still feeling slightly anxious, I ask, "What exactly is your brother sulking about?"

"Our brother," she reminds me with a grin. Then she shrugs and says, "Who knows? He's always sulking about something."

Well, even if Dorian is pissed about my existence and my being here, at least one of my siblings seems nice. When we walk into the kitchen, I'm greeted by a huge, black and white Great Dane who sniffs me all over while wagging its tail. I giggle and scratch the top of the dog's head, only looking up when I hear clanking by the stove in the kitchen.

"Hey," Henry says, giving me a nervous smile. "Thanks for coming."

His wife stands beside him, and I'm relieved to find her smiling at me. She's way shorter than me and Henry, and she's super pretty with long, auburn hair and freckles all over her face.

"Hi, Harriet. I'm Audrey. It's so nice to meet you," she says. And she sounds genuine. Just as genuine as Elsie was at the door. "Why don't you have a seat? Dinner will be ready in just a few minutes."

Thanking her, I take a seat at the big oak table in the dining room where five places are already set. Elsie insists again that I sit next to her, and Henry sits at the end of the table on my other side. Everything smells delicious, and the entire family has been welcoming so far. I try to force myself to relax, even reminding myself of all that sentimental stuff Mattie said to me last night. Weirdly, it actually helps.

"What's your dog's name?" I ask. The Great Dane must not be allowed around the table because he's sitting right outside the dining room, staring at us with a pitiful expression while he thumps his tail.

"That's Puddles," Elsie says. I giggle at the silly name, and she grins excitedly at me. "We have two cats too, but they always hide around strangers. Scarlett and Ginger. Dad says you have a cat too?"

Nodding, I tell her about Circe. How she scared me in the yard my first day in town while I was moving boxes, how she forced me into adopting her, and then how I found out that she's having kittens. There's a chance Henry already told her about that last part, but Elsie seems to hang on my every word and reacts enthusiastically to the whole story. From the corner of my eye, I catch Henry staring at me with a mixture of awe, sadness, and joy. Sort of like how he looked at me when he came over to talk yesterday.

Audrey walks into the dining room, a bunch of dishes floating in the air behind her. She twirls her fingers, and the dishes land delicately on the table. My stomach rumbles at the sight of homemade lasagna, garlic bread, and a large bowl of tossed salad. After texting Henry back last night to accept his invite to dinner, he asked me if I was allergic to anything or had any food preferences. Thankfully I'm not, but it was still thoughtful of him to ask.

As she takes her seat at the opposite end of the table from Henry, Audrey twirls her fingers in the air and quietly says, "Dorian, please come downstairs. Dinner's ready."

It's the same spell my mom uses whenever she's trying to summon me from another room in the house. My heart stutters nervously in preparation for meeting my half-brother. I really hope he's just as nice as the rest of his family. Or at the very least, disinterested in me. I have enough asshole witches to deal with at school. As corny as it is, I do want to be able to think of Henry's family as my family too someday. I want these people to like me.

It only takes a few moments until Dorian makes an appearance. I turn to watch him walk into the dining room, and he pauses when our eyes meet. He's tall and thin like I am, and he has the same gray-blue eyes that Henry, Elsie, and I share. His hair is dyed a dark green, and it's messy like he rubbed his hands through it a million times. As we stare at each other, his lips curve into a half smile, and I notice a dimple appear.

"Nice to meet you, almost-twin." He chuckles, walking closer to the table. He pauses again right beside my chair and adds, "Your hair color is fucking sick. May I?"

Not completely sure what he's asking, but not wanting to appear unfriendly or hesitant, I shrug and say, "Sure, thanks."

He quickly strokes his hand over my hair, and I watch as his hair gradually turns the same color. I've never seen a witch use this particular trick, and I have to admit, it's pretty fucking impressive. He grins when the process is over, walking around the table to sit across from me.

Once everyone is seated and settled, Audrey says a quick prayer to the Goddess and Henry begins serving himself. Nobody else moves to fill their own plates, so I sit awkwardly and wait while Audrey quietly makes small talk with her kids. As soon as Henry's finished, the table erupts into magical chaos. Food begins flying all over the place, serving itself onto Audrey, Elsie, and Dorian's plates. They're already digging in by the time I shake off my surprise. My mom uses magic around the house all the time, but not for everything. At least not around me. The only other witch family I've been around frequently is Sage's. Her parents use magic like this, but Sage and her siblings aren't allowed to use their powers for chores or menial things like serving themselves dinner.

When I go to grab the dish of lasagna to serve myself, Elsie turns and looks at me like I'm crazy. "You don't have to do that. We're allowed to use magic at the table. We only wait for dad to get his food first since he can't do magic and is slower than we are."

Henry chuckles from my other side. "Thanks for that."

I swear I can feel the color drain from my face, and I stare at the food on the table in a panic while I think of what to do or say. I wasn't planning on telling Henry or my half-siblings about my lack-of-magic any time soon, if ever. Part of me feels shame, like I always have. But maybe I shouldn't? Owen, Spencer, and Mattie have made me feel pretty awesome about my powers lately, and Sage never made me feel bad or inferior either. Since there's no way for me to lie or get out of this situation, I figure it's best if I just tell the truth straight away. Better to know how my newly discovered family will react sooner rather than later, right?

"Actually," I mumble, clearing my throat. "I can't do magic. Not like you guys, anyway."

"What?" Elsie exclaims. She looks as shocked as I imagine

she would if I sprouted an extra head. "How is that even possible? You seriously can't do *any* magic?"

Her mom hisses a reprimand at her, and I do a quick sweep around the table to judge the rest of the family's reactions. Audrey looks embarrassed by her daughter's reaction, but Henry and Dorian are just watching me curiously. When Dorian catches me looking at him, he even grins in a way that doesn't seem malicious or judgmental.

I turn to face Elsie and give her an anxious half smile. "Well, I get that tingly feeling whenever I recognize another witch. But otherwise, no. I've never been able to do any sort of spellwork, and I'm even useless with potions and things that seem like they'd be more hands-on."

"And there's nothing wrong with that," Audrey says, giving everyone in her family a pointed look. I kind of love her for being so defensive of me, especially when nobody has even said anything rude.

"Of course not," Henry says. He picks up my plate and quickly serves me before I can protest, shooting me a big grin when he's finished. "Now I won't feel left out all the time when the rest of the family's using magic for every little thing."

It never occurred to me that it might be nice to have a fully human parent. Someone to make me feel normal in comparison to my mom and the rest of the community.

"You said you can't do magic like *we* can," Dorian says, making me turn my attention to him. His eyes light up with curious excitement as he asks, "Does that mean you can do magic in a different way?"

"Sort of." I shrug, feeling a lot less uncomfortable than I expected I would. "I can see and talk to ghosts."

After dinner, I end up sitting in the living room with Elsie and Dorian while Audrey cleans up the kitchen and Henry takes a work call. Dinner went super well. Everyone was really accepting of my strange, witchy abilities. More than that, they all seemed just as interested and excited as Owen, Mattie, and Spencer did when I told them. It made me feel good enough to relax and open up, and in no time, the five of us were talking and joking around at the table like I've known the family forever.

And now, while I listen to Elsie chatter about her classes and cheerleading squad at school, I can't stop smiling. There's been a warm, hopeful feeling in my chest pretty much all evening that I hope never goes away. Part of me still feels bitter that I was robbed of so many years having Henry as my dad, but I can't deny that I'm happy I have the chance to know him and my half-siblings now.

"Have you ever thought about being a cheerleader?" Elsie asks me.

Dorian snorts from the opposite end of the couch, proving he's paying attention to our conversation even though he's been pretending to scroll through his phone while watching an episode of *Midnight Mass*.

I giggle when Elsie rolls her eyes at her brother—*our* brother—and shake my head at her. "No way. I'm way too awkward and antisocial for something like that."

Elsie pouts. "Ugh, I don't know *any* witches who are into cheer or regular human stuff at all. Like football games or shopping at the mall. They all dress goth, listen to weird music, and watch horror movies. Like Dorian. He's the perfect witch even though he never hangs out with anyone from the covens around here."

That's surprising. I glance over at Dorian curiously to find him frowning down at his phone. Totally still listening, even though he's trying to play it cool. The reason it's surprising to hear he doesn't hang around with a coven is because he totally gives off this cool, aloof vibe that makes it impossible not to want to get to know him, and he seems to have a typical witchy style. Plus, I get the impression that he's super advanced with his magical powers based on a few comments that were made during dinner and the impressive trick he did with his hair. Witches love that type of shit. They're always drawn to power, and it hardly matters that Dorian's dad is human or that his mom doesn't come from a prestigious witch family.

"Most of your friends are human, I guess?" I ask Elsie sympathetically.

Even though I admittedly fit the stereotypical witchy vibe with my style and hobbies, I've never gotten along with other witches either. For different reasons than Elsie, but still. I know what it's like to feel like you don't fit into our community.

"Yeah." She sighs, reaching over to scratch Puddles's head. The dog plopped down on the couch with us as soon as we came into the living room. He's way too massive to be a lapdog, but he seems like he hasn't quite gotten that memo based on the way he's sprawled across both my and Elsie's laps. Elsie smiles at Puddles fondly when he thumps his tail, and then she looks up at me with another pouty look. "What about you? You probably have a ton of witch friends, right?"

"My best friend Sage back in Oregon is a witch," I admit. "But that's it. I usually don't get along with other witches because of the power thing. All my friends here are human, actually. But three of them know I can see ghosts, and one of them also knows I'm a witch." I almost mention Spencer too–I don't want to lie to Elsie, but it's easier to lie since he's technically not allowed to know like Owen is.

"Oh my Goddess! You're so lucky," Elsie whines. "I wish I could tell my best friends about being a witch."

Yet another thing I can totally sympathize with, and absolutely something I constantly feel lucky and relieved about lately. "Well, Owen's stepmom is a witch, so he already knew about me as soon as we met. I won't lie, it definitely makes things easier. But Spencer and Mattie at least know about the ghost stuff, and it's nice being able to confide in them."

Elsie's eyes light up at the guys' names. "Your friends are boys? Ooh, are any of them your boyfriend?"

"No!" I deny it way too quickly to sound convincing, and I feel a flush spread across my cheeks. "I swear, they're just friends."

Just because I have a massive crush on both Spencer and Owen doesn't mean anything's going to happen. Ever. Even if they keep acting like they like me too. I still can't figure them out, so I'm determined to keep them both locked in the 'just friends' box in my head.

My sister looks more delighted than ever, like she's barely holding in a squeal. Dorian's smirking at his phone too, which makes me blush even harder. Nope. Definitely *not* talking about boys and crushes with my siblings. Not yet, anyway.

"Elsie?" Audrey walks into the living room, giving her daughter a stern look. "It's still a school night, and you have an essay due tomorrow you still need to finish."

"Ugh, mom!" Elsie throws her head back dramatically. "Harriet's here!"

"And you'll have plenty of opportunities to hang out again," Audrey says.

Before Elsie can argue further and get herself into trouble, I nudge her and grin. "Yeah, we'll definitely hang out soon. I can't make any promises about football games, but I'll definitely go to the mall with you and do whatever other stuff human teenage girls usually do."

She giggles and nods, making me swear I'll text her. We exchanged numbers already earlier, luckily. As soon as Elsie gets up, Puddles slinks off the couch and follows her upstairs. It's pretty adorable to see his devotion. I've spent even less time around dogs than I have cats, but I've got to admit that Puddles is the perfect amount of cute and obnoxious that makes me consider wanting a dog too.

Audrey mumbles something about needing to finish some work too and walks out of the room, leaving me and Dorian alone. I only feel awkward for a few seconds before Dorian turns to face me with a lazy grin.

"Thanks for being so nice to Elsie," he says. "She can be fucking annoying and overbearing, but it means a lot to see you making an effort with her. She was so excited when our dad came home the other day and told us there was a chance we have another sister."

"I think she's sweet," I say honestly with a shrug. "Goddess, I was nervous as fuck to meet you guys. I thought you'd hate me. But I've always loved the idea of having siblings. My best friend has a bunch of younger brothers, and I was always jealous of her for it."

Dorian glances at the hallway his mom just walked down, and then he waves his fingers as he mumbles a quick spell. Maybe a soundproofing charm? I immediately tense up, mentally preparing myself to deal with whatever he's going to say or do now that we have real privacy.

"Sorry," he says, giving me a guilty smile when he sees my reaction to him using magic. Scooting a little closer to me on the couch, he adds, "I just don't want my parents to overhear us. The stuff with your mom has been a pretty, uh...touchy subject."

Glancing down at my lap in shame, I chuckle humorlessly. "Yeah, I can imagine. When I realized you're only a couple of months older than me, and that your parents were already together when Henry and my mom—"

"It's messy, yeah." Dorian laughs, cutting me off. I meet his silver-gray eyes, surprised to find him smiling genuinely at me. "But all the shit that happened between our dad and our moms way back then? My parents dealt with it ages ago. So, you shouldn't feel bad about it. It's not like it's your fault any of this happened or that you didn't get the chance to meet us sooner. I swear to the Goddess that nobody in our family hates or blames you."

Stupid, embarrassing tears sting my eyes, and I get another warm and fuzzy feeling in my chest. Desperately trying to hide what a crybaby I am, I nod and clear my throat. "Thanks."

Pretty sure he sees right through me because his grin widens. "You're welcome, almost-twin."

I snort at the ridiculous nickname despite how accurate it is. Not only are our birthdays close together, but we look a lot alike. Especially now that he's borrowed my hair color. If only I could pull off the same cool-and-collected vibe he does.

"So, no coven for you?" I ask, still curious to know why that's the case after hearing what Elsie said about him.

"Fuck no!" He laughs loudly. "Most witches are assholes."

A wide grin stretches across my face, and I turn in my seat to face him better. Dorian is officially the second witch to ever agree with me on this fact. After Sage, of course. "True, but *most* witches seem completely unaware of their asshole-ness."

He fidgets with his phone, like he needs an excuse to do something with his hands. When he meets my eyes again, he looks almost vulnerable. "Elsie wants a witch best friend so badly. She has a hard time with the other witches in her grade since she has nothing in common with them, and the human girls tend to find her just a little too odd. Know what I mean? I'm sure it doesn't help that we go to fucking private school, which sucks. But I wish I could just get her to realize that a lot of witches aren't worth being friends with. At least around here. They're all power-hungry, constantly manipulating and using each other to improve their own status in our toxic society."

Dorian seems a little embarrassed when he finishes speaking, like he worries he might have said too much or possibly offended me. But honestly? I couldn't agree with him more. The witch community should be welcoming and supportive, but it just isn't. Not from what I've seen, anyway, though I always assumed I was the only one who thought so since I'm basically an outsider without magic. Not wanting Dorian to feel bad for being so honest, I decide to tell him the truth about my experience with most witches.

"It's not just here. I'm pretty sure witches are like that everywhere—at least they were in Oregon too. Back home, I never got along with witches my age because I couldn't do magic. Sage was the only one who hung out with me, and people were dicks to her because of it. I was constantly told I wasn't a real witch, and that I didn't belong. When I moved here, I decided I wasn't going to tell anyone about my lack of powers or seeing ghosts if I could help it. It's kind of been biting me in the ass though because the witches at school have been hazing me. And the longer I go without defending myself or retaliating, the more it's escalating."

"Shit." He whistles, brushing his fingers through his already-messy hair. "I think you just managed to make me hate the covens around here even more than I already do. Let me guess—Blaze Alden has been the biggest asshole to you so far?"

Just hearing his name makes me grimace. I've managed to avoid him since the incident at my house last weekend, but I doubt I'll forget any time soon how dangerous he is. "Yeah. He and Amethyst Redferne have been the fucking worst. Leading the charges and all that."

Dorian leans closer, his eyes lighting up mischievously. "Want me to hex them?"

I let out a choked laugh. I'm not entirely certain whether he's joking or not, but it's still a nice way to remind me that we're on the same side. I have a good feeling that after tonight, Dorian and I are going to be good friends.

"What are we watching?" Henry walks into the living room carrying a large bowl of popcorn. Dorian grins, scooting back to the opposite side of the couch so our dad can sit between us. Once he sits and offers us both the salty, buttery treat, he glances at the screen and groans. "*Midnight Mass* again? Can't we watch something, I don't know, a little less scary and depressing?"

Dorian and I snicker, meeting each other's eyes. If my almost-twin likes horror shows and movies as much as I do, I'm pretty sure Henry's outvoted.

CHAPTER 19

SPENCER

I grudgingly hand the stack of yearbooks to Mattie, feeling like a giant fucking failure. I've been poring over these books all week, desperate to find any hint of Ryan's time as a student at Weeping Hollow High. It's become terrifyingly clear over the past couple of weeks that I'm in way over my head when it comes to Harriet. I think at this point I'd do just about anything to make her happy. It's almost embarrassing how much I like her.

And even more embarrassing that I managed to fail at the one task I swore I'd do everything I could to help her with.

"Do you really think you'll have any better luck than Owen and I did?" I ask, my voice giving away my bitterness.

Mattie doesn't even look at me. Just sets the yearbooks on his bed next to the others he somehow convinced Harriet to let him borrow. I still don't understand how that happened. Since when do they talk and hang out outside of school? Jealousy burns hot in my chest, and I have to remind myself that Harriet's not my girlfriend. Not yet, at least. Probably not ever, if I'm being realistic.

"Absolutely," Mattie says, shuffling through his new collection of yearbooks before pulling out the class of 2009 and of 2010. Finally glancing up at me with a triumphant grin, he arrogantly says, "I already found something, actually."

"What?" I ask incredulously, leaning over him like I'll magically see the proof we've been looking for written all over the front of the yearbooks in his hand. "How is that possible? I've looked at these things a thousand fucking times. Owen and I even search Facebook groups for all the graduating classes, and we checked Myspace! There's no way you found something that we didn't."

My best friend gives me a cocky grin and shrugs. "Guess we all just have different talents."

Shoving his shoulder and taking a seat on the bed next to him, I glare at the fucking yearbooks. "You're such an asshole. And you're full of shit."

He smirks, casually flipping through one of the yearbooks like he isn't aggravating the fuck out of me. "You're just mad Harriet trusted me with her secret and asked for my help. Now you and Owen can't hog her attention all the time."

I hate how right he is. It's been weird enough getting used to the fact that Owen's interested in Harriet. Whenever he flirts with her, which is something we've both started doing frequently and openly, I have to constantly remind myself that Owen is my best friend and he's been through a lot of awful shit. He's never shown interest in anyone, and he deserves to be happy. Sometimes I can't help feeling like an asshole, like I can't help but get in the way of him pursuing Harriet.

But somehow Owen's made it really easy not to feel jealous or resentful about us liking the same girl. I don't get how he does it, but every time those feelings start to creep in, he says something that sounds so chill and logical that I can't help but agree with him in the moment. Harriet's awesome, so of course

219

we both like her. And no, we *don't* have any control over whether she likes either of us back. If Harriet ever becomes my girlfriend, by some fucking miracle, I have no doubt that Owen will genuinely be happy for me and her. So, I'm determined to show him the same courtesy with no hard feelings if things work out in his favor instead.

Mattie smirks at me again, and I physically rub my hand over my chest like that will somehow make my anger and jealousy go away. It's stupid and unfair that I feel this way. Mattie's just as much my best friend as Owen and Nolan are, even if I've only known him since middle school instead of since kindergarten like the other guys. So, why is it so fucking hard to feel as chill about him liking Harriet as I do about Owen liking her?

"Well?" I nudge him, probably harder than necessary. "Are you gonna show me what you've supposedly found, or what?"

He hisses and rubs his arm, shooting me a glare before opening the Class of 2007 yearbook. "Alright, chill. I'm pretty sure this one was his freshman year, so I'm hoping I'll find more evidence in your yearbooks for his junior and senior year. Harriet mentioned he was possibly on the baseball team—"

"Yeah, I checked all the baseball team photos already," I cut him off. Rolling my eyes, I add, "I even checked past team rosters for his name."

Mattie flips to a page he's marked with a sticky note where he's made a mark next to a small picture of a group of students sitting together on the gym bleachers. With a flourish, Mattie points at a kid wearing a baseball cap and a red hoodie. He's smiling and holding up a peace sign with his fingers, as are most of the other people in the photo.

"I think that might be him," Mattie says.

There aren't any names attached to the photo, which is less than helpful. I dubiously grab my phone from my pocket and pull up one of the pictures that Owen took of Ryan and Harriet. The kid in the yearbook picture looks younger, which would make sense if Mattie's right about how old Ryan was then. But it's just really, really hard to tell. The kid in the yearbook picture could literally be anyone. There are no defining features or characteristics that are noticeable in the yearbook photo.

"Maybe." I shrug. "Is that all you've got?"

"No." Mattie rolls his eyes. "But it made me pay better attention when I was going through this book. Now look at this!"

He flips forward in the book to the freshman class photos. On the final page of them, he points out the short list of students who weren't pictured for whatever reason. Highlighted is the name *George Nichols*.

"Uh..." I glance sideways at Mattie, waiting for an explanation. When he keeps his mouth shut and stares at me silently—a first for him—I sigh in exasperation. "Who the fuck is George? And why is this relevant?"

A smug grin blooms across Mattie's face again, and he quickly opens the next year's yearbook. Wordlessly, he flips to the sophomore class photos and shows me the list of students not pictured there. Again, the same name is highlighted. Only, this time, it's listed as *George R. Nichols*.

"I know it probably looks and sounds like a longshot, but what if Ryan goes by his middle name? From what Harriet said, he can't remember anything. Even his own fucking last name or birthday."

It is a longshot, but he's right. It's not like we have anything else to go on. I grab the Class of 2009 yearbook—one of the ones I've looked through countless times—and I flip straight to the junior class photos. There on the list of students not pictured is the same damn name again. *George R. Nichols.*

"What the fuck?" I mumble. "How does someone not get their yearbook picture taken three years in a row?"

Mattie wastes no time in checking the next yearbook's senior photos and the not pictured list. Only, there's nothing there. He taps his finger against the page, staring off into space thoughtfully. "Kind of makes sense it wouldn't be here if he died sometime between his junior and senior year. I'm assuming you didn't come across any sort of memorial or mention of a student's death in either of these?"

"No. Nothing." I shake my head. Curious, I flip to the page with the baseball team's photos for the Class of 2009. I managed to miss it completely, or else deemed it irrelevant the first dozen times I saw it. But in tiny, nearly illegible print are the words: *'not pictured: George R. Nichols.'*

When I point it out to Mattie, he smiles triumphantly. "See? I fucking knew it, dude. This *has* to be him."

"We need to tell Harriet."

Before I can type a single word to her, Mattie smacks my phone out of my hand. It lands on his bedroom floor with a thud, and I turn to glare murderously at him. I can normally deal with him being energetic and obnoxious, but not when he's purposely keeping me from talking to my girl.

"What the fuck is wrong with you?" I ask, standing up and angrily picking my phone up off the floor. Thankfully it isn't cracked or anything. If it were, I doubt I'd be able to stop myself from punching my best friend in the face.

"We can't bug Harriet with this shit tonight. She's at her dad's house," he says, looking at me like I'm fucking stupid. "Don't you get how important that is for her?"

The way he says it, like he thinks he understands Harriet better than I ever could, makes all my jealousy flare and rage all over again. "Yes, I get how important it is. Owen and I spent pretty much the entire fucking day reassuring her it was going to be great. You're not the only person she talks to about personal shit, Matthew."

His nostrils flare angrily at my use of his real name. I expect him to argue with me about Harriet, or even to bitch at me for not using his nickname. What I'm not expecting is for him to jump up and shove me as he practically snarls in my face.

"Why do you always have to like the same girls as me?" he asks, raising his voice to nearly a yell. "It's not fucking fair. Why can't you just back off and give me a chance? I've never liked anyone as much as I like Harriet."

"Are you fucking serious?" I hiss. "First of all, she's not a prize to win. If she likes me, great. If she likes you instead, that's cool too. I'm not going to *back off* to make you feel better about your chances with her. You're not entitled to her just because you like her. I like her a lot too. And so does Owen, in case that wasn't obvious."

It's like he doesn't hear a word I'm saying. His hands shake at his side as he trembles in anger. "It was the same with Amethyst. You knew I liked her, and you started dating her, anyway. And the whole time you were together, you fucking rubbed it in my face."

I rub my hand over my eyes in exasperation. I thought we were past all that drama with Amethyst. Sure, I knew Mattie liked her too, but Amethyst liked *me*. And at the time, that felt pretty fucking awesome. Now I know it was because she's a witch, but back then, being with Amethyst was intoxicating. Every red flag in our relationship was easy to ignore for so long because she made me feel like any attention she gave me was a gift. Amethyst never wanted to hang out with my friends anyway, but I always hated the idea of Mattie being around her because he never made it a secret that he still liked her the entire time I was dating her. But he hasn't brought her up to any of us in so long. Amethyst and I broke up forever ago, and

I'm definitely over her. If he's still bitter about all that stuff, why is he just now saying something after such a long time?

The last thing I want to do is fight with Mattie. Especially about Amethyst or Harriet. Channeling the patience and logic Owen always seems to carry, I sigh and give Mattie an apologetic look. "I'm really sorry you felt that way and that you're still upset about it. But can we please agree that no matter how we feel about her, Harriet's our friend? She asked for our help with this. Plus, this is legit the first *real* paranormal investigation we've ever had."

Guilt flashes in his eyes, and all of the anger drains out of him at once. He swallows and turns his gaze away from me as he nods. "Yeah, you're right. I'm sorry. I don't want to fight either. It's just..."

"Just what?" I ask.

Mattie shrugs, still not looking at me as he brushes his hand through his hair. "Harriet thinks I'm annoying. Most of the time she acts like she hates me, and any time she seems like she's finally starting to see me as even just a friend, I manage to fuck it up. But for you and Owen? It just seems so fucking easy. You guys are always flirting with her and hanging out with her, and she definitely never acts like she hates you guys."

I roll my eyes and chuckle. "Dude, for real? Harriet doesn't hate you. I'm pretty sure she's just like that with everyone. Even me and Owen. I guess I can't speak for him, but Harriet hasn't once flirted back with me. But I also know she's secretly a huge marshmallow once you get her to let her guard down. She sits with us at lunch every single day. She's invited us to her house and asked to hang out multiple times. Shit, we're having a goddamn sleepover at her place tomorrow night! She drew a logo for our stupid club, even when she originally acted like she wasn't all that interested in it. I'm pretty sure if she hated you, or hated any of us, she wouldn't do any of that stuff. She'd tell you to fuck off and never speak to you again."

"Yeah, I guess you're right." He finally meets my eyes again and says, "I'd still rather not bug Harriet with this stuff about Ryan tonight. Can we please wait until we're at school tomorrow? That way she'll be able to talk to Ryan right away and see if we're right."

"If he tells her the truth."

Mattie snorts at the annoyed tone in my voice. "Yeah. I've wondered if he's lying to her or not about not being able to remember shit. But she'd know better than us, right? Everything we know about ghosts is only from speculation and research."

"I really wish you guys wouldn't encourage her."

We turn to find Nolan standing in Mattie's doorway, his arms crossed and his eyebrows furrowed. Mattie groans and gives his cousin an irritated look. "Would you shut up?"

"She's sick!" Nolan insists. "How do either of you think you're helping Harriet by going along with her lies and delusions?"

"Wait." I shake my head. "You don't believe her about being able to see ghosts? You, who believes in all sorts of wild and improbable supernatural phenomena? Why the hell not?"

Nolan clenches his jaw and lifts a hand to adjust his glasses. "This is different. She knows we like supernatural stuff, and she's probably just trying to impress you guys. That, or she's convinced herself she really can see ghosts when she can't. Sometimes, people with certain mental illnesses—"

"Enough with the schizophrenia talk," Mattie scoffs and rolls his eyes. "Fuck off if you don't believe her. I do, and so do Spence and Owen."

"You know she can literally prove it, right?" I laugh, smirking at Nolan in disbelief. He and Mattie may not know

Harriet's a witch—or that a ton of people at our school and in this town are also witches—but they've always believed wholeheartedly in stuff like this for as long as I've known them. Honestly, I would normally have expected Nolan to be the first person to believe that someone can see and speak to ghosts.

Although, the more I think about it, Nolan's been pretty weird about Harriet since day one. He's constantly embarrassed around her and extremely defensive and protective of her. Never when she's around or where she can hear him, but always with us. Then when he's around her, he barely talks to her. Fuck. He probably likes her too. Knowing him though, and adding in the fact that Mattie, Owen, and I have already made it clear we like her too, Nolan will never admit it.

"If you want proof, I bet we can test her tomorrow." Mattie grins, bouncing on his toes. "Either at school with Ryan, or later at her house with Old Creepy. Harriet's going to make you feel like an idiot for doubting her, Nolan."

Nolan raises his hands like he's fed up with us, sighs, and turns to skulk back to his room. When he closes the door, Mattie and I grin at each other and laugh. For the first time, I'm genuinely fucking glad that Harriet decided to share at least part of her secret with Mattie.

CHAPTER 20
HARRIET

This is officially the worst morning of my life. I shove my dead, useless phone into the front pocket of my backpack and glare out the window of my mom's crappy Jeep Wagoneer. I was so caught up hanging out with Henry, Dorian, and Elsie last night that I totally lost track of time and didn't go home until after midnight. By that point, I was so tired and irritated about the looks my aunt kept giving me on the drive home that I completely forgot to plug my phone in before falling asleep.

Which means my alarm didn't go off, and I woke up less than ten minutes ago. While I had time to shower, I didn't have time to dry my hair or do my makeup. I know it's stupid and vain of me, but Goddess, I'm so upset Owen and Spencer are going to see me like this. I have a makeup bag in my locker, but the guys will probably be looking for me first thing since I never texted Owen this morning asking for a ride.

"You shouldn't worry so much," my mom says. She sounds way too pleasant and chipper for how early it is. "You're a beautiful girl with or without makeup, and I'm sure your boyfriends will agree."

Goddess, please kill me. I groan and tug on my wet hair. "First of all, they're not my boyfriends. The guys are just my friends. Second of all, nobody except for you would ever think I'm beautiful when I look like a drowned rat with bags under her eyes!"

My mom cackles. No matter how mad I've been at her, I can't help but fight a smile at the sound.

"If you're a drowned rat, you're a very cute one." She reaches over to brush her finger through my wet locks. "If you're really upset about going to school like this, I don't mind doing a quick spell. At least to dry your hair, if nothing else."

I sigh and lean back in my seat. The temptation is strong, but I've taught myself not to accept magical help from my mom or other witches for small, petty things like this. It just reminds me of how useless I am at being a witch, and it's better not to get used to those types of spells when it's not like I can use them myself. It sucks, but I'll just have to suffer through the day until I can find time to do my makeup in the bathroom.

"No, thanks." I force myself to give my mom a smile. "Is it still okay if the guys stay over tonight?"

She said yes before when I asked, with a few embarrassing rules included as a compromise. But since things have been kind of weird ever since I found out about Henry, I want to double check. Owen's the only one who's actually allowed to stay over. The rest of the guys told their parental guardians they're sleeping over at Owen's tonight. I feel sort of bad forcing them all to lie, but I get it.

"Of course. As long as you promise to take a contraceptive potion before they come over." She arches an eyebrow at me and adds, "In fact, I'd prefer if you take one daily from now on.

I know you say those boys are only your friends, but I know exactly how promiscuous teenagers can be. Especially a young witch, and *especially* when that young witch meets the right boy. Or boys."

Ugh, I hate the stereotype that witches are slutty. I hate even more that it's usually true. But that's just another reason I don't fit in with the community. I'm way too awkward with guys, and embarrassingly inexperienced. I've never even been kissed. But I'm not going to argue with my mom, especially when I can't even lie to myself about my crushes on Owen and Spencer and how I've definitely imagined what it would be like to kiss both of them.

"Yes, okay. I promise," I whine.

There's a moment of silence that feels almost awkward, so I glance sideways at my mom suspiciously. I already agreed to take the stupid potion, and I agreed to her other rules about the guys not being allowed to sleep in the same room as me. What else is she going to insist on?

"I really am glad you're making friends here," she finally says. Keeping her eyes on the road instead of looking at me, she continues. "But I do wish you were making more of an effort with some of the witches around here. The witch community in Weeping Hollow is unlike anywhere else, and I really feel like you could thrive here if you gave more people a chance."

"Are you serious, mom?" I laugh humorlessly. "What, you think my powers are suddenly going to manifest just because we moved to a new town? Why can't you just accept the fact that I'm a dud? And I'm okay with that."

"That's not what I'm saying," she says quickly and defensively. "Just that it wouldn't hurt to try to get more in touch with your heritage and magic here."

I breathe angrily out of my nose while I decide how to respond. It would be really easy to tell her off or to stay angry and silent until I get out of the car in a few minutes. But I desperately want my mom to understand me. To maybe for once try to see things from my perspective.

"Sage is still my best friend, and I think Dorian and I could become close too if we hang out some more. Other than them, I'm not interested in making friends with other witches. The witches here? They've been awful to me, mom. I haven't gone a day at school without them hazing me and trying to embarrass me with spells where they literally take control of my body. Owen and Spencer know I'm a witch, and they know why they're messing with me. But the other guys? They think I have Tourette's Syndrome or something, and they *still* accept me and want to be friends. Do you really, honestly think any of the witches around here would be nicer to me if they found out I can't do magic and barely count as a witch?"

My mom grips the steering wheel tight enough that I see her knuckles turn white, and she turns to give me a guilty, horrified look. "The witches are hazing you? But you never said anything. Neither did Kamal, and he swore he'd look out for you."

I shrug defensively. "I haven't told Principal Di Rossi. I didn't want to tell you either because it's just proof that I'm *not* like other witches. I never will be. It sucks, and it's always made me feel really shitty about myself. But the friends I've made here? They don't make me feel that way. I feel like I can finally be totally myself with them and in Weeping Hollow. What you said about feeling more connected to my magic? Well, I do. Old Creepy isn't the only ghost I've seen."

We pull up in front of the school, so I pull my seatbelt off and get ready to bolt. I've said more than enough to my mom. Before I can open the passenger door, she grabs my arm to stop me.

Her eyebrows are furrowed when I turn to face her. "Would you wait a minute, please?"

"Mom," I groan. "I have to go to school." And I really, really need to try to do my makeup before class starts.

She sighs and slowly lets go of my arm. "We need to talk about this, Harriet. You've been keeping so much from me. I'm not even sure where to start."

I should have known better. I've been keeping all this stuff from my mom for what feels like forever, and blurting it all out when she's not able to keep me trapped for more than a few minutes felt like the easiest way to go about it.

After I spend a few minutes squirming in my seat uncomfortable, my mom sighs and rubs a crease between her eyebrows. "You can still have your friends over tonight, but after they leave tomorrow, you and I are going to have a long talk. We have so many things to discuss. Alright?"

"Yes, alright." I agree with an eye roll. I finally open the door and start to step out, turning to give my mom one final look. "Thank you."

She gives me a sad smile. "And I'm sorry, Harriet."

It's the one thing I feel like I'm constantly desperate to hear from her. I've wished she could tell me she's sorry for so many things for as long as I can remember. Sorry for the things she's said in the past about my lack of magic. Sorry for always having to be the center of attention and for never listening to me when it counts. Sorry for forcing me to move to Weeping Hollow without so much as talking to me about it first. And most recently and probably more than anything else, I wished for her to tell me she's sorry for keeping Henry's existence a secret from me.

Now that she's said those two small words, I have no idea how to respond. So, I don't. I slam the car door shut and hustle toward the front doors of the school.

As soon as I walk into the school, it becomes obvious I don't have much time before the first bell. I nearly groan out loud from frustration, adjust my backpack, and quickly head to my locker. Unsurprisingly, I find all the guys huddled around it. Spencer, Mattie, Nolan, and Owen are sort of standing in a circle while Ryan floats near them and watches them curiously.

Spencer is the first one to look up and see me. He instantly straightens and grins. "Hey! Where have you been?"

I give him and the other guys a grimacing smile. "I've had a rough morning."

They move so I can open my locker. While I'm switching out my books and looking for my makeup bag, Owen leans against the locker beside mine and lifts a hand to brush a strand of still-damp hair behind my ear.

"You're okay though?" he asks. "I was worried when you never texted me back this morning."

Even though I look like an absolute nightmare, he's still looking at me like I'm the most stunning girl he's ever seen. My face heats up when I meet his gorgeous blue eyes, and my voice comes out sounding all stupid and squeaky. "Yep. Sorry. I forgot to plug my phone in last night, so it died and I accidentally slept in. I didn't even have time to do my hair and makeup."

Owens blinks and stares at me like it's only just occurred to him that I look different than usual. His smile widens as his eyes travel over my face. Mattie shoves him out of the way with a scowl, quickly changing his expression to something more smug when his eyes land on mine.

"Don't worry, Harriet." Mattie smirks. "You look just as hot without makeup as you do with it."

I make a face at him. He's probably trying to be nice, but ugh. I'm a makeup girl. For those who can go without and not only look amazing but also feel super confident? That's awesome for them. But for me, I rarely leave the house for anything without wearing a full face of makeup. It's, like, the only thing about my appearance I have control over since clothes rarely fit me the way they should. I've spent countless hours watching YouTube tutorials for makeup techniques, and even more time in front of the mirror practicing.

"Thanks, but I'm still gonna head to the bathroom to try to do my makeup before class."

I slam my locker closed and give the guys an apologetic look, wishing I had more time to talk and catch them up on my night at my dad's house. Plus, I'm anxious about our plans tonight and need to double check they still want to stay over and hang out.

"Can we come with you?" Nolan blurts out.

Spencer and Ryan laugh while the rest of us stare at him incredulously. His cheeks flush bright red as he fusses with his glasses. I raise my eyebrows and slowly ask, "You want to watch me do my makeup in the girls' bathroom?"

Not that it's *that* weird, if I'm being honest. Ryan follows me to the bathroom all the time, so I'm pretty used to it.

"I—um..." Nolan stutters, rubbing his hand over the back of his neck.

Shaking his head with another laugh, Spencer leans closer to me and lowers his voice to an almost-whisper. "Mattie and I have something to tell you. Something we may have found about Ryan. Unfortunately, Mattie opened his fat mouth and told Nolan your secret, and now Nolan wants proof."

"Hey!" Mattie says, frowning. "I didn't mean to. It just sort of slipped out when I was telling him what I was looking for in the yearbooks."

I roll my eyes and give him an unamused look. "Just try not to 'accidentally' tell anyone else, please?"

I'm not really mad he told Nolan. It makes being friends

with their group easier, and I know I'd feel bad if he was the only one left out of being told my secret. While I'm still not convinced Nolan likes me, he at least tolerates me being around. He's been nice and helpful for the most part, and he's never made fun of me or made me feel badly about my supposed issues.

"If you're all skipping first period to hang out in the bathroom together," Ryan starts, grinning in amusement. "Then you should use the bathroom down the hall from the library. There are no morning classes in that area, so nobody ever goes down there this time of day."

After I relay the information to the guys, Mattie enthusiastically leads the way. We manage to make it to the secluded bathroom before the bell rings for class, so nobody stops us or asks where we're headed. I waste no time in situating myself in front of the mirror so I can get my makeup done as quickly as possible. While Mattie, Owen, and Ryan crowd around me, Spencer and Nolan stay closer to the door.

"So, you guys said you found something?" I ask, finally allowing Spencer's words to sink in. "Something about Ryan?"

"I'm excited to hear this too!" Ryan beams, floating so it looks like he's sitting over the sink beside me. "I didn't get to hear any theories about *me* before you got here. Nope, they were all too busy worrying and arguing about you."

"We think so," Spencer answers me, still hovering near the door so he can keep watch in case a teacher or student comes by for any reason. "In some of the yearbooks, we found—"

"I'm the one who found it!" Mattie yells, scowling at Spencer. "Fuck you. You're trying to take credit when you wouldn't have found shit without my help."

Glancing at both guys through the mirror, I frown. I don't want them to fight about something they're only doing because I asked. "Hey, I seriously appreciate you guys helping at all. No matter what you found or who found it. I've been hopeless at finding anything by myself."

Mattie deflates like he's embarrassed by his outburst, refusing to meet my eyes. Spencer smirks at him and gives me a soft smile before continuing. "Sorry. *Mattie* discovered that in a few of the yearbooks, there was a student who was on the baseball team in their junior year but who wasn't photographed in any team or class photos for their freshman, sophomore, or junior year. Every year, his name was only listed as 'not pictured.' It's a weird fucking coincidence, but we're pretty positive it was Ryan."

I pull my eyebrow pencil away from my face and pause, watching Spencer for a few seconds to see if he'll say anything else. A quick glance at Ryan proves my ghost best friend is hanging on Spencer's every word. My chest tightens. Goddess, I really hope the guys are right about having found something. It'll kill me if we've gotten Ryan's hopes up for no reason.

"If Ryan is even real," Nolan mumbles, just loud enough to be heard by everyone.

That seems to snap Ryan out of his serious mood. He shakes his head and snorts, turning to grin at me in amusement. "Wow. The leader of the ghost hunting club is the only one of these guys who doesn't believe in ghosts? Didn't see that one coming."

"He believes in ghosts. He just doesn't believe in me." I roll my eyes, trying to hide my stupid hurt feelings. And it is stupid to feel hurt because most people who aren't witches would never believe I can see ghosts either. Normal people would think I'm crazy too, just like Nolan does. I seriously shouldn't hold it against him, but I guess I've gotten used to feeling safe around these guys. Like, comfortable enough to be myself without worrying about being shunned, laughed at, or judged.

Owen reaches out to stroke my hair, almost like he's doing

it absentmindedly, while he looks over at Nolan. "Why don't you believe her?"

Nolan's cheeks flush bright, cherry red as he hesitantly steps closer to us at the sink. "It's nothing personal, Harriet. It's just—the statistical probability of you being able to see ghosts is astronomically low, and the coincidence of you moving here and making friends with us make those odds even more unlikely. I'm not saying you're lying. I'm sure you truly believe you *can* see ghosts."

There it is. He's telling me to my face he thinks I'm nuts without actually saying it. I almost roll my eyes again, but instead I sigh and go back to finishing my eyebrows in the mirror. "Alright. So, how can I prove it to you? You make up a test for me or something?"

"Uh..." he mutters, nervously adjusting his glasses. "I guess we could do a test? But you don't have to."

Luckily, it seems the rest of the guys all feel a mixture of annoyance and amusement when it comes to Nolan not believing me. They enthusiastically come up with the idea that Nolan should stand at the other end of the bathroom away from the rest of us where he can write down words in a notebook for me to read out with Ryan's help.

It's laughably easy. While I focus on finishing my makeup, I repeat the words Ryan rattles off for me. "Botany. Necrophobia. Telepathy. Extrasensory Perception. Haunted House. Clairvoyance. Alchemy." After a handful of these words, I giggle and stare at Nolan through the mirror. "Kinda have a one-track mind over there, don't you?"

He frowns at me and shrugs, shutting his notebook. "I can't think of anything else. I don't get how you're doing this, but—"

"Seriously?" Mattie groans, cutting him off. "How do you

still not believe her? How else would she fucking know what you're writing?"

Without missing a beat, Owen sets his backpack on the sink counter and pulls out his polaroid camera. "How about you tell us how Ryan is posing, and I'll take a picture to prove it?"

Ryan loves that idea. He immediately floats to look like he's lying on his back across the sink counter with his arms above his head like Kate Winslet in Titanic. In a high-pitched, 'girly' voice, he croons, "Paint me like one of your French girls."

I shake my head and tell the rest of the guys what Ryan's doing and make sure I'm standing in the frame when Owen snaps the photo. Everybody huddles around the photograph while we wait for it to develop. Even though most of them—minus Nolan—are expecting the photo to depict exactly what I described, they all completely flip out when they see the image.

"Dude, that's so fucking awesome." Mattie bounces on the balls of his feet excitedly. "Has he seriously been chilling with us this whole time? Like, every day?"

"Pretty much, I think." I shrug. "He's been with me constantly since my first day, but he says you guys were some of his favorite people to follow around even before I got here. Probably because of your fascination with ghosts."

Nolan gapes back and forth between the photo and where Ryan is still sprawled across the sinks. Fluttering his eyelashes, Ryan smirks and says, "Tell him to stop staring at my dick like that, or else I'm going to think he's flirting."

A laugh bursts out of me, and I smile crookedly at Nolan. "Ryan says you're staring at his dick, which apparently means you're flirting with him."

Everyone laughs, except for Nolan. His face reddens again as he sputters and lowers his eyes to the ground. Maybe it's mean to tease him, but he *did* pretty much call me crazy to my face. I finish putting on my lip gloss, the final touch to my look, and close my makeup bag to put it away in my backpack. I feel a million times better now that I look more like myself. My hair is mostly dry now too. So, with a giddy smile, I turn and hop up to sit on the sink so I can enjoy skipping the rest of first period with my guys.

The guys, I mean. Not my guys.

"So, have you decided you believe me yet?" I ask Nolan.

He gives me a grimacing smile and rubs the back of his neck. "Uh, yeah. I do. Don't really see how I could doubt you now, honestly. I'm really sorry about before."

"It's okay. I get it." And I really do. Hopefully now that we're over this weird bump, Nolan and I can become actual friends like I've become with the others.

A curious expression comes over his face. "How long have you been able to communicate with ghosts? Do you remember your first experience with the paranormal? Or how about your most memorable experience?"

Before I can think of a good enough response without lying about growing up as a witch, Mattie cuts in with a glare at his cousin. "No, dude. You don't get to be an ass about Harriet seeing ghosts and then turn around and ask her all these nosy questions. I've been waiting for hours to tell her about Ryan!"

"Yes, please. Let's get back to talking about me." Ryan floats over to sit beside me, swinging his legs back and forth with an eager expression on his face.

"What did you find?" I ask Mattie, making it clear I'm happy with the subject change. I'm anxious to hear if he really found something concrete. Something we can use to help us discover who Ryan was and how and why he died. "You said something about his picture not being in the yearbooks, but his name was? How did we not catch that before?"

"Because," Mattie says, a feral grin spreading across his face. "The name wasn't Ryan. I have a theory that Ryan's just his middle name, and that his full name is George Ryan Nichols."

Any other time, I'd probably laugh or roll my eyes. But Ryan's reaction tells me everything we need to know. His eyes practically bulge out of his ghosty skull, and he makes this awful gasping sound like he's taking a breath after holding it for a very long time. He moves so fast, he's no more than a blur to me.

"That's me," Ryan rasps, standing in front of me with a wild look in his eyes. When he places his hands on my shoulders, my eyes widen in alarm and a quiet gasp escapes me. Because I can actually feel him. Not just a wispy, cold feeling either. Like, I can physically feel him touching me as though he were no different from Owen, Spencer, or anyone else alive. He doesn't seem to notice my shock, shaking me gently as he continues, "Holy fuck. Harriet! How did I forget my fucking name? George Ryan Nichols."

Placing my hand on his arm, which still feels eerily solid and barely cold at all, I try to smile to hide how much I'm internally freaking out. "Maybe because George is a stupid name?"

"It is!" He laughs gleefully. "It's a really stupid fucking name. The only people who call me George are my mom when she's pissed at me, or my older sister when she's being an asshole. Shit. I think I remember my mom and sister."

"Was I right?" Mattie asks.

With the way Ryan reacted, I nearly forgot we had an audience. But now that the guys know I'm talking to a ghost— and that I'm not crazy—it's freeing to be able to nod and be honest about my conversation. I also notice that Mattie's holding his phone up like he's recording us, and it looks like

Owen may have taken a couple of photos while Ryan was freaking out too.

"Yeah." I laugh breathlessly. "His real name is George, and I think revealing that is helping him remember some other stuff."

Spencer wastes no time in pulling a notebook and pen from his backpack. With an excited and determined look on his face, he focuses his gaze in Ryan's direction. "Go ahead and tell us everything new that you remember."

CHAPTER 21
HARRIET

"This looks good, right?"

Old Creepy twists her hands in her long, ratty skirt and hums a dreary tune. I wait for one of her spooky nursery rhymes, but she only gives me a strained smile and floats away while humming softly to herself.

I roll my eyes and huff. It's not like she can tell me outright, but I'm pretty sure Old Creepy disapproves of my sleepover with the guys. It's not that she doesn't like them. She always seems happy whenever any of them are over, and she's taken a special liking to Mattie since he started coming over to hang out this week. It's only the sleeping over part she's not a fan of. She's obviously ancient, so I should have known she'd be old-fashioned too. Putting my hands on my hips, I raise an eyebrow at Circe.

"Well? What do you think?"

Circe blinks slowly up at me from her spot on the sofa I shoved against the wall to make space for the sleepover. My mom let me set up a ton of blankets and pillows on the floor of the upstairs sitting room. I even gave in and asked her to use a spell to make the floor and blankets a million times softer and more comfortable. So, the guys should be super cozy up here. I still have to sleep in my own room because of my mom's rules, but I totally plan on sitting out here with them to watch movies and hang out.

After giving the blanketed area a cursory glance, Circe yawns and goes back to licking her paws. I might love the little demon slut cat, but she's still a huge asshole any chance she gets.

"Harriet!" my mom calls, using one of her spells to make her voice carry through the house. "Come downstairs, please."

I rub my hands over my torn jeans and sigh. I've been waiting for her to jump down my throat for the past hour to finish our conversation from this morning. She picked me up from school, seemingly in a good mood, but hasn't brought it up yet. She's probably planning to do it now.

The guys will be over soon, so I don't have much time to deal with her. They headed home first to grab their stuff for the sleepover and for another paranormal investigation. They're extra excited now that they know about my gift and the fact that Old Creepy will more than likely cooperate. I'm not sure what they have planned exactly yet, but I'm looking forward to finding out.

When I make it to the kitchen to find my mom, I raise my eyebrows at the sight of all the food set out on the counters. There are bowls filled with popcorn and pretty much all the best types of Halloween candy, five large homemade pizzas with different toppings, fresh caramel apples, and what have to be a million cookies and cupcakes all sporting cute Halloween decorations.

"What's all this?" I ask, gaping.

My mom laughs, stepping away from the oven holding another sheet of cookies with her favorite oven mitts. She's wearing her favorite apron too, which means she's in an even better mood than I realized.

"This is for you and your friends, silly."

"All of it?" I ask incredulously. It's so much food. I know they're teenage guys, but can they really eat this much? You'd think my mom was making enough food to feed an army at this rate.

After setting the cookie sheet down to cool, my mom props her oven-mitted hands on her hips and frowns at me. "Yes, Harriet. I wanted to make sure you and your friends had everything you could possibly want or need. I wanted to prove that I'm very proud of you and happy that you've made friends with these boys. If what you said this morning is true about them making you feel accepted, then they're even more special than I realized."

My cheeks warm up. I didn't mean to sound ungrateful. It's really sweet and thoughtful for her to go to so much effort for my friends.

"Thanks," I mumble. Maybe I should finally take Mattie's advice and stop holding a grudge against her.

Pulling off her oven mitts and setting them on the counter, she nods distractedly down at her iWatch. "Of course, dear." Looking back up at me, her smile tightens. "I'm leaving in a few minutes to meet Kamal for dinner and drinks, and I might stay over at his place depending on how the night goes. Do you mind? I didn't want you to feel like I was intruding on your privacy tonight."

"Oh." I blink, trying not to sound as wounded as I feel. It's completely stupid of me, really. It's not like I want my mom hovering or saying embarrassing shit about me to the guys. But I also didn't expect to have the house to myself with them tonight either. I should have known better. My mom's always like this when she meets a new guy, at least until she gets tired of him.

"Flora left for New York this morning too," my mom reminds me. "She'll be back Sunday evening though."

Unlike my mom, who quit her job and sold nearly everything we owned as soon as she received her mysterious letter from my great-grandmother about the Abbot House curse lifting, my aunt Flora decided to keep her job and apartment in New York. As a freelance graphic designer, she almost exclusively works from home, but she still has plenty of friends in the city she wants to visit every now and then.

So, I'll really, *really* be alone with the guys tonight. Goddess. My cheeks feel so hot that I'd swear I'm about to burst into flames just thinking about it. It's not like anything is going to happen. Even if Owen and Spencer flirt with me, Mattie and Nolan will be here to distract me. And Old Creepy will totally be the fussiest, sternest chaperone ever once she finds out there's no adult supervision here tonight.

When I don't answer my mom, she finishes plating and decorating the rest of the cookies with a few spells to speed the process along. I've always loved watching my mom bake. Something about it settles me. Even though I'm terrible at it, it's the only time I can remember not feeling annoyed by her overuse of magic. She's spectacularly talented at it too, and I know the bakery and tea shop will be a hit once she and Flora get it up and running in a few months.

"Alright, all done." My mom claps her hands together and looks around at her work with a pleased expression. "I used a spell to keep everything warm and fresh so you and your boys can eat throughout the night without having to reheat anything."

I thank her again, and she reminds me that I still need to drink her stupid birth control potion. She gets it ready for me while repeating her list of rules. There aren't many, other than my promise to drink the potion and to not let any of the guys sleep in my room with me. But a tiny, rebellious part of my brain wants to sneer and tell her it's not like anyone will be here to make sure I follow her rules. But I don't want her to make me cancel my plans, and I know I'm way too chicken to break the rules regardless of her or Flora being home.

It's not until she's finished cleaning up in the kitchen that I realize she never brought up our conversation from this morning.

RIGHT ON TIME, AND ALSO WAY TOO SOON, THE DOORBELL RINGS.

I rub my sweaty hands on my jeans and walk as slowly as possible to answer the door. Why am I nervous? It makes no sense. I've been looking forward to this all week, and it's not like I'm uncomfortable around the guys anymore. I hang out and talk to them every day. Still, these last-minute nerves are making me rethink this entire night. Why didn't I just suggest they come over to watch movies or do ghost hunting stuff without the sleeping over part? That would have been way more normal.

After quickly smoothing my hair down, I open the door to find all four of the guys standing together on the porch. Mattie grins and shoves Spencer aside to wrap me in a hug. I'm still not big on hugging, but I'm used to him enough by now that I just chuckle and roll my eyes as I hug him back.

"Hi," I say, sounding stupidly shy. Feeling myself blush, I push Mattie away and open the door wider. "Do you guys wanna take your stuff upstairs first? Or do you want to eat?

My mom made enough food and snacks to feed a fucking army."

"Fuck, that smells delicious." Mattie dumps his bags by the stairs and heads straight for the kitchen. Decision made, I guess.

The rest of the guys laugh and set their stuff near Mattie's. Nolan follows after his cousin, but Owen and Spencer hang back with me. Spencer gives me a lopsided, flirty smile and holds his arms out. "Well? Mattie got a hug, so I get one too, right?"

I playfully roll my eyes, ignoring the fact that I'm definitely blushing, and step forward so Spencer can pull me into a hug. Only, this hug is way different than the friendly one I shared with Mattie. Being the same height, Spencer rests his cheek against mine and wraps his arms around me tight enough that our bodies are pressed flush together. He feels good, and he smells even better. Goddess, this crush is going to consume me.

My eyes meet Owen's, and the butterflies stirring in my chest multiply by about a million. He doesn't look jealous as he smiles down at me. He never does. But when Spencer finally pulls away from our hug, Owen pulls me into his arms instead. He's much bigger and taller than Spencer, and I feel strangely small and fragile in his arms. It's not something I'm used to feeling around guys. Or, well...anyone. And Goddess, I think I love it.

"Okay." I practically jump away from him, giggling nervously. Avoiding eye contact with Owen and Spencer, I point toward the kitchen. "I hope you guys are hungry."

In the kitchen, we find Mattie shoveling a slice of pizza into his mouth while Nolan stands beside him with an anxious expression. Looking up at me while he fusses with his glasses, Nolan asks, "Are we really allowed to eat all this stuff? I said we should wait for you, but Mattie started stuffing his face as soon as we walked in."

"It's fine." I laugh. "My mom made all this stuff for you guys."

And that's when I learn that four teenage guys apparently can eat enough to feed an army. I manage to grab some pizza for myself, thankfully, but they devour the rest of it in the time it takes me to eat two slices. They move onto the cupcakes after that, though slower than they ate the pizza.

"Where is your mom, anyway?" Nolan asks after swallowing a bite of his cupcake. Watching him eat so much more than I normally see him eat during lunch at school worries me. My feelings must be evident on my face because Nolan gives me a small, timid smile. "Don't worry. I checked my blood sugar and took the insulin I needed before you came into the kitchen. I'm fine, Harriet."

"Okay." I nod, feeling only slightly better. But he knows his disease better than I do, right? I want to ask him if he's sure he's alright, or even suggest he let me know if he feels sick at any point tonight. Instead, I drop it and clear my throat, answering his original question. "She's upstairs, getting dressed. She has a date with Principal Di Rossi, so she'll probably be leaving soon."

Nolan's eyes widen, and Spencer chokes on his food before grinning wildly. "Whoa, the principal? Really?"

It's not like I can tell him that Di Rossi's a witch. Not while Nolan and Mattie are standing here. It never occurred to me that Spencer might not know which of the faculty at school are witches. I wonder if Owen knows because of his stepmom? But he looks just as surprised as the other guys. Giving them a look, I nod. "Yeah. He and my mom have a lot in common. Apparently, they were friends when they were kids."

Owen seems to understand my silent implication before

Spencer does. He looks almost startled when he mumbles, "I had no idea."

"Why would you?" Mattie frowns at him obliviously. My energetic friend turns to me, holding a cupcake in one hand and a stack of cookies in the other. "Are we allowed to take any food upstairs?"

My mom never said we couldn't, so I tell him and the others they can as long as they're careful not to make a mess. The guys somehow manage to carry a bunch of snacks along with their bags upstairs while I lead the way. My mom walks out of her bedroom as soon as we reach the landing, and she gives me and the guys an amused smile. She looks amazing, as always, wearing a velvet dark green dress that enhances her curves and sultry red lipstick. Her ebony hair is styled to perfection, and I spend a few seconds staring at it enviously.

"You look great, mom." I try to give her a real smile.

"Thank you, darling." She adjusts her clutch under her arm and reaches out to stroke my hair. "Do you need anything before I leave?"

I shake my head, glancing sideways at the guys. Mattie's met my mom a bunch of times now, and Owen's waved at her a few times after dropping me off after school. The two of them smile at my mom like they're completely comfortable, but Spencer and Nolan seem slightly anxious. I nearly hold my breath, waiting for my mom to embarrass me or insinuate I'm romantically interested in all four of them.

Thankfully, she doesn't say anything. But the anticipatory dread I feel at the possibility makes me determined to never, ever tell her about my crush on Owen and Spencer. Even if I tell her everything else I've been keeping a secret, the only person who will ever get me to admit *that* is Sage.

"Nope, we're all good." Giving my friends a teasing smirk, I add. "I guess you called it about the amount of food. They already devoured the pizza."

My mom cackles. "I'm glad you boys enjoyed it."

"It was freaking awesome, Ms. Abbot. Best pizza I've ever had." Mattie gives her a charming grin and pats his stomach. "I can't wait for you to open your bakery. I'll probably be one of your best customers."

Flattery always goes a long way with my mom, so I'm not surprised when she preens and thanks him. She leaves us, reminding me to behave and follow her rules before she bids us goodbye. Part of me is glad to see her go so I can relax with the guys, but I still feel a twinge of hurt at her ability to leave me to my own devices so easily.

"This is where you guys will sleep," I say, leading the guys into the large sitting room where the cushy blankets are set up for the sleepover. Unlike the first time they came over to do their preliminary paranormal investigation, there's a huge TV set up for us to watch scary movies. I point out the main bathroom on this level and suggest, "We can get into our jammies now if you want, and then we can either do ghost hunting stuff or just chill."

Nolan groans and rubs his hand over his face. "Jammies? Seriously?"

The other guys snicker, which makes me blush. But surprisingly, I don't feel embarrassed. I put my hands on my hips and glare at Nolan, raising an eyebrow. "Yes, seriously. You agreed to this sleepover, didn't you? You're lucky I'm not planning on forcing you guys to do facials and manicures like I would with my bestie, Sage."

"Alright." Nolan raises his hands defensively.

"We can get in our jammies," Spencer says teasingly, his eyes full of mirth.

I stick my tongue out at him and turn to head into my room. "I'll be right back."

They can tease me all they want, but what's wrong with wanting to get comfy? Especially if we're gonna spend most of the night sitting around. I pick through my dresser, grumbling to myself that I don't need to wear anything special or try to look cute for the guys. Because they're my *friends*. Just friends. And I'm determined to keep it that way with all four of them. Not that Mattie or Nolan are interested in me like that, but they're still two of the cutest guys I've ever met. I've got to remind myself to treat them completely normal and act like I would around Sage or even Ryan.

In the end, I decide to wear a pair of sleep shorts with cute little Saint Bernard puppies all over them and an oversized, teal Olympic State Park hoodie. I throw on a pair of fuzzy pink and white striped socks just in case my feet get cold.

When I walk back into the sitting room where I left the guys, I find Owen, Spencer, and Mattie sitting on the blankets laughing about something. I'm pleased to see that they've all changed out of their jeans into either sweatpants or basketball shorts, and I can only assume Nolan's still changing in the bathroom.

Mattie looks up at me just as he brings a large handful of popcorn to his mouth, and he immediately starts coughing and choking as he stares at me with wide eyes.

"Goddess, chew your food!" I frown at him, crossing my arms. When neither Spencer or Owen say anything, I glance over to find them gaping at me like I've grown an extra head. I triple checked my appearance in the mirror before I left my bedroom, so I know I'm not flashing them or anything. "What's wrong with you guys?"

"I—" Mattie wheezes, still struggling to swallow his food. He shakes his head, his cheeks turning bright red as he grabs one of the pillows beside him and places it over his lap. "What are you *wearing?*"

"Um, pajamas?" I ask sarcastically, moving to sit on the floor with them. I am not going to admit I'm embarrassed or change back into my regular clothes, no matter how weird they're making me feel. Still feeling Owen and Spencer's eyes on me, I turn to glare at them.

Owen bites down on his bottom lip, which does nothing to hide the stupid smile he's fighting. Spencer chuckles, sounding more nervous than amused as he rubs his hand over his longish, messy black hair.

"Well, first of all, I'm pretty sure none of us has ever seen you wear anything that's not black, white, gray, or hunter green." Spencer clears his throat, his eyes falling onto my long, pale legs. "Second of all, I knew you were hot, but I was really not expecting to be this turned on just by seeing your fucking legs. I'm assuming Mattie feels the same since he's using a pillow to try to hide his boner."

"Shut the fuck up," Mattie hisses, making it obvious that Spencer has the right idea about him.

Heat flares across my cheeks, my gaze flitting between the three guys. Are they for real? They're freaking out about me showing my legs like they've never seen a girl wearing shorts or a skirt before? I'm embarrassed, flattered, and extremely amused. It doesn't take long before I end up giggling uncontrollably.

"You guys are so fucking dumb!" I exclaim between bouts of laughter.

Spencer laughs quietly, and Owen smiles bashfully as he shrugs. Letting his eyes travel back down to my legs, Owen's smile widens. "There are puppies on your shorts."

"Yeah. And look at her cute little socks," Spencer says with a chuckle. He reaches out to touch my left foot, his fingers

251

slowly inching up until he softly caresses my ankle. For something so simple and innocent, it feels incredibly sensual. I have the strongest urge to stretch my leg out so he's forced to move his fingers higher up on my leg. With a heated expression, Spencer smirks at me and teases, "What did I say? I knew you were secretly a big marshmallow deep down."

I roll my eyes at him and smile. They don't realize that I'd dress way differently if I could. That I love pretty, girly clothes, but that they never fit me properly. Thankfully, Nolan puts a halt to our ridiculous conversation when he comes out of the bathroom and joins us on the floor. He's wearing a plain black tee shirt and a pair of dark green plaid pajama pants. I almost say something sarcastic about him coming prepared for the sleepover despite his bitching and groaning, but I decide to keep my mouth shut when he gives my shorts and socks a cursory glance without commenting on them.

"Did the guys tell you what we were thinking as far as our investigation tonight?" Nolan asks, making himself comfortable.

I shake my head, looking around for Old Creepy. She's floating in the corner, silently keeping an eye on us. When she catches me looking at her, she offers me a kind smile. "No, but I'm up for whatever. I assume you want to take more pictures of Old Creepy?"

"I brought a few different cameras," Owen says.

Nolan nods, giving his friend a quick glance before focusing on me once more. "Definitely, yeah. More pictures would be awesome. But I was also hoping we could interview her? Mattie can record it like we did with Ryan today. His voice sounds surprisingly clear when you play back the recording Mattie took with him. I only listened to a few seconds, so I wanted us to listen to it together and see if there were any extra details to pick up on that you might have missed."

252

"Really? That's fucking awesome. I'd love to listen to that with you guys, especially if you think we can learn anything else." I grin enthusiastically. It's one thing for the guys to see a picture of a ghost and to take my word for it when translating, but the thought of them being able to hear Ryan as clearly as I did is so exciting. Tilting my head thoughtfully in my ghost roommate's direction, I add, "I'm not sure how we can interview Old Creepy though. She doesn't talk. Like, she listens, and she makes it clear she can understand me. But she always answers back in nursery rhymes."

"I have an idea of how to work around that," Nolan says with a shy smile, lifting his hand to adjust his glasses. "But if not, we can still try to work with the nursery rhymes. Figure out the context and what she's actually trying to say with them."

"Okay." My smile gets bigger with every word out of his mouth. Talking to Old Creepy would be amazing. I don't want to get my hopes up in case Nolan's idea doesn't work, but it's awesome he's already thought of something. With these guys around and with their knowledge of ghosts, I'm going to learn so much. I'm determined to turn my gift into something useful.

"You know we're in," Spencer says, gesturing between him and the other two guys. "Let's listen to Ryan's recording first. You have it on your phone, Mattie?"

Mattie jumps at the sound of his name, blinking at Spencer in surprise. "Huh?"

Was he seriously not paying attention? I furrow my eyebrows and ask, "Do you have your phone so we can listen to the recording you took when we were talking to Ryan?"

"Oh, right." He chuckles awkwardly. He reaches over to grab his backpack, careful to keep the stupid pillow over his lap. I almost roll my eyes because I still think his reaction to seeing me in shorts is weird and ridiculous. Our fingers brush when he clumsily hands me his phone, and his forest green eyes bore into mine. "Um, Harriet?"

My eyebrows furrow at the nervous tone in his voice. "Yeah? What's wrong?" Goddess, if he brings up the fact that he has a boner, I'm going to die of embarrassment.

The other guys stare at him curiously, and Mattie lets out another nervous laugh while he runs a hand through his curly hair. Taking a deep breath, he blurts out, "Would you ever go out with a guy who's shorter than you?"

"Oh, Jesus." Nolan groans quietly, pinching the bridge of his nose.

I clear my throat, feeling my cheeks flush. Why the hell would he ask me that? It's so fucking random and humiliating. It's not like *he's* even interested in me, which he continues to make clear almost every day when he gushes about how hot Amethyst is. Granted, yesterday and today, he insisted on walking a different route through the halls, and we never ended up passing her. But still, I'm not going to forget about it or assume he's suddenly decided he likes me instead of her just because he reacted like an idiot when he saw me in a pair of shorts.

Feeling irritated and flustered, especially after realizing Owen and Spencer are staring at me like they're just as keen to hear the answer to Mattie's stupid question, I shrug defensively. "I guess? Maybe? Most guys are shorter than me, and it's not like that's going to change."

"Okay. Cool, cool." Mattie rubs his hands over his knees, a dopey, lopsided smile forming on his face.

Spencer snorts and mumbles under his breath. "You're a dumbass."

Before Mattie can respond to him or ask any other random,

personal questions, Nolan sighs and takes the phone out of my hands. "Can we get back to this?"

Everyone agrees, thankfully. Nolan spends a few seconds clicking around on Mattie's phone, and he sets it down in the middle of the blankets as he presses play. All of us move closer and lean over the phone so we can see the screen. You can't see Ryan though, which is disappointing but not surprising. The only thing you can see on screen is me, which is slightly cringey. While I know I was looking at Ryan, on screen it seems like I'm staring off into space. No wonder Nolan and Mattie originally suspected I was nuts.

For several minutes, we listen to the conversation we had with Ryan this morning at school. Nolan and Spencer took turns asking questions while we hung around in the bathroom to interview Ryan, and Spencer scribbled everything down in his notebook. While Mattie and Owen were mostly quiet at the time, spending the time either recording or taking photos, it's easy to see their excitement now as they listen to the recording.

"Do you remember where you lived?" Nolan asks on screen.

Ryan hums before answering the question. *"Shit. Umm…it was a yellow house with blue shutters? And there was a garden out front. Yeah! One time, I snuck out of the house through a front window, and when I got caught, my mom was more pissed about me ruining her flowers than the fact that I snuck out to go to a party."*

Ryan sounds wistful and happy, and the memory of his facial expressions every time he remembered something new makes my heart ache. Even though I remember the conversation perfectly well, my throat feels thick while I listen to it all over again. Goddess, I hope we can find a way to help him after all this. At the very least, I'm glad the guys can hear his voice now too, so they can hear for themselves how grateful my ghost friend is. Now they can hear for themselves that they're seriously making a difference.

In the video, I repeat the information for the guys and stand up to stretch after sitting on the counter for too long. Nolan asks a follow-up question about Ryan's mom that Ryan seems to struggle with. We can hear him humming thoughtfully, but I vividly remember the way he fidgeted and tried not to show how frustrated he was when he couldn't remember.

"Hey, Harriet." Ryan's voice becomes overly cheerful, and I picture that stupid smirk on his face as I listen to the next words out of his mouth. *"Did you know Spencer's staring at your ass right now? He's not even trying to hide it. Please tell me you plan on screwing him sometime soon. Better yet, you could have a threesome with him and Owen!"*

Spencer coughs loudly, looking up at me with a stricken expression like he's been caught with his hand in the cookie jar. I try to ignore him, grimacing as I keep my eyes on the phone screen. In the video, my lips purse as I sigh heavily. I look more pissed than embarrassed, which isn't exactly how I felt at the time. Through gritted teeth on screen, I tell the guys, *"He doesn't remember. Next question."*

"Come on!" Ryan snickers. He loves getting me riled up. *"He's still staring. He can't help himself. If you don't hook up with one of those guys, I'm going to die. Again! And then how will you feel? Please just let me live vicariously through you. You're supposed to be my best friend."*

Owen reaches out and pauses the video. When I risk a glance at him, his eyes are blazing with amusement and he looks like he's seconds away from laughing. "Does this, um, happen often with Ryan?"

Judging by the guys' expressions, it's pretty clear none of them are going to let this go or pretend like they didn't hear anything. I try to shrug nonchalantly, avoiding eye contact with all of them. "Well, yeah. But I'm pretty sure he only did it during the interview so he didn't have to admit to not being able to remember things."

"He called you his best friend," Nolan says thoughtfully.

"That's what you're focusing on!?" Mattie exclaims. He runs his fingers through his hair and stares down at his phone in horror. "He told Harriet to have a threesome with Owen and Spencer. Why the fuck would he suggest something like that?"

His tone makes me feel tense and prickly, and I can't help but give him an annoyed look. "What, are you seriously going to slut shame me for something that literally came out of somebody's mouth? I told you, he's obnoxious. And even though he's been dead for a long time, he's still a horny teenage guy. He's constantly saying dumb shit like that to me about all of you, ever since my first day. I've learned to ignore him for the most part."

Owen finally breaks and laughs. He scoots a little closer to me, brushing his fingers against my knee as he stares down at me with a bemused smile. "He told you what I wrote in your notebook on your first day, didn't he?"

I give him a tiny smile and shrug, which is answer enough. He laughs again. While this whole conversation is sort of humiliating, I'm glad he's not making it weird or freaking out like Mattie is. I glance nervously at Spencer to gauge his reaction. While his cheeks are slightly pink, the smile he gives me is genuine.

"Do you guys want to keep listening?" Nolan asks. He looks thoughtful and excited, and not at all like he's fazed by Ryan's drama. With a smile aimed in my direction, he says, "This is great news though. I didn't realize how close you were, but if Ryan considers you his best friend, that means he's more likely to be honest and cooperative."

"You thought he was going to lie?" I ask, blinking in confusion. Nolan grimaces and shrugs, a blush spreading across his face. My frown deepens. "Or did you still think I was making everything up about him?"

He raises his hands defensively and shakes his head. "That's not what I said. But, well...we had to consider those possibilities if we were going to investigate this issue."

My heart sinks. I guess I understand where he's coming from, but it still sucks to be constantly doubted. Especially after I trusted Nolan enough to open up about my gift and to ask for his help.

"Dude." Spencer shakes his head and sighs like he's disappointed. Owen and Mattie throw Nolan disapproving looks too, which sort of makes me feel better. The three of them have never questioned me. They believed me right away about my gift and about Ryan.

Their support gives me the encouragement I need to straighten and settle my gaze on Nolan. "I haven't lied to any of you about anything, and I've never once felt like Ryan's lying to me either. And yeah, we are close. I mean, as close as you can be to someone who's dead and invisible to everyone but me and who I've only known for a few weeks. But Goddess, I want to help him. I've never wanted to help a ghost before like I want to help Ryan. And honestly, I'm not sure I can do that without you guys."

"Of course we'll help," Owen murmurs. He places his hand over my knee, soft and hesitant at first. His touch makes my skin tingle all over, and I feel dizzy at the onslaught of butterflies writhing in my stomach. When I blink dazedly at Owen, he gives me one of his brilliant and disarming smiles. "And you know I always believed you. Right?"

An embarrassing giggle escapes me, but I find myself nodding all the same.

258

Mattie makes a disgruntled sound, reaching forward to snatch up his phone. I guess that means we're done listening to the recording. His expression suddenly changes, and he looks up at me with this wild, manic grin. "We can finish listening to that later. But I also brought the yearbooks from when Ryan was in school. I figured we could go through them to see which faculty members still work at the school. But if you don't wanna do that right now, we can always interview Old Creepy instead. If you're not up for any ghost hunting shit, then let's just watch horror movies and chill. I call dibs on sitting next to you though so we can snuggle."

By the time he finishes speaking, he seems mostly back to normal, with a flirtatious smirk on his face as he smoothly runs a hand through his hair. After the way I reacted to Owen touching my freaking knee of all places, there's no way in hell I'll be snuggling with any of these guys. Ever. But I am glad to see that Mattie's dropped his weird attitude, so I playfully roll my eyes at him.

"All of the above sound great, so we can seriously do whatever you guys want." Before I can stop myself, I smile and say the cheesiest thing I've probably ever said in my life. "I'm just happy you guys are here."

CHAPTER 22
HARRIET

"Here it is!" I spin around, holding up the spirit board triumphantly.

Spencer closes the trunk he was searching through and turns to grin at me excitedly. "Awesome. I really hope Nolan's idea works."

So do I. After the guys agreed we should take a break from the Ryan mystery and try to interview Old Creepy instead, Nolan told us his plan to try to communicate with her with regular words and sentences instead of only through nursery rhymes. He mentioned seeing an old, dusty spirit board the last time he was here when the guys did their first preliminary paranormal investigation. Our hope is that she'll be able to talk to us through it instead of worrying about trying to physically talk.

Tracking the board down has been a slight pain, however. Since my mom and Flora have been doing almost nothing but cleaning and organizing the house over the past few weeks, it was nearly impossible to find. While the rest of the guys have been searching in the spare rooms on the second floor, Spencer and I have been looking for the spirit board in the attic. Pretty much everything up here is still dusty, including the things my mom and aunt have shoved up here in their efforts to clear out the rest of the house.

Spencer crosses the room to me and brushes some of the dust off the board. It's definitely super old, made of some kind of wood and painted black with white and gold lettering. A few of the letters and paint around the edges are faded, but not so much that it's unreadable. The paint on the small, wooden planchette is even more chipped and faded.

For the first time since I've known him, Spencer looks doubtful. Before I can ask him what's wrong, he meets my eyes and asks, "We're not overstepping, are we? Does Old Creepy want to talk to us? I never thought to ask her opinion before deciding we should do this."

Old Creepy stayed downstairs when I came up to the attic with Spencer, but she smiled at me and made sure I knew she was still sticking around. Just like always. It's not like she didn't hear us talking about her either, as she's been hovering nearby since the guys got here.

"I can ask her before we start, just to make things clear. But I'm sure she would have let me know if she was uncomfortable or didn't want to talk to us. She likes you guys." I tilt my head and grin wryly. "Well, she doesn't like that you're sleeping over. She's chaperoning us, making sure nothing inappropriate happens."

He barks out a laugh. "Well, I can't really blame her." Glancing down at the spirit board, he sighs softly. "I think I'm just feeling like a bit of an asshole. For years, the guys and I have been chasing ghosts, and I've never once thought of them as real people. Even after everything you told me and Owen about Ryan, I still never expected him to seem so alive. And fuck, Harriet, I feel terrible that he caught me, uh, staring at you like that."

I giggle and focus my gaze on Spencer's hands while he fidgets with the planchette. I'm worried if I meet his eyes, I'll admit something embarrassing or say something I'll regret. "You're not an asshole, and you shouldn't feel bad. Ryan was only trying to tease me."

Spencer lifts his hand and brushes his fingers over my jaw, tucking a strand of my hair behind my ear. My breath stutters, and I glance up to meet his warm chocolate brown eyes before I can stop myself. His lips curve into a tender, crooked smile.

"Now that I know he's keeping an eye on us for you, I'll have to be smoother about checking you out and flirting with you."

Oh, Goddess. It was one thing when he was flirting with me before, when I was able to fake ignorance to it. Now he's not only admitting to it, he's making it clear he's going to keep it up. I feel dizzy from the way my heart keeps flipping around in my chest, and I'm suddenly all too aware that we're only standing a handful of inches apart. It would take nothing for him to step forward and press his lips to mine.

A shrill, choking laugh escapes me, and I quickly avert my eyes and take a step back as I hug the spirit board to my chest. "Um. You know I'm really terrible at this, right?"

I want to cringe as soon as the words are out of my mouth. First, because I shouldn't respond when he talks about flirting with me. I don't want there to be any drama between him and Owen, and I don't like either one of them more than the other. But even the part of me that wants nothing more than to give in to this all-consuming crush recoils at the fact that I just admitted how absolutely fucking inexperienced I am. What guy wants to hear that from a girl he's interested in?

He chuckles, his sweet smile transforming into a teasing smirk. "Maybe that's one of the reasons I like you so much."

That's it. I'm going to combust from a mixture of embarrassment, shock, and giddiness. Or I might just pass out. What am I supposed to say to that? This was so much easier when he was tiptoeing around this thing between us—I could ignore it then and pretend to be ignorant. But what the hell am I supposed to say to him now!?

Before I explode, faint, or blurt out that I like him too, Spencer turns and heads for the stairs. "Come on. The guys will be stoked we found the board."

Taking a deep breath, I rub my hands over my cheeks like that will make any blushing disappear, and I follow him downstairs. Spencer calls out to the rest of the guys that we found the spirit board, and they quickly rejoin us on the blanket pile in the sitting room. Old Creepy makes an appearance too, taking a seat on the couch near us where she hums softly to herself.

"So, how do we start?" Mattie asks, looking excitedly around the room. "Is Old Creepy in the room with us?"

"Yeah." I point my thumb over my shoulder in her direction. "She's been in here with us the whole time."

The guys perk up and turn to look where I'm pointing. Even though they can't see her, Old Creepy sits up and smiles fondly at them. Spencer meets my eyes, gently placing his hand on my knee. I feel my cheeks flame, but try my best to ignore it. Owen sits on my other side, and he glances down at Spencer's hand on my knee with a stupid, secretive smile. Goddess, how did I end up sitting between these two? I swear, they're going to kill me.

Remembering what Spencer said about feeling badly for not asking Old Creepy's permission, I clear my throat and hold up the spirit board for her to see. "Do you want to try to talk to us using this? The guys have all kinds of questions they want to ask. You know they love ghosts."

She giggles and gives me one of her creepy, toothless smiles as she floats over to sit with us. When she hovers behind Spencer with a slightly disapproving look on her face, I gesture for him to scoot over. He hesitantly pulls his hand away and moves, leaving enough room for another person to sit. When it becomes clear to the others that Old Creepy is sitting in our circle, they jump up to get some of their equipment ready.

Mattie sets up a tripod with his phone to record us, and he has another, smaller recording device he tells me is strictly for the audio rather than a video. Owen grabs his fanciest camera —the one he told me he loves to use for developing film—and sets a polaroid and a couple of other backup cameras within reach. Nolan and Spencer both have notebooks and pens, and Nolan also has his EMF meter. He doesn't technically need it, but he tells me he wants to periodically check the readings on it throughout the interview to see if there are any changes at any point. To my amusement, he also pulls out a fancy-looking thermometer to keep track of the temperature in the room for the same reasons.

"Ready?" I ask Old Creepy.

She reaches out and brushes her fingers over my cheek. All I feel is a cold wisp of air, making me shiver slightly. When Nolan sees my reaction, he glances at his thermometer and quickly scribbles something in his notebook. Old Creepy hums solemnly, swaying back and forth slightly as she sings,

> *"I'll tell you a story*
> *About Jack a Nory,*
> *And now my story's begun;*
> *I'll tell you another*

Of Jack and his brother,

And now my story is done."

I smile and shake my head, taking that as a yes. Since the guys will most likely play back the audio recording of this later, I figure it's not worth me repeating the creepy old nursery rhyme. Turning my attention to the spirit board in the center of our circle, I contemplate what to do. I've never actually used one of these. Despite spirit or Ouija boards being popular with people into occult stuff, they're typically frowned upon in the witch community. Honestly, I'm surprised this one was in the house, and I'm curious to know which of my late relatives was daring enough to use it. Did someone else know about Old Creepy? Did they use this spirit board to try to talk to her?

Placing the tips of my index fingers gently against the little wooden planchette, I glance at Old Creepy and ask, "Can you touch this too?"

She leans forward and attempts to touch the planchette and the board, but her long, bony finger goes right through it. A morose, wistful sob escapes her. I give the guys a sad shrug and let them know she's not able to use the spirit board on her own, even with me touching it.

"How about she just points at the letters for her answers, and Harriet can tell us what she says?" Mattie suggests.

Before I can agree, as that seems like the simplest solution, Nolan grunts and shakes his head as he scribbles something in his notebook. "We can't simply take Harriet's word for everything, especially for something we can't prove scientifically. Old Creepy's voice might show up in our recordings, but we still won't be able to see her answering our questions non-verbally."

I wonder if this guy will ever believe me about anything, with or without any stupid proof. While Spencer, Owen, and

Mattie argue with him and give him dirty looks in my defense, I focus on Old Creepy and try to think of another plan that will satisfy Nolan.

"Um, I think I have an idea," I mumble, clearing my throat. Everyone goes quiet and stares at me expectantly. I wasn't sure if or when I was going to mention this. Truthfully, I'm still a bit freaked out about it. But the guys are the closest thing I have to experts for anything ghost-related. "You think the only reason Ryan or Old Creepy show up in photographs is because of me, right? I think maybe I can make ghosts stronger."

"What do you mean?" Owen asks.

"Normally, when a ghost touches me, it feels like a cold breeze. They can't *really* touch me, and I can't touch them. But then today, when we asked Ryan about his real name in the bathroom, he sort of grabbed my shoulders. I don't think he even noticed because he was so excited, but I *felt* him. Like, the same way I'd feel any of you guys. It freaked me out, but I didn't want to ruin his excitement or the chance to learn any new information. Also, a few days ago, I was looking for him at school. He was nowhere near me, but he said he somehow felt me calling for him. I have no idea how that's possible, but I've also never really had the opportunity to test or explore my power until now."

The guys exchange looks. Surprisingly, it's Nolan who shrugs and slowly nods his head. "I think it's reasonable to suspect you're somehow enhancing their presence. So, maybe if you touch her, Old Creepy might be able to touch the spirit board on her own?"

That was my idea. Nodding, I turn to smile nervously at Old Creepy. The thought of being able to feel her as though she's alive is both exciting and nerve racking. I'll feel a bit silly if it doesn't work after making a big deal about it, but I figure there's no harm in trying. Especially in a controlled area like this, in private and surrounded by people I trust.

Before I take Old Creepy's hand, I touch my adder stone necklace. I haven't taken it off once since Circe helped me find it under my floorboards. I know it's the only reason I haven't had any migraines, or worse, during the past few weeks while I've spent so much time around my ghost friends. Is it possible the necklace is helping my gift wake up even more, making it possible for me to physically touch ghosts or summon them?

Not wanting to take any chances, I wrap my fist around the stone and hold my other hand out for Old Creepy. Taking a deep breath, I concentrate on feeling her and helping her communicate clearly with us. She hums a quiet, eerie tune, and slowly places her hand over mine.

I feel her immediately, and I inhale a sharp gasp. Her skin is warm and soft, and she looks just as shocked as I feel as she slowly brushes her wrinkled, gnarled fingers over mine.

"It's working," I tell the guys. Nolan's eyes light up as he writes something in his notebook. Spencer does the same while Owen snaps a photograph of us. Turning my focus to the ghost holding my hand, I ask again, "Can you touch the board now?"

Old Creepy leans forward and effortlessly slides the planchette across the board, leaving it over the word *yes*. I hear Mattie whisper 'holy shit' under his breath, but nobody else moves or says anything to interrupt.

"Do you remember your real name?" Spencer asks.

It's not a question I've ever thought to ask, and shame makes me grasp my adder stone tighter. Of course Old Creepy has a real name. I'm the one who gave her such an awful nickname. She gives me a soft, almost motherly smile before leaning forward to move the planchette across the board. She pauses briefly over the letters *S-O-P-H-I-A* before she finishes.

Sophia. I swear to myself then and there to never refer to her as anything else again.

When I glance at the guys, they look completely entranced and beyond excited. Both Spencer and Nolan are writing rapidly in their notebooks while Owen and Mattie simply watch me and the spirit board in awe.

"Do you know what year you died?" Spencer asks next.

Her answer is immediate. *1898.* She's so quick and confident with her answers. Hopefully, that's a sign she doesn't have the same issues as Ryan when it comes to her memory.

Spencer's next question takes me by surprise, even more than his first two questions. "Are you stuck inside this house?" When she quickly answers *yes,* Spencer follows with, "Is it because of a curse?"

I must be the world's biggest idiot. How did I never consider she was stuck here, the same way Ryan's stuck inside the high school grounds? She's never come outside with me, and I stupidly assumed it was because she didn't like going outside.

Sophia answers with the letters *M-O-R-E.*

"More?" I exclaim, feeling angrier at myself by the second. "What does that mean? How could something keep you stuck here like this?"

"It's alright, Harriet." Owen gently rubs his hand over my back. "Please don't get upset. This is why we're interviewing her. So we can help her."

I know he's right, but it doesn't make me feel any better. For weeks, I've been calling this poor, cursed woman old and creepy to her face daily, and I've never made any effort to figure out who she is or how she ended up like this before now. I squeeze my adder stone tighter in my fist and thread my fingers through Sophia's, concentrating harder on my intense feelings of guilt and my desire to learn everything I can about her in order to help her.

My vision gets spotty, and the room around me begins to flicker in and out of view. I feel Owen's hand on my back, and I hear his concerned voice. But it's like I'm underwater, and it's impossible to make out anything he's saying. I shake my head and force any thoughts of Owen out of my mind, focusing only on Sophia.

After blinking several times, I realize I'm no longer in the sitting room with Sophia or the guys. Instead, it looks like I'm downstairs in the foyer. Only, the furniture and décor are all wrong. I stare around in confusion, flinching when there's a knock at the front door. A woman walks out of the kitchen to answer it. She looks young, like she's maybe in her early twenties, and she's dressed in a long, old-fashioned gown. I gape at her, but it quickly becomes evident she can't see me. It's like *I'm* a ghost. What the fuck is happening?

"Yes?" she asks when she opens the door.

The voice on the other side of the door answers, "Good morning, madam. My name is Sophia. I'm here about the available nanny position?"

I nearly shove in front of the young woman at the mention of Sophia's name. Standing on the front porch is a plain woman who looks like she's in her mid-to-late twenties. Her dress is old-fashioned like the first woman's, but even to my untrained eye, it's obvious she's nowhere near as wealthy as the woman who answered the door.

"Oh, yes, of course." The first woman opens the door wider and lets Sophia step through. I quickly jump back to get out of her way, though I'm fairly certain she wouldn't notice me, anyway. My eyes travel over her face, searching for any familiar features. This has to be *my* Sophia, right? Why else would I be here? The longer this goes on, the surer I am that I'm seeing some sort of memory.

I follow them into the kitchen, trying my best not to worry about how this is possible. I have a feeling that if I freak out or panic, this vision will break. Within a few minutes, I learn that the woman interviewing Sophia is called Rebecca Abbot, which means she's a distant relative of mine. I also learn that the Abbot House has only recently finished being built, and Rebecca Abbot is one of the first witches ever to live in it, along with her husband and daughter.

The women speak politely to one another, and Sophia seems thrilled to be given the nanny job. I don't know why I'm here, witnessing this point in her life. It'll be years before she dies. But my being here at all means it has to be important for some reason.

Rebecca asks Sophia if she wants some tea, waving her hand in the air to summon a kettle and two teacups. After pouring their tea, Rebecca uses magic to mix milk and honey into hers. Sophia uses a spoon instead. I can't help but squint suspiciously at her. I've always assumed she was a witch simply because she lived in the Abbot House, and she clearly isn't surprised by Rebecca's casual use of magic.

"Oh." Rebecca laughs nervously. "Is it true, then? Your uncle mentioned that you don't have very many magical abilities."

"It is true, I'm afraid." Sophia grins wryly. "Both my parents are witches, but I've never been able to do a single spell or charm in my life. I promise it won't affect my job performance, Mistress Abbot."

They continue speaking, but all I hear is a ringing in my ears as I stare at Sophia. My breathing becomes shallow, and the room becomes spotty again, like I'm losing the vision. I try my best to hold on, but I'm too close to crying. Panic sets in when I realize I can no longer breathe, and I uselessly grip my throat while I search for any sign of Sophia, either dead or the version in her memory. Whispered shouts reach my ears, but they're too far away for me to make out.

There's a sharp pain on my hand, and I gasp. It's the first breath I've been able to take in what feels like forever, and I greedily suck in another gulp of air. This time when I blink, I'm back in the sitting room with the guys. Owen's holding me cradled in his lap while the others surround us, and I realize they all look completely panicked.

I take a few more steady breaths and ask in a croaky voice, "What happened?"

"You stopped breathing," Mattie says, sounding close to tears. When I turn my attention to him, I notice he's holding Circe and petting her with trembling hands. "We couldn't get you to snap out of...whatever the fuck that was. Not until Circe ran over here and bit your hand."

A pitiful meow escapes Circe, and Mattie lets out a shaky laugh as he leans down to kiss the top of her head.

"Are you okay?" Owen asks, brushing his hand over my cheek.

That's when I notice there are tears running down my face. Maybe I should be embarrassed about that, or about the fact that Owen's still holding me in his lap. But I'm too overwhelmed and exhausted to care. Everything comes rushing back—everything I learned about Sophia, and the fact that she used to be a witch just like me. A useless witch who couldn't do magic. I desperately want to confess this information, but Mattie and Nolan still don't know the truth about witches. They can't know.

"Do you remember what happened, Harriet?" Nolan asks softly. He adjusts his glasses when our eyes meet, and I see him subtly reach for his notebook and pen. "It seemed like you

271

were in some sort of trance. You were completely unresponsive to us. Did you see something? Maybe a vision?"

Words completely fail me, and I shake my head in agitation. Where is Sophia, anyway? I search the room frantically, and I find her hovering against the far wall with her arms wrapped around herself.

"Dude, just back off." Spencer glares menacingly at Nolan. He scoots closer to me and Owen, lifting his hand to gently stroke his fingers through my hair. "Can't you see she's fucking upset?"

Nolan looks a little guilty, but more than anything, he looks disappointed. I try to settle my breathing and the stupid, chaotic thoughts in my head. How am I ever going to help Sophia if I can't get my shit together?

"I did have a vision," I mumble. "Like, a memory, I think? It was from when Sophia was young and first came to work here. I—I think I messed up and broke the vision when I got upset. But maybe we can try again?"

"No!" Mattie, Owen, and Spencer shout in unison.

Spencer gently grips my chin, tilting my face toward his as he gives me a nervous smile. "Let's just call it a night with the ghost stuff, okay?"

"But—" I start to say before Mattie cuts me off.

"It's not fun when it makes you cry, or when there's even the slightest chance you could get hurt." Mattie reaches his hand out like he's going to grab mine, but he changes his mind at the last second and simply continues petting Circe. "That shit was really fucking terrifying."

Everyone seems to agree. As much as I want to argue, it's obvious they're way more freaked out about my vision and how it all ended. I don't know how to tell them it's more important than ever that we get to the bottom of this mystery. How can I possibly explain that I feel a kinship with her I've never felt with anyone else? I've never known another witch like me, and I feel responsible for her. It may just be a hobby for the guys, but this is my purpose in life. I have to figure out how Sophia died and how to help her escape her cursed fate somehow. She's counting on me, just like Ryan is.

"Why don't we watch some horror movies?" Owen asks, hugging me a little tighter. "Plus, we still have all those snacks to eat."

I don't want to upset them, so I don't make any more fuss. While they put their ghost hunting gear away and grab the rest of the snacks from downstairs, I take a moment to sneak to my room so I can hopefully talk to Sophia. She follows me after I subtly motion to her, but she seems apprehensive.

Once she and I are alone, she anxiously wrings her hands in front of her and keeps her eyes on the ground, humming the most melancholy tune I've ever heard from her.

"It's not your fault," I say. Tears prick the corners of my eyes, and I quickly wipe them away. "I'm sorry I haven't done more to help you. But I swear, I will. I'll do whatever it takes."

She shakes her head and reaches out to stroke my cheek. I can't feel her anymore, like before. Her touch is a cold tingle against my skin, but her intention is easy enough to figure out. She's always been sweet, almost grandmother-like with me, and her concern for my well-being is beyond clear.

I'm not deterred. Somehow, with or without the guys' help, I'll figure this out. But for tonight at least, I'll have to set the issue aside and figure out how to proceed later. After reassuring Sophia that I'm not hurt, and making sure as well as I can that she's not somehow hurt either, I head back to the sitting room to try and enjoy my sleepover with the guys.

CHAPTER 23
Harriet

The next week leading up to Halloween day passes quickly and uneventfully. After the sleepover, the guys are adamant about taking a break from any ghost hunting mysteries. It's incredibly frustrating since I feel like I'm finally getting somewhere with being able to legitimately help both Ryan and Sophia. But I get why the guys are apprehensive. I really freaked them out when I fell into that trance to look at Sophia's memories. I explained the truth to Owen and Spencer—that Sophia and I share something in common as far as our lack of magic—in the hopes they'd give in and keep going with our investigations. But they weren't swayed, and they continue to agree with Mattie and Nolan that we need to wait and do more research before attempting another interview like the one we did with Sophia.

Despite the halt in ghost business, I've spent nearly every free minute with the guys. The sleepover definitely brought us closer and made my friendship with them stronger. Owen continues to drive me back and forth to school every day, and Mattie still comes over after school to hang out and to do our homework together. During school, I'm constantly with at least one of them. Even Nolan has been way more talkative. It's been really nice, and it makes it so much easier to ignore the petty witches I go to school with. In a matter of weeks, Weeping Hollow has genuinely started to feel like home.

That's not to say everything has been easy. My fellow witches still fuck with me at school daily. Amethyst is the worst of them all, but truthfully, Blaze makes me feel the most uneasy. Every time I see him in class or the hallways, he gives me a malicious smirk that instantly reminds me of how easy it was for him to corner and hurt me.

Almost as bad as dealing with witches at school is the fact that my mom has been totally absent at home. I swear I've barely seen her all week. Part of me can't help but be irritated that she hasn't brought up our talk in the car last week. She hasn't asked me any more about the guys, about the ghosts I've seen, or about the hazing I've been experiencing at school. I can only assume she's forgotten all about our conversation now that she's distracted by reconnecting with old friends and with her blossoming relationship with Principal Di Rossi.

"What are you thinking so hard about?"

I turn to give Ryan a bashful smile and shrug. "Nothing. Just spacing out, I guess."

He gives me a knowing look. Ryan knows all about my drama with my mom as well as last week's events during my sleepover with the guys. I ignore his judgy little smile and shove through the door of the bathroom. We seriously need to find somewhere else to hide during class, but it's too risky to sneak into the library or an empty classroom. This bathroom is rarely used as it's in a fairly secluded corner of the school.

Ryan glides through the wall instead of using the door like me. "I hate to say this, but you probably shouldn't keep skipping class just to hang out with me."

His smug grin proves that he could give two shits about me skipping class. I roll my eyes at him and make myself comfortable sitting on the counter beside the sink.

"Whatever. I doubt Mr. Fuller will even notice." I scoff. "Plus, it's Halloween. Do you really think anyone is paying attention in any of their classes? I'm not missing anything."

It's true. My Latin teacher is totally ancient and oblivious to pretty much everything. It's also my last class of the day and the only one I don't share with any of my friends. Normally, I love Halloween. But Goddess, if I have to hear one more mention of all the *exclusive* Samhain parties happening tonight and over the weekend, I'll scream. Every witch I go to school with seems to have made it their mission today to make sure I overhear their plans while making it clear I'm not invited. As if I'd ever want to go to any of their douchey parties or coven meetings, anyway.

"You're hanging out with Spencer tonight, aren't you?" Ryan asks, wiggling his eyebrows obnoxiously.

"Shut up." I giggle. "You know it's nothing like that. I'm going trick-or-treating with him and his nephew. Totally innocent."

"You're killing me with this slow burn bullshit, Harriet."

There's no point in responding. Ryan knows I'm crushing hard on Spencer and Owen, and he also knows damn well that I have no intention of doing anything about it. Ryan hovers beside me and tries to nudge my elbow. When his elbow goes straight through mine and all I sense is a cold, tingly feeling, his shoulders droop. Since I told them about the incident with Sophia, he's constantly trying to touch me to see if I can feel him, and he's always disappointed when it doesn't happen. I don't know why I've kept it from him, but I haven't told him that I felt him too the day we discovered his full name.

"So, what's on your mind?" he asks, shaking off his

disappointment. "There must be something you want to talk about if you were willing to skip class and chill in the bathroom with me."

"It's been a weird week." I shrug, pulling my knees up to my chest. Giving Ryan a half smile, I add, "And maybe I kind of miss you. I feel like we barely get to talk anymore."

Technically, we talk every day during the week. He still finds me first thing in the morning when I get to school, and he stays by my side all day until I leave. But it's rare we get any time alone where I can talk to him without at least one of the guys around. Sometimes, I can get away with writing notes to Ryan during class, but there's always the chance of being caught by a teacher or of someone reading over my shoulder. And now that it's Friday again, I'm dreading going all weekend without seeing or hearing from him.

"I get it." He chuckles. "Too bad ghosts can't use cell phones."

Maybe if I learn more about how to use my gift, I can figure out how to make it possible for him to physically touch and move things. Then he *could* use a cell phone, and I'd probably be way less worried about leaving him trapped and alone in the school. Then again, the real goal is to get him un-stuck and to potentially help him cross over. Making him strong enough to use a cell phone would be selfish on my part as it would only make me feel better rather than helping Ryan in any real way.

For the rest of class, Ryan and I talk about random things. He's getting better at remembering small glimpses from his life, and he shares a few new details about his family. Mostly though, we talk about Sophia. Ryan seems extremely intrigued by her and the fact that her situation is similar to his. He knows how guilty I feel about calling her Old Creepy, and he understands why I feel desperate to help her.

"I'm thinking of trying to see her memories again on my

own," I admit. I'm not sure Sophia would cooperate, to be honest. She's been fussing over me all week like I'm the most delicate thing in the world, and she's been careful not to get too close or to accidentally touch me. But Goddess, I hate sitting by and doing nothing when there's something I can do to help her.

Ryan shakes his head. "I don't think that's a good idea."

"Why not?" Surely, he understands better than anyone. I want to help him too, but I don't think I'd be able to search through his memories the same way.

He sighs, furrowing his eyebrows in exasperation. "I know you want to help her, but you could have been seriously hurt. The guys are right. Until you have a better idea of what you're walking into and how to deal with it, you're better off waiting. Sophia will understand."

"But she's stuck, and I feel like I'm the only one who can help her." My voice trembles, and I meet his eyes with a frown. "Just like you. Goddess, I hate it. I feel like I'm failing you both."

"Harriet," Ryan says softly. He places his hand over mine, and I try to take comfort in the tingly, numbing coldness that seeps into my skin. "What if your cat hadn't bit you, and what if the guys still couldn't figure out how to break your trance? You could have died. It's too risky to do this shit alone. Sophia is already dead, and she has been for hundreds of years. Fuck, *I'm* dead, and I think you forget that sometimes. You make it too easy to forget because you make me feel so alive, but we're dead. A few more weeks, months, or however long it takes you to solve the mysteries of our deaths? It won't make a difference."

Tears prick my eyes, making me feel like a giant baby. "What if I never figure out how to help you?"

He smiles, and I feel the barest touch from his hand. The

sensation ends so quickly, I'm not sure whether or not I imagined it.

"You have this insanely cool power that lets you see me and talk to me. That's a gift. Knowing you at all is a gift, and I guarantee Sophia feels the same." Ryan's eyes drop to our hands, and a faint blush rises to his cheeks. Which makes no sense, because as he just reminded me, he's dead. But it happens all the same. "Just because you can see us, that doesn't mean you're responsible for what happened to us or for helping us with anything. You've gotta stop letting this weigh you down."

Quickly wiping away my ridiculous tears, I let out a choked laugh. "When did you get so sweet and sentimental, huh?"

He smirks. "Oh, I'm sorry. Would you rather listen to me list all the reasons you should hook up with Owen and Spencer again? You know I'm always up for that discussion."

I flip him off and laugh for real.

"I'LL MEET YOU AT YOUR PLACE AT FIVE?" SPENCER ASKS.

"Sounds good." I smile at him like a nervous idiot, glancing sideways at Owen. I can't explain why, but it feels a little awkward making plans and saying goodbye to Spencer while Owen silently watches and waits to drive me home. It's not like Spencer and I are going on a date tonight. Like I told Ryan, I'm helping Shiloh with his costume and going trick-or-treating with them, which is completely innocent. I must be letting Ryan's ideas about these guys get to me.

Spencer smiles and pulls me into a quick hug, waving goodbye to us one last time. When he walks away, Owen opens the passenger door of his truck for me. Before I get in, I look back at the front entrance of the school to try and catch a glimpse of Ryan. Unfortunately, he's nowhere to be seen. He took off when we finally left the bathroom after class ended, giving me some bullshit excuse that he needed to check on something. I think he realizes how hard it is for me to say goodbye to him for the weekend, so he disappeared before I could get too caught up in my head about it.

"You okay?" Owen asks as he pulls his truck out of the student parking lot.

It's not a far drive to my house, but I know for a fact that it's slightly out of Owen's way. It's sweet of him to insist on driving me. Then again, pretty much everything about Owen is sweet. My stomach squirms uncomfortably. Eventually, he and Spencer are going to ask me bluntly if I like either of them, and I have no clue what I'm going to say or what's going to happen.

"Yeah." I'm definitely not going to bring up my crush, and I don't want to get into another argument about Ryan or making progress with our ghost mysteries. So, I change the subject. "What are you doing tonight? I'm not sure I ever asked."

I know Mattie and Nolan are staying home to babysit Nolan's younger sister. She's twelve, which makes her too old to find trick-or-treating cool but too young to be left alone by herself for most of the night. Mattie spent most of lunch whining about it, dropping several hints that he'd rather be hanging out with me and Spencer or possibly coming over to my house for more horror movie binging instead.

"I'm not sure yet." Owen shrugs, keeping his eyes on the road. "I might stay home, or I might go over to Nolan and Mattie's to hang out."

"Oh." My cheeks flush before the next words are out of my mouth. "You don't want to go trick-or-treating with me, Spencer, and Shiloh?"

He laughs, glancing over to give me an amused smile. "Spencer told me and the guys we weren't allowed to come. I'm pretty sure he's hoping you two will be able to hang out alone after Shiloh's dad picks him up later tonight."

Oh, Goddess. Was Ryan right? Does Spencer think tonight is sort of like a date? This is just like that time I went over to his house, completely oblivious to the idea that he was most likely asking me out. Even worse, Owen sounds so fucking casual about it. Like he's not bothered at all that Spencer supposedly tried to stake some kind of claim.

"It's why Spence and Mattie kept bickering all through lunch," Owen adds when I stay quiet for too long. "Mattie's jealous that Spencer's hanging out with you."

"That's stupid," I blurt out. They've been picking at each other a lot lately, but I assumed that was normal for them. "Why would Mattie be jealous? He doesn't even like me. I mean, not like *that*."

Owen laughs again, his amused smile growing wider. "Yes, he does."

He's wrong. Totally wrong. Mattie likes Amethyst, which I'm reminded of almost daily. He still gets all fucking moony about her every time he and I pass her in the hallways at school. But ever since I called him out for it, he's been making more of an effort to walk a different route to class with me so there's less of a chance of seeing her. I know that's probably only because he's embarrassed or doesn't want to make me mad. Definitely not because he likes me. Seriously, what guy would talk about how hot one girl is to another girl he supposedly likes?

Still, I'm dropping this subject with Owen immediately. I'm not going to tell him that Mattie's crushing on Amethyst. She's a sore subject with most of the guys because of how things ended between her and Spencer last year. Plus, Owen

281

dislikes her even more than the others because he knows she's been harassing me more than any of the other witches at school. It's also probably not smart to keep talking about this because I don't want Owen to ask me questions about *my* feelings. Nope, I am definitely not prepared for that conversation.

"You should hang out with them," I say, attempting to revert the conversation to safer grounds. "Chilling with Nolan and Mattie sounds more fun than being alone."

He hums noncommittally. We're quiet for the rest of the drive, but the silence between us is comfortable. Owen is usually pretty quiet, especially compared to his friends. But I don't mind. He's always open and talkative if I start a conversation with him, and the other guys have told me more than once that Owen only talks to people he genuinely likes. It's flattering to know he makes the effort for me.

When he parks in front of my house, I grab my backpack and give him a bright smile. "Thanks for driving me. You seriously are the best."

He smiles back at me, lifting a hand to rub the back of his neck. "You're welcome. It's really no trouble."

I pause with my hand on the door. I'm sure we'll text each other over the weekend, but we never made plans to hang out. Since the guys are adamant about this ghost hunting break, I assumed I'd be spending most of my weekend hanging out in my room with Sophia and waiting for Circe to have her babies. Henry says she's getting closer to giving birth, but it's hard to tell when it might happen exactly since we have no way of knowing when she got pregnant.

"So, I guess I'll see you Monday?" I ask.

"Actually," he says, clearing his throat. "I was wondering if you wanted to hang out with me tomorrow?"

"Oh." The squirming feeling in my stomach ramps up, and

my heart flutters. Is he asking me out? Why is it so hard for me to tell? It feels like he is after what he said about Spencer and Mattie. "Just the two of us?"

He smiles bashfully and nods. "Yeah, if that's alright. I thought maybe we could walk around some of the shops downtown. You haven't explored much since you moved here."

No, I haven't, and I definitely want to. There's so much of Weeping Hollow I still want to see and learn about. I've just been so busy with school, the guys, Ryan, Sophia, and all the drama around meeting my dad. Plus, as anxious as it makes me, I *want* to say yes to Owen. I've wanted to say yes to him since my first day of school when he wrote that sweet note to me in English class. I'm just so afraid of what will happen if I do. If he thinks Spencer and Mattie are fighting because of me, then what's going to happen between Owen and Spencer if I go out with either of them?

"Okay," I blurt out before I fully make up my mind. The smile he gives me in return is blinding. I let out an embarrassing, high-pitched giggle and practically throw open the door to make an escape before I have a chance to humiliate myself. "Um, text me later?"

"I will," he says sweetly, still smiling at me like I've totally made his day.

As I walk up to my house, I glance backwards twice to see Owen still watching me from his truck. I'm blushing like crazy by the time I make it to the front door, and there's a cheesy smile glued to my face.

CHAPTER 24
HARRIET

"I think you've had enough, buddy. Your pail is overflowing with candy!"

Shiloh pouts at Spencer and reaches for my hand. "But Harriet wants to keep trick-or-treating too!"

It takes a lot of effort to stifle my giggles as I squeeze Shiloh's tiny hand affectionately. I hate to shatter his hopes, but I agree with Spencer. We've been out for hours, and even I can tell that Shiloh's starting to get tired, as much as he tries to fight it. Plus, Danny is supposed to meet up with us soon to pick Shiloh up for the night.

Trick-or-treating with them has been awesome though. Nearly every house we've been to has been decked out with Halloween decorations, and Shiloh and I have gotten so much candy. His pumpkin-shaped pail has been overflowing for a while, so Spencer had to use another bag to carry extra candy for him. Shiloh's costume came out amazing too, if I do say so myself.

It was ridiculously fun to do his makeup to make him look like a creepy mermaid. Using a few really cool techniques I learned from watching about a million YouTube videos, I managed to make it look like he has dark green and blue scales scattered over his face, arms, and hands, and I even gave him realistic-looking gills. I also came through with my promise to make it look like he has fish hooks sticking out of his mouth, which he was ecstatic about. And earlier this week, I found some old fabric and a net that I dyed dark blue and added some shiny beads to before sewing them into the shape of a mermaid tail. The fins at the end swish around perfectly when he walks, making it look as close as possible to a mermaid tail while allowing him to move freely. For something homemade, his entire costume looks professional as fuck, and so many people handing out candy have complimented Shiloh's look.

"How about this?" Spencer bends down to Shiloh's height and gives him a conspiring smile. "We can finish going to the last few houses on this street, and then we can head over to the diner. I'll get you and Harriet some milkshakes, and we can text your dad to have him meet us there instead."

Shiloh happily agrees to that plan. Luckily, Rosemary's Diner is a much closer walk from here than my house. It takes us no time at all before we walk into the 1950s-styled restaurant. The place is packed and completely chaotic. By some miracle, we find an open booth. Spencer and Shiloh take up one side, and I slide into the seat across from them.

My nose itches something fierce and there's a tingling feeling on the back of my neck as I settle into the booth. Thanks to my adder stone, the signs are a lot less irritating, but they're there all the same. I subtly glance over my shoulder and find the same old man ghost glaring at me that I saw the first time I ate here. He's sitting in the same spot I last saw him—on a stool at the bar in front of the kitchen where a newspaper is spread out in front of him.

"You okay?" Spencer asks quietly.

After checking that Shiloh is still distracted by digging through his candy pail, I nod at Spencer and mouth the word 'ghost.' His eyes light up with recognition, and he turns to glance in the general direction of the ghost. When the ghost sees Spencer looking, he curls his lip in a sneer before going back to staring daggers at me. I'm not anywhere near him or bothering him, so I have no clue what his problem is. Most ghosts I've met before befriending Ryan and Sophia just ignored me, even when I knew they were aware I could see them. This guy is the first ghost to ever act so hostile toward me, and it definitely makes me uncomfortable.

"Shit, I forgot," Spencer whispers. I mentioned the diner ghost to him and Owen when I first told them my secret, but we've been so caught up with WHISPER's attempts to solve Sophia and Ryan's death that I don't blame him for forgetting. He gives me a guilty look and asks, "Do you want to leave?"

That gets Shiloh's attention. He looks up from his candy collection with wide puppy dog eyes. I chuckle and shake my head. "I'm fine. I think you promised us some milkshakes?"

Spencer laughs and looks around the crowded diner. When he sees someone who works here, he sits up slightly and waves at them with a grin. My mom and aunt's friend April approaches our table with a frazzled look.

"Thank god you're here, Spence." She sighs and gives him a pleading look. "I know you were supposed to be off tonight, but is there any chance you can help out for a bit? Shawna and Rob called out, and we're completely slammed."

"Seriously? They always call out." Spencer groans. He glances worriedly down at Shiloh and shakes his head. "I wish I could help, but I'm watching my nephew until his dad picks him up."

When Spencer meets my eyes with an unspoken question in his expression, I give him a small smile. If I didn't think he was looking for an excuse to avoid stepping in, I'd keep my mouth shut. But I know Spencer generally likes working here, and he seems like he genuinely wants to help April out.

"I don't mind keeping an eye on him," I offer.

Spencer grins and ruffles Shiloh's hair. "You okay with that?"

"Duh." Shiloh rolls his eyes, making us laugh. He looks up at Spencer suspiciously and asks, "We still get our milkshakes though, right?"

April laughs, a relieved expression taking over her face. "Milkshakes and any other snacks you want are on the house."

After assuring him that she only needs him to fill in for an hour tops until another worker can make it in, Spencer gets up and follows April back to the kitchen to get to work. For the next half hour, Shiloh and I talk and goof around together while eating our candy and drinking the apple pie flavored milkshakes Spencer brings out for us. Shiloh cracks me up with stories about his first-grade class at school and about funny things Spencer has said or done at home. Shiloh makes the time pass quickly, and he makes it easier to forget the ghost glaring at me from across the restaurant.

A tingling feeling erupts across my skin, alerting me to the presence of a witch. It shouldn't be surprising, especially after tonight. The amount of witches who answered doors while we were trick-or-treating was telling. I thought there were a lot of witches my age at school, and tons who came over to my house when my mom and aunt threw their party a few weekends ago. But based on tonight, I would guess that a significant percentage of the population in Weeping Hollow are witches.

Still, I'm certainly not excited at the possibility of having to deal with any catty witches after having such a fun night so far. I self-consciously touch the brim of my witch's hat. Back home in Oregon, it always felt funny to dress up as witches with

Sage. Spencer and Shiloh love my costume too, but I definitely got a lot of funny looks from some of the witches around town while trick-or-treating. I'm glad I didn't wear it to school because I'm sure Amethyst, Blaze, and some of those other witchy dicks never would have let me live it down.

My shoulders tense when I realize the witches who just walked into the diner are around my age. Shiloh remains oblivious, still prattling on about a girl in his class he finds annoying while he pops a mini Snickers bar into his mouth. Thankfully, I don't recognize any of them from school. At least until one of the guys turns and looks in my direction. A relieved smile spreads across my face when I meet my half-brother's eyes.

I haven't seen Dorian since I had dinner at his house, though I have been texting Henry and Elsie regularly. Dorian grins at me in response, saying something to one of his friends before heading in my direction.

"Hey!" he says excitedly. "I didn't expect to run into you tonight."

"Same to you." My lips twitch as I take in his long, black cloak and the witch's hat atop his head that's incredibly similar to mine. While my hat is decorated with a purple ribbon, bow, and flowers, his is decorated with small orange flowers, maple leaves, and acorns. I raise my eyebrows and teasingly ask, "No coven parties tonight?"

"No, thank you." He chuckles and turns his gray-blue eyes to Shiloh. The six-year-old has gone silent in Dorian's presence, staring up at him with a distrustful expression. Dorian gives him a goofy smile and asks, "Who's this?"

"This is my friend Shiloh." I wave my hand at my half-brother and introduce him. "And Shiloh, this is Dorian."

"Cool," Dorian says. "Can I hang with you guys?"

I scoot over to make room for him automatically. Judging

by my interactions with Dorian so far, I doubt he'll start any trouble or say anything to make Shiloh feel uncomfortable. Still, Shiloh's expression only becomes more dubious when Dorian joins us.

"Are you Harriet's boyfriend?" he asks.

Dorian bursts out laughing and throws his arm around my shoulders. "Definitely not. Harriet's my sister."

"Oh." Shiloh relaxes instantly and finally gives Dorian a smile as he goes back to unwrapping another piece of candy. I swear, this kid is going to make himself sick at this rate. "I didn't know Harriet had a brother."

"I have a sister too," I tell him. "But they live with my dad, not with me and my mom."

The explanation seems to appease Shiloh because he excitedly regales Dorian with the story of our night and trick-or-treating. When Dorian asks who helped him with his costume, Shiloh proudly preens and credits me, Dorian gives us both tons of enthusiastic compliments.

"Are you sure you don't need to get back to your friends?" I ask Dorian quietly after we've been talking for a while. I glance nervously at the group of witches sitting in a booth a few down from ours. They keep periodically looking in our direction.

Dorian waves his hand dismissively. "Nah. They're more acquaintances than friends, honestly. I'm only hanging out with them because I figured it was better than sitting at home with my parents."

His honesty makes me laugh. Dorian really seems to generally not like other witches. It's something we have in common, even if our reasons are different.

"Uh, hey." Spencer walks over and sets a large plate of cheese fries on our table, frowning down at Dorian with a confused and jealous expression. "What's going on over here?"

My cheeks flush at how obvious he's being. Seriously, he's

almost as bad as Shiloh! I give him a timid smile and quickly introduce him to Dorian. At the sound of my brother's name, Spencer relaxes and gives him a friendly grin.

"Your dad should be here in a few minutes," Spencer tells Shiloh, sliding into the seat beside him. To me, he says, "And the rush has died down, so April says I'm good."

In no time at all, Danny arrives at the diner to pick up Shiloh. After I give the kid a big hug and thank him for letting me tag along tonight, Spencer tells me he'll be right back and walks Shiloh outside to Danny's car. Once we're alone, Dorian turns to me with a teasing half smile.

"What?" I ask with a nervous chuckle.

"Do you want me to leave?" he asks. When I furrow my eyebrows, he snickers. "I'm serious. That guy is clearly into you, and even his little nephew was all fucking territorial when he thought I was some dude making a move on you. Is this supposed to be a date now that the kid's gone?"

"It's not a date," I insist. Dorian's smirk widens as he tilts his head, clearly not believing me. I giggle nervously and whisper, "I know he likes me, but no. I swear we're not on a date."

"Why not? Do you not like him? He's kind of good-looking, if you're into emo guys."

"I do like him." Goddess, it's way too easy to open up to Dorian. "It's just, um, complicated."

"Why? Because he's human?"

The disapproving look he gives me is more proof that he and I agree about how the witch community views certain things, and it makes it even easier to be truthful. I scoff and shake my head, still keeping my voice low. "No, of course that's not why. It's because I also really like his best friend. I'm pretty sure he likes me too, and this whole thing is just getting ridiculous. I refuse to pit them against each other or choose between them. So, we're just friends."

"I see."

The smile Dorian gives me is devious. My face heats up when I spot Spencer walking back into the diner, so I make a face at Dorian and hope he gets the hint to stay quiet. He chuckles at me and mimes zipping his lips.

"Sorry about that," Spencer says.

We decide to stay and hang out here. Dorian orders a milkshake, and I get a soda to drink while the three of us snack on the delicious cheese fries Spencer brought out to share. Spencer and Dorian get along easily, and it's nice to sit with them while we talk and joke around. I've never felt as comfortable so quickly as I do around Dorian. His jokes about us being practically twins are starting to feel a little too close to the truth. Running into him outside of a nerve-racking family dinner gives me even more hope that he and I will be able to become close friends.

"What do you keep looking at?" Dorian asks after a while.

I jerk my gaze away from the grumpy ghost man and grimace at Dorian apologetically. I'm glad I already told him and the rest of his family about my gift, or else I'd probably feel super awkward. "Sorry. It's just that there's a ghost over there who's been glaring at me since I got here."

Dorian's eyebrows raise in surprise, and he turns his head in the direction he caught me staring. "For real?"

Spencer chuckles at his question and slides his arm across the table to gently place his hand over mine. "Do you want to go talk to him and find out what his deal is?"

Quirking a teasing smile, I sarcastically ask, "Is that allowed? I thought you and the guys were against any WHISPER or ghost business for the time being."

He rolls his eyes in response, a light blush dusting his cheeks. "Just please promise to be careful?"

I turn my hand over to thread my fingers through his, giving him a soft smile. I know I scared him and the others with everything that happened with Sophia, so I understand where they're coming from. But that doesn't mean I want to stop investigating or dealing with any ghosts in the future. "I promise."

We leave our table and head over to the ghost. Luckily, there are a couple of open stools next to him, and Spencer and Dorian agree to do their best to make it look like I'm talking to them instead of the ghost in case we catch anyone's attention. My palms get sweaty as we get closer to him. I've never been so bold as to approach a ghost for the first time in public like this, and I've also never dealt with a ghost so hostile right off the bat.

As I lower myself onto the stool beside the ghost, I catch Spencer taking his phone out and subtly pressing the record button on a video. I'm sure he wants to try and capture the audio. As much as he's able to in a busy, noisy place like this, at least.

"Stupid, meddling kids." The ghost grumbles, glaring between the three of us. "I don't want your help. Just leave me alone."

Goddess, he's such a dick. I furrow my eyebrows and say, "We haven't offered to help you with anything. Why do you keep glaring at me?"

"You know why," he spits.

I glance at Spencer and Dorian. I know they can't hear anything, but the wonder and curiosity in their eyes makes me feel brave enough to keep talking. I clear my throat and tell the ghost, "No, I really don't."

He sighs in annoyance and reaches his arm forward to flap

his arm around my head. "You've got that damned light with you. I know what you're trying to do, and I'm not ready to go yet. Nope, I'm content right where I am."

I blink at him stupidly before quickly relaying the conversation to Dorian and Spencer. Dorian snorts and shakes his head in disbelief while Spencer stares at the ghost with a thoughtful expression.

"He thinks you're going to force him to cross over?" Spencer asks. "Huh. Have Ryan and Sophia ever mentioned you carrying around this light that he's talking about?"

"Never." I shake my head. That's definitely something I'd remember.

Dorian hums and asks the ghost, "Why don't you want to cross over yet?"

The man practically growls at my brother and says, "None of your damn business."

I let out a frustrated sigh. Clearly, we're getting nowhere. Spencer suggests we start with more basic questions, like his name and how long he's been dead. To my surprise, the ghost actually answers, though he doesn't look happy about our continued conversation with him. We learn that his name is Ernest Williams, and that he died a little over five years ago.

Spencer grins triumphantly when I relay the information. "I thought so. That's April's dad, the original owner of the diner. He used to come in here every day even after he retired, and he always sat in the same seat. It's why April puts a newspaper out every day, and nobody else ever sits here."

Ernest grumbles a rude comment about Spencer being nosy. Now we know who he is, and he's made it clear he wants nothing to do with us. So, we should just walk away. But that doesn't feel right to me. A fierce determination comes over me, and I grip my adder stone tightly in my fist as I glare at Ernest.

"Tell me the truth," I say. "Why would you rather stick around here like this instead of crossing over?"

April walks by just then, too busy to give us more than a cursory glance and smile. It's apparent that she's oblivious to her dad's ghost sitting with us, and she has no reason to suspect us doing anything weird by sitting here. Ernest's expression shutters as his eyes follow her, an almost palpable cloud of sadness enveloping him.

"I need to keep an eye on my girl," he says softly. "It was just me and her after her mom died, and now she's got nobody looking after her. There were lots of things I should have said to her before I did, and now I worry she's carrying too many burdens and responsibilities that aren't hers to bear."

Well, that's surprisingly sweet. I bite my lip, staring at Spencer and Dorian at a loss. After I tell them what Ernest said, they both look equally thoughtful and sympathetic.

Leaning in closer to me and Spencer, Dorian whispers, "Maybe you could talk to his daughter? Then he can say all the stuff he wants to say to her."

I don't see any other way to help Ernest either—not that he *wants* my help—but that's an incredibly risky plan. April isn't a witch, and the chances that she knows about anything truthful about the supernatural world despite living in Weeping Hollow are slim. What if she freaks out and says something to my mom? Even though my gift of talking to ghosts is considered to be something different and separate from a witch's powers, I could still potentially get into trouble with the Witch Council. Worse, I could get Spencer into trouble. What if April fires him because she's angry or offended?

"You know April better than I do," I tell Spencer. "How do you think she'd take it if I told her I can talk to her dad's ghost?"

"Uh…" He grimaces and rubs the back of his neck. "I have no idea. But I think Dorian's right, and we should try, anyway."

Grabbing his hand, I give him a worried look. "What if she fires you? It's one thing if she bans me from the diner or even talks to my mom, but I don't want you to face any backlash if she gets angry."

His face lights up with the sweetest smile. While he twines our fingers together, he lifts his other hand to softly caress my cheek. "Don't worry about me, babe. If that happens, I'll find a new job. This is your calling. So, if you wanna do this and help this ghost, I'm here to support you however I can."

Gah, just melt my heart, why don't you? I'm sure my face is on fire, and I can't keep the cheesy grin off my face. A quick glance at Dorian shows him biting his lip to hold back a laugh, but he thankfully doesn't say anything to embarrass me or ruin the moment.

With my mind made up, I awkwardly wave April over the next time she walks by. She looks much less frazzled than she did earlier, which is a mild relief. My stomach is in knots as she walks over to us with a smile. This might be one of the stupidest things I've ever done.

"Can I get you kids anything else?" she asks happily when she stops in front of us. With a genuine smile for Spencer, she adds, "You seriously were a lifesaver earlier."

"Actually, I sort of have to tell you something?" Ugh. My voice sounds pathetic and terrified, and that wasn't meant to be a question even though it sounded like one.

April gives me an inquisitive smile. "Alright. You're Della Abbot's daughter, right?"

I nod and clear my throat, looking around us to make sure nobody but Dorian and Spencer will overhear our conversation. Spencer squeezes my hand, giving me another small burst of courage.

"This is going to sound crazy, but please don't freak out." I pause to gauge her reaction so far. She looks concerned, but not irritable or anything. I force myself to keep going and get it all out at once. "I can see ghosts, and your dad's ghost is sitting here beside me. He, um, has some unfinished business, I think? He says there's a bunch of stuff he never got to say to you before he died, and I think he wants a chance to say it to you now so he can finally cross over."

She gapes at me for several seconds, and I hold my breath while I wait for her to shriek at me to get the fuck out of her diner and never come back. Spencer soothingly rubs his thumb over the back of my knuckles, and Dorian stays close enough that our shoulders are touching to let me know he's here for me too.

"Is this some kind of joke?" April hisses, her eyes darting around the diner before landing on me with a glare.

The hesitantly hopeful expression on Ernest's face drops, and he crosses his arms as he grumbles at me. "I told you stupid kids to mind your own business."

Ignoring him, I widen my eyes imploringly at April. "Please. Like I said, I know it sounds nuts. I'm only trying to help."

"Maybe you can ask Harriet a question only your dad would know the answer to?" Dorian suggests calmly.

She still looks dubious and more than a little pissed off. But she nods, leaning her elbows on the counter in front of us to get closer. "Fine. What were the last words my dad ever said to me?"

Ernest chuckles humorlessly, never tearing his eyes from his daughter. "I was in the hospital after having a stroke. She never left my side. Not until I yelled at her to get her ass back to the diner before it burned down without either of us here."

I stare at him for a moment, trying not to show my shock or

dismay at the depressing and heartbreaking story. Clearing my throat and hoping to keep any emotion out of my voice, I quickly repeat the story to April. It seems to be enough to convince her because she lets out a quiet gasp and stares at her dad's ghost with tears welling up in her eyes. I know she can't see him or feel him, but he lifts his hand to her cheek and pleads with her not to cry.

"Um, do you want to hear whatever it is he wants to say?" I ask awkwardly.

She nods wordlessly, her eyes flickering between me and the spot her dad's ghost is occupying. Taking a deep breath, she whispers, "Please."

Ernest wastes no time in speaking the words he's been waiting all his death to say. "Tell her I'm sorry. God, I'm sorry, April. You don't need to feel any guilt about not being there when I died. It's my fault, but I'm glad you weren't there to see it. I'm sorry you had to go through that all on your own. I'm also sorry that I spent so many years giving you hell about this damned place. The diner was my and your mother's dream, and I never should have made you feel like you had no choice but to take our dream on as your own. I never wanted you to feel burdened or like you were stuck here. If you want to burn this whole goddamn diner to the ground, if that would make you happy...then damn it, you do that. All I ever wanted was for you to be happy and find peace. I'm sorry I never said that while I was able to."

I repeat everything word for word so nothing accidentally gets lost in translation. A few tears fall from April's eyes before she quickly wipes them away.

"Thank you," she says, giving me a small smile. She sniffles, more tears forming at the corner of her eyes. "I just—thank you so much. I, um, think I need a minute. Excuse me."

April hastily walks away, heading back to the kitchen. I

don't blame her. That was a lot of heavy shit to drop on a person, let alone a person with little knowledge of the supernatural world and who only learned about my ability a few minutes ago. Letting out a deep breath, I turn to look at Dorian and Spencer.

"That was really fucking cool of you," Dorian says, beaming. Spencer nods along with him enthusiastically.

Ernest grunts, grabbing my attention. His expression is unreadable at first. But as I maintain eye contact with him, a look of pure serenity comes over him. "Thanks, kid."

He touches my shoulder, causing a sharp, tingling feeling to trickle across my skin. When Ernest's form begins blurring around the edges, I blink rapidly in an attempt to clear my vision. But as the seconds pass, all of him slowly becomes blurry until he slowly disappears from my sight entirely. The moment he's gone, I feel an intense warmth fill my chest. It's so strong and overwhelming that I gasp, unable to breathe for a few seconds. When it fades, all that's left is this strange blanket of peace enveloping me until I feel it deep in my bones down to my soul.

"Are you okay?" Spencer asks, squeezing my hand as his eyes frantically search mine.

I nod, feeling dazed. "He's gone. I, uh, I think he just crossed over?" I phrase it as a question, glancing at Spencer. He and the rest of the guys are still better ghost experts than I am. I can't think of another explanation for what just happened.

"Holy shit," Spencer whispers, staring at me in awe. He lets out a quiet, reverent laugh and lifts his hand to cup my cheek. "You are fucking incredible."

Dorian seems just as awed, grinning at me brightly as he laughs. "Seriously? Wow. Have you ever done that before?"

"Never." I shake my head, still reeling over everything that just happened. "I didn't even know I could do that."

"Are you feeling okay?" Spencer gently rubs his thumb over my cheek, a hint of worry in his gaze.

Knowing he's worried there will be weird side effects, like what happened when I fell into Sophia's memory vision, I slowly nod my head and tell him honestly, "I think so. I'm a little freaked out, and I'm feeling sort of drained."

He nods in understanding. "I'm gonna go check on April really quick, and then how about I walk you home?"

We're only a couple blocks from my house, so walking makes sense. I agree with his plan, giving him a grateful smile as he quickly heads back to the kitchen area to make sure April is alright.

"He's right," Dorian says. I turn to find him grinning cheekily at me. "You are pretty fucking incredible. Coolest witch I've ever met."

I snort and playfully roll my eyes. "No way."

"Yes, way." He nods, his expression sobering until he has the same awestruck, reverent look Spencer was giving me. "Almost every witch I know is selfish and pretentious. What you just did was not only badass, but it was also kind and selfless. You put yourself in a risky, uncomfortable situation for no gain of your own. You did that because you're a nice, caring person."

A shy smile tugs at my lips. Maybe he's right, but I also didn't think about it all that hard. How do I explain that once I spoke to Ernest, I felt like I didn't have any choice but to try to help him?

He grins at me even though I'm not sure what to say. Laughing quietly, he throws his arm around my shoulders and gives me a side hug. "When are you coming back over to the house? Elsie won't stop talking about how great her big sister is, and I know my parents would love to have you around more."

299

"I don't know." I shrug, smiling happily. "It feels a little weird to ask or invite myself over, but I've been texting with Elsie and Henry."

"You have an open invitation," he assures me. "But I'll ask my parents which day next week works best to do another family dinner if you're cool with that. It would be fun to hang out again away from the rest of the family too. With or without your emo boyfriend."

My cheeks flush, and I open my mouth to remind him that Spencer isn't my boyfriend. But when I see Spencer walk back through the swinging door behind the bar, I snap my mouth shut. Dorian snickers quietly beside me, and I subtly shove my elbow into his side.

"You ready to go?" Spencer asks when he rejoins us.

Dorian fist bumps Spencer and gives me another hug before we head out, giving me one final grin. "I'll text you later, almost-twin."

Outside, Spencer laces his fingers with mine as we begin walking in the direction of my house. The action gives me a fuzzy feeling in my stomach, and I just know there's a goofy smile on my face. Even though I know it's a bad idea, I can't bring myself to pull my hand away.

The walk home is nice and peaceful. Even though it's dark, the streetlights, the moon, and the Halloween lights from all the houses we pass give us plenty of light to see by. We recap the night and quietly discuss Ernest's ghost and how I managed to help him complete his unfinished business.

When my house comes into view, I realize I don't want the night to end. And then a thought occurs to me. "I'm so dumb. How are you going to get home?"

Spencer gives me a swoon-worthy smile and shrugs. "I'm gonna head over to Nolan and Mattie's for a bit. Owen's over there now, and he said he'll drive me home."

The reminder of Owen makes me feel slightly guilty for holding Spencer's hand. Still, I'm glad he ended up going to their house instead of staying home alone. I swallow back my feelings and smile awkwardly at Spencer. "Okay. You gonna tell them about Ernest?"

"Fuck yes!" He laughs. "They're gonna be so jealous when they hear what they missed out on."

I don't want them to be jealous, but I hope it makes them rethink taking a break from trying to help Sophia and Ryan. "Well, make sure to tell them I say hi. If I wasn't so worn out, I'd come hang out for a little while."

"I'll let them know." We stop outside my front door, and the porch light lets me see Spencer's expression soften as his eyes travel over me. "Thanks for coming with me tonight. I'm pretty sure you made this the best Halloween I've ever had."

A giggle escapes me, and I awkwardly swing my cauldron full of Halloween candy at my side. "I had a lot of fun too."

Spencer steps closer, letting go of my hand so he can reach up to touch the brim of my witch's hat. He grins as he looks it over. He already told me earlier I looked cute wearing it, and the memory makes my face warm up even more. The look he gives me when he finally meets my eyes again totally sets my heart on fire.

"God, I'm fucking crazy about you," he whispers, dropping his hand to caress my cheek. When his thumb brushes over my bottom lip, I swear I stop breathing. That swoopy feeling in my stomach is more intense than it's ever been, and I can't tear my eyes from his. Before I realize it's happening, Spencer leans forward and softly presses his lips to mine.

My first kiss is everything. Fireworks explode inside my brain and my chest, and every thought that isn't about Spencer completely disappears until he's all that's left.

Way too soon, he pulls away. I make this horribly

embarrassing whining sound, which makes him chuckle and lean in to give me another quick peck. I manage to keep any more noises to myself, but I know I'm staring at him like a lovesick idiot. Because a lovesick idiot is exactly what I am.

"Thanks," I say. And then I immediately want to cringe and slap myself for being such a fucking moron.

"You're welcome." He chuckles, the smile on his face more than a little smug. Neither of us says anything for a moment. Not until he hesitantly steps away from me. "I'll text you tomorrow?"

"Okay." My voice is all weird and breathy. Goddess, I need to get inside to process what just happened before I completely humiliate myself.

Spencer laughs again and shakes his head, staring at me like he thinks I'm adorable and not just incredibly stupid. "Goodnight, Harriet."

CHAPTER 25
HARRIET

Circe walks into my room, dragging a long piece of yellow ribbon with her. I have no idea where she found it, but she's been adding random shit to the pile of blankets I set up for her to nest in in the corner of my room near the heater. She drops the ribbon into her little nest and starts kneading the blankets, purring so loudly that I can hear her clearly from my bed all the way across the room.

"You realize you're a cat and not a bird, right?" I ask her.

She pauses her movements, glancing up to give me an unimpressed look before going back to the important task of kneading her blankets. Seriously, that cat is ridiculous. The mysterious yellow ribbon is only her newest treasure. Over the past several days, she's also stolen several of my socks and brought in leaves, a doily, and a dish towel for her nest. When I tried throwing the leaves out, she retaliated by immediately bringing in more, along with two pinecones. I gave up and let her continue adding to her weird little collection after that.

If Henry's right, then she's probably going to give birth any day. I'm equal parts excited and anxious. I have no experience with animals, so I definitely feel lucky to have a dad who's a vet. He's reassured me several times that he'll help out if anything goes wrong with Circe or her kittens.

A knock at my door has me glancing up from my bed where I've been lounging and scrolling through my phone for most of the morning. My mom pops her head in, giving me a wide, red-lipped smile.

"Good morning," she says. Despite being out late last night to celebrate Samhain, she looks just as beautiful and well-rested as she always does. "Flora and I are going out to brunch with some Council members and a few other witches to celebrate All Saints' Day. I think some of your classmates will be there. Do you want to come?"

That literally sounds like my worst nightmare. Did my mom just completely forget what I told her about the witches at school hazing me? Instead of bringing that uncomfortable topic up, I roll my eyes and sigh. "All Saints' Day isn't even a pagan holiday, mom."

She cackles and waves her hand dismissively. "Oh, you know we just use it as an excuse to keep celebrating once Samhain is over."

I'm pretty sure there's something not right about that, but I'm not going to argue with her. I shrug and turn my attention back to my phone. "Have fun, I guess."

"Are you sure you don't want to go?" she asks. "It might be good for you to spend more time with other witches and get more in touch with your heritage."

Yeah, she's completely forgotten everything I said to her last week about my experience in Weeping Hollow so far. I don't know why I'm surprised. There's no point getting angry, so I just shrug and give her a slightly annoyed look.

"No, thanks. I'm hanging out with Owen today."

Thinking about it makes my stomach flutter, in a good way

and a bad way. I always love spending time with Owen, but I'm kind of freaking out about Spencer. I know he told the guys about Ernest at the diner because Mattie blew my phone up about it last night. Did Spencer also tell them that we kissed? If Owen knows about that, is he going to act any differently around me? It's not like Spencer asked me to be his girlfriend or anything, but I still feel really weird and torn about it. I've replayed the moment about a million times in my head, and I feel giddy about it every single time. At the same time, I'm very aware that kissing Spencer last night was one of the stupidest things I could have done.

"That sounds lovely," my mom says. She gives me another smile, oblivious to the turmoil going through my head. "Have a wonderful day, sweetheart."

She leaves, and I go back to mindlessly watching TikTok videos on my phone. Seconds later, a text from Owen pops up, asking if he can pick me up in an hour. Relief, excitement, and worry fill my chest. I'm glad he still wants to hang out, and I'm genuinely looking forward to spending the day with him. But I still don't know if it's supposed to be a date or not, especially after kissing Spencer. I'm certainly not going to embarrass myself by asking.

After texting Owen back, I finally get up from bed and head to my closet to get dressed and ready. While I'm doing my hair and makeup, Sophia floats into my room. As usual, she's humming a gloomy song and nervously wringing her hands together. Ever since the sleepover last weekend, she's been slightly distant. I've told her a million times she has no reason to feel guilty about anything, and I've reassured her I'm perfectly fine.

"Hey." I give her a genuine smile. At this point, I don't think there's anything I can say to make her feel less bad about what happened with the spirit board and everything, so I've decided

I'm just going to act normal and talk to her like I always do until she hopefully chills out. "Do I look okay?"

She smiles softly in return, floating closer until she's practically hovering over me. It's the closest she's gotten since the sleepover, so I'll consider this progress. Giving me a questioning look, she traces the letters S, M, O, and N along with a question mark against the surface of my mirror.

Feeling my face warm up, I shrug a little defensively and say, "Owen. He asked me to hang out today."

Sophia giggles teasingly. She knows about my crush. I really want to tell her about my kiss with Spencer. Even though she can't easily give me advice or talk to me about it, I'm sure it'll feel good to get it all off my chest. I thought about calling Sage a million times last night, but I forced myself to wait. We have plans to FaceTime later tonight, thankfully, but the distance and time difference between us is seriously taking a toll.

Before I can make up my mind about blurting everything out to Sophia, I hear the doorbell ring downstairs. Rushing over to my window, I spot Owen's truck parked on the street outside. Butterflies swirl in my stomach, and I make a stupid squeaking sound as I rush back to mirror to finish putting on my lip gloss. Once I'm sure I'm set, I grab a black mini backpack, shove my phone, wallet, and a small makeup bag inside, and tell Sophia and Circe goodbye as I hurry downstairs.

Realizing I'm breathing heavily and probably look like a crazy person, I take a couple of seconds to compose myself before I calmly answer the door. Owen stands on the porch before me, his hands shoved in his pockets.

"Hey." I smile nervously, stepping outside and shutting the door behind me. "No way it's been an hour already!"

"Maybe I'm a little early." He gives me a shy smile. "I was

excited to see you, but I don't mind waiting if you need a little more time."

Well, he's not acting like he knows Spencer and I kissed. And of course, he's just as sweet as ever. Anxiously running a hand over my hair, I let out a nervous giggle and shake my head. "No, I think I'm fine."

We walk side by side to his truck together, and Owen even opens the passenger door for me. I seriously need to get ahold of myself. The butterflies are fluttering so hard in my stomach that I feel like I'm going to throw up.

When Owen gets in on the driver's side, he throws a gorgeous smile at me as he puts his seatbelt on. "You look beautiful, by the way."

That is not helping the butterfly situation in the slightest.

Seemingly unbothered by my lack of response, Owen pulls onto the street and asks, "Are you hungry enough for an early lunch?"

SEVERAL HOURS LATER, IT'S HARD TO REMEMBER WHY I WAS SO nervous when Owen picked me up. We've been having so much fun, and everything between us has been completely natural and easy. As quiet as Owen can be sometimes, conversation has never lulled between us, and even the few flirty remarks he's made have been innocent and low-key enough that I haven't freaked out or found a way to embarrass myself over them.

After we ate lunch at a cute deli place downtown—where we spent most of our time discussing Ernest's ghost and how I helped him cross over, much to Owen's awe and excitement—

we decided to visit an antique shop next door to the restaurant. After looking through the collection of old, dusty knickknacks and pieces of furniture for only a few minutes, we quickly decided to turn our outing into a game to see which of us could find the weirdest item for sale in the store.

And now, I think we must have been to every single antique shop in Weeping Hollow. There's no shortage of them, and I swear we've been to at least fifteen different shops. Most of them are really similar, but our hunt for all things weird and creepy has made it one of the most fun days I've ever had.

"Harriet!" Owen whispers my name, beckoning me over to the shelf he's perusing. This shop is much smaller than some of the others we've been to today, but the owner overcompensated by shoving as much crap as possible onto the many shelves crammed close together. This place is definitely one giant fire hazard waiting to happen, but that means the chances of us finding something extra cool are higher. When I walk over to stand beside Owen, his eyes light up with a wicked grin. "I think I found it."

My eyes follow where he's pointing, and I bite my lip to hold in a horrified giggle. The entire shelf is filled with taxidermy mice and rats all posed and wearing different costumes. There are several scenes depicted in some of the pieces, like groom and bride rats or a group of mice sitting down for a Thanksgiving dinner. But the one Owen's pointing to absolutely takes the cake. It's a display of a rat in a hospital bed with a rat doctor and mice nurses surrounding it.

"Oh my Goddess," I hiss quietly, lifting my hand to cover my mouth. We're the only customers in here, and I don't want the woman at the register to hear us. When I'm sure I'm not going to burst out laughing, I lower my hand and grin up at Owen. "I think this wins the whole day, if I'm honest."

He snorts. "You think this beats the mosaic made of antique, prosthetic glass eyes we saw earlier?"

"I don't know." I giggle, my eyes darting around at all the taxidermy art pieces. There's a sign beside the displays that says the rats and mice were ethically sourced. I know tons of people love this kind of stuff, but I'm personally not one of them. "They might be tied."

The bell chimes over the door of the shop, signaling that someone else is coming in. Owen and I decide to call it a day because there's no way more than two people can comfortably walk through this shop.

Outside, it's drizzling lightly. Owen places his hand on my back and frowns up at the dark clouds covering the sky. "Shit, I'm sorry. If I knew it was going to rain, I would have brought an umbrella for you."

"It's not your fault." I chuckle. "And I'm not going to melt."

Because we've been walking downtown all day, we're nowhere close to Owen's truck, unfortunately. It takes us more than ten minutes to get there, and by then, the light drizzle of rain has turned into a torrential downpour. We end up running the rest of the way to his truck, laughing the entire time. Despite both of us being soaked, Owen still takes the time to open my door for me.

Once we're both inside the truck, Owen turns the vehicle on and cranks up the heat. I wipe my face and brush my hair over my shoulder as I smile over at him. How is it that he can look so damn cute with wet hair while I probably look like a drowned rat?

"It'll take a few minutes for the truck to heat up," he says. Glancing over at me worriedly, he asks, "Are you cold?"

Now that we're sitting still, the chilly air combined with my clothes and hair being soaked make it impossible to hide the fact that I'm shivering. Not wanting Owen to feel bad, because the weather definitely isn't his fault, I shrug. "I'll be fine in a few minutes once the heat kicks in."

His frown deepens. Without warning, he reaches over and wraps his arms around me, pulling me flush against his side. While he tucks my head under his chin and rubs his hand up and down my arm, he hums softly. "This probably won't help much since my clothes are just as wet as yours, but it's better than nothing, right?"

"Um, yeah," I squeak.

Goddess, I'm glad he can't see my face. I'm definitely blushing, and even I can't decide if I'm horrified or elated by the position I'm in. Either way, the cold is now the last thing on my mind. I hesitantly rest my hand against Owen's broad chest, feeling stupid and guilty but unable to stop myself. I've hugged Owen several times, and he held me in his lap for a long time last weekend when the guys slept over at my house. But this feels different and way more intimate. Maybe it's because we're alone. Or maybe it's because I kissed Spencer and now I feel a million times more aware of my feelings and attraction toward both him and Owen.

We're quiet for a few minutes, listening to the rain pelt the windshield while Owen continues rubbing his hand over my arm and waits for the truck to heat up. My body already feels like it's on fire everywhere he's touching me, but I keep my mouth shut and greedily allow myself to enjoy every second of this while I can. I know it's not going to last. Sooner rather than later, I'm sure, I'm going to have to tell Owen and Spencer how I feel and that we can only be friends before things get any messier or someone's feelings get hurt.

When the heat finally starts working enough to make the cab of the truck feel warm and toasty, I move to pull away. But Owen keeps his arm around me and snuggles me closer, reaching over with his other hand to buckle my seatbelt in the center seat. He looks down and gives me a cheeky smile, so I let out a soft chuckle and keep my head on his shoulder while he drives.

"You ready for me to take you home?" he asks quietly.

I want to say no, that I want to keep hanging out or that I never want this day to end. Instead, I grudgingly admit, "Yeah. I still have some homework to finish before Monday, and Sage is planning on calling tonight."

The drive is quiet but comfortable. Too soon, he parks along the street in front of my house. I slowly lift my head from Owen's shoulder and glance out the window. There aren't any lights on in the house, making it look dark and foreboding. Obviously, my mom and aunt aren't home yet.

"Thanks for everything today," I say to Owen, turning around to face him. "I had a lot of fun."

"Me too." His voice is deeper than usual, sending shivers up my spine. When his eyes fall to my lips, my heart stutters in my chest. And then my heart stops altogether when he says, "I really want to kiss you, Harriet."

I'm not in control of my voice or my body as I stare up at him silently with my lips slightly parted. He meets my eyes and slowly leans closer, giving me plenty of time to pull away or reject him. But I don't. It's a horrible, *horrible* idea, but Goddess, I want to kiss him so badly!

When his lips press against mine, I completely lose my mind and melt against him. His kisses are soft, sweet, and hesitant at first, but when I kiss him back, he becomes more confident and slides his arm around my waist to pull me closer. When his tongue caresses my bottom lip, it's like something snaps inside of me and every thought escapes my brain except for the desire to be closer to him.

A needy whine leaves my throat when he deepens our kiss, and I desperately climb into his lap until my legs are straddling either side of him. I slide one of my hands behind his head and bury my fingers in his dark hair, and my other hand falls to his chest where I grip his shirt between my fingers. He groans and places his hands on my hips, trailing kisses from my mouth down to my throat. I had no idea something could feel so fucking good. My breath escapes in sharp pants, and I press myself impossibly closer to him until his hands fall to my ass.

Somehow while we're making out, one of us bumps the steering wheel and causes the horn to beep. It startles me enough to jerk me back to reality, and I pull away from Owen with a shocked gasp. He stares back at me dazedly, his lips curving into a crooked smile.

"Oh, Goddess." My eyes dart around as embarrassment floods through me. How did I let this happen? The windows are completely fogged up, and I still have my hands tangled in Owen's hair and shirt. I quickly pull my hands away and squeak when I notice the very obvious bulge in his jeans.

Before I can scramble off his lap and apologize profusely, Owen gently grabs my hand. "Hey, I'm sorry. I didn't mean to get so carried away."

Him!? What about me? Is this why so many witches are super promiscuous? I lost my fucking mind from one kiss. That felt so good, and I already know I could easily get addicted or push things much further if I let it happen again.

Owen squeezes my hand, bringing my attention back to him. His cheeks are flushed, but he's got the sweetest, happiest smile on his face. "I like you so much. I've wanted to kiss you since we first met, but I never expected it to happen like that. We can take it slow, okay?"

"I—" Words completely escape me. What can I possibly say to him? He's so sweet and perfect, and I don't deserve him. Tears fill my eyes as guilt threatens to consume me. I should have put a stop to this when Owen and Spencer first started flirting with me, but I was too fucking selfish. "I'm sorry."

"What do you have to be sorry about?" Owen wipes a tear from my cheek that manages to escape.

Forcing myself to put some distance between us, I climb off him and sit as far away as I possibly can against the passenger door. As terrified as I am at the drama this will probably cause, I know I need to tell him the truth.

"I kissed Spencer last night," I blurt out.

There are a few seconds of silence between us before Owen responds, "Okay?"

His expression is completely unreadable, giving absolutely no indication of how he feels about my admission. My stomach squirms uncomfortably under his gaze, and then every stupid thought I've had for weeks spills from my mouth.

"I like you both so much. Goddess, so fucking much, it's stupid. I've been crushing on you and Spencer from pretty much the first second I saw both of you, and then we became friends and my crush got so much worse. I've spent the past few weeks letting you guys flirt with me and pretending to be oblivious to it because I didn't know how to tell either of you how I feel. I'm no better than Amethyst or my mom. I never wanted to be a cheater or someone who leads a guy on, but now I've gone and kissed you both and created this whole complicated mess. I'm really, really sorry."

Owen bites his lip and turns to look out his window. It's still too foggy for him to see out of, but I'm sure he needs an excuse to look anywhere but at me. My heart feels like it's in my stomach as I wait for him to say something. When he doesn't, I clear my throat and say, "I totally understand if you don't want to be friends anymore."

He whips his head back around to stare at me with his

eyebrows raised. "I still want to be friends. To be honest, I still want to be more than friends."

A hysterical giggle bubbles in my throat, but I choke it back. No way can he mean that after everything I just said! Staring at him incredulously and desperately trying to ignore the way my heart's flipping over in my chest, I shake my head. "We can't. I can't choose between you and Spencer, and I don't want to ruin your friendship. It'll be easier for us to stay just friends."

He frowns, but he doesn't argue or disagree with me. I take that as a sign that I need to go. He clearly needs space. When I open the passenger door and start to climb out, Owen moves to open his door too. "Do you want me to walk you up?"

"No, thanks." My voice is all stupid and squeaky again. Can he seriously just stop being perfect for two seconds so I can think straight? Clearing my throat, I give him a smile that probably looks more like a grimace. "I'll see you later."

I practically sprint up the path to my front door. The second I'm locked inside, I slide onto the floor with my back against the door and cover my face with my hands. Only I could find a way to turn such a wonderful day into such a disaster. I just hope Owen doesn't hate me once he has some time to think.

Realizing Spencer still needs to hear the truth too, I pull my phone out of my pocket to text him. *'I'm sorry, but I think we should just be friends.'* When he reads the message and calls me a few seconds later, I ignore the call and put my phone on Do Not Disturb. It's super dickish of me, but after talking to Owen, I don't have the energy to have the same conversation with Spencer right now. Not yet. At least now he'll know where we stand, and I can explain everything later if he still wants to hear it.

CHAPTER 26

SPENCER

'*I*'*m sorry, but I think we should just be friends.*'

My fingers type out another desperate response to Harriet's text, but I force myself to delete it before I press send. She didn't answer my calls, so I doubt she'll answer a text. I don't need to send her something that makes me sound like more of an idiot than she probably already thinks I am. Even if she did answer me, what do I expect? I can beg her to reconsider and go out with me, but she'll just think I'm pathetic. If Harriet only wants to be friends, I need to respect that. And as much as I might want an explanation after how well everything went last night, she doesn't owe me anything.

A knock at the door has me sighing and setting my phone on the side table beside the couch. I lean over and ruffle Shiloh's hair. He's sitting on the floor playing his Nintendo Switch, and he bats my hand away without ever looking away from his screen. Chuckling to myself, I get up to answer the door. Any kind of distraction is welcome right now to help me stop obsessing over Harriet.

"Hey, man." I grin when I open the door to find Owen

standing on the porch. It's weird he didn't text before showing up, but I'm definitely not upset to see him. "What's up?"

He shrugs. "Just wanted to talk. You busy?"

Owen never wants to talk. Normally, getting him to talk about anything is nearly impossible. Whatever it is must be pretty important. I open the door wider to let him in and say, "Not really. Zoe just ran to the grocery store, so I'm chilling with Shiloh and waiting for her to get back."

He follows me into the living room and sits down on the couch, reaching over to ruffle Shiloh's hair the same way I did a few moments ago. "Hey, kid. Whatcha playing?"

Shiloh spares Owen a quick side glance. "*Kirby and the Forgotten Land.*"

I sit down on the other end of the couch, shoving my hands into my hoodie pocket to avoid the temptation to grab and check my phone for the millionth time. As soon as Shiloh is distracted by his game again, Owen looks at me with an almost nervous expression.

"So, what's up?" I ask.

Owen hesitates, making me wonder if I should wait until Zoe gets home to press him in case he wants to talk in private. But eventually, he answers, "I just dropped Harriet off at home."

I swear I can physically feel the blood drain from my face. There's no way it's a coincidence that he was with Harriet when she sent me that text. Is that why she sent me that message? Because she finally decided she likes Owen more than me and wants to go out with him instead? It's the only explanation I can think of. Harriet's always so skittish about shit like that, so a random and vague text from her makes sense if she was too nervous to tell me the truth.

"Did something happen between you guys?" I force myself to ask calmly. If Owen came over to break the news to me in

316

person, I know it's because he's nervous or feels guilty. Not because he's rubbing it in my face.

He clears his throat, avoiding my eyes as a blush spreads across his face. "We, uh, made out."

Shit. I knew it. I stare at my best friend, waiting for anger or jealousy to kick in. But all I really feel is sad and really fucking stupid. I knew she was into Owen, and it's my own damn fault for getting my hopes up or for thinking she liked me back too. That's not her fault or his.

Still, I'm too hurt to respond properly. I know this is a huge deal for Owen. He's never kissed a girl before, and I'm sure part of him wants to relive it and talk about it with someone. I don't want shit to be weird between us just because he got the girl and I didn't. So, I clear my throat and force a smile, reaching a hand out to him to fist bump. "Congrats, man."

He stares at my hand like I'm insane for a second, and then snorts and fist bumps me back. "Thanks. You're not pissed?"

My knee bounces up and down, giving away the nerves I feel. "No, of course not. Don't get me wrong. I'm sad because I really like her, but I knew you liked her too. You guys deserve each other. You've been way happier since she started hanging out with us, and you're even talking more. I think she's good for you."

"Is Harriet your girlfriend now?" Shiloh asks Owen, his game temporarily forgotten.

Owen slowly shakes his head and clears his throat. "No."

Hope burns in my chest for about a millisecond until I remember Harriet's message. I really want to ask Owen what happened, but I don't want to sound like a dick by appearing too excited that he's not officially dating her yet. Not like it's gonna change anything for me, anyway.

"Then that means she can still be your girlfriend, Spencer!" Shiloh tells me excitedly. He gets a thoughtful look on his face and hums. "Or maybe she can be both your girlfriend. If I was older, I would want Harriet to be my girlfriend too."

This is not a conversation I want my six-year-old nephew butting in on. Especially not when he says shit like that. I give him a stern look and say, "Stop being so damn nosy, and go play in your room until your mom gets home."

He sticks his tongue out at me as he stands up, grabs his Switch, and storms down the hallway to his room. I wait until I hear the sound of his game resume, and then I turn to Owen and sigh.

"Sorry. So, what happened? Did you just not ask her out, or what?"

Owen stares at me with a blank expression and deadpans, "She told me she kissed you last night too."

I choke on my own spit which leads to a coughing fit. Owen chuckles at me, and I flip him off as I struggle to regain control of my breathing. Seriously though, that has to be the last thing I expected him to say. I didn't tell him I kissed Harriet because I didn't want him to feel weird or self-conscious. I'm really fucking surprised she told him though. Maybe she felt guilty about it? That sounds like Harriet. Though honestly, it makes me feel even more pathetic to think she feels badly about something that made me feel like I was on top of the world.

"I kissed her goodnight after I walked her home last night," I admit, feeling awkward as fuck. "It's not like it's going to happen again. She just texted me before you got here and told me she thinks we should just be friends. She obviously likes you more than me."

He laughs, surprising me again. "No. She told me she only wants to be friends with me too because she likes both of us and feels guilty about it." He pauses, a bashful smile forming on his face. "I didn't know what to say to her in the moment, but I think Shiloh makes a good point. What if we both ask her out?"

I gape at him in shock. No way did I just hear him correctly. "Wait, what?"

"It wouldn't be that weird." He shrugs, blushing again. "At least for me, it doesn't bother me to think of you liking her or dating her while I'm dating her too. You're my best friend, and we've been honest with each other so far about wanting to be with her."

The fact that the idea doesn't immediately put me off should be alarming. Instead, I remember going to the pumpkin patch with Harriet and Owen, and how we both held her and cuddled her when we slept over at her house. It wasn't weird then, and after a while, it didn't bother me to know that Owen liked her as much as I do. I figured Harriet liked us both. I just stupidly assumed she'd end up liking one of us more than the other at some point. If Owen's right, and she genuinely likes us both the same, could I really be okay being in an exclusive relationship with her while she's also dating Owen?

It takes me about five seconds to decide that I think I could. It's worth trying, at least. I've never liked anyone as much as I like Harriet. The first time I ever saw her at the diner, I thought she was insanely hot, and seeing how flustered she got over her mom and aunt teasing her was seriously fucking cute. After I found out she went to school with us and that she's a witch, I tried to keep my guard up even though everything about her drew me in. But it became apparent very quickly that she's nothing like Amethyst or any of the other witches I know, and it was easy to let myself fall for her after only knowing her a week. Not once has Harriet ever judged me or my family, and underneath her grumpy exterior, she's one of the kindest and most selfless people I've ever met.

"Do you think she'd be okay with that?" I ask hesitantly.

319

"She's never had a boyfriend before. Having two at once might feel like too much to her."

"I was thinking we could talk to her about it together?" Owen grimaces. "You know I'm not great at talking. It's easier with Harriet, but I still always feel like I'm going to say the wrong thing or freak her out. She seemed like she felt really guilty about liking both of us, and she acted like she expected me to be angry that she kissed you."

"You didn't get mad, did you?" I really can't see Owen getting pissed about something like that, so I'm not surprised when he shakes his head. "Okay, good. It's not like she cheated on anyone. Neither of us were officially dating her when she kissed us."

"Yeah, but maybe it felt like cheating to her? She made a comment about being no better than Amethyst. I felt so bad when she said that, like we'd completely fucked up by openly flirting with her over the past few weeks. But I couldn't think of anything to say that wouldn't sound desperate or like I was trying to convince her to pick me over you. Plus, I wasn't sure if you felt the same way I did. I know Amethyst really hurt you, and I agree with Harriet that I'd never want to put you in a position where you felt like you did when you were dating her."

My stomach drops when I hear that Harriet compared herself to my ex. Like Owen, I can't help but feel shitty for making her feel like that. I've been trying to take things slow with Harriet since I know she's inexperienced. It never occurred to me that she'd feel guilty about anything that Owen and I started with her because of what I told her about Amethyst.

"She's nothing like Amethyst," I say firmly. "It's not the same thing at all. Even if Harriet agrees to go out with both of us, it's not like she's going behind our backs. We're being really fucking open about everything."

"Alright." He grins, looking relieved and excited. "So, when do you want to talk to her?"

Sighing, I turn and grab my phone from the side table. Still no response from Harriet, which isn't a surprise now that I understand better where her head is at. "I don't know. She's not answering my calls. Plus, I'm technically watching Shiloh until Zoe gets back from the store."

As if my words summon her, the front door opens and Zoe walks in carrying bags full of groceries. She pauses when she sees Owen sitting on the couch with me, grinning at him warmly. "Hey, Owen. Do you guys mind helping me bring the groceries in?"

Between the two of us, we manage to get all the groceries inside in one trip. As a thank you, Zoe invites Owen to stay for dinner. Away from my sister so she doesn't overhear us, Owen and I agree that we'll head over to Harriet's house after we finish eating.

All through dinner, I keep my fingers crossed that Harriet gives us and our crazy idea a chance.

CHAPTER 27
HARRIET

"Ugh, stop laughing!" I whine. "Nothing about this is funny. I've literally been freaking out about this for hours."

Sage cackles over FaceTime. "Girl! You need some perspective. Two incredibly sweet, incredibly *hot* guys, who not only like ghosts but encourage you to explore your powers, admitted they have romantic feelings for you and gave you the best kisses of your life. That's fucking awesome, and you should feel like you're on top of the world!"

I feel my face heat up as I murmur, "Technically, they're the only two times I've ever been kissed."

"Regardless!" Sage snorts. "Why aren't you jumping for joy? From what you said, it sure didn't seem like Owen was pissed or even surprised when you told him about Spencer. Those guys aren't stupid. If they've been flirting with you as much as you've said the past few weeks, they probably expected this. You need to chill out, put your big girl pants on, and straight up ask them if they both want to be your boyfriends. Chances are, they'll probably say yes. You're fucking awesome, and it's about time someone other than me realized that!"

"You're insane. That sort of thing only happens in those smutty romance books you read."

She laughs so hard that she drops her phone, and I have to wait several seconds for her to get control of herself and reposition her phone so we can see each other. I give her an unamused look before we both burst into hysterical giggles together. Goddess, I miss her. Talking to her over the phone every few days will never be enough when we used to hang out literally every single day when I still lived in Oregon.

"Seriously, Harriet." Her voice becomes softer after our giggle fits die down. "I really think you're overthinking everything."

She's probably right, but I feel like there's nothing I can do except see how Owen and Spencer act when I see them at school on Monday. Whatever happens, I'll just deal with it then.

"Whatever." I sigh. "Let's talk about something else. Anything new with you?"

Sage instantly groans. "Well, school has been absolute shit without you. The covenettes have been kissing my ass and begging me to sit with them at lunch, which is hilarious and pathetic." The covenettes are what we call the other witches I used to go to school with. They always ignored us when I was around, so it's both obnoxious and insulting to hear they've changed their tune so quickly with Sage now that I'm gone. She rolls her eyes, and then a wicked grin spreads across her face. "My magic's been getting more unpredictable lately though. It's freaking my parents out enough that they want to hire someone from the Council to help guide me. I've been trying to convince them I'll have a better shot at getting help if we move to Weeping Hollow since the community is so big there. I think they might actually be starting to consider it!"

"For real?" I ask excitedly, my eyes widening.

Sage's magic has always been a little wonky. It's part of why we were first forced together as kids by our parents. Sometimes her magic doesn't work at all, like mine, and other times it's like it explodes out of her to the point she's unable to control it. I know it bothers her, even when she pretends it doesn't, so I'm sure getting some sort of mentor would be helpful. But if she ended up moving *here* in order to find help? That would be the best outcome either of us could ever imagine.

"Yes!" she exclaims. "You know I was planning on visiting over winter break, but now my parents are talking about getting an Airbnb for our whole family so my parents can talk to other local witches and representatives from the Council."

I cross my fingers where she can see them on her screen, grinning ear to ear. "I'll be praying to the Goddess every night."

We enthusiastically discuss the possibility of Sage's family moving here, making theoretical plans and coming up with about a million what-if scenarios. Talking and giggling like nothing has changed between us after all these weeks apart makes my soul feel lighter and helps all my worries concerning Owen, Spencer, and helping my ghost friends drift away for a little while.

In the middle of yet another mutual laughing fit, there's a pinging sound at my window that catches my attention. I shush Sage and turn to face my window with my eyebrows furrowed, noticing that Circe is glaring at the window with her tail swishing irritably behind her.

Another pinging sound has me sighing and standing up from my bed. "Hold on, Sage. I think there's something at my window." Narrowing my eyes teasingly at Circe, I add, "I already ended up with one aggravating familiar. The last thing I need is some creepy little bat fluttering around."

She cackles as I walk across my room and pull the curtain back on my window. It takes my eyes a second to adjust to the darkness outside, and I don't see anything flying around the window like I first suspected. When something small hits the window right in front of my face, I jump back and curse. "What the fuck. I think a rock just hit my window!"

Muffled laughter makes me look down, and my mouth drops when I spot Owen and Spencer standing in the yard below my window.

"Sage," I hiss. She stares at me questioningly. I think she even asks me a question, but my heart is pounding too loudly for me to hear anything else. "Spencer and Owen are outside... throwing freaking rocks at my window!"

She gasps and then squeals, excitedly demanding, "Turn the camera around and show me."

Somehow, my brain functions enough for me to flip my camera and to slide open my window. Shaking my head in disbelief and angling my phone so Sage can see their dark silhouettes down on the lawn, I yell down at the guys in as hushed a tone as I can. "What are you guys doing?"

They glance at each other before looking up at me again. Spencer cups his hands around his mouth and says in a slightly raised voice, "We want to talk to you. Can you come downstairs?"

My heart beats faster, if possible, and it takes me several seconds to remember how to speak. "Why didn't you just knock on the front door? It's not even late."

There's enough light from the porch, moon, and street lights that I see Spencer grin. "We thought this would be more romantic."

Romantic!? Oh my Goddess. They are actually going to kill

me. A hysterical giggle escapes me before I manage to slap a hand over my mouth. When I'm sure I'm not going to erupt into anymore stupid laughter, I drop my hand and tell them, "You are such idiots."

The guys laugh, and Sage snorts through my phone. I quickly flip the camera back around so she can see me again, and she shakes her head in exasperation. "You lucky witch. I told you that you had a good shot at making them both your boyfriends. Only happens in smutty romance books, my ass."

I tell the guys I'll be down in a minute and slam the window shut, back away into my room where they can't see me as I stare at Sage like a deer in headlights. "They showed up here *together*. Sage, I seriously think I'm going to have a heart attack."

Because if they're here together now, trying to be *romantic*, then they've definitely talked about kissing me and everything I blurted out to Owen earlier. Part of me feels incredibly embarrassed at the thought of them discussing that, but mostly, I'm relieved that they don't seem like they're angry at each other or at me. The fact that they want to talk is good news, right?

Unless this is all a desperate ploy to get me to choose one of them over the other.

"You're not going to have a heart attack," Sage says calmly. "You're going to go downstairs, hear them out, and then have crazy-hot make out sessions with both of them after agreeing to be their girlfriend." She pauses, grinning mischievously before she tacks on, "And then you're going to call me right after and tell me all the delicious details."

"Okay, fine." I laugh nervously. We say goodbye after I promise to update her as soon as possible, and I toss my phone onto my bed.

As I quickly search for a pair of slippers to wear outside,

Sophia floats past me to the window where the curtains are still open. She giggles softly when she sees the guys, turning to give me a teasing look. She was giving me privacy during my conversation with Sage, but apparently, she doesn't feel that courtesy is necessary when the guys are involved. I roll my eyes and grunt, nearly tripping as I hurry to pull the slippers on.

It's not until I'm opening the front door downstairs that I realize I could have changed out of my pajamas into something more presentable. My hair's up in a messy bun, and I already washed my makeup off my face. Standing with the door cracked, I raise my hand to touch my hair self-consciously and nearly jump out of my skin when someone calls my name from behind me.

"Harriet?" I spin around to find my mom standing in the doorway of the kitchen, a concerned look on her face. "Where are you going?"

"Oh, um." I anxiously rock back and forth on my heels. "Owen and Spencer are outside. I'm just going to talk to them really quick."

Understanding lights her eyes, and she grins almost as mischievously as Sage did when she asked to hear all the delicious details. "Ah, I see. Well, if it gets too cold, make sure to invite them in."

I nod distractedly, totally not in the mood to talk to my mom when I'm still not one hundred percent sure what I'm walking into. Without letting myself think about it anymore, I walk outside and quietly close the door behind me.

"Hey," Owen whispers, him and Spencer waiting for me at the bottom of the porch steps.

"Hi," I say shyly. When I reach the bottom of the steps to join them, I awkwardly gesture at the front door. "Um, my mom said to invite you guys in if it's too cold."

Spencer chuckles, shoving his hands into his jacket

pockets. I keep my eyes trained on his chest because it's too hard to meet his eyes. Still, I can practically feel him smiling at me. "We thought talking outside might be easier so you don't feel trapped or like you can't walk away if you get too nervous."

While his words are thoughtful, they make my heart skip like crazy. What are they going to say that they expect me to run away from?

"We can always sit in my truck to talk if you prefer that," Owen says.

My eyes snap up to meet his, a squeak leaving my mouth as my face burns hot. He bites his lip to cover his smile, and I dart a nervous glance at Spencer to find him smirking at me. If I wasn't suspicious already, that proves it that Owen already told him exactly what happened between us in his truck earlier.

"Um, that's okay. This is probably fine." I twist my hands together anxiously, shoving them into my hoodie pocket as I clear my throat. "So, what are you guys doing here?"

They share another look before Owen gives me a bashful smile. "I told Spencer that we kissed and what you said about liking both of us."

Well, they're certainly not beating around the bush. While part of me was expecting the conversation to go like this, I'm still absolutely mortified. I have absolutely no idea what to say, so I stay silent and stare at the ground between them.

When Spencer takes a step closer to me, I jump and lift my eyes to meet his. He smiles softly, a hint of nervousness in his expression. "Neither of us are mad, and we don't want to pressure you about anything. So, please don't feel nervous or scared, okay? We just thought it would be easier to talk and put everything out in the open. I'm pretty sure it hasn't been a secret that Owen and I like you, so this doesn't need to be a secret either."

"Okay, that's fair." I take a deep breath. "I really like you both a lot for about a million different reasons. I figured you guys liked me back, but I've never dated anyone so I almost never know how to react or what to say. It's so much worse whenever I feel flustered, which is pretty much anytime either of you flirt with me. Plus, I felt guilty for liking both of you and I've been too afraid to say anything or accidentally hurt your feelings. I'm sorry I kissed both of you without talking about everything and for making it seem like I was going behind anyone's back. I, um, really hope we can still be friends."

"You didn't do anything wrong, so you have nothing to be sorry about," Spencer says, his nerves falling away as his grin widens. "Also, it's really fucking cute whenever you get flustered."

Owen chuckles and nods in agreement. "Definitely cute."

Spencer grins and shuffles slightly closer to me. "So, Owen and I were wondering if you might consider going out with both of us? We talked about it, and we agreed that we trust each other and we both like you enough to give it a chance."

"Oh my Goddess," I squeak, my hands flying up to cover my flushed cheeks. I can't believe Sage was right and that this is actually freaking happening.

The guys chuckle, and Owen reaches out to soothingly rub his hand up and down my arm. "If you really only want to be friends, that's okay. Or if you truly like one of us more than the other but are still worried about hurting someone's feelings, that's alright too. We're not going to hold your feelings against you, and I swear we'll do our best not to make anything weird or uncomfortable. But I just want you to know that I like you so fucking much, and I'd feel incredibly lucky to be your boyfriend."

"Won't you guys feel jealous?" I ask, glancing guiltily at Spencer. "Or like I'm cheating on you?"

Spencer shakes his head vehemently. "No. It wouldn't be like cheating at all. Not if we're open about it. As far as feeling jealous, I'm sure sometimes things might be weird or difficult, but that's any relationship. We can figure out our boundaries as we go, as long as we promise to tell each other when something bothers us. Unconventional relationships like this really aren't that unusual nowadays."

Hearing him say that makes me feel like a weight has been lifted off my shoulders. After he told me what happened between him and Amethyst, I never wanted to be someone who made him feel like she did. A giddy feeling rises in my chest as butterflies flutter like mad in my stomach. If Owen and Spencer are serious about wanting to be a throuple, then I would have to be the stupidest girl in the universe to turn them down.

"I'm probably going to be a terrible girlfriend." I glance back and forth between them, a smile blooming on my face at the adorable looks of anticipation they're wearing. "But if you guys really mean it, then yeah, I would love to be with both of you."

"Fuck yes!" Spencer exclaims, laughing happily as he leaps forward and captures my lips in a kiss. When he pulls away, softly cupping my cheeks, he gives me a crooked smile. "Sorry. Is that okay?"

When I glance over at Owen, he gives me a reassuring nod. Feeling slightly breathless, I smile timidly at Spencer and nod. "More than okay."

He grins in relief and quickly kisses me again. This time when he pulls away, Owen steps closer and wraps his arms around me as he leans down to press his lips to mine. My heart races and my head feels like it's going to explode as I let myself melt against him.

Just like Spencer, Owen keeps his kisses short and sweet.

But I'm still completely breathless when he pulls away. I giggle and bury my face against his chest, turning my head enough so I can grin at Spencer.

"I'm pretty sure I'm going to pass out if you guys keep doing this."

They laugh, but I'm honestly worried I might die from swooning too much if they kiss me again tonight.

Fortunately—or maybe unfortunately—neither of them kisses me again while we stand outside and talk for a little longer. But they continue touching me and hugging me, making it clear they're just as ecstatic about our arrangement as I am. I have no idea how I ended up lucky enough to somehow call Owen and Spencer my boyfriends—*boyfriends*, plural! —but I'm absolutely going to try to be the best damn girlfriend I can be and make the most of this while it lasts.

CHAPTER 28
HARRIET

"What are you so dressed up for?"

My mom smiles coyly and checks her makeup in the rearview mirror. "Oh, I have a meeting this morning. That's all."

I side-eye her curiously and a little suspiciously. My mom always looks amazing and dresses like a knockout any day of the week, but it's obvious she's made even more effort than usual this morning. She's even wearing one of her favorite vintage dresses that she typically only wears to witchy events. What the hell kind of meeting could she possibly be going to that she needs to make this sort of impression? She and my aunt agreed to move into my great grandma's house with the intention of converting the house into a bakery and tea shop. I haven't heard much about their progress lately, but I've been busy with my own stuff to ask much about it. I can only assume my mom's meeting has something to do with their business.

Deciding to leave it alone, I shrug to myself and turn to

look out my window. There's no point pushing her about it. If my mom wants me to know her plans, she'll tell me.

"I have a surprise to share with you later," she adds after a short silence.

Oh, no. Historically, my mom's 'surprises' are usually bad news for me. Dread fills my chest as I narrow my eyes at her. "What is it?"

"Nothing bad! Don't worry," she cackles, waving her hand at me. With another sly smile, she says, "I don't know why you're so grumpy this morning. I thought you'd be in a good mood after looking so cozy with your boys yesterday."

My cheeks flush, and a nervous giggle escapes me. She's not wrong. Owen and Spencer came over yesterday and we spent pretty much the entire day snuggling and watching horror movies together. If I thought they were flirting with me a lot before, that was nothing compared to now after agreeing to be in a relationship with them. Honestly, the whole day was super nice and by the end of it, I stopped feeling so embarrassed to snuggle against them or even kiss them.

Owen was going to drive me to school this morning like he usually does, but my mom insisted on driving me instead. I can't deny I'm sort of bummed about it, but not enough to make a fuss. It's not like I won't get to spend time with him or Spencer at school today, and Owen already promised to drive me home.

Instead of pulling up at the drop-off area in front of the school like she usually does whenever she drives me, my mom parks in the visitor's lot. I make another face at her and say, "Don't tell me your meeting is with Principal Di Rossi."

She huffs irritably and purses her lips. "Kamal is a good man. It's been a long time since I considered settling down, so I wish you'd give him a chance, Harriet."

I try not to roll my eyes as I shrug her off. I don't have any issues with my principal, even though it is slightly embarrassing to know my mom's dating someone who works at my school. But I don't believe for one second that she's serious about the guy. She never is. I stopped feeling bad for the men my mom strings along years ago.

"Okay," I say when she keeps glaring at me. Adjusting my backpack over my shoulder, I give her an awkward smile. I'm sure as hell not going to walk with her. Ryan's probably already waiting for me, and it won't be long until the rest of the guys find me too. "I guess I'll see you later."

Before she has a chance to say anything, I quickly walk away and head into the school by myself. To my relief, I find Ryan floating near my locker. A grin spreads across my face as I rush over to him,

"Hey!" For a split second, I think about hugging him. Which is so not like me. And anyway, it's not like he'd be able to feel me. I clear my throat and shove aside the thought. "I have so much to tell you. The whole weekend was so crazy."

Ryan's eyes light up as he leans closer to me. Close enough that I feel a chill against my arm as he wiggles his eyebrows at me. "Oh, this better be good. Please tell me you hooked up with Spencer on Halloween like we talked about?"

My whole face heats up as I giggle nervously in response. His eyes widen and his jaw drops. Flapping his hand in front of my face, he gasps. "Shut the fuck up. Are you serious? You really hooked up?"

I giggle again, flooded with warmth and a mixture of giddiness and embarrassment. "Well, I don't know if I'd call it hooking up? Certainly not by your definition. But Spencer kissed me on Friday night. And then I hung out with Owen on Saturday, and we made out. I sort of freaked out about it all right after and confessed how I was feeling about him and

Spencer, and then both guys came over together Saturday night and asked me out. Like, officially."

I don't mean to blurt the whole thing out, but it's always so easy and natural to confide things in Ryan. Maybe part of it is because he can't really tell anyone my secrets—unless the guys record him talking, I guess—but mostly, he's just a good listener and a really good friend. By the time I finish telling him how things turned out with Owen and Spencer, Ryan looks shocked.

"Holy shit." He laughs, still gaping at me. When he shakes off his initial shock, he grins and asks, "You said yes, right?"

"Of course," I whisper, laughing nervously. "They're both my boyfriends now. At least until they realize how crazy they are."

Ryan crosses his arms, smiling even bigger as his eyes soften. "No way. Those guys would be idiots to ever let you go. They know exactly how lucky they are if they agreed to share you so quickly. Honestly, I'm impressed. I hoped this would happen for you, but I really expected there to be way more drama or fighting on their part."

The past few weeks he's been teasing me about my crushes on Owen and Spencer, I really thought it was just that— teasing. Feeling a little more vulnerable than usual, I bite my lip and whisper, "Do you really think they're lucky? I'm kind of a disaster, and the chances of me fucking this whole thing up are pretty high. I have literally no idea what I'm doing, and they're both...ugh, they're both seriously amazing."

"Of course they're lucky." Ryan chuckles, stepping closer to me until we're only standing a few inches apart. I force myself to stay still, even when I feel a blush rise to my cheeks. He lowers his voice, his eyes never leaving mine. "You're a little oblivious sometimes, but I've seen the way they look at you. Those guys are fucking crazy about you and have been since you showed up here. I don't blame them. Because if I was still alive, I'd be shooting my shot with you too."

I blink rapidly, my face burning hotter. There's no way I heard him correctly. "But—you like guys!" It's not the most eloquent thing to say, but they're the first words out of my mouth regardless.

He laughs, his eyes squinting in amusement. When he lifts his hand like he's going to touch my face, I feel a numb, tingly feeling against my bottom lip that causes butterflies to stir in my stomach.

"I like anyone who's hot," Ryan says with a cocky shrug. "And not only are you insanely fucking hot, but you are really something special. My memories still suck, but I'm pretty sure you've been a better friend to me in my death than anyone I ever knew while I was alive." Some of the arrogance falls from his expression, and his smile becomes shyer. "Plus, I don't know. You've got this light that sort of follows you around. I can't explain it, but it's intoxicating. So, yeah, I can name about a million fucking reasons Owen and Spencer are lucky as shit to be with you, and I'll make sure to tell them that the next time they want to record me."

His words instantly bring me back to Halloween night and everything that happened at the diner. Ernest mentioned a light following me too. Somehow, the entire incident slipped my mind after all the drama with Owen and Spencer.

For Ryan to mention the light thing *now*, after basically telling me he has feelings for me? I'm at a complete loss for words. I don't know what to say, let alone feel, and the fluttery feeling in my chest isn't helping me think clearly. Ryan is important to me, but he's dead. Not only that, but what about Owen and Spencer? If it wasn't already crazy for me to like two guys, now I'm sitting here pondering my feelings about a ghost?

"Harriet!"

I swear I nearly jump out of my skin at the sound of Mattie's voice. I quickly pull away from Ryan even though it's not like anyone will be able to see how close we were standing. When Mattie stops in front of me with a bright, energetic smile, I feel completely flustered and unprepared to talk to him.

"Hey," Mattie says, flicking his hair away from his eyes. "I never heard back from you yesterday."

"Oh." I clear my throat, feeling guilty all over again. Mattie texted me and asked to hang out, but I never messaged him back. Owen and Spencer said they want to be open about our relationship, but I didn't want to break the news to Mattie over the phone. I also didn't want him to come over and pop the bubble I was in with Owen and Spencer either. In retrospect, I should have at least texted him back to let him know I was busy. "Uh, I'm sorry. I got distracted."

Ryan snorts at me, which isn't helpful at all. But I'm relieved to see him giving me his usual teasing smile. Despite the bomb he just dropped on me, I'd be devastated if that made things weird between us.

"You gonna break the news to him about your new boyfriends?" Ryan asks with a smirk.

No, I am absolutely not doing that. Not until Spencer and Owen are here to help me through that conversation.

Mattie shrugs, setting his backpack on the ground before proceeding to dig through it. "That's alright. I wanted to talk to you more about that ghost from the diner, and I also wanted to show you some research I've been working on. I figured if you're feeling better, there's no reason we shouldn't continue our investigations on Ryan and Sophia's deaths."

"Really?" I can't hide my excitement, everything negative falling away for the time being. Even after Spencer witnessed the incident with Ernest in person, he never suggested picking up our other investigations. Nobody else has either, so I've felt stuck. I could seriously hug Mattie right now.

"Sure. What happened with Sophia was scary, but you know your limits better than we do." Mattie's eyes blaze with enthusiasm as he shoves a piece of paper at me. "So, I went back through Ryan's yearbooks and made a list of all the teachers and faculty who were around then and still work here now. I also tracked down some retired teachers, his baseball coach, and some of the other guys on the team. A bunch of them still live locally or within a couple hours' drive, at most."

My eyes scan over the long list of names, addresses, and phone numbers. I'm seriously in awe. The fact he even thought to track these people down is impressive, but I'm even more amazed he managed to find so much information about them.

"This is incredible!" I exclaim, giving in to my soft side and pulling him into a hug. Mattie smiles at me like he's slightly dazed when I pull away, so I bring his attention back to the paper in my hand. "So, you think we should start calling or visiting these people? Maybe asking them what they know?"

"Well, yeah, but we should try to be subtle," he says, looking around the hallway to make sure we're alone. Thankfully, we're here early enough that not many students are roaming the halls yet. "I think it's safe to assume at this point that somebody covered up Ryan's death. It's better if nobody knows we're looking into it."

My heart seizes in my chest at his theory, but I admit that I agree. It's the only thing that makes sense. Scanning the list of names again, I try to figure out if any of the teacher's names are familiar. The only one I recognize is my history teacher, but there are a handful of surnames on the list that are well known family names in the witch community. I quickly pull out a pen and mark a star next to all of those.

Looking at them grouped together that way makes me feel uneasy. Were witches responsible for Ryan's death and for trapping him here? It makes a sick sort of sense, especially considering Sophia's similar situation and the fact that she lived and died in the Abbot House.

"We should look more closely into these names first," I say.

Mattie takes the paper back, and Ryan peers over his shoulder to read it. I'm not sure if Ryan recognizes any of the names or not. The expression on his face is incredibly hard to read. But Mattie looks curious and mildly confused. "Any particular reason why?" he asks.

Shit. How can I explain my reasoning without telling him anything about witches and still sound convincing enough for him to take me seriously? If witches really were responsible, is it a good idea to let Mattie or Nolan help me investigate these deaths? I'm not sure if I can do it without them. Especially Mattie.

Footsteps in the hallway behind us save me from answering, and we turn to find Owen and Spencer walking toward us. My heart races, and a cheesy smile tugs at my lips. I'm stupidly excited to see them considering I saw them just last night. They smile back like they're just as thrilled to see me as I am them, and I nearly swoon on the spot.

"Hey, baby." Spencer greets me first, giving me this insanely sexy and confident grin. He steps closer until he's caging me against my locker, raising his arm to rest beside my head. I get lost in his chocolatey brown eyes as he slowly leans closer and closer.

The second he presses his lips to mine, it's like my body has a mind of its own. I throw my arms around his neck and pull him closer until our bodies are pressed flush together, swiping my tongue across his bottom lip until he groans and deepens the kiss. I might be new at this, but I don't think I'll ever get tired of kissing either of my guys.

When Spencer places his hands on my hips and trails his fingertips under the hem of my shirt and jacket, the sudden chill against my skin shocks me enough to remind me that we're at school and that we have an audience. I jerk away, grimacing as my cheeks flush. "Goddess, I'm sorry."

"Don't be." Spencer grins widely. He quickly leans forward and gives me another peck before stepping away from me with a chuckle.

Ryan catches my eye first, mouthing the word 'hot.' Feeling even more mortified that I completely lost my mind, I turn to stare guiltily up at Owen. While his eyes are full of heat, he also looks amused.

"I thought we told you to stop apologizing for that," Owen teases, leaning down to give me a quick kiss of his own.

It's true. When I hung out with them yesterday, I probably ended up apologizing at least a dozen times for either kissing them in front of each other or getting so caught up like I just did with Spencer before the guys told me to cut it out and not to be sorry. They told me that after weeks of not being sure whether I liked them or not, the fact that I'm so eager to kiss them and be close to them is majorly reassuring.

"What the hell? Since when are you guys kissing her?" Nolan asks with a groan. I turn toward him, only just realizing he's joined our group. There are other students walking through the hallway and stopping at their lockers near us too now that it's getting closer to first bell. When Nolan meets my eyes, his cheeks flare red as he glares harshly at me. "This is going to fuck up our friendship dynamic so much."

His words make my heart drop. I was originally worried Spencer and Owen would be upset about me liking both of them, which thankfully isn't the case. But I never thought I'd have to worry about Nolan or Mattie being affected by my feelings or by me being in a relationship with the others. Was that completely naïve of me? These four have been close friends for years, well before I ever moved here and started hanging out with them or joined their ghost hunting club.

A glance at Mattie only makes my heart sink further. He looks shocked and utterly devastated as his eyes dart between me, Owen, and Spencer. His fists are clenched at his sides, the paper of names he showed me partially crumpled in his left hand.

"Shut the fuck up," Spencer says, throwing his arm around my waist. He tries to give me a reassuring smile before glaring at Nolan. "You don't know what you're talking about. This isn't going to ruin shit."

Nolan clenches his jaw and adjusts his glasses, tearing his eyes from me to glare at the floor instead. "It is. This is going to be just like Amethyst, only worse."

I inhale sharply, my eyes suddenly stinging with unshed tears that I desperately try to hold back. Goddess, if I cry at school, that's going to make everything a million times worse. I knew this was a terrible idea. It doesn't matter how much I like Owen and Spencer. I never should have let them talk me into this. If their best friends can't accept us and think so horribly of me, what are other people going to think? Spencer said that lots of people have unconventional relationships these days. While that may be true, it's still not the norm. People will always judge us harshly and unfairly.

"That's not true," Spencer says to me, tightening his arm around my waist like he's worried I'm going to run away.

Owen threads his fingers through mine on my other side, shaking his head slowly at Nolan. "Harriet is nothing like Amethyst, and you know that. Spence and I have been really obvious about our feelings for Harriet over the past few weeks.

341

We haven't hidden anything from each other or from her, and over the weekend, we both asked if she'd be our girlfriend. She said yes, and now we're a throuple. It's really that simple."

"Oh my god," Ryan whispers loudly, beaming when he catches my eyes. "I wish so fucking badly I could eat popcorn right now."

I make a face at him. This is so not the time for his bullshit. Mattie seems to be the only one who notices where my attention is because he shakes off his agonized expression and glances in Ryan's direction. Taking a deep breath, Mattie meets my eyes with a forced smile.

"That's great. A throuple, wow." Mattie swallows audibly, his smile wobbling a bit. "I'm really happy for you guys."

He certainly doesn't look like it. Part of me isn't surprised by Nolan's nasty reaction. He's been up and down with me since we met, continually making it clear he doesn't like or trust me. I thought things were getting better ever since he learned about my ability to see ghosts, but obviously I was wrong. With Mattie though, his approval means so much to me. He might be annoying sometimes, but he's become one of my best friends. Somebody I feel like I can trust with almost anything. I would be devastated to lose him as a friend or to make things strained between him, Owen, and Spencer.

"Really?" I ask Mattie quietly.

The tension in his body seems to evaporate and his smile softens enough that it almost looks genuine. "Yeah, Harriet. If you're happy, then I'm happy for you. I was just taken by surprise at first."

Things still feel a little strained and awkward after that, like there's an invisible barrier separating Nolan and Mattie from me, Spencer, and Owen. But Mattie's sweet declaration and acceptance definitely help diffuse any animosity between the guys. Once I'm sure that nobody's going to start fighting, I attempt to change the subject by bringing up the list of names Mattie curated.

Spencer and Owen seem just as impressed as me, and they excitedly ask Mattie a bunch of questions as they smooth out the paper and look over the names marked down. Thankfully, without asking why I specifically marked the names of witches. I'm still not sure how to explain that, but hopefully Owen or Spencer will have an idea once I can talk to them about it privately. Nolan stays silent while they talk, and I purposely don't look anywhere near him.

When the first bell rings, I say goodbye to Spencer and Owen without letting them kiss me and head to class with Mattie while Ryan floats by my side. It's silent between us, which is practically unheard of for Mattie. He's always talkative and energetic, even first thing in the morning. My stomach churns guiltily as I dart side glances at him. He has to still be feeling weird about learning I'm in a relationship with two of his best friends.

"Don't worry about him too much," Ryan says softly. "He and Nolan are probably just jealous."

Yeah, right. While I could technically see Mattie feeling that way, strictly because he hates feeling left out, there's no way in hell that's why Nolan snapped at me like he did. The thought is so unbelievable that I accidentally snort out loud.

Mattie startles at the sound, looking up at me with an awkward smile. "Sorry. I know I'm being weird. Just trying to wrap my head around things, you know?"

"I guess," I mumble, even though I don't really get that at all.

"It's just—" Mattie clears his throat, anxiously fidgeting with the straps of his backpack. "I didn't realize you even liked Spencer or Owen. We've been hanging out so much, and you never mentioned it."

343

That's not quite what I expected him to say, but at least he sounds genuine and not like he thinks badly of me the way his cousin seems to. I nervously smooth my hand over my hair and shrug. "Well, I was trying to hide how I felt. I'm not really good at talking to guys in general, and I felt guilty for liking two people at the same time. Plus, I know we're friends, but they were your friends first. I assumed if I told you anything like that, you'd turn around and tell them about it."

He nods slowly as we walk into our health class together and take our seats. While I'm taking my stuff out of my bag, Mattie leans closer until our heads are nearly touching.

"Is it not weird for you though?" he asks, whispering. "Dating them both, I mean? Like, you don't like either of them more than the other, and you're not worried things will get messy or that someone will get their feelings hurt?"

A nervous laugh bubbles in my chest, and I subtly move away to put a little distance between us. "The throuple thing was their idea. I never would have suggested something like that myself, but now I'm glad they did. Even if it gets messy or whatever, I think it's worth trying. I like them both so much, and I definitely don't like either of them more than the other."

Mattie blushes, running his hand through his hair until it's sticking up in multiple places. When the bell rings and he still hasn't said anything, I assume the conversation is over. But then he lets out a shaky breath and whispers again.

"What if you also liked someone else?" He taps his pencil rapidly against the desk between us. "Would you consider having three boyfriends then instead of just two?"

Just two? Like that isn't already a lot? Embarrassingly, his question immediately makes me think of Ryan and what he said to me this morning. About how he apparently not only thinks I'm hot, but that he thinks I'm special and that Owen and Spencer are lucky to be with me. When I shyly glance over at Ryan where he's floating beside my desk like always, he smirks back at me like he knows exactly what I'm thinking.

"I don't know," I snap at Mattie, feeling flustered. "I've never had a boyfriend, period, and I certainly never expected to have two. Three sounds fucking impossible."

He grimaces, opening his mouth like he's going to apologize. But we're interrupted when our teacher clears her throat loudly. To my dismay, she's scowling in our direction when I look up front.

"I'm so sorry to bother you, Miss Abbot," Ms. Askew says sarcastically. A few students snicker in response around the room. "You've been excused from class and are expected in the auditorium."

Another girl—the only other witch who shares this class with me—is standing in front of Ms. Askew's desk holding a hall pass. Confused, I shrug at Mattie and shove my stuff back into my bag before joining the other witch up front. Ms. Askew hands me a hall pass and waves her hand at us dismissively.

CHAPTER 29
HARRIET

In the hallway, the witch from my health class hums and shoves the hall pass into her pocket with a shrug. "Must be coven business. I don't see why else we'd be called out together."

I don't know why either, but I secretly cross my fingers and pray she's wrong. It's hard enough avoiding my fellow witches during school without being forced together in a group setting. The girl raises her eyebrow at me like she's waiting for me to respond, but I keep my mouth shut. I've never talked to her before, and I have no idea what her name is. But she sits with the other witches during lunch, so I automatically don't like or trust her. Maybe that makes me a judgmental hypocrite, but whatever.

She seems to know where she's going, so I silently follow her through the hallways until we reach the auditorium. Dread sweeps over me when I see another group of witches heading through the doors ahead of us. Looks like my classmate called it, though I hate that I'm potentially being grouped into 'coven business' when I want absolutely nothing to do with it.

"Do you have any clue what's going on?" Ryan asks me.

I subtly shake my head. Having him by my side is a huge relief, and I step closer until my arm brushes against him. I don't care if my arm goes numb. The tingly feeling I get when I touch him is a small comfort, letting me know I'm not alone through this.

The unease festering in my chest worsens when I walk into the auditorium and see what has to be every witch I go to school with seated in the audience. I normally only deal with the witches in my year, but it looks like there are freshman, sophomore, and senior witches here too. There have to be over fifty of us altogether, which is a ridiculously high number considering this school isn't that big to begin with.

Thankfully, I manage to take a seat in the last row where everyone is sitting. While there's a guy I don't know sitting on my left, the seat on my right is left empty so Ryan is able to sit there without anyone's knowledge. He places his hand over mine, which is as close as he can get to holding it.

"Abbot, right?" the guy beside me asks, pulling my attention to him. His eyes sweep over me, and a pompous smirk curls at his lips. "I'm Rowan Sullie. I'm in the year above you, which is probably why we haven't met before."

Sullie is a common family name in the witch community, but I'm fairly certain they're not affluent or as well-known as families like mine, Amethyst's or Blaze's. Still, the emphasis he puts on his name and the creepy way he's looking at me are enough for me to know he's no different than any other asshole witch at this school. I give him a thin smile and stay silent, turning away from him to face the stage up front. I don't care if he's offended.

It feels like I'm sitting there forever, listening to the quiet muttering of the witches around me. Several of them are showing off spells for everyone to see, clearly too comfortable in their surroundings despite being at school where such outward displays should never be allowed. How do they know human students or teachers won't be joining us? The chance of someone walking in who shouldn't see is too high, and clearly none of them care. My entire body is tense while I watch them and wait to find out what this is all about. At least Amethyst and Blaze are sitting nowhere near me, but my guard is still up in case anyone tries to mess with me.

"Isn't that your mom?" Ryan whispers to me, pointing to the stage.

To my absolute horror, he's right. There's my mom, standing on stage alongside Principal Di Rossi and three other witches. Two of the strangers are dressed just as formally as my mom, and one of the men has taken it a step further by wearing indigo-colored ceremonial robes. Everyone else seated in the audience with me finally seems to notice their presence, quieting within seconds.

"Good morning, young witches," the man in the robes says, his voice rolling over us with palpable authority and a hint of a European accent. "Before we get into why we're here, I'd like to introduce you all to the newest member of our Council, Madame Della Abbot."

My mom steps forward, smiling her most charming smile as my classmates applaud politely. I don't move a muscle as I stare up at her, a deep sense of betrayal burning in my veins. *This* is the meeting she was talking about this morning? Since when is she a fucking Council member?

"Thank you, Chancellor Bernauer," my mom says to the man in the robes.

I swear I feel the blood drain from my face, and I grip the arm rest between me and Ryan until my knuckles turn white. I feel him looking at me in concern, but there's no way for me to explain anything to him right now.

But seriously, something major is about to happen if the leader of the Witch's Council is here at my high school of all places. He's supposedly the most powerful witch alive, and he has the final say on any laws passed by the Council. I can tell I'm not the only one affected by his presence. I can all but feel the thick tension along with a mixture of fear and excitement in the air.

"I'm here today to announce that there will be some changes going forward," the Chancellor announces. "After several recent claims and complaints, the Council has come to the conclusion that our youngest coven members need more guidance than you are currently being provided. As the future leaders and members of our society, you must be held to a higher standard. New rules will be implemented for all underage witches after today. You will no longer be permitted to use magic during school hours, and the consequences of revealing your nature to any human not approved by the Council will be much more permanent and severe."

Shocked and outraged whispers fill the room. I must be the only one here who's not upset by the new rules. Hopefully now, I won't have to worry about the constant hazing and bullying from my fellow witches every day at school. Ryan smiles in relief at me, clearly thinking the same thing.

"That's enough," Principal Di Rossi says loudly. I've never heard or seen him get angry, and the change from the usual friendly demeanor I'm used to is slightly shocking. He looks around at my classmates with a stern expression until the room is silent once again. "Show some respect to your elders and superiors. You have all become too comfortable and careless, so you have nobody to blame but yourselves for the new laws. These laws will be implemented to all underage witches, but we are starting in Weeping Hollow because of the staggering number of complaints received over the past few weeks. A student has been bullied relentlessly using magic, nearly always in the presence of non-approved humans."

I barely manage to stifle a gasp, widening my eyes in alarm. Principal Di Rossi continues speaking, but all I hear is an awful ringing in my ears as my heart nearly beats out of my chest. He might as well have called me out by name at this rate. Several people turn in their seats to send me nasty glares, so I know I'm right to assume everyone is going to blame me for this. How could I have been so fucking stupid? I never should have told my mom anything about what I've been going through.

When I look at my mom on stage, I find her watching me with a smug smile on her face. At this moment, I absolutely loathe her and I don't see how I can ever forgive her for what she's done. My classmates may not be able to use magic to bully me during school anymore, but what's to stop them from harassing me or hurting me outside of school? Before, they were only testing me. But now, anything they do to me will be for revenge.

Feeling like I'm in a nightmare-induced trance, I line up with my classmates and wait my turn to walk on stage. The Council members explained that we'll each be given a silver bracelet infused with a spell that will make it impossible for us to use magic during school hours or within the parameters of the school, period. We won't be able to remove it either—only a Council member has the ability to do that. From my understanding, it will also make any pre-made charms or potions useless during those times too. The only silver lining is that at least I won't have to worry about being poisoned or hexed by one of my classmates during school if they try to whip something up at home and use it here later.

Ryan stays glued to my side when it's my turn to step on stage. I purposely avoid eye contact with my mom, tensing further when I have to walk past her to stand in front of

Chancellor Bernauer and the other two Council members. They explain the way the spell works to me once more as I hold my wrist out. It doesn't occur to me until they place the silver cuff around my wrist that this spell could possibly affect my ability to see ghosts. I stare fearfully at Ryan, waiting for him to vanish before my eyes. Thankfully, several seconds pass, and nothing happens.

Stumbling out of the way for the next student to receive their bracelet, I stare at the silver cuff on my wrist curiously. It's intricately designed to look like two snakes forming a circle with their heads intercrossing.

"Well? How do you feel?" Ryan asks, still looking as anxious as I feel.

Quickly glancing around to see if anyone's watching me, I quietly murmur, "I feel fine." Which is the truth. Several of my classmates are muttering about how they can already feel the bracelets draining their energy. A few of them even look like they're in physical pain as they rub at their wrists. I don't feel any different, and clearly my abilities weren't affected. I've always wondered if my ghosty abilities were related to being a witch, and this just proves that they aren't.

First period is almost over by the time everyone is dismissed. Before I can dart out the auditorium doors behind my classmates, my mom calls my name. I consider ignoring her or pretending I don't hear her, but it's impossible to do so when she walks up behind me and grabs my arm before I manage to escape.

"I have to get to class," I hiss at her under my breath.

She gives me a tight smile, clearly trying to appear calm in public. "You have plenty of time. I only need to talk to you for a moment."

With no other options, I let her drag me through a door next to the stage to what looks like a large storage area. Her grip on my arm tightens the moment we're out of sight of my classmates, my principal, and the Council members. Thank Goddess my mom has no idea that Ryan exists. He's able to stay with me without her realizing, continuing to keep me calm and give me silent support.

"Well?" my mom asks, crossing her arms with a haughty expression on her face.

I grit my teeth. "Well, what?"

She scoffs. "Well, you could say thank you, to start."

Is she serious? I blink rapidly, feeling like my brain is short-circuiting. I really think she's fucking serious right now. "What exactly should I be thanking you for? For lying to me and betraying me?"

My mom has the audacity to look hurt at my words. "Excuse me? How have I lied or betrayed you?"

"Let's start with why we moved here in the first place?" My entire body trembles with anger. It's too overwhelming to keep my guard up any longer, so I say exactly what I'm thinking instead of keeping my mouth shut like I usually do. "You said you wanted to move into the Abbot House because of all the great childhood memories you had there, and that you wanted to use the house to open a bakery. Not once did you ever tell me that all you really wanted was to climb the power-hungry social ladder in our society to join the Council. I don't know why I continue to be amazed after all these years at how absolutely selfish you are, mom."

Her jaw drops, fire lighting in her eyes. "I joined the Council for *you*, Harriet. Yes, I've always dreamed of living in the Abbot House, and I still plan to open a bakery and tea shop. But the Council was the only way I could help you! How else was I supposed to stop your classmates from hazing you? It was the only way to ensure this new law would be passed."

"You are so full of shit!" I laugh humorlessly, waving my

hands in frustration. "Did you ever think of maybe just fucking talking to me? Or for once, just listening to anything I have to say? All you've done with this law is ensure I'm blamed and targeted even more by the witches here. Do you seriously believe none of them will try anything outside of school? Blaze Alden cornered me and burned my hand at *our house* after you invited him and his family over. After this, I sincerely doubt that will be the last time I'm hurt by one of my classmates because of you."

She opens her mouth, but no words come out. I'm fucking done. Spinning on my heel, I storm out of the room. I'm the only student left in the auditorium, and luckily none of my fellow witches are lingering in the hallway outside.

"Are you sure you're okay?" Ryan asks, brushing his hand against my arm. "That was—wow, that whole thing was really fucking scary and kind of fucked."

"Yeah." I take a deep breath, walking aimlessly down the hall. My face feels hot, and I'm still trembling slightly from anger. "I think I'm okay. I'm just pissed at my mom and scared about how the other witches are going to act going forward. Thank you for staying with me. It seriously helped a lot."

His eyes soften, and he brushes his hand over my arm again until goosebumps rise across my skin. "Always." Glancing down at my wrist, his mouth twists with concern. "Are you sure you're feeling alright with the bracelet? I was worried it would make it so you couldn't see me anymore."

"I was worried about the same thing at first," I admit. Lifting my hand, I frown at the horrible piece of jewelry. "But I honestly don't feel anything. Guess I'm not really a witch, after all."

The bell rings, meaning first period is officially over and the halls will soon be crowded with people heading to their next class. I huff in irritation, wishing I could talk to Ryan for longer.

I've skipped too many classes to hang out with him lately to keep getting away with it.

Since I'm not familiar with this part of the school, Ryan helps me find my way to my history class. On our way there, I run into Mattie. He grins in surprise, gently grabbing my arm to stop me so we can talk.

"Hey! I was wondering if you'd make it back from wherever you went in time for second period," Mattie says. His eyebrows furrow. "What did you get called to the auditorium for, anyway?"

Goddess, I wish I could tell him. I have so much I feel like I need to get off my chest. For the millionth time, I'm so grateful Spencer and Owen know about witches so I can confide in them. Making up a lie on the spot, I shake my head and sigh. "Nothing. It was this stupid volunteer thing my mom signed me up for."

Mattie smiles sympathetically. Even if he doesn't know about witches, he knows how complicated my relationship with my mom is. He'll at least be able to understand my frustration with her, if not the exact reason why I'm so mad.

Before we turn to head the rest of the way to class, someone shoves me from behind. I stumble and fall to the ground, landing hard on my knees. I groan and turn to see who pushed me, not surprised in the least to see Amethyst glaring daggers at me.

What *does* surprise me is the venomous look Mattie gives her. "What the hell is wrong with you?"

I've never seen him look at her with anything other than heart eyes. Honestly, I'm shocked he's not coming up with excuses or pretending she pushed me by accident. Mattie bends down to help me up, asking me in a hushed and worried voice if I'm okay. Feeling completely speechless, I nod wordlessly and let him help me up. He doesn't let go of me right away. Instead, he keeps his hand around me like he's worried I'm going to fall again.

My intention is to ignore Amethyst entirely, but she refuses to let that happen. She lets out a shrill screech and shoves me again, practically snarling in my face. "You stupid witch. Do you have any idea what you've done?"

"I haven't done anything," I hiss. Still, my face heats up from shame. I know exactly what she's referring to, and I can't help feeling responsible.

Completely ignoring Mattie's presence and the fact that he's a *non-approved human*, as the Council likes to say, she lifts her arm and gestures angrily at her silver snake bracelet. "This is your fault. You just had to run and cry to your mommy instead of doing what any decent witch would do. This could have been over weeks ago if you'd used just one single spell to defend yourself. The rest of the coven will never forgive you for this. Your last name doesn't make you special, and the fact that your mom is on the Council doesn't either."

She has seriously lost her fucking mind. A quick, nervous glance proves that there isn't anyone else in this hallway aside from me, Amethyst, Mattie, and Ryan. Mattie's eyes are wide as saucers as he stares back and forth between me and Amethyst, and he drops his arm from my waist as he shuffles nervously on his feet.

"Newsflash. It doesn't make you special either, you stupid cunt," I say to her. I know for a fact she has at least two family members on the Council, so that's a really rich comment coming from her. Gesturing at Mattie, I also remind her, "And shut the fuck up before you get us into trouble."

Amethyst rolls her eyes, renewed anger taking over her expression. "He's an idiot. Plus, he's practically in love with me, so he won't say anything."

Mattie isn't an idiot. Not by a longshot, and my mind is

already reeling with how I'm going to explain this conversation to him later. But what seriously pisses me off is that she can sit there and talk down about him, knowing how he feels about her, and make it clear that she can disregard him so easily. Goddess, I hate her, and Mattie deserves so much better. Feeling angry and defensive of my friend, I shove her the same way she shoved me and tell her, "Just leave us the fuck alone. I don't give a shit about you or your precious coven."

I turn away to drag Mattie to class, completely over today and the witches at this damn school. I've only taken one step when Amethyst grabs a fistful of my hair and yanks me back. I let out a yelp, turning to slap her away. Her palm lands clumsily against my cheek, like she was trying to hit me but didn't follow through all the way. I've never been in an actual fight with anyone, but even I can tell this is pathetic.

"Goddess, just stop!" I shove her back harder, causing her to stumble over her platform sneakers.

Screeching like a fucking banshee, Amethyst reaches out like she's going to hit me again. Only this time, she grabs the adder stone around my neck and yanks until the twine breaks. Instant and excruciating pain brings me to my knees, and I press my hands to my temples in a sorry attempt to make the horrible feeling go away.

The pain in my head and rushing through my body is like nothing I've ever experienced before. It's been weeks since I've had a ghost-induced migraine, and this is ten million times worse than one of those. I can't hear anything except for an awful ringing sound, and I'm so dizzy that I shut my eyes when I feel myself swaying. My face feels hot and wet, but I don't know if that's from blood or tears. All I can do is wait for the pain to end.

After what feels like eternity, the pain disappears all at

once. I feel completely disoriented, and I have to blink several times before I realize I'm lying sprawled on the floor with my head in Mattie's lap. He's fussing with my hair, brushing it away from my face as he wipes his hoodie sleeve over my cheeks. When he pulls his hand away, I see streaks of mascara and eyeliner along with some dried blood on his sleeve.

"Goddess, you're so dramatic!" Amethyst yells. I wince at the sound of her voice, still not feeling back to normal after my episode or whatever that was. Amethyst, either oblivious or uncaring, continues her tirade. "And you're such a cheater! Your bracelet obviously doesn't work since you just used magic in front of a human. You're going to pay for this!"

The sound of her footsteps retreating allows me to take a breath of relief. With a groan, I sit up with Mattie's help and rub a hand over my forehead. "What happened?"

Mattie's forest green eyes are filled with uncertainty and fear, and he swallows audibly before he answers. "Uh, I'm not really sure. When she pulled your necklace off, you fell. Your nose started bleeding, and you started whimpering and crying. I wasn't sure what to do, and then your necklace floated over here, and I tied it back together around your neck. It's the only thing that seemed to help."

When I turn my head, I'm not surprised to find Ryan kneeling behind me. He looks panicked, twisting his hands in front of him. "I grabbed the necklace and handed it to Mattie. I'm not sure how I managed it, but..."

He trails off, like he's at a loss for words. So much has happened so quickly, and I know he and Mattie both have a million questions. Mattie most of all. Sucking in a breath, I quietly ask, "Did anyone else see?"

"No, thankfully." Mattie bites his lip, gazing at me intently. "The bell rang while you were out of it. Even before that, nobody came by when Amethyst was saying all of that stuff."

357

There's an unspoken question in his voice, but I don't know where to start. My heart races wildly in my chest. After Amethyst's outburst, there's no way I can lie to Mattie or convince him not to pay attention to anything she said. He's way too smart, and he's already fairly knowledgeable when it comes to anything paranormal or occult. Since he hasn't asked outright, I decide to ignore the major elephant in the room and grip the adder stone between my fingers instead.

"So, you know I've been able to see ghosts my whole life," I start. "But I always used to get these horrible migraines, and sometimes nosebleeds, every time I was around them. That's the biggest reason why I never really tested my powers or tried to interact with them much. But a few days after I moved here, I found this necklace stashed under the floorboards in my room. There was a note with my name on it from some distant relatives who died a long time ago. When I wear it, I don't have those symptoms around ghosts anymore. I haven't taken it off for weeks..."

"And you've been spending a lot of time with ghosts and pushing your abilities," Mattie finishes for me. He nods like everything makes sense. "Having it torn away so suddenly like that must have forced any delayed symptoms to hit you all at once. Fuck, I'm sorry, Harriet. That sounds horrible."

"It's not your fault. Ryan somehow grabbed the necklace off the floor, which is how you saw it floating. I—I didn't use magic." Goddess, I nearly choke over the words, my heart beating rapidly in my chest.

Mattie snorts. "I don't see how you could have with the state you were in." His hand trembles as he slides it through his hair. "But I'm assuming that means it's true? All that shit Amethyst said about witches and magic?"

"You're not supposed to know," I whisper in a panicky voice.

Ryan moves so he's sitting beside Mattie where I'm able to see them both. With a grimace, Ryan says, "It's alright. You can trust him, Harriet."

It's not about trusting him. Of course I trust Mattie. But I certainly don't trust Amethyst or any of the other witches at this school. I don't want anything bad to happen to Mattie because he found out this way, and I definitely don't want him to be freaked out or to stop trusting me. Then again, Spencer knows about witches, and he's not approved by the Council either. Maybe this will be okay, and it will make things easier going forward if I don't always have to make up stupid lies.

"Maybe we should just go to class. And then maybe we can talk later?" Mattie phrases it as a question.

I nod, and we finally stand up from the floor. Mattie keeps his hand on my elbow to keep me steady and grabs my backpack before I can get it myself. He's being really sweet, if not a bit frantic. I should probably tell him that I feel fine and really don't need help, but I'm honestly relieved to see that he's more worried about me being hurt than he is about me being a witch.

Unfortunately, we don't make it to class before running into Amethyst again. She's with a teacher who I'm unfamiliar with, but the light tingle I feel on the back of my neck is enough to tell me they're a witch. Amethyst smiles at me smugly as the teacher tells me and Mattie that we need to report to the principal's office.

PRINCIPAL DI ROSSI'S OFFICE IS WAY TOO CROWDED. NOT ONLY AM I here with him and Amethyst, but my mom, Chancellor

Bernauer, and the other two Council members are here too. Mattie was told to wait outside. Ryan's by my side too, of course, but obviously nobody can see him but me.

"Explain what happened, please." Principal Di Rossi gives Amethyst a stern look.

Her lips curve into another ridiculously smug smile as she meets my eyes across the room. Is she actually stupid? How can she be so smug when she's most likely going to get into at least as much trouble as I am? Not only did she start the fight, but she revealed the truth about witches to Mattie!

"I ran into Harriet on my way to class, and we had an argument," Amethyst says innocently. "Things escalated when she hit me. I mean, look at her. She's nearly a foot taller than I am! When I tried to defend myself, I accidentally pulled her necklace off. Harriet fell into a rage, and she used a spell to make her necklace float over to her. She did it right in front of Matthew Baxter, and he saw the whole thing! He didn't even look that surprised, so I can only assume Harriet illegally told him about magic and our community."

That lying fucking bitch. I clench my fists at my sides and seethe. "None of that is true!"

To his credit, Principal Di Rossi stays calm and collected as he nods at me. "We'd like to hear your side of the story, Harriet."

I take a shaky breath to calm myself so I don't appear weak or too heated. "While Mattie and I were walking to class, Amethyst came up behind me and shoved me to the ground. After I stood up, I was going to walk away rather than confront her, but she started yelling at me about our bracelets and our new laws. She blames me, apparently. I reminded her that she shouldn't be talking about that in front of Mattie, and she not only dismissed my concerns, but called him an idiot. That made me angry, so I shoved her."

Principal Di Rossi nods, encouraging me to continue. I don't want to lie, but I also don't want to get Mattie into trouble or give them reason to question him. I also don't want to mention Ryan, especially after my epiphany that witches were most likely responsible for his death and curse. There's a chance that someone in this room knows what happened to him and why.

Deciding I care more about protecting Mattie and Ryan, I don't feel the slightest bit guilty for the next words out of my mouth. "That's when Amethyst hit me and ripped my necklace off. I fell to the ground, totally disoriented. The next thing I knew, Amethyst was screeching at me about using magic in front of a human. After she walked away, Mattie helped me clean some of the blood off my face and called Amethyst a psychopath. I swear on the Goddess that I never used any spells or magic in front of him, or any other human for that matter."

Amethyst's jaw drops in outrage. If there weren't so many people looking at me, I'd be tempted to give her a smug smile of my own. My story has to be more believable. I'm pretty sure there's still some dried blood around my nose since I never had a chance to clean up before being dragged here.

Stomping her foot like a child, Amethyst shrieks, "She's lying! I know what I saw. She used magic to move her necklace."

"I'm sorry, but that's impossible," my mom says, speaking up for the first time since I walked in. I force myself to look at her, which I've managed to avoid until this point. She gives me a saccharine sweet smile before addressing the rest of the room. "Harriet has never been able to do magic, despite our best efforts. Test her abilities if you'd like, but I can assure you there's no way she did a spell in front of that boy."

Shame washes over me. While I know this knowledge

might end up saving my ass—and Mattie's—it seriously fucking burns that my mom just shared my biggest failure with a room full of some of the world's most powerful witches and a girl I consider my enemy.

Ryan's hand brushes against mine. It's the only way he can show me any comfort or support right now, and Goddess, I can't describe how much it means to me. My face feels hot and my throat feels thick as I look around the room to gauge everyone's reactions. Principal Di Rossi appears sympathetic but unsurprised—I already suspected my mom told him about my deficiency from my very first day of school. Amethyst, on the other hand, looks so shocked that it would be comical if I wasn't so embarrassed.

One of the Council member guys hums thoughtfully. I wasn't paying attention enough in the auditorium, so I can't recall his name. "Your daughter can't do magic, Della? None whatsoever?"

It's almost a relief when the chancellor interrupts, not allowing my mom to humiliate me further. "It seems the only real issue here is whether the human boy overheard anything important. If one of these girls let slip the truth about witches, we may have to wipe his memories. If that becomes necessary, then Miss Redferne and Miss Abbot will be investigated further to see which of them is at fault for this travesty. Our youngest members of our community have become much too careless with who they reveal our secrets to, as well as where and how they perform magic. If the human boy's memories need to be altered, drastic measures will be taken. Not only will your magic be bound until further notice, but both of you will be denied the opportunity to ever apply for a position on the Council."

I couldn't give two shits about either of those 'consequences,' but the thought of witches fucking with

Mattie's brain makes my heart skip erratically. I will do anything to keep that from happening. I don't care how powerful the chancellor is. Altering memories is one of the most difficult forms of magic to perform, and the risks are insanely high that something could go wrong. Widening my eyes in fear, I stare at Ryan and silently ask him for help. I know there's nothing he can do, but I'm at a loss. His expression matches mine. Without a word to me, he rushes from the room, floating straight through the wall to the main office where Mattie is waiting.

"It won't be necessary," I say, my voice desperate.

Amethyst nods in agreement, looking every bit as scared as I feel. I grit my teeth in annoyance, knowing her reasons are completely selfish and have nothing to do with Mattie's well-being.

"Let's hope so," the chancellor says. Gesturing to the door, he commands, "Call the boy in, Kamal."

CHAPTER 30
MATTIE

Waiting outside the principal's office is torture. I can't stop fidgeting, twisting my hands together, and bouncing my knee up and down while a million thoughts run rampant through my head. Dragging my eyes away from Principal Di Rossi's door, I sigh and rest my head in my hands as I desperately try to settle my nerves.

I don't know why I'm so surprised, to be honest. It's no secret that Weeping Hollow is a town known for its occult history, and I've always felt like plenty of folklore or stories about the supernatural are probably true. There's enough evidence if you know what to look for, and I've become very good at researching shit like that since moving here. Fuck, I wasn't even that shocked when Harriet told me she can see ghosts. Unlike Nolan, I never doubted her for a second.

So, why is the idea that Harriet and Amethyst are witches freaking me out so much?

Maybe because from the way they were talking, it's obvious it's not just them. Amethyst mentioned the words *coven* and *council.* Which means there's an entire network and government of witches, apparently living right under my nose. The more I think about it, learning that Harriet is a witch isn't that strange. There's always been something a bit ethereal about her. Plus, she's already proved she has at least some magical ability with the ghost stuff. Knowing that and now learning she's a witch isn't that big of a leap.

Like a magnet, my gaze falls on the principal's door again. I think I might feel better if I could just talk to Harriet. Really talk to her, and ask all the questions popping up in my brain. As worried as she seemed about me hearing everything Amethyst said, I know she'll tell me the truth and help put me at ease. I think it's just the idea that I've been so blind to something so big without realizing it that has me feeling out of my depth. That, and I'm not sure if I should be scared or not. What kind of magic are witches capable of? Is Harriet going to get in trouble since I heard things I wasn't supposed to? Am *I* going to get into trouble? There's just so much I don't know.

Aside from all the witch stuff, I'm worried about Harriet. The teacher who brought us to the office never stopped to ask if she was okay, and I think Amethyst really hurt her. First, when she pushed her down, but especially when she pulled her necklace off. Seeing Harriet fall and writhe in pain like that was fucking awful. So much worse than what happened with the spirit board at her house.

It's crazy to think that an hour ago, all I could think about was the fact that Harriet is going out with Owen and Spencer. I was an emotional wreck when I first found out. I was heartbroken and jealous, wanting nothing to do with my friends—which I realize isn't fair or healthy, but it's how I felt at that moment. At least until after I talked to Harriet and got the ridiculous idea in my head that I might still have a chance with her. After all, if she's cool with dating two guys at the same time, then why wouldn't she be cool with dating three? I know she doesn't think of me like that, but maybe she could someday? I really want to talk to Owen and Spencer to find out how they came up with their throuple idea and how they can go through with it without feeling jealous of each other.

While I'm still interested in hearing what they have to say, and secretly hopeful Harriet might eventually see me as more than a friend, all this stuff about witches has definitely shifted my perspective and priorities.

I sigh loudly, willing the principal's door to open. Harriet and Amethyst have been in there forever. Why is this taking so long?

A crashing sound by the receptionist's desk causes me to look over. The older, meaner receptionist must be out sick today because there's currently only one behind the desk. Since I've been sitting here, she's been not-so-subtly watching TikTok videos on her phone and paying me absolutely no attention.

"Oops," she says with an annoyed sigh, pushing out of her seat. "Must have bumped my computer."

That's when I notice the cup of spilled pens and pencils on the ground in front of her desk. Losing interest, I move to turn away. Until I notice a sharpie floating away from the rest of the mess on the floor. It drops to the ground a few times, making slow progress across the floor, until it falls one final time when the receptionist walks around her desk.

"Let me help you," I say, slightly frantic as I jolt forward.

It has to be Ryan. The way the sharpie moved was way too similar to what happened with Harriet's necklace. But with her out of the room, it's probably harder for him to move an inanimate object like that again. I quickly hide the sharpie in my sleeve before haphazardly picking up the rest of the pens and tossing them in the cup. I place the cup on her desk and rush back to my seat, anxiously waiting for the receptionist to go back to looking at her phone.

As soon as she does, I pull the sharpie out and pull the cap off. "Ryan?" I whisper. I know I won't be able to hear him answer, so I really hope I'm right. Not knowing what else he'd be trying to move a sharpie for, I hold the marker tip to the back of my palm and quietly ask, "Can you move it if I hold it like this?"

I'm relieved to discover I'm right about Ryan trying to talk to me. It's the weirdest sensation ever, holding the pen while feeling and seeing it move on its own. When the sharpie stops moving and I see the word scrawled on my hand in the ghost's handwriting, my heart drops into my stomach.

LIE. That's all it says. What else could that possibly be but a warning? I stare at the principal's door again, anxiety prickling under my skin as I feel the urge to run. Without giving it much thought, I use my sleeve to roughly wipe the word away. The sharpie only smudges, but I keep rubbing until my skin is red and the word is illegible.

Seconds later, the door opens and Principal Di Rossi steps out. He gives me a stern look and gestures at me to follow him. "Mattie, can you come in, please?"

My heart is in my throat as I stand up, and I do my damned best to hide all signs of nervousness as I walk into his office. I had a feeling this might happen, didn't I? It's why I felt so jittery in the first place. Harriet told me I wasn't supposed to know this shit, so of course I'm going to be questioned. Ryan's last-second warning is another hint to let me know what to expect, and I feel grateful to him and Harriet for doing what they can to give me a heads up.

Principal Di Rossi closes the door behind me, clicking the lock shut. My pulse jumps at the sound, but I'm not stupid enough to outwardly show my shock when I look around and see how many people are in the room. Harriet and Amethyst are here, obviously, both of them staring at me in alarm. That's not a great sign. Harriet's mom is here too, along with three other adults. One of the guys is wearing these weird robes that make him look like a mage from one of the fantasy books Owen's obsessed with. Another not-great sign. If I wasn't suspicious already, that would be more than enough to let me know that everyone in this room aside from me is clearly a witch.

"You okay?" I ask Harriet, genuinely concerned. She's beautiful as ever, but she still has some dried blood around her nose, and her makeup is messy and smeared across her cheeks. I tried to clean as much of it off as I could when I was holding her on the floor in the hallway, but I could only help so much.

She nods slowly and releases a shaky breath, but I don't believe her. There's a furrow between her eyebrows, and she's staring at me with terrified eyes like she's trying to warn me about something.

"I understand Harriet and Amethyst were in an altercation," Principal Di Rossi says, pulling my attention back to him.

"Um, yeah." That's a fucking understatement, but I'm not about to offer up any more information unless specifically asked.

"Can you tell us what happened?" he prompts.

Shrugging to try and appear nonchalant, I nod. "Sure. I ran into Harriet on my way to class, and we stopped to talk. Out of nowhere, Amethyst came over and shoved Harriet to the ground and started saying a bunch of nasty stuff to her. After I helped Harriet up, we tried to walk away without further confrontation, but then Amethyst pulled Harriet's hair and started hitting her." I pause to rub the back of my neck, glancing up at Harriet. Her expression is the same, still just as worried as when I walked in. Without putting much thought into it, I add a white lie that I hope fits whatever story Harriet told. "Harriet tried to defend herself by shoving Amethyst back, but then Amethyst hit her pretty hard and Harriet fell again. It all happened really fast, and there wasn't anyone else in the hallway. By the time I helped Harriet up, Amethyst had already walked away."

"And what about Harriet's necklace?" the creepy guy in the robes asks.

A lightbulb goes off in my head. This is what they're most worried about, isn't it? Amethyst accused Harriet of using magic in front of me, and that must be a hell of a lot more worrisome than anything I overheard the girls say to each other. Words can be explained away easily, but seeing a necklace floating in the air? Not so much. If they're asking me about the necklace, then Harriet probably didn't tell them about Ryan.

I try to look as puzzled as possible, hopefully not overdoing it too much. "Uh, yeah? Her necklace broke while the girls were fighting. After Harriet fell when Amethyst hit her, I grabbed the necklace and helped her put it back on. Maybe it's stupid, considering she was hurt, but I knew it was important to her. She told me it's a family heirloom."

That part is true. Didn't she just tell me before we came in here that she found it in her room with a note from some long-dead relatives? Textbook definition of a family heirloom, if you ask me.

Principal Di Rossi hums thoughtfully, a smile tugging at his lips. I can't tell if that's a good sign or not. "Mattie, do you happen to know what they were fighting about in the first place?"

"Umm..." I rock back and forth on my heels, shooting Harriet an apologetic look. There's only one thing I can think of that will make sense and also help me look oblivious to the existence of witches and magic. I just hope she's not mad at me for mentioning it in front of her mom and these other people. "Well, I think Amethyst was mad because Harriet's dating my friend Spencer. Amethyst and Spencer used to go out, and Amethyst has been jealous of Harriet ever since she started talking to Spence."

One of the adults I don't know chuckles under his breath, and the robe guy looks incredibly annoyed as he settles a glare on Amethyst. She practically shrinks under his gaze when he grumbles, "I think we're done here."

The principal dismisses me, telling me to get a late pass from the receptionist on my way out. I hesitate, wanting to ask about Harriet. She didn't do anything wrong, and she certainly doesn't deserve to get into trouble. But I'm out of my element here with these people. What more can I do? I'm fucking lucky it seems like I didn't screw things up any more as it is.

When Harriet gives me a subtle nod, I finally take my leave. But after I get my pass, I linger in the hallway instead of heading to class. I can't just pretend like everything is fine and normal without knowing if Harriet's going to be okay or not.

To my relief, Harriet and Amethyst walk out into the hallway just a few minutes later. I completely ignore Amethyst and stride over to Harriet, throwing my arm around her.

"Are you alright?" I whisper, my eyes scanning her face.

She nods, glancing over her shoulder to watch Amethyst walk in the opposite direction. "I—I need to go to my locker. I'm suspended for the week."

"You're fucking kidding!" I say angrily, tightening my hold on her. When she leans against me, my heart flips in my chest. I know this isn't the time to worry about shit like that, but I can't help feeling happy that I can offer her any sense of safety or comfort. Shaking my head, I focus on the situation. "But why? She's the one who started the fight."

"Some bullshit about a zero-tolerance policy for fighting. It doesn't matter that I didn't start it. I'm guilty for being involved at all." Her mouth twists, and she stumbles over her feet as she turns her head to look at me. "It doesn't matter though. I'm just so glad you're okay, Mattie. I was so fucking worried. They were talking about erasing your memories."

My heart drops into my stomach, and I suddenly taste bile in the back of my throat. Hearing how close I was to something truly fucked up and out of my control brings all my earlier panic back. But when Harriet throws her arms around me and hugs me tightly, all the bad feelings slowly begin to slip away. I hug her back, glad she can't see the cheesy smile on my face. She might be a few inches taller than me, but holding her like this feels so fucking good.

"I'm fine. I made sure they all think I'm an oblivious idiot, didn't I?" I joke. Harriet doesn't look amused, so I try to soften my smile. "Seriously. Don't worry about me so much. I had a feeling it might be like that after what Amethyst said, and Ryan managed to give me a warning before I was called in too."

"He did?" Her eyes flick to my left. While I know Ryan's always around, it still throws me off every time Harriet looks at or talks to him. I wish so fucking badly I could talk to the guy too, and not just through Harriet or a stupid recording.

"Yeah. Thanks for that, man," I say, hoping I'm looking in his general direction.

We walk the rest of the way to Harriet's locker, our steps slow while I quietly describe how Ryan was able to give me his warning with the sharpie. Talking about it is definitely a big distraction from all the things I really want to ask, but I don't want to push Harriet too much. She still seems so nervous and concerned about what almost happened.

The first thing she does when we get to her locker is text somebody on her phone. The jealous part of me wants to ask if she's talking to Owen or Spencer—or both, I guess—but I force myself to keep my mouth shut. It's none of my business. I'm Harriet's *friend*, which is still a million times better than being nothing. And we've been through a lot of shit together over the past half hour. Something that Owen and Spencer aren't a part of.

"I still can't believe you're suspended," I say angrily. "If you want, I can bring you your homework and shit every day so you don't get too behind."

"Thank you." She smooths her hand over her hair nervously, glancing sideways at me as she slowly shuffles her books around in her locker like she's stalling for as much time as possible. "I really am sorry, you know. I never would have put you in a position like that on purpose. I'm also really sorry it was Amethyst's fault, and for what she said about you. I know how you feel about her..."

My brain short circuits at her words. "What? I don't like Amethyst. I don't give a shit if she thinks I'm an idiot or whatever."

"Mattie." Harriet sighs, leaning back against her locker. "You drool over her every single day, and you're always talking about how hot she is and how into her you are whenever we see her."

My face heats with shame. Of course she thinks I'm into Amethyst. Why wouldn't she assume that after the dumb shit I see and do around the other girl almost every morning? That's when it occurs to me that today is the first time I've looked at Amethyst in years without feeling like I'm in a dream or a stupor. I barely spared her a glance except to glare at her when she started shit with Harriet. And after everything that happened? I don't see how I can find anything about her the least bit attractive ever again.

Desperate to defend myself, I shake my head and try to explain, "I had a crush on her back in middle school when I first moved here, and I admit I was jealous when Spencer started dating her last year. But I haven't thought of her like that in years, Harriet. I can't explain why, but when I see her every morning, it's like...my brain shuts off and it feels like I'm dreaming or something. Like she's the only thing I can see or focus on. As soon as she walks away though, I always feel so fucking confused, and I swear I never think of her at all until I happen to run into her again."

Harriet's eyes are huge as she stares at me with her lips parted in disbelief. I wonder if I should tell her that *she's* the one I like? That Amethyst is nothing compared to her? Or would that be pushing it too much? It's just so fucking frustrating that she's so oblivious to my feelings for her and that she honestly believes I like somebody else.

Before I open my mouth again, Harriet's lips curl with anger and her eyes fill with fury. Surprising the shit out of me, she turns and kicks the locker next to hers and curses, "That fucking bitch! She's probably been using some kind of love spell."

That anxious, jittery feeling I experienced while I was waiting in the office hits me once more, rushing through my whole body. Can that be true? Has Amethyst seriously been using a love spell to make me feel a certain way around her? The thought makes me want to throw up. Did she do that to Spencer too?

Side-eyeing Harriet, I can't help wondering if she's been doing the same thing. I hate myself for thinking it, but how can I not? I have been obsessing over this girl for weeks and fighting with my friends because of her. Is anything I feel around her real, or is it all because of fucking magic?

"I'm sorry, Mattie," Harriet says quietly. Her voice is so earnest and full of concern that I immediately dismiss the idea of her using magic on me against my consent. Maybe I don't know everything about witches or magic, but I do know Harriet. She would never use magic on me or anybody else against their will.

"Do you really think she's been doing that?" I ask, brushing my hand through my hair.

Harriet hesitates before nodding. "It seems like something she'd do, yeah. A lot of witches put love potions in their perfume. It probably wasn't something aimed directly at you specifically, but something that would affect anyone nearby who already had a natural attraction to her to start with. It's not your fault."

"Oh." I'm not sure if that makes me feel better or worse, to be honest. But I do know it's fucking humiliating having this conversation with Harriet. "Have you ever, um, used a potion like that?" I really don't think she would, but I still want to hear her say it.

To my relief, Harriet widens her eyes in outrage and hisses, "No! Of course not." Her expression fills with shame then as she lowers her gaze. "I would never do that anyway, but I actually can't do magic. Or mix potions, or anything like that. My family is known for being really powerful, but I'm pretty much considered a dud in the community. Being able to see and talk to ghosts isn't considered a magical power, and it doesn't have anything to do with being a witch."

It probably makes me a giant asshole, but my first reaction is to feel happy and relieved to hear it. But fuck, Harriet looks so sad and ashamed. I hate seeing her look like that. My fingers twitch with the urge to touch her hair or face. Anything to make her look at me. Anything to comfort her.

"Hey, it's alright," I say softly. "Who gives a shit? You're still the coolest, most badass girl I've ever met. Seeing ghosts is way more awesome than mixing stupid love potions."

She lets out a choked laugh, but I'm horrified to see tears forming in her eyes when she finally looks up at me. She looks completely drained and overwhelmed, like she's seconds away from falling apart. Before I can pull her into a hug and tell her everything's going to be okay, the sound of footsteps walking over interrupts us.

"Hey," Owen says, his eyes roaming over Harriet with worry as he quickly approaches. "Are you okay? What happened?"

"What are you doing here?" I ask, sounding annoyed. I'm a fucking asshole for it, but I can't help feeling like this was *my* moment with Harriet. Owen is supposed to be in class and completely ignorant to all the shit that's been going on.

He barely spares me a glance as he pulls Harriet into his arms. "She texted me and said she got suspended, so I left class as soon as I could to see if I could catch her before she left. What are you doing here?"

Even though the question is directed at me, it's Harriet he's looking at. When she looks up to meet his eyes, he brushes his fingers over her jaw and asks her again what happened. Her face crumples as she collapses against him, burying her face against his chest as she begins to sob.

"Oh Goddess, Owen," she cries. "It's all so fucked up. My mom apparently joined the fucking Council, and she just had a new law passed because I stupidly told her I've been being bullied by the other witches at school. The Council leader came here today and called all the witches into the auditorium where we were given these horrible bracelets that are supposed to make it impossible for underage witches to do any kind of magic on school grounds. They all know it's because of me. If I wasn't a huge target before, then I definitely am now."

She cries harder, going on to tell him about the altercation with Amethyst in the hallway and everything that took place after. He continues to hold her and stroke her hair while he listens, staying completely calm the entire time. I watch his face carefully, waiting for the moment he appears shocked by anything she's telling him. But it never happens.

By the time I realize that Owen's not surprised because he already knows that Harriet's a witch, I feel like the world's biggest dumbass. When did Harriet tell him? And why did she tell him and not me? I don't understand why she'd tell me about the ghost stuff but not this. More than that, I feel stupid that I've completely underestimated Harriet's relationship with Owen. It obviously isn't just mild infatuation or lust. The way he's holding her and listening to her, and the way she's confiding in him...they're way closer than I realized.

"It'll be alright," Owen tells Harriet. He lifts her hand and pulls back her sleeve enough to reveal a silver bracelet designed to look like two snakes. Frowning in concern, he taps on the bracelet and asks, "Does it hurt? Is it bothering you at all?"

"No." She shakes her head, pulling away from him just enough to wipe her tears away. "I don't feel anything, but some of the other witches said it was painful for them."

Owen lifts her hand higher and places a kiss against her palm. My chest burns with jealousy the longer I watch them, but it's not my place to say anything or to offer Harriet any comfort. Not right now, anyway.

"Do you want me to drive you home? I don't mind skipping the rest of the day," Owen says.

She shakes her head again. "My mom is waiting for me

outside. I've already spent too long talking to you guys. She'll probably come looking for me if I don't leave soon."

Pulling her against his chest once more, Owen kisses the top of her head and offers me a nervous smile. "Well, listen. None of this is your fault, okay? Everything will be fine. I'll talk to Mattie and answer any questions he has, and then we can drive over to your house after school."

"I already offered to bring her homework and stuff over," I say, desperate to feel included. Somehow, it only makes me feel like more of an idiot when Owen grins wryly at me.

Harriet grimaces, glancing back and forth between us. "No. I don't want you guys anywhere near my mom if I can help it. I don't trust her. But maybe I can come over to Mattie's house?"

She looks so unsure of herself. Like I'd ever say no to her for anything. But coming over to my house? Yes, absolutely fucking yes. I beam at her and nod emphatically, agreeing right away. Owen and I offer to walk her to the front of the school— we're out of class already, so what's the harm in missing the rest of the period? But Harriet shyly says she wants to walk alone so she can talk to Ryan.

After she walks away, leaving Owen and I alone in the hallway, he and I stare at each other silently for several long, awkward seconds. Eventually, Owen rubs the back of his neck and hesitantly asks me, "Are you okay, dude? It sounds like you came pretty close to dealing with some really scary shit."

I scowl and shove my hands into my pockets, shrugging defensively. "I'm fine. How long have you known that Harriet's a witch?"

"Since her first day of school," he says, completely deadpan. When I stare at him in shock, envy burning hot in my chest, he chuckles quietly. "I get that you're trying to play it cool, but I know this is a big deal and you have to be freaking out. My stepmom is a witch, so I've had a while to get used to all of this. Because of her, I knew Harriet was a witch as soon as I met her without her ever having to say a word."

"Oh." I blink several times, letting that process. "So, Harriet didn't tell you just because you guys are dating?"

He snorts like he's both annoyed and amused. "No. There are all sorts of laws about humans knowing the truth. I doubt Harriet would have given me the time of day or even told me about being able to see ghosts if my stepmom hadn't gone to her house for a coven thing and mentioned me. You know Harriet's skittish about, well, everything. Do you honestly think she would have broken the law and told me such an important secret after only knowing me for a couple of weeks?"

"I don't know. Maybe. She said she really likes you." It occurs to me that Harriet originally decided to trust and open up to Owen because he already knew about witches. That's probably how and why they managed to get so close. And if she feels just as strongly about Spencer... "Does Spence know too? About witches?"

Owen nods, smiling apologetically. "Yeah. Even though she wasn't supposed to, Amethyst told him when they were dating."

So, Amethyst not only told me about witches—even if it wasn't technically her intention—but she also told Spencer. Which is apparently against their witchy laws. And yet she still tried to get Harriet in trouble for supposedly using magic in front of me? That's fucking rich. For the first time in my life, I feel legitimate hatred for another person. Gritting my teeth, I admit to Owen, "Harriet thinks Amethyst has been using some kind of love potion that's been making me act loopy around her."

After explaining what I already told Harriet, how I normally feel whenever I'm in Amethyst's presence, Owen looks incredibly troubled. I even guiltily tell him that I think it's why things have been so tense between me and Spencer the past couple of years. Because even when he was dating her, I still felt like I was in that weird dreamy state every time I saw Amethyst, and the arguments Spencer and I got into after he witnessed me act like that later made me resent him for being liked by her when I wasn't.

"I'm sorry, man. I never noticed. If I had, I would have asked Iris to make you a charm or something to make you immune to magic like that."

I slump back against the lockers, feeling both relieved and completely emotionally drained. Like he said, even though I'm trying to play it cool, I feel like my brain has way too much shit to process. I'm just glad Owen is here, answering my questions and making me feel validated. I was jealous when I saw how he was with Harriet, but it's hard to feel that way right now.

"Do you think your stepmom can still make me a charm like that? It feels, I don't know, kind of gross to realize I'm being manipulated to act and feel a certain way." Hoping he'll be understanding and not feel offended, I nervously say, "And not just by Amethyst, but anyone. I asked Harriet if she's ever used a potion like that. She said no, but...dude, I feel fucking crazy around her. It's different from what I usually feel around Amethyst, but now I can't stop worrying that none of my feelings are real."

He rubs his hand over his jaw, his expression completely unreadable. After what feels like a long, awkward silence, he nods. "Yeah, I can ask her to make you a charm. But I don't think you should worry about Harriet. The way I feel about her is really intense too, but I know it's real."

Yeah, no. It definitely wasn't a good idea to bring up how we feel about Harriet. The last thing I want to do is listen to how intense Owen's feelings for her are. My chest burns, and I have to look away from him before I say something really fucking dumb.

"Listen, we should go back to class. Just get through the rest of the day," he suggests. All I want is to go home, but I don't think I could get away with that as easily as he could. "We can talk after school, and I'll answer whatever questions you have. Since you already know witches exist, I'm not technically breaking any rules at this point."

"What about Nolan?" I ask. Nolan is not only my cousin, but my best friend in the fucking world. How can I go on living with this secret and leave him out, especially knowing my other two best friends already know about it?

Owen shrugs, giving me a sly smile. "If he finds out because you told him, then I'm still not breaking any rules. And you're not technically supposed to know, so you're not really upheld to the same rules Harriet and I are. Just please be careful, alright? The Council is not something you want to fuck with. Especially if they already came as close as they did to wiping your memories."

A shudder runs up my spine. God, he's fucking right.

And that's when I have an epiphany. I inhale sharply as I stare at Owen in alarm. "Shit, dude. Do you think that's what happened to Ryan? Do you think maybe witches wiped his memories before he died?"

CHAPTER 31
HARRIET

"Where do you think you're going?"

I pull my hat down over my head and turn to glare at my mom where she's sitting and drinking tea beside my aunt Flora in the downstairs sitting room. I haven't spoken a word to her since our conversation in the auditorium today. She tried getting me to talk when she drove me home after I was suspended, but I refused. There's nothing I want to say to her that I haven't already, and I know whatever bullshit she tries to tell me now will only make me angrier.

Gritting my teeth in frustration, I give in and finally speak to her, if only to be defiant. "I'm going to Mattie's house."

If she tries to tell me I'm grounded on top of being suspended, that's seriously fucked up. She knows I wasn't responsible for the fight with Amethyst. Even Principal Di Rossi seemed apologetic when he broke the news to me, stating repeatedly that it was school policy and his hands were tied. I haven't heard from Mattie—or the other guys, for that matter—but he should have gotten home from school by now. I've been anxiously waiting for hours to go see him and talk to him so I can make sure he's really okay after the shitshow that happened this morning.

My mom sighs and sets her teacup down on the coffee table before giving me a concerned look. I doubt she's truly concerned about me or literally anything that doesn't have to do with her. "Are you sure that's wise, sweetheart?"

I fume silently as I stare her down. What does she expect me to say? There's no fucking way I'm going to tell her the truth now that she's on the Council—that Mattie lied earlier and he's now aware that witches exist. I'm still desperately hoping she's conveniently forgotten that I slipped and told her about Spencer.

"Come and sit down, Harriet." She pats the sofa beside her.

"Will you let me leave after?" I ask, not bothering to disguise the irritation in my tone.

She rolls her eyes and nods. "Yes, I suppose that's fair."

Flora stands up and gives me a tense smile. "I'm going to start dinner and let you two talk. Are you going to eat here tonight?"

Since I've never been to Mattie's house or met his aunt before, I don't want to assume anything. Even if I would jump at the chance to stay away from home for as long as possible. "I'll be home."

She walks into the kitchen, leaving me alone with my mom. I sigh heavily and take a seat on the opposite end of the sofa from her, staying as far from her as possible as I settle my glare on the fireplace in front of us.

"I thought about what you said earlier," she starts slowly. "And you're right. I should have talked to you more about what's been going on in your life lately, especially with the hazing from other witches at school. I also should have told you I was aiming to find placement on the Council. I see now how cruel it must have seemed to you, leaving it a surprise like that."

This has to be the first time she's ever admitted to being wrong. But it's still not an apology, and it's impossible to believe her. I can't trust her. Just because she's capable of being sympathetic for ten seconds doesn't mean she's not going to turn around and make my life harder than she already has. Or worse, she could get the guys involved with the Council. Mattie came way too close to having his memories fucked with today.

When I refuse to acknowledge her, my mom continues. "You were also right about some of my reasons for joining the Council being selfish. The Abbot family used to be renowned throughout the community, and we always had a place on the Council until your great grandma Sylvia died. My mother pulled away from the community after that happened, and I feel like I've been fighting my whole life to find a way to bring honor back to the Abbot name. But I promise it's not the only reason we moved here. Weeping Hollow is the only place I've ever truly felt at home, and Flora and I are still planning on opening the tea shop and bakery. In fact, we're on track to have the business up and running by Yule! My responsibilities as a Council member will still leave me plenty of time to focus on you and the business. More than all that, I swear I honestly believed joining the Council and pushing for the new laws to be passed would help you. It never occurred to me that the witches at your school might blame or target you for the laws."

I swallow the lump in my throat, still keeping my eyes glued to the fire so I don't have to look at my mom. "Well, they do blame me. You saw that for yourself earlier after that whole incident with Amethyst Redferne. Even after you put me in that position, you made things even worse by announcing the fact that I can't do magic."

"Harriet," she says, reaching out to touch my shoulder. I shrug away from her, and she sighs quietly. "I was protecting you. I knew you were innocent, but the chancellor and other Council members didn't. The Redfernes have had a stronger standing in society than us for too long, and after the lies and abhorrent behavior that girl exhibited, it's clear the family needs to be knocked down a peg. And as much as you seem to think your lack of magical ability is shameful, you're wrong. I've done a horrible job of making that clear, but it is perfectly fine that you can't do magic the way most of us can. You're still just as much of a witch as anyone in this family or our community, and I'm proud of you regardless of any abilities you have or don't have. I'm also absolutely thrilled you've found people here who encourage you to embrace your unique magic and who want to help you discover who you are and what you can do."

Tears form in the corners of my eyes. My mom has never once told me she's proud of me, and she's never said that it's okay that I can't do magic. I hate how fucking happy it makes me to hear those words out of her mouth. And I hate myself even more when I feel some of my anger slip away. I'm not ready to forgive her—I'm not sure I'll ever be ready.

"I wish I could believe you," I whisper.

"I'm sorry. All I can do is promise I'll try harder to make you see how wonderful and special I think you are. And I'll be better about talking to you before making major life decisions too."

Feeling itchy and uncomfortable, I fidget in my seat and dart a side glance at her. She looks genuine, but I refuse to let her off so easily. How can she possibly understand what it's like to be me? Or how difficult things have been for me, being unable to do magic when our world is the way it is? One day and one short conversation isn't going to fix everything between us. Not by a longshot.

"Can I go to Mattie's house now?"

She looks hurt that I have nothing else to say or add, but she nods slowly. Before I can jump up and make a break for it, she places her hand on my arm. "Please remember to be cautious, at least for now. Mattie and the rest of those boys are good kids, and it's obvious they care about you very much. I'm not sure how much Mattie knows, but I suspect he put on a very good show for the Council today. After this incident has blown over and been forgotten in a few weeks, we can submit a request for Mattie, Spencer, and Nolan to be approved by the Council. If they're as important to you as I suspect they are, it's better to get them approved sooner rather than later."

Crap. She totally knows Mattie was lying, and she clearly remembers me mentioning that Spencer knows about witches. I'm glad she's not asking me outright, and for once it really seems like she's on my side. Things would be a million times easier if the guys were approved by the Council, but there's no way in hell I'm going to admit anything for sure. She can't do anything if all she has are suspicions. I nod jerkily but keep my mouth shut, and she finally lets go of my arm and tells me I'm free to leave.

MATTIE'S HOUSE IS ONLY TWO BLOCKS FROM MINE, BUT THE COLD, sharp wind makes the walk feel like an eternity. It doesn't help that I'm a nervous wreck. Mattie seemed okay at school. At least, he didn't seem angry with me and he acted like he took everything in stride fairly well. He wasn't very surprised when he found out that I can see ghosts either. In fact, he was thrilled to learn about that, so I can only hope that he'll feel the same about the witch stuff after he's had some time to process.

My heart does a stupid little flip when I spot Owen's truck outside of Mattie and Nolan's house. Knowing he's here and on my side makes me feel about a million times less anxious as I knock on the front door. Moments later, a woman close to my mom's age answers. She's tall and willowy with the same dark, wavy hair as Nolan.

"Hi," she says, smiling brightly as she takes in my appearance. "You must be Harriet. My boys have been talking about you nonstop for weeks."

"Oh." I shuffle my feet, feeling a blush rise to my cheeks. I can't imagine what exactly Mattie or Nolan could have been saying about me, but it must be something nice to garner such a welcoming smile and reaction. "Yes, I'm Harriet. It's nice to meet you, um..."

Shit. What is Nolan's last name? I know Mattie's, but Nolan's mom is Mattie's aunt from his mom's side of the family. Meaning they most likely don't share the same name.

The woman chuckles and opens the door wider as she gestures for me to come in. I quickly wipe my feet on the mat outside as she properly introduces herself. "You can call me Sally. Please, make yourself at home. From the way Mattie talks about you, I can assure you that you're more than welcome here any time."

My face heats up even more at the implication, and I'm suddenly reminded of my conversation with Owen the other day when he bluntly told me that Mattie likes me. I dismissed the idea immediately because of Amethyst. But after learning today that Amethyst has most likely been using a love spell or potion around Mattie at school, and Mattie's own admission that he doesn't actually like her, maybe I should rethink

Owen's theory. *Does* Mattie like me? He doesn't flirt like Owen or Spencer, but he's always very enthusiastic and attentive whenever he's around me. Plus, he asked me if I'd ever date a guy shorter than me.

The longer I think about it, the warmer I feel all over. When stupid butterflies start flapping around in my stomach, I want to slap myself. Goddess, what is wrong with my brain? I've had two boyfriends—two! —for literally two days, and in the past twelve hours alone, I've found myself thinking about two other guys aside from Owen and Spencer. Granted, one of those guys is dead, but I'm clearly failing horribly at this girlfriend thing already by considering Ryan or Mattie like that.

Sally chuckles at my silence. "The boys are all upstairs if you want to head up."

I thank her and head up the staircase she indicates as quickly as I possibly can without seeming rude. At the top of the stairs, there's a long hallway with a few doors on each side. Thankfully, I hear the muffled sound of the guys' voices coming from behind the second door on the left, so I don't have to make any guesses about where they are.

Lifting my hand to knock, I pause when I hear Nolan's slightly raised voice. "I'm not sure we should be hanging out with her anymore. Clearly, associating with her at all is dangerous."

My throat feels thick as I drop my hand and take a step away from the door. If I had any doubts Nolan was talking about me, Mattie's response to him makes it clear. "That's not Harriet's fault."

Nolan's kind of right though, isn't he? Mattie wouldn't have had to face members of the Council if it weren't for me, and my mom wouldn't know that he and Spencer know about witches either. Plus, I've somehow managed to drag them into a murder investigation that seems more dangerous and disturbing the more we look into it. Is solving the mystery of Ryan's death really worth putting Nolan, Mattie, Spencer, and Owen at risk?

I need to leave. If I get out of here quickly and quietly enough, the guys will never know I was here. Unless Sally says something, of course, but I have no control over that. I practically sprint down the hallway to the stairs to make my escape, stupidly tripping over my own feet and making a thumping sound against the wall when I do. The door where I was listening to the guys opens, and Mattie pops his head out.

"Harriet?" He looks puzzled when he sees me standing by the stairs at first, but a huge grin takes over his face as he strides over to me. "Hey! When did you get here? I was waiting for you to text me to make sure you weren't grounded or anything stupid like that."

I fidget with my hoodie sleeve as I stare down at the floor between us. It's impossible to meet his eyes, especially when he sounds so happy and earnest. In my peripheral vision, I see Nolan and Owen step into the hallway too, but I can't bear to look at them either.

"Um, I should probably go," I whisper. Really, I don't even know why I'm still standing here.

Mattie grabs my arm when I turn to head down the stairs, his voice pleading. "Wait! Don't leave. You just got here."

"I—" My eyes move over Mattie's shoulder to Nolan, completely out of my control. The second our gazes lock, he grimaces and his entire face turns bright red.

"You heard what Nolan said?" Mattie asks softly, his fingers brushing up and down my arm. When I meet his forest green eyes, unable to hide my hurt expression, his frown deepens and the tone of his voice becomes angry and slightly desperate. "Don't listen to him. He's an asshole and an idiot. I might have been kind of freaked out when everything happened this morning, but I never blamed you. And I'm *fine* now. For real. So many things make sense the more I think about everything, and I have about a million questions that I'm dying to ask you."

This energetic curiosity and enthusiasm is the norm for Mattie. While I'm definitely relieved to see he's fully back to himself and no longer solemn or shell-shocked, I can't help but repeat Nolan's words over and over in my brain. A deep sense of shame settles in my chest, and I slowly shake my head. "I'm glad you're okay, but...maybe Nolan is right. I'm sorry."

I don't give him the chance to say anything else as I jerk my arm from his grasp and rush down the stairs. I hear somebody on the stairs behind me. Assuming it's Mattie, I don't bother turning to face him. But when I reach the front door, a large hand slaps the wood in front of me, keeping me trapped inside.

"Let me drive you home," Owen insists quietly, leaning close enough that I feel his breath against the back of my neck.

Glancing over my shoulder, I find him staring down at me with an unreadable expression. I was so excited at the thought of finding him here, but now I just feel embarrassed and desperate to be alone. Swallowing the lump in my throat, I mumble, "It's a short walk. I'll be fine."

His mouth curves into the slightest smile, and he leans down far enough to kiss my cheek. "But it's fucking cold out. And I missed you today."

Despite feeling like crap literally two seconds ago, Owen's words have me melting into a puddle. So much so that I find myself leaning back against him until he chuckles quietly in my ear.

"Okay," I tell him. "Thank you."

Owen lets out a quiet breath of relief and opens the door, keeping his hand on my back as he leads me to his truck. He sweetly opens the passenger door for me before rushing around to his side. Once he's seated behind the wheel, he gives me a shy smile and beckons for me to scoot closer. "Come here."

Giggling nervously, I crawl across the bench seat until I'm sitting flush against his side with his arm around me. It feels so strange but so *good* to be like this with him. Warm, affectionate, and intimate. The butterflies I always have whenever I'm around Owen wreak absolute havoc on my stomach as I grin timidly. "You're impossible to resist."

His eyes light up, and his smile broadens. "Good. I still can't believe you actually like me back." He leans forward to kiss me softly, his smile even brighter when he pulls away. "And it's even more unbelievable that you're mine. God, I feel so damn lucky."

"Pretty sure I'm the one who's lucky." It dawns on me that this is the first time I've been alone with Owen since we became official. Biting my lip, I anxiously brush some of my hair over my shoulder and ask, "And you promise you're really not jealous that I'm dating Spencer too?"

"No." He pulls his truck onto the road, slowly driving toward my house. "Spence is my best friend. I'm happy for him. Plus, Iris told me that witches are naturally, uh, *sensual*. I think it's probably pretty normal for witches to feel strongly about more than one person. But unlike some, you're open and caring enough for a healthy polyamorous relationship to be possible."

Tears prick at my eyes at his genuine, casual acceptance. I've always known witches tend to be more promiscuous than most normal humans, or that they're fickle when it comes to romantic commitments. My mom is a perfect example, constantly moving from one brief relationship to another and always bragging about having multiple lovers. But nobody has ever made the reasoning sound as simple or as normal as Owen just did.

I nuzzle closer to Owen, feeling totally and completely smitten. With a relieved sigh, I ask, "Where is Spencer, anyway? I didn't see him at Mattie's house." Owen reassures me that Spencer had to work, but that he's been caught up on everything that happened at school this morning with me, Mattie, and the Council. "And Mattie really is okay?"

"Oh, yeah." Owen laughs. "He got over his shock pretty quickly. Spent most of the day bombarding me with questions. I didn't even know how to answer most of them, so I know he really is dying to pick your brain. Mattie got into ghost hunting and the supernatural stuff way later than the other guys and I did, but he's definitely the most enthusiastic about it."

More of my anxiety fades. It's crazy that just a few minutes in Owen's presence has helped me feel lighter and more relaxed considering how I ran away after overhearing what Nolan said. Now, I almost feel silly, like I might have overreacted. But at the same time, I can't deny that hanging out with me could be risky. Especially with my mom being on the Council. I want to talk about it with Owen, but I'm not sure how to start.

Luckily, he beats me to it. "You really shouldn't worry about what Nolan said either. I don't think he really meant it, to be honest. It's just like this morning when he first saw you with me and Spence. Nolan always reacts to things defensively without thinking them through or taking the time to consider what he's saying. I guarantee he's going to beat himself up for weeks for what he said to you this morning, and probably even longer for what you overheard him say in Mattie's room. I know that doesn't make what he said okay, but..."

He trails off with an awkward shrug. Owen might know Nolan better than I do, but I'm not sure I can believe that he didn't mean what he said. Personally, I still don't think Nolan likes me very much, even before he found out that I'm a witch or that I'm Spencer and Owen's girlfriend. That doesn't mean Nolan is *wrong* though.

"Whether he meant it or not, my mom being on the Council *is* dangerous. Like, I seriously can't trust a word out of her mouth anymore. I already slipped and told her that Spencer knows about witches before all this, and she seems pretty sure that Mattie lied in front of the Council and that he knows about witches now too."

"Do you think she'll do anything to get them in trouble?"

I hesitate before shaking my head slowly. "I don't know. I don't think so. But like I said, it's impossible to trust her. She said she'd help me submit something to have Mattie, Spencer, and Nolan officially approved by the witch's Council in a few weeks once this all blows over, but even thinking about that right now freaks me out."

Owen hums, his fingers rubbing over my arm soothingly. "Well, we can talk about that in a few weeks. If she's serious, that's really not a bad idea. I still don't think we have anything to worry about. Hanging out with you is no more dangerous than going to school and talking to the same witches the guys and I have known our whole lives."

He has a point. It's not like I'm the only witch in this town. Not even close. And honestly, anywhere outside of Weeping Hollow, it's not unusual for witches to be friends with humans. There's absolutely nothing wrong with me being friends with the guys, and as long as my mom really doesn't say or do anything with her newfound power and authority, the Council has no reason to suspect me or my friends of anything.

"Honestly, I'm more worried about you guys helping me with the ghost stuff," I admit. "That list of names Mattie showed us this morning of potential people to ask about

Ryan's death? At least a third of them were witches. And the more I think about it, the more sense it makes that witches were involved in his death and covering it up. There's no way you can deny that investigating this is dangerous if that's the case. For all of us, but especially for them when they're not supposed to know anything about witches or magic. There's no way I can give up trying to find out what happened to Ryan, but...it would be horrible and selfish for me to ask you guys to help."

Owen parks in front of my house. I knew it would be a quick drive, but it's disappointing to realize it's already over. Owen turns and cups my cheek in his hand, smiling down at me with this undeniably sappy expression.

"You don't need to ask, Harriet. Fuck the risks. I'm all in— with you, and with investigating the deaths of any ghosts you meet. I know the other guys feel the same. Nolan too, even if he's shit at saying so."

Before I can argue or mention any more of my insecurities, Owen presses his lips to mine. There's nothing soft or hesitant about the kiss, and my entire body flushes with pleasure as I press myself closer to him and moan against his mouth. I'm about to climb into his lap when he pulls away with a chuckle.

"I'm pretty sure I'm never going to get tired of that," he says. There's a faint blush on his cheeks and so much open adoration in his light blue eyes.

Now that the moment is over, I can't help but feel a little embarrassed. Every time he or Spencer kiss me, I totally lose my mind. "Goddess, you must think I'm ridiculous. Especially considering the fact I'd never kissed anyone until only a few days ago."

Owen huffs a quiet laugh, shaking his head as his eyes light with amusement. "No, I don't think you're ridiculous. I think you're beautiful and sexy, and I think I'm really fucking lucky. I guess I haven't exactly mentioned this, but I've never had a girlfriend before either. Actually, you were my first kiss."

All I can do is gape at him. It never occurred to me that I wasn't the only inexperienced person in this relationship. Owen is incredibly hot, sweet, and pretty much perfect as far as I can see. I assumed he's dated girls before, just like Spencer, but I never wanted to ask or hear any details. Knowing I'm his first kiss and girlfriend makes me feel all warm and giddy. For probably the first time, I feel confident as I lean forward and initiate another kiss.

CHAPTER 32
HARRIET

I jerk awake with a gasp, completely disoriented as I blink in the dark. My heart races in my chest, beating so loudly it's the only thing I can hear for a moment. Did I have a nightmare? I don't remember, but I never usually wake up in the middle of the night like this.

Reaching blindly for my phone on my bedside table, I shiver against the intense chill in my bedroom. My mom and Flora usually charm the house so it's always comfortably warm, so I don't understand why I'm freezing right now. Once I grab my phone, I turn the flashlight on and look quickly around the room.

The first thing I notice is Sophia standing in the corner, facing the wall. I sit up and call out to her, but she doesn't answer. Dread blooms in my chest as I slowly approach her. She's always been a little creepy, but she's never done anything weird like this. Do ghosts sleep? I guess I never thought to question what she does when I'm asleep at night. When I'm only a few feet away from her, the faint sound of her melancholy humming reaches me.

"Sophia?" I whisper her name again, softer, and slowly reach out to touch her arm. She's freezing cold but solid against my touch, and I pull my hand away with a choked gasp. Sophia still doesn't react, and I try really hard to keep myself calm. This isn't the first time I've been able to physically touch a ghost, so I figured it was possible for it to happen again. And maybe Sophia really is just sleeping, or stuck in some sort of weird stupor? I'm probably freaking myself out for no reason.

A quiet meow grabs my attention, and I whip around to lift my phone's flashlight and check on Circe. She's curled up in the bed I made for her, but it's too dark to see much more than her bright yellow eyes, even with my phone.

"What's wrong, girl?" I coo at her as I walk over.

After turning on a lamp so I can see without my phone, I sit on the ground beside her. She purrs and nuzzles my hand. She seems okay, and thankfully it looks like she hasn't gone into labor yet. But it's way too cold in this room for her. From everything Henry's told me, I'm pretty sure Circe will have her kittens any time.

I grab a few more old blankets I'd set aside for Circe and place them around her nest, hoping they'll make do until I can get the heat issue figured out. When I tiptoe across the hall, I discover that my mom isn't in her bedroom. Flora's room is empty too, and neither of them are in the kitchen or anywhere else in the house. It's after one in the morning, and neither of them mentioned leaving the house tonight.

Panic laces my throat as I clumsily call my mom. The phone rings three times before she answers, sounding completely normal and carefree. "Hello?"

"Where are you?" I ask.

"Oh, Harriet." She sighs like she's amused. "It's a full moon tonight. Your aunt and I decided to come down to the river to do a few spells. The moonlight is the best down here. Is something wrong?"

I vaguely wonder if the river she's talking about is the same one where my adder stone necklace was originally found, but I quickly shake my head and focus on why I called my mom in the first place. "There's no heat in the house. I assume your charm broke or something."

"That's odd. Flora and I will take a look and get it fixed as soon as we're back in the morning. Do you need anything else, sweetheart?"

I'm irritated that she's gone when I legitimately need her help with something, but I'm too pissed and stubborn to ask her to come home now. I'll figure something out to keep Circe warm, and then I'll try to find out what's going on with Sophia. I end the conversation with my mom, letting her know I'll be fine until morning, and then I trudge upstairs to the fireplace in the large sitting room.

When we first moved in and got the place cleaned up, I insisted on learning how to get a fire going in these old fireplaces even though my mom and aunt called me silly and repeatedly said it was unnecessary when they can use their magic to start fires. Now, I'm glad I didn't listen to them. It's not ideal to move Circe, but getting a fire started and moving her out here now is better than potentially trying to move her after she goes into labor. I don't want to have to rely on my mom's magic for this when her charm shouldn't have been broken so easily in the first place.

My phone chimes with a text while I'm working on the fire. I almost don't check it, assuming it's my mom. But then I remember that Sage is three hours behind me, so it's also just as likely to be her texting me this late.

It's not my mom or Sage though. It's Nolan. *'Are you still awake?'*

He's never texted me before other than in a group chat. I stare at the message for a long time while I debate answering. I could totally ignore it and pretend like I'm asleep. But my curiosity outweighs any ill feelings I have toward Nolan or about anything he's said to me or about me today.

I text him back a short and simple *'yes'* before getting back to my task. Seconds later, he calls me instead of just texting me back. I'm more confused than ever, but I already answered him so it would be really shitty to ignore him now.

Feeling nervous and hesitant, I answer and put it on speakerphone so I can keep working on the fire while we talk. "Hello?"

"Hi." His voice is high, and he quickly clears his throat. "Um, I'm sorry to be bugging you so late. I couldn't sleep and... well, I feel really terrible about what I said today. So, I wanted to see if we could talk in person so I can apologize properly?"

"You want to talk in person now?" Maybe I shouldn't be that surprised—Owen told me that Nolan probably felt bad and would beat himself up over this—but I still never expected him to reach out to me. And I definitely never expected Nolan of all people to ask if we can meet up in the middle of the night.

"Yeah. I can come over." Nolan pauses, his voice rising in pitch again. "Or is that too weird? Do you think your mom will be pissed?"

I snort humorlessly. "No. It's a full moon, so she and my aunt went out. You can come over if you want." Maybe I should ask if his mom will have a problem with him leaving the house this late, but I decide not to worry about it. Coming over to talk is Nolan's idea, not mine. I'm genuinely curious to hear what he has to say, and hopeful we can put this behind us and work toward being real friends. Owen, Spencer, and Mattie have become such important people to me, and I don't want things to be weird between me and one of their best friends.

Nolan lets me know he'll text me as soon as he's outside before we end the call. The thought of being alone with him makes me nervous. If he really just wants to come over and apologize, I already know I'm going to forgive him and do whatever it takes for us to get along. I never want to be the reason he fights with his friends. Still, no matter what he says or how the conversation goes, I can't imagine this interaction being anything other than awkward. To avoid thinking about it too much, I put another log on the fire and move Circe's bed, litter box, and food and water bowl to a cozy spot nearby. She's slightly irritated with me at first, but she seems pretty content once I get her to settle down in her new bed.

By the time Nolan lets me know he's outside, all of Circe's things are moved and she's purring happily as the fire continues to grow. I scratch her head before heading downstairs to let Nolan in, shivering at the icy gust of air that follows him through the door.

"Fuck, it's cold," he says, rubbing his hands over his arms as I quickly close the door behind him.

If the walk between our houses was bad for me earlier, I can only imagine how miserable those two blocks were for him this time of night when the temperature has dropped even lower. I give him a wry smile. "I can make some tea or hot chocolate if you want. And I just started a fire in the fireplace upstairs, so we can sit up there."

He fidgets with his glasses, avoiding my eyes as he quietly thanks me and takes me up on the offer of hot chocolate. The kitchen is somehow even colder than the rest of the house. It's so bad that I can see my breath while I rush around to make the hot chocolate as quickly as possible. While I'm waiting for the milk to heat on the stove, I turn to face Nolan. He looks as nervous as I feel, his cheeks red as he rocks back and forth on his heels.

"I don't remember your house being this cold when the guys and I slept over." He chuckles awkwardly.

Since he already knows I'm a witch, I don't see the point in hiding anything at this point. I shrug and grumble, "Yeah, sorry. I don't know how, but the charm my mom uses to keep the house warm stopped working. That's why I lit the fire upstairs in the first place. I think Circe is getting ready to have her babies any time, so I want to make sure she's as comfortable as possible."

Nolan's eyes light up with interest, some of the awkward tension between us dissipating. "That must be convenient. Being able to heat a house this big with a charm like that."

"It's only convenient if my mom or aunt are actually home to do it." I know I sound bitter, but I'm still irritated they didn't tell me they left tonight. "I'm not sure if Owen or Mattie mentioned it? But I can't do magic like other witches."

"They mentioned it." He rubs the back of his neck and lowers his gaze from mine. "Harriet, I'm really sorry. I never meant for you to hear what I said earlier, about it being dangerous to hang out with you, but I also never should have said it in the first place."

"It's alright," I mumble. "I really like hanging out with you guys, but I understand why you said that."

He shakes his head, finally meeting my eyes. "I like hanging out with you too. And obviously, so do the rest of the guys." I must look doubtful because he blushes and gives me a grimacing smile. "You have no reason to believe me, but I mean it. I know I've been an asshole to you, but it's not because of you. Mattie, Spencer, and Owen have been through a lot, so I can't help feeling protective of them. Even when it's uncalled for or unnecessary. They all like you so much. And I'm not an idiot—I can see why. You're beautiful, interesting, and mysterious, and that was before learning you're a witch and that you can see ghosts. Sometimes I feel like you're too good to be true, so I'm constantly looking for reasons to not like or trust you. It's stupid and unfair, and I promise I'm gonna be better because I really want us to be friends."

It's so much more than I expected him to say when he asked to come over. From the tone of his voice and the way he's looking at me, I can tell he's genuine. My face flushes from the strange, unexpected compliments in his confession, but it also helps me understand Nolan a little better. It makes sense for him to be protective of his friends after everything they've been through with their families.

Still, the only thing I can think to say in response is, "I'm really not that interesting."

Nolan laughs in surprise, squinting his eyes at me in amusement as he adjusts his glasses. "Sure, Harriet."

He's definitely teasing me, so I give him a shy smile. The kettle on the stove begins to whistle, so I finish fixing our hot chocolates. When I hand Nolan his mug, I smile again and tell him, "Thanks for saying all that stuff. I really want us to be friends too."

It seems like he still wants to stay and talk for a while, so we make our way upstairs to the only place in the house where it's currently warm. I'm proud to see the fire crackling and burning strong, but I still add another log as we sit down in front of the fireplace to make sure it stays that way. Circe is curled up in her new bed, blinking at us lazily for a moment before going back to sleep.

Nolan nervously asks me what happened at school this morning that led to the incident with Mattie in the principal's office. Since he only got to hear my side of the story secondhand through Owen, who only heard a short version of the story, I tell Nolan all the details about the assembly in the auditorium, the new laws, the fight with Amethyst, and the meeting in Principal Di Rossi's office before Mattie was called in. He's horrified to learn that Amethyst and the other witches at school have been hazing me—I guess it still hadn't occurred to him that I wasn't having episodes because of some sort of disorder—and extremely intrigued to learn how the Council works in the witch community.

He asks me tons of questions. And somehow, it doesn't feel weird to open up about everything. Now that we're past all the drama, it's a relief for Nolan and Mattie to know that I'm a witch. I don't have to lie or hide anything from them anymore, and already, I can feel a true friendship finally forming with Nolan. The more we talk, the more curious he seems—and he definitely doesn't seem nervous or scared. I even hesitantly tell him about the fears I already shared with Owen, about the risks of investigating Ryan's death. But he tells me he's way too invested in the mystery to give up now, no matter how dangerous it might be.

"So, that's why we weren't able to break in before you moved in? Because the house was cursed?" Nolan asks after I tell him the truth about my great-grandma Sylvia. When I nod, he hums thoughtfully. "But why? Why put the curse on the house in the first place? And for so long?"

"No clue. I'd love to know the truth, but I feel like we've got enough mysteries on our plate between Ryan and Sophia."

"True." He chuckles. "But maybe we can put a pin in the Abbot House mystery and look into it later, after we figure things out with the ghosts. Where is Sophia, anyway? Is she sitting with us?"

He glances around the room curiously, but I shake my head. "Actually, she was in my room the last I saw her. She was being really weird."

I explain how I woke up to find Sophia creepily humming in the corner of my bedroom, ignoring my presence even when I reached out and touched her. He suggests checking on her again and follows me to my bedroom to do just that.

My room is colder than ever, and when I flip the light on, I find Sophia standing in the same place I last saw her. Before I can take a step closer, Nolan makes a choking sound. When I turn to him with concern, he's staring straight at Sophia with a horrified expression.

"What the fuck?" he mumbles. "Why can I see her?"

My mouth drops in surprise, and I quickly shake my head. I have no idea how that's possible. Alarm bells ring in my head as I glance at Sophia again. Something strange is clearly going on if she's acting like this, and if I'm easily able to touch her and Nolan can see her without any help from me or a camera.

"Sophia?" I call out softly. She doesn't move or react. I slowly walk closer toward her. After only a slight hesitation, Nolan follows closely behind me without ever once taking his eyes off her. When I'm only a few inches away, I reach out and touch her shoulder. Just like earlier when I first woke up, she feels solid under my touch. "Sophia, can you hear me?"

She sways slightly and hums a little louder, but otherwise, there's no change in her behavior. Nolan swallows audibly and whispers, "I don't like this. What should we do, Harriet?"

I don't like this either, and I don't know what's wrong with her. But as to what to do? It feels so obvious to me. I hesitate for a second before turning to Nolan. He freaked out just as much as the other guys did the last time I did this with Sophia.

"I think maybe I should search through her memories," I say, sounding way more confident than I feel. "We can finally find out how she died and maybe why she's like this."

"What?" Nolan's eyes widen. "But—but the rest of the

guys aren't here to help. What if something bad happens like last time?"

He has a point, but now that the idea has planted itself in my brain, there's no way I'm not going to try. Walking away or waiting feels impossible. It's like there's this sudden buzzing beneath my skin, and I'm desperately itching to reach out to touch Sophia so I can dive straight into her memories.

"I'll be fine," I insist, reaching down to squeeze Nolan's hand. "Just, um, slap me or something if it looks like I'm stuck or if I stop breathing."

To my surprise, he pulls me into a hug. His breath tickles my neck as he softly says, "Just please be careful."

I pull back with a nod, turning to face Sophia again. I trust Nolan. I'm glad he's here and that I'm not doing this totally alone. I know if it looks like something's wrong, he'll do whatever it takes to make sure I'm okay. With a steadying breath, I rest my right hand on Sophia's shoulder and grip my adder stone in the other.

STEPPING INTO SOPHIA'S MEMORIES IS EFFORTLESS. MAYBE IT'S because I semi-know what I'm doing this time, or maybe I'm just better prepared and know what to expect. When I blink, I find myself still in my bedroom. Only now, there's light coming through the windows, and the room is clearly being used as a nursery. There's an old-fashioned crib against one wall and a shelf full of children's toys nearby. In the corner, Sophia is sitting in a creaky old rocking chair with an infant cradled in her arms as she softly sings a lullaby.

I spend a few moments watching, unsure if I should do

anything else. But as soon as the thought enters my head and I blink, I open my eyes to discover that a few years have passed in Sophia's memories. Sophia still appears young, but the baby she was holding in the rocking chair now looks to be about three or four years old. A smile tugs at my lips as I watch Sophia chase the little girl around her room while they laugh and play. They run out into the hallway after a few moments, and I follow. And again, it seems a few more years have passed when I find Sophia cleaning the room while the little girl sits by the fire with a book, now appearing to be maybe ten years old.

It continues like this, where I watch a scene for a few moments before we jump ahead a few years. It should be disorienting, but it's not. It feels more like I'm flipping through a living scrapbook, peeking into small moments of Sophia's life here in the Abbot House. In every new scene, I always find her either cleaning or taking care of children. Each time, she's a little older, but she's almost always singing lullabies or nursery rhymes. I watch the first child she nannies grow into an adult until she becomes the head of the household, and Sophia becomes the nanny for *her* children.

While it's fascinating to watch Sophia's life unfold like this, I can't help feeling prickly and suspicious. Everything I've seen so far has been so domestic and idyllic. But I have a feeling it won't end that way. What is this all leading up to? For the most part, it seems like Sophia was a happy, simple woman who genuinely enjoyed caring for the young Abbots of the house.

My heart quickens when I finally reach a part in Sophia's memories where she looks the same as she does as a ghost. Well, not exactly the same, obviously. Her skin isn't translucent, her eyes aren't pitch black, and she still has her teeth—unless they're dentures or whatever the equivalent is for this time period. But she's older, her skin appearing soft and wrinkled, and I catch her making the same nervous gesture where she fidgets her hands that I always see her do as a ghost. I must be getting very close to finding out how she died.

I follow Sophia closely as she hums one of her familiar tunes and dusts all the rooms on the second floor. We're completely alone for several minutes—much longer than I've spent in any of the other snippets so far. Eventually, a group of teenage girls come upstairs, laughing and talking amongst each other. Two of them are Rebecca Abbot's grandchildren—both girls I just spent the past however-long watching Sophia help raise. They're grown up now, both of them aged somewhere between fourteen and sixteen. Two other girls are with them, a blonde and a brunette. The girls ignore Sophia's presence entirely until they sit around the sitting area by the fireplace.

One of the granddaughters sniffs and gives Sophia a haughty look. "Get us some tea."

Sophia purses her lips, but she bows her head and says, "Yes, Miss Josephine."

It's been difficult to keep track of all the kids' names that I've seen Sophia care for with how quickly I've sifted through her memories. But I'm fairly certain Josephine's younger sister is named Gladys. I eye the girls with disdain as I follow Sophia downstairs. I've never witnessed the girls act rudely toward Sophia, but my ghosty friend doesn't seem particularly surprised. Do the girls only act like this in front of their peers?

While Sophia gets a tea set together, she quietly hums one of her favorite songs. Her hands shake as she carries the heavy tray back up the stairs, and my fingers itch to reach out and help her. But I know I'm useless here. All I can do is stand by and watch events unfold that already happened over a hundred years ago.

When Sophia reaches the second floor, none of the girls move to help her as she sets the elaborate tea tray on the small table in the sitting area. The granddaughters' brunette friend giggles maliciously and says, "Your housemaid is so slow! Ours would have already had our tea set up ages ago."

"Well, Sophia is getting rather old," Gladys says. When her sister and friends look unimpressed, Gladys sniffs and quickly adds, "Besides, she's hardly even a real witch. She can't use magic to make our tea like your maid can."

The girls laugh cruelly, and Sophia winces as she lowers her gaze submissively. Anger burns in my chest, but I quickly try to calm myself. If I let my emotions take over, I could end up getting stuck or have trouble breathing like last time. It takes so much effort to keep my rage in check. Sophia is one of the kindest people to have ever existed, before and after death. To talk less of her for any reason, but especially because she can't do magic? It hits way too close to home.

"Can't do magic?" The blonde friend cackles. "How droll."

The brunette girl nods, her eyes lighting up mischievously. "We should practice our spells with her."

Sophia stiffens, slowly backing out of the room. The younger granddaughter, Gladys, blanches at the suggestion, but Josephine's eyes light up with curiosity.

"What did you have in mind?" Josephine asks.

"Miss Josephine, don't make me fetch your mother." Sophia tries to sound stern, but the nervous wobble in her voice is undeniable.

With a flick of her fingers, the brunette snickers. "Well, we start with this, obviously."

Sophia's arms snap to her sides as her back straightens and her lips clamp shut. If I had to guess, my assumption is that the nasty brunette witch has used a spell to make it impossible for Sophia to move or speak.

I hold my hands over my mouth, forcing myself to keep quiet and stay as calm as I possibly can while I watch the scene unfold. At first, the girls take turns using magic to force Sophia to jump up and down or march across the room. Gladys is the only one who doesn't partake, but her pleas for the other girls to stop are half-hearted at best. The girls' sickening game only escalates further when they force Sophia to kneel in front of the fire. Bile rises in my throat when Sophia thrusts her arm into the flames. Her sleeve catches fire, and the scent of burning flesh fills the air after only a few seconds.

The girls laugh loudly, and it seems that Sophia is released from their spell as she gasps and jerks her arm back and quickly pats the flames on her sleeve away. Tears stream down her cheeks.

My face is wet from silent tears too. This is the most horrifying thing I've ever witnessed. Even though this has absolutely nothing to do with me, I can't stop comparing Sophia's experience to what I've had to deal with at school with the other witches and with Blaze when he burned my hand. The biggest difference is that I've always had someone there to help me or step in. Sophia has nobody here to save her.

I want to turn away. To leave and try desperately to erase this vision from my brain. But I force myself to stay and watch every awful moment. I owe it to Sophia. This could be the only way to learn the truth about her death and her curse. The only way to save her soul.

"She's going to tell on us!" Gladys whispers frantically. She's more worried about getting into trouble than what they've just forced poor Sophia to go through.

"No, she won't," Josephine says, but she peers down at Sophia nervously.

The granddaughters' friends share a look, and the blonde says, "That shouldn't be a problem. Have either of you ever altered someone's memories before? My father's been teaching me at home, and it isn't so hard."

"Please," Sophia whispers, her voice cracking as she cradles her arm. Tears continue to fall freely down her face. She remains kneeling beside the fire, too hurt, afraid, and frail to run away or call for help.

One of the girls casts another spell to force Sophia to go still and silent once more. Josephine walks over and stands in front of Sophia, placing her hand on top of Sophia's head. With a quick glance over her shoulder at her friend, Josephine asks, "How do I do it?"

The blonde whispers advice in Josephine's ear. It's hard to tell what's happening or what Josephine actually manages to do. The fear never leaves Sophia's eyes, but there are several moments she appears slightly dazed or that her jaw falls slack. When Josephine finally pulls her hand away, Sophia sways like she's about to faint.

"How do we know if it worked?" Gladys asks anxiously.

After some coaxing, the girls get Sophia to stand up. She still appears lost, her eyes glazing over. I'm growing angrier and more confused by the moment. Did Josephine really manage to steal Sophia's memories? If that's true, then how am I able to witness this so easily? Sophia pulled me into her memories the first time, something that felt very purposeful. This incident hasn't been forgotten at all, even in her death.

"Sophia?" Josephine asks, raising her voice slightly until the old nanny startles and makes eye contact with her. Josephine smiles innocently and asks, "Do you remember what just happened?"

Fear fills Sophia's eyes again, and she jerks away from the girls. When she opens her mouth to speak, the only sound that comes out is a sharp, hysterical laugh. She grips her throat, shaking her head back and forth, and when she opens her mouth again, she begins singing one of the creepy old nursery rhymes I've recently become familiar with thanks to her.

This goes on for several moments. Every time Sophia tries to speak, the only words she's capable of are the nursery rhymes she lovingly sang to the Abbot children she cared for. The girls begin to laugh, eventually turning away from Sophia entirely as they sit and enjoy their tea. They even have the audacity to complain that their tea has gone cold while Sophia stands by, crying and babbling her nursery rhymes with rising panic.

Josephine didn't take Sophia's memories at all. No, all she did was steal Sophia's voice.

A sob escapes my throat, and my vision blurs from tears. I wipe my eyes, but it's impossible to stop crying. It's all too much, and I know I'm not even done here. I still haven't discovered how Sophia died. Through my tears, I force myself to take deep breaths until I'm sure I'm not going to lose it and accidentally yank myself out of her memories.

When I open my eyes again, I'm not sure where I am at first. The room is large with a high, vaulted ceiling and wood beams. It's not until I see the small, circular stained glass window to my left that I realize I'm in the attic of the Abbot House.

I'm also not alone. Chills run up my spine as I slowly approach the center of the room where Sophia is sitting in a wooden chair. Her hands are trembling, but otherwise she's perfectly still, staring straight ahead at the wall. There's nothing else up here. No other pieces of furniture and no sign of other people. It's chilling, and I can't even guess at what sort of horror I'm about to witness this time.

I don't have to wait long. The sound of footsteps on the stairs breaks the eerie silence. Sophia's fingers tremble harder, and she lets out a soft, terrified whimper. All I want to do is put my hand on her shoulder and whisper something comforting to her, but it's pointless. It won't change this. I have to remind myself over and over that this isn't happening *now*. It already happened, and I'm only here to spectate.

A group of men and women enter the attic, all of them wearing ceremonial witch's robes in shades of dark blue, red, or green. They form a circle around Sophia, remaining silent. Once everyone is settled, a man wearing maroon robes steps forward, roughly grabbing the shoulder of a girl in emerald green robes. She gasps when he yanks her hood down, revealing a teary-eyed Josephine.

"Josephine Abbot," the man says in a harsh, authoritative tone. "You have admitted your guilt in attempting to alter this woman's memories. An act which resulted in breaking her mind to an extent that no Council member has been able to correct."

Josephine's lips tremble as she nods her head and lowers her eyes. "Yes."

I can't help feeling a sick sense of glee. Maybe it doesn't change what happened to Sophia, but at least Josephine is being held responsible.

My delight is short lived when the man looks at Josephine with disdain and says, "You have wasted the life of a fellow witch, and it is now your responsibility to give this tragedy a sense of purpose."

Another witch steps forward and holds out a sharp, silver dagger. Sophia whimpers again when Josephine hesitantly reaches out to grab it. Josephine stares down at the dagger for a moment before raising her eyebrows expectantly at the man in the maroon robes.

He places his hand on Josephine's shoulder, some of his anger slowly receding. "Today you will join the Council just like every eldest Abbot child before you. As you know, the

Council and this town were formed by the five most powerful families in our community. To keep our power, and in turn, to keep our community safe and prosperous, one member from the five families must make a sacrifice once per generation. While we would have ideally had you wait another year or two, the Council has decided this woman's wasted life would be better put to use as your generation's sacrifice."

I swear I can literally feel the blood drain from my face. I even try to convince myself I'm mistaken, that this guy can't possibly mean what I think he means. But it becomes all too clear that he's serious when Josephine walks over to stand beside Sophia and holds the dagger's blade against her throat. The man in the maroon robes says a few more bullshit words about protecting our history and how important these sacrifices are. All the other witches in the room form a tighter circle around Sophia and Josephine as they begin chanting some sort of spell in unison.

My eyes are glued to Sophia as I watch with absolute dread as Josephine slashes the dagger across her throat. It's not a quick death. It takes several minutes for her to bleed out, and she spends that entire time gasping in pain while staring at the witches around the room with pleading, terrified eyes. She's incapable of moving or fighting, thanks to whatever spell they've used to keep her in place. By the time she finally slumps in her seat with a vacant expression, dead at Josephine's hands, her body and the floor around her are covered in her blood.

Bile rises in my throat and tears blur my vision again. I clamp my hands over my mouth, trying so fucking hard to keep myself from throwing up or from breaking down completely. I have to keep watching. Now I know how Sophia died. And I can probably safely assume that the way she was sacrificed by these horrible, wicked people has everything to do with her curse and the reason her soul has been stuck in the Abbot House all these years instead of being able to cross over. But how do I fix it? Is knowing the reason enough for me to find a way to fix everything?

My mind races, a million thoughts assailing my mind at once. The man said that someone from the Council makes a sacrifice like this every generation. Have witches in this town seriously been killing innocent people for centuries just for some sick, misguided attempt to keep witches safe? Or is it more about keeping the families powerful?

The Abbot family has always had a family member on the Council, at least until my great-grandma Sylvia died. And I don't have powers. Is that because nobody in our family stuck around long enough to be part of a sacrifice like this? Goddess, does my mom know about this ritual? She must know if she's a Council member.

The vision before me becomes fuzzy around the edges. I expect to be thrown out of it any moment now that Sophia's dead, but I spot her ghost looming in the corner of the room as she watches the witches finish the ritual. Someone uses a spell to clean up Sophia's blood and to heal the wound on her throat. Two of the witches leave the room, quickly returning with a wooden casket lined with obsidian.

Several of the witches draw symbols with white chalk on the inside of the casket, and I notice a few others mutter spells or charms as they touch each corner. Once they're done, Sophia is placed inside the casket. It feels like I'm standing there forever, and at the same time, for only a few seconds, as I watch them place the casket inside the walls of the attic. When they're finished, they use their magic to close up the wall so it looks as though it's never been disturbed.

I keep my eyes locked on the place where I now know Sophia's body was stashed as the memory slowly fades around me. I know I'm being pushed out—that I've seen everything I need to see by now—and I don't fight it.

The next time I blink, I'm back in my bedroom and my own mind, standing in the same spot I last remember with Sophia's ghost in front of me. I gasp, taking deep breaths as I reorient myself. Nolan is standing beside me, squeezing my hand tightly between his. Someone else's arms are around me though, and I turn my head in confusion to find Spencer and Owen holding me close. Mattie's with us too, and everybody looks scared out of their minds.

"Are you back?" Nolan croaks.

I nod slowly. My mind is all over the place, and I still feel sick from everything I saw. It takes me a second to get any words out. "Yeah. What are you all doing here?"

"Nolan called us," Owen says, forcing me to meet his eyes. He looks undeniably worried as he lifts his hand to my cheek. That's when I realize I wasn't only crying inside Sophia's memory. My face is wet and streaked with tears.

Spencer touches my other cheek, grabbing my attention. "You've been trapped in whatever vision you saw for over an hour. You've been crying almost the whole time. We were going to try to call your mom, but none of us have her number and we couldn't unlock your phone."

"No," I gasp out. It's become clearer than ever that my mom is not somebody who can be trusted. Not for one fucking second. Everything comes rushing back to me, and I jerk away from the guys to face Sophia.

She stares back at me with a sad, haunted expression. Fresh tears fill my eyes, and my stomach churns uneasily until I know I'm definitely going to throw up. I held back while I was inside her memory, but I can't anymore. I pull away from Sophia and the guys, collapsing to the ground a few feet away as I puke my guts out.

"Shit, shit, shit." Mattie says, the first to rush over to my side. "I knew we should have tried to pull you out sooner. What can we do, Harriet? Please, talk to us."

While he rambles, he gently pulls my hair back. I don't have it in me to feel embarrassed as I sit up and wipe my sleeve over my mouth. What I do feel is grateful that the guys are here —constantly proving that they're with me through any tough or scary shit that might possibly happen in my life. Nolan stayed with me when I jumped into Sophia's memories without much of a thought or plan, and the other guys clearly didn't hesitate to come over as soon as he called them. It didn't matter to any of them that it's the middle of the night. Them being here means so fucking much to me. I'm also fucking livid about everything I learned in Sophia's memories, and I feel a fierce determination to do whatever it takes to fix things for her and any other innocent person who was sacrificed so cavalierly by the Council.

"I'm fine," I insist, standing up even though the guys try to get me to sit down and rest. I shake off their concern and sweet touches and try to explain. "I saw Sophia die, and I know why and how she was cursed. It was fucked up. Beyond fucked up. But I'm going to fix it."

CHAPTER 33
HARRIET

It takes very little to convince the guys to help me. After I tell them what I saw, Nolan is the first to suggest we go up to the attic. The room is dusty and full of clutter just like it was when Spencer and I came up here to look for the spirit board. The lighting also sucks, but I can sense the same frantic energy in the guys that I feel. There's no way any of us can wait any longer. There's this insistent pull I feel inside my chest that's urging me to push forward, and it's impossible to fight against.

"Which wall was it?" Spencer asks, looking around the messy attic.

My hand shakes as I point out the spot I saw Sophia's casket placed. There are tons of boxes and miscellaneous antiques hiding that section of the wall, and everybody jumps to help me move things out of the way. The boxes and smaller items are shoved to the side until the only thing in our way is a large, ornate mirror with the glass cracked in multiple places. Nolan, Mattie, and I are way too scrawny and barely manage to move the mirror more than a few inches. Spencer chuckles at us and asks us to move aside while he and Owen lift the mirror effortlessly and set it on the other side of the room.

I'm all too aware that this is definitely not the time, but I can't help the smile that crosses my face as I stare heatedly at my boyfriends. Why is watching them show off how strong they are so hot?

Mattie catches the look on my face and makes a disgruntled sound as he rolls his eyes. "You guys are such show-offs."

"You're just jealous," Spencer says with a grin. He throws his arm over my shoulders and kisses my cheek.

"Can we please focus?" Nolan groans, rubbing his temples. "We're literally about to uncover a dead body."

He's not wrong, and his words definitely do the trick in making the mood in the room more serious. Now that the wall is visible, we need to figure out a way to break through it. In Sophia's memory, the wall was only made of wooden panels, but somebody has plastered over it since then.

After searching around the attic, Mattie finds a large box full of random tools. He very enthusiastically picks up a sledgehammer and begins tearing down the wall where I know we'll find Sophia's body.

Nolan rubs the back of his neck and grimaces every time the sledgehammer hits the wall. "What if your mom comes home early and finds us demolishing the house?"

"It will be fine," I say, trying to sound convincing. I really don't think my mom or Flora will be home before morning, but if I'm wrong? I genuinely don't know how she'd react if she knew what we were doing. She hasn't asked me much about Sophia's ghost since we first moved in, and I don't think she realizes that Sophia was one of the Council's sacrifices. Still, I'm not exactly itching to explain anything for my mom or for her to find out that we now know the Council's secret. "We should probably try to hurry though, just in case. What about you guys? Won't you get in trouble for being out so late?"

"Oh, me and Nolan are definitely going to be grounded." Mattie gives me a manic grin as he hands Owen the sledgehammer to take over. "But this is more than worth it."

"Zoe will be pissed, but whatever." Spencer shrugs.

I glance at Owen, and he smiles bashfully as he rests the sledgehammer over his shoulder. "I'm not in trouble. I woke my dad and Iris up before I left the house and told them you needed my help with something. They were understanding, but they really want you to come over for dinner soon now that we're together."

The simple reminder of our relationship is so sweet and unexpected, especially with everything currently going on. I grin back at Owen and nod, silently agreeing that I'd love to have dinner with his family. This isn't the first time he's mentioned talking to his parents about me, and just thinking about what he's possibly told them if they're already this supportive of us makes me swoon.

Owen makes quick work of the wall until the original wood paneling and Sophia's casket are visible. He steps back, and all of us stare silently at the wall. The tension in the room is so fucking thick, and I don't think any of us know what to do next. I've just been winging it so far, following whatever crazy thing my intuition is pushing me toward.

"Now what?" Mattie asks, voicing my thoughts out loud.

The guys look at me expectantly. My hands feel clammy, so I rub them over my pajama shorts and say the first thing that comes to mind. "Um, I think maybe Sophia should be up here with us?"

She stayed downstairs when we came up to the attic. I don't blame her for wanting to stay away from this part of the house if she can help it. But the moment I mention wanting her here, she floats up through the floor until she's standing in front of me with a worried expression on her face.

"Fuck me!" Mattie exclaims as he jumps back. His eyes widen as he stares at Sophia, laughing at his own reaction. "Knowing a ghost is there and seeing it right in front of me are two very different things. How do you ever get used to this, Harriet?"

The guys were so focused on me when I came out of Sophia's memory that I didn't stop to wonder if they were still able to see her or not. Mattie's declaration answers that question though. I still don't know why the guys can suddenly see her or what's so special about tonight that all of this is happening. But figuring it out certainly isn't the priority right now. All I can do is go with it while we get through this and try to break the curse.

"It's normal for me." I shrug at Mattie before turning to face Sophia. I reach out to grab her hand, shivering at the icy cold feeling of her touch. "You know what we're doing up here, right? We want to break the curse, but we don't know how. Do you know?"

She points her long, bony finger at the casket and hums one of her lullabies, her voice higher in pitch than usual.

It's not much of an answer, but at least I can assume I'm on the right track. The feeling that's been compelling me to search her memories and then to find her body still sparks in my chest. I've never felt my witch's intuition flare so brightly like this, but it's the only explanation I have.

"Alright." I clear my throat, my heart thudding rapidly in my chest. "I guess we should open the casket?"

"Oh, god. I've never seen a dead body before," Nolan hisses, just loud enough for us to hear.

Mattie punches his arm and gestures at Sophia. "But you've seen a ghost. How is that any different?"

419

It feels pretty fucking different to me, and judging by how pale Nolan looks, he agrees. I've never seen a dead body either, so this will be a first for me as well. Hoping to make him feel better, I smile sympathetically at Nolan and give him an out. "You don't have to be here for this. I wouldn't blame you. You've seriously already helped so much."

His shoulders straighten as he adjusts his glasses, a look of determination crossing his face. "No. I'm going to see this through. We're a team, right?"

I'm pretty sure none of the guys ever imagined forming WHISPER or getting into ghost hunting would lead them to a situation like this, but the certainty in Nolan's words warms my heart. We are a team, and the guys have more than proven that they're on my side and willing to help me no matter the cost.

Owen and Spencer pull the casket out of the wall and set it on the ground. It's pretty obvious from looking at it that the casket is encased in magic because the wood still looks fresh and new, like it was placed here yesterday rather than over a hundred years ago. I worry that it will be difficult to open because of some stupid spell, but Owen manages to open it without much trouble.

The guys and I move closer and peer inside. Lying at the bottom of the casket is Sophia's skeleton, still wearing the clothes she was killed in. The same dress she wears as a ghost. I'm not surprised that her body is fully decomposed, but there's still something heartbreaking about finding it this way. Unlike her skeleton, the casket is pristine, and all of the chalk markings appear clear and fresh.

"Okay." Mattie takes a deep breath, his eyes never leaving Sophia's skeleton. "We should, uh, bury her somewhere else, right? Like with a proper grave. And maybe find a way to destroy this casket?"

Those aren't bad ideas, but I can't shake the feeling that I need to do something else first. Without really thinking it through, I reach down into the casket and grab skeleton-Sophia's hand. One of the guys makes a weird, grossed out sound, which I try to ignore. Following my instincts, I turn to look at Sophia's ghost and offer her my other hand to hold. She floats closer, darting a frightened glance at her casket, and hesitantly places her hand in mine.

"I see you," I say softly. The words feel natural on my tongue, so I don't overthink what I'm saying or doing. "I'm here for you, and I release you."

My adder stone necklace grows hot against my chest, and there's a sudden pressure surrounding us that feels like it's going to suffocate me. Before I can question whether I just severely fucked up or check to see if the guys feel anything too, the pressure disappears like it was never there.

Sophia's ghost slowly begins to fade. She stares at me, shocked for a split second, and then she smiles widely with pure joy and relief. As she continues to fade from existence, she whispers, "Thank you."

And then she's gone. I drop her skeleton's hand and take a ragged breath, glancing around the attic like Sophia will pop up somewhere else. There's no way it could be that easy.

"Is that it? Is it over?" Nolan asks, blinking rapidly like he's still waiting for Sophia's ghost to come back too. "Did she cross over?"

Spencer's eyes blaze with excitement as he turns to me. "Is that what it looked like when you helped the ghost in the diner cross over?"

I shake my head, feeling dazed. "I don't know. It felt really different."

"Yeah, that was fucking nuts," Mattie says. "Your necklace

started glowing and the air got really thick. Like I couldn't breathe for a second."

Owen pulls me close to his chest and softly rubs his hand over my back. I melt against him, feeling completely exhausted and overwhelmed from all of the events over the past twenty-four hours. He seems to understand that without me having to say a word, simply holding me and offering me some comfort.

While Owen holds me, the other guys quietly discuss what we just witnessed. They seem pretty optimistic that I managed to break Sophia's curse and that her ghost really did cross over. I guess there's no way to truly know for sure, but they also agree we should still bury her bones and burn the casket just in case.

Just like everything else they do, the guys are extremely efficient when it comes to coming up with a plan and complete a task. My entire body feels like jelly, making me useless as they search the attic for a different box to place Sophia's bones in. Nolan is still too creeped out by the skeleton to help, but Mattie and Spencer seem to have no problem moving her bones to the new box. It's smaller and simpler than the casket, but anything has to be better than the awful way she was stowed away in the wall before.

After cleaning up the wood and plaster from the floor, placing the casket back in the wall until we figure out how to deal with it later, and placing the mirror back in front of the destroyed wall to cover it up, the five of us head outside to my backyard. It's even colder than it was earlier, but I have way too much adrenaline running through my body to feel much of the chill.

"Maybe we can bury her by the garden?" I suggest quietly. "My dad told me that my great grandma Sylvia used to grow all sorts of plants and flowers out there. I was going to try to bring it back this spring, so it will be pretty for Sophia. Eventually."

"I think that sounds perfect," Owen says.

I bite my lip, reconsidering. "Or do you think we should go somewhere else, further away from the Abbot House?"

Nolan offers me a reassuring smile as he tucks his hands into his pockets. "I think giving her a proper burial anywhere is what will make the difference. She's not a secret stashed away anymore."

"Besides," Spencer says, wrapping his arm around my waist. "She might have died in this house, and in a really fucking awful away, but it sounds like she was happy here too. She lived in the Abbot House most of her life, and I'm sure she loved all the kids she cared for, even if they didn't love her back the way they should've. I also think it will be nice for her to be close to you."

Tears form in the corners of my eyes, and I nod my head as I lean against him. Seriously, what would I do without these guys? "Thank you."

There's an old, beat up shed near the garden where we thankfully find a few only slightly-rusted shovels. Using our phone flashlights to see by, we choose a spot in the garden beside a large maple tree and take turns digging. It's messy and difficult, but the work keeps us warm.

Despite it being the middle of the night, and despite our task being morbid as fuck, the guys talk and joke around and make the entire thing feel not-so-scary. There's no way in hell I could have ever done this alone.

By the time we finish burying Sophia's bones, we're covered in dirt and the sun is peeking over the horizon. We stand around her makeshift grave in silent reverence, and a sense of peace washes over me.

"Thank you guys," I whisper softly. "You've been amazing. I have no idea how I'm going to make this up to you."

"There's nothing to make up for," Spencer says. "We wouldn't have stuck around if we didn't want to."

Nolan nods. "We did the right thing."

"And now you're stuck with us forever." Mattie grins wildly, bumping his elbow against mine. "Now that we've literally buried a dead body together."

I snort in amusement, but I can't exactly argue with his logic. Peeking at the rising sun, I sigh sadly. "I wish you guys could stay, but you should probably go home soon. It's still early enough that you might not even get caught sneaking back in."

None of them seem to want to leave either, but they agree it's best if they leave too. I spend a long time hugging each of them—and giving Owen and Spencer a few kisses—before the guys pile into Owen's truck so he can drive them home. Owen and Spencer promise to come over straight after school tomorrow while Nolan and Mattie let me know they'll keep me updated on whether they're grounded or not.

After they leave and I walk back inside, I'm overcome with loneliness and exhaustion. The house has never felt so empty and strange, and I realize it's because Sophia's ghost is truly gone. There's a pang in my chest at the idea that I'll never talk to her again. I'll never hear her sing one of her creepy nursery rhymes that I found a weird sort of comfort in. But while I'll miss her, I know Nolan was right about us doing the right thing. I hope that wherever Sophia's soul ends up, she's happy and at peace.

On my way upstairs with every intention of taking a shower before falling into bed for the rest of the day, I hear Circe meow. I completely forgot about her after Nolan got here and I jumped into Sophia's memories. I didn't even think to check on her when we came downstairs from the attic because I was so preoccupied.

"Circe?" I rush up the rest of the stairs and into the sitting room where I moved her bed. Thank Goddess, the fire is still burning and keeping the upstairs area warm. "Is everything okay, girl?"

She blinks up at me with her bright yellow eyes, and I gasp as I spot three tiny, squirming kittens beside her. A squeal escapes me as I crouch on the floor in front of them. "Holy crap! You had your babies!"

I can't believe I missed the birth, and I spend a few moments panicking while I search for any signs of distress or anything that Henry told me to keep an eye out for. But Circe seems calm and happy as she purrs softly, and all three of the kittens seem to be nursing without any issues. I couldn't have hoped for a better outcome.

This whole night was so crazy after such a long, terrible day, but it couldn't end more perfectly. When I send a picture of Circe and her kittens to the guys along with Sage, Henry, Dorian, and Elsie, the peaceful feeling I felt outside turns into something bright, warm, and fuzzy in my chest. I never thought in a million years that I'd feel such a sense of belonging and meet so many people I care about when I moved to Weeping Hollow.

And that makes all the drama with various ghosts and the community of witches more than worth it.

ACKNOWLEDGMENTS

We've reached the end! But like I promised, there's no big cliffhanger. So, you can't be too mad at me!

This story is so dear to my heart. If you've been following me for a while, you might know I actually started Harriet's story several years ago, way back before I ever published anything and just wrote stories on Wattpad. I had a few chapters of this book posted there back then, and I finally decided that it was time to finish this book.

Shadows and Curses ended up being so much *more* and taking me so much longer to finish than I originally planned. I thought it would be be, like, 80K words tops and take me 1-2 months to finish writing. Instead, this book ended up somewhere around 130K words and took me something like 5-6 months to finish! Aside from the length being crazy long, I also found out I was pregnant while writing this book. (Which has absolutely nothing to do with Harriet's cat being pregnant —that was already planned and written in years ago, haha). Pregnancy brain is a struggle, for sure. So, I am extra proud of how this book turned out despite my plans and deadlines changing so much!

And now it's time for my thank-you's.

Thank you first and foremost to my husband, David, for always being helpful and supportive. And this time, for majorly picking up the slack around the house while I spent the first several months of my pregnancy sick and exhausted.

Thank you so much to Taryn, Kiersten, and the rest of my moon slut besties for beta reading and giving me so much love, support, and encouragement even when my brain felt like total mush.

And thank you so, so much from the bottom of my heart to all of my readers who have been so sweet and beyond supportive of me over the past several months. You've made me feel so much better about taking my time to write this, and for choosing to publish this book before working on an already-ongoing series instead. I'm so excited to see what you all think of Harriet and her guys. Especially a certain Ghost Boy, as I haven't decided what the future holds for him in Book 2 just yet. ;)

ABOUT THE AUTHOR

Willow Hadley is a self-published author who primarily writes sugary sweet reverse harem romance. She lives on the coast of North Carolina with her husband, their dog, ferret, and two cats. She started writing in early 2018, and decided to pursue publishing in 2020. She loves character driven stories and fluffy books that give you a warm, fuzzy feeling. She's also obsessed with Disney movies, and her favorite candy is licorice.

Sign up for her newsletter here.

Join her reader's group here.

You can also find more info on her website here.

Also by Willow Hadley

Cricket Kendall Series

Cricket

Wildflower

Wandering Star

Luna Witch

Rises the Moon (Cricket Kendall Spin-off)

Charlotte Reynolds Series

Smile Like You Mean It

Everything Will Be Alright

Of Moons and Monsters Series

Of Moons and Monsters

Of Dreams and Demons

Standalones

Dark Paradise

Made in the USA
Middletown, DE
19 October 2023

41095754R00245